John Ledbetter

Deadbeat Escapement

John Ledbetter is an American writer. He was born in the EAST in 1979, and raised in the SOUTH, only to move WEST at the last turn of the century. He will likely die somewhere up NORTH, completing his cardinal BINGO card—DEADBEAT ESCAPEMENT is his first novel.

VIKON VILLAGE

Deadbeat Escapement

John Ledbetter

VIKON VILLAGE BOOKS

California, U.S.A.

Deadbeat Escapement

Published by Vikon Village Books, Montrose.

ISBN 979-8-218-94602-9

FAIR USE DISCLAIMER: This book is a work of satirical fiction intended for entertainment and educational purposes only. *Deadbeat Escapement* is an amalgamation of people, places, things, and events; both real and invented. Every attempt has been made to integrate accurate details when opportune, but, in lesser cases, tremendous artistic liberties have been taken; a barrel of monkeys method for a writer working in satire, which *Deadbeat Escapement* is. I, JOHN LEDBETTER [author], do not draw any conclusions within the following pages, but instead, correlate and format hundreds of publicly available leads so that any truth-seeking, curious individual may further independently investigate and form their own opinion—s'all tongue-in-cheek, mate.

> *Experience teaches us all that, as with any complex human event examined scrupulously and in detail, it will reveal improbabilities, inconsistencies, and awkward gaps in our knowledge. Only in fiction do we find all the loose ends neatly tied. It is one way that we identify something as fiction. Real life is not all that tidy*—WALTER CRONKITE

Library of Congress Cataloging in Publication Data

Ledbetter, John, 1979-

[English]

Deadbeat escapement / John Ledbetter.

First edition.

LCCN 2026901805

Front and back cover artwork, book design & type setting by John Ledbetter

10 9 8 7 6 5 4 3 2 1

CONTENTS

DEADBEAT ESCAPEMENT

JOHN LEDBETTER

For All Post-humans

PREFATORY NOTE

IT MAKES LITTLE SENSE TO MAINTAIN A DIARY when the newspapers will do it for you, yes? On occasions, such as this one, the best and most immediate illustration of a relatively unknown American icon, of whose life journey you are about to hitch a ride on, is with a concise obituary: *The Press Democrat,* October 27, 1992. Page 6:

> VITO PAULEKAS, Cotati artist Vito Paulekas, one of Cotati's leading firebrands and a friend to the disparate likes of Frank Zappa and former "Tonight Show" talk show host Johnny Carson, died at a Santa Rosa hospital Sunday following a long battle with cancer. He was 79. Paulekas, born in Lawrence, Mass., spent his life in the world of arts and entertainment, beginning as a 15-year-old performing vaudeville in Boston, said his son, B.B. Paulekas. "He also was a marathon dancer. One time, he danced for five months," Paulekas said. But Paulekas, a renowned sculptor who operated a studio for 20 years in Los Angeles before moving to Cotati in 1969, was more than an artist. "In Los Angeles, he was a human rights activist. He joined Martin Luther King Jr. when they marched on Washington," said his son. Former 12-year Cotati City Council member Linda Shorey said Paulekas "was the spirit of Cotati." Paulekas, known for his great thunderous oration at council meetings during the '70s, built the city's first bandstand in LaPlaza Park that became the focal point of the town's cultural events and a centerpiece for the city's fostering of free speech. City leaders granted Paulekas the honorary title of "keeper of the bandstand." "If a light bulb went out, he'd change it before our public works crews could get out there," Shorey said. Paulekas also sculpted the 10-foot-tall statue of Chief Cotati that adorns the city's downtown park, a statue that honors the Miwok Indians on whose land Cotati was founded. Cotati Vice Mayor Richard Cullinen vividly remembers moving to Cotati in 1973 and being entertained by Paulekas' own form of

guerrilla theater, Cotati Free Store, made up of a colony of artists that followed Paulekas from Los Angeles. While he lived in Cotati, he returned numerous times to Los Angeles to appear on "The Gong Show," a wacky half-hour of sometimes outrageous amateur entertainment. "He was very famous in L.A.," said Shorey. "He was a good friend of Johnny Carson, who called him the 'cosmic hippie.'" Cullinen said Paulekas also was good friends with Frank Zappa and was pictured on the cover of Zappa's 1965 album "Freak Out." "It's hard to eulogize someone as flamboyant as Vito. He was a remarkable individual. He was dancing all the way up to this year," Cullinen said. During his years in Cotati, he taught dance classes at Sonoma State University, was a member of Cotati's 1975 Citizens Advisory Committee to the General Plan, and was a member of the city's Community Services Commission since 1987, a position from which he resigned two weeks ago due to his failing health. Paulekas is survived by his six children, including sons B.B., Sky, and Mark Paulekas, all of Cotati; daughters Gruvi Paulekas of Cotati, and Mary and Sophia Paulekas, both of Areata; and a sister, Alberta Kaufman of Cambridge, Mass. Private family services will be Saturday.

Santa Rosa, CA

HOLLYWOOD

—most beautiful suburb of America's most famous residential city, set amid charming scenery where the mountains blend into the plain, blessed with all-the-year sunshine, fanned by ocean breezes, surrounded by one of the most fertile regions of the world, and peopled by men and women who appreciate and demand the best of everything in their community life, invites the stranger and sojourner of like mind with them to make his home here where nature and civilization have united to produce ideal living conditions.

DEEP WATER IS DARK AND FULL OF PEACE—It was at the close of February 1914 that California state government agencies surveyed all of Los Angeles County after three days of catastrophic flooding, and estimated an excess of ten million dollars in damages. Legislature quickly formed the LA County Flood Control District, which spent the next three years systematically terraforming the soppy county—draining creeks and brooks, backfilling them with busted boxcars and plastered film set-pieces. Ancient ceremonial mounds, now in the way of a fantasy downtown, get pancaked, creating makeshift valleys that will one day host purse shops, pilates studios, and yogurtoriums. Very few lomas survived. Prehistoric marshlands covering a hundred thousand acres with tall, sharp, golden grasses were given the old concrete treatment, rolled over, and turned into the boulevard of the Cienega. And, for all their destructive efforts, the developers still had to come to terms with the everlasting simple truth that Los Angeles County proper was, is, and forever shall be, a desert. The small ranching community of Los Feliz borders Hollywood to the east at Van Ness Avenue, which includes areas known today as Silver Lake, a significant chunk of Griffith Park, and the desert oasis. The Feliz familia was among the first Spanish descendants to put down roots in the Southland, choosing this temperate, rocky landscape to stripe with citrus orchards and dot with banana tree groves. The rancherias were built from repurposed Tongva/ Gabrielinos villages ... er ... inherited when Spanish Governor Pedro Fages deeded this purdy parcel to José Vincente Feliz in 1795. Alas, many decades of quick-drawing and digging have made this plot ripe for reconstructive surgery, so Los Feliz gets a major bioturbation to meet the growing demand for a landing zone—a shopping stop-off for those commuting between the hills and flats of Beverly, and that calcifying pearl downtown.

Near Hyperion Avenue, where Tracy and Monon Streets helix together, Sacatella Creek once snaked between rolling lomas all the way to the main branch of the Ballona Creek, pacing Fairfax Avenue into Ballona Bay before finally feeding into the Pacific. Sacatella Creek will soon be slabbed over and gain recognition as the LA River. Wise men once gathered at the intersection of St. George Street & Rowena Avenue, where the waters of knowledge sprang from a natural springhead that the Tongva/Gabrielinos believed summoned forth spirit animals into our world beyond the fissure. The custodians sowed and reaped the land before new decorative vegetation was planted in 1910. The spirit animal faucet was capped, redirecting water into a youth fountain that cuts a timid channel through an anointed section of Ferndell, down the hill toward Los Feliz Boulevard, where it quietly re-joins the groundwater table. Sheesh. The Tongva/Gabrielinos will take none of the credit, but all of the blame.

It is going to rain, rain more, and flood in 1917, so L.A. had better be prepared. The Flood Control District has installed nearly twenty major storm drains that all feed floodwaters into the 48-mile concrete channel, the Los Angeles River. A series of concrete and steel cubes and sheets, floating on buried creeks and redirected rivulettes. Under the futile threat of outdoor malls, or high schools, or animation studios, the water swears that it will find a way unless handled. Enough of that, let's get away from this whirlpool and move west, inching into Hollywood, at the intersection to be home to the Vista Theatre once this corner develops into a convergence of the two famous boulevards: Sunset and Hollywood. The Vista will eat up the corner in a building that houses offices, one of which becomes Edward Davis Wood's first production headquarters. Today, on the hottest day so far in August of 1919, there is no theatre or bustling boulevards, only a trickling stream running the length of a modest Temple Avenue. There is the elephant in the city—the rotting set from D.W. Griffith's *colossal spectacle, Intolerance.* Production wrapped in 1916, and much of the massive structures have been left to spoil into a quarter mile of jagged crud, anointed in dirt and horse shit and bug legs, pieces crumbling against the tropical backdrop after holding out as long as possible. What remains doubles as a shelter; a sanctuary for a dozen depraved and infirm, the hopeless and lost, homeward-bound. The 2x4 ribs splinter under the ply skins, creating a canopy or blanket for some to sleep under. Here come the boys in blues. The ragged foreman chalks shards and marks, indicating what is to be broken down, dismantled, and destroyed by the arriving crew of work-release prisoners. It takes 30 destitute men, two entirely dirty days of blowing up shit, tearing shit down, hacking massive chunks into tinder sticks to set ablaze. They are soiled harbingers; creators of endless pasts. At the close of the second day during the criminal round-up, some spooked officers discover that two inmates are, uh, *unaccounted for.*

Every affluent American community of the West needs an equally alluring putting green, something to make Tubal Caine proud, maybe even a little jealous. Jog a 3.5-mile zig-zag southwest to arrive at the Los Angeles Country Club, where Rossmore Avenue and Temple Street cross. Although the club is open to the public, it will take another three years to complete construction of the links, creating California's first double 18-hole golf course. For the time being, the courses are bisected by a shallow lake that, since the end of the war last November, has become a stagnant wetland left to swell atop the groundwater table while some suits propose and finance solutions. The coveted fairway poses the most significant and immediate problems, one of which is the 100-yard section of exposed creek that cuts through it. It is abundantly clear that a herculean sponging-up effort is necessary. And, so it be done by thy city's blessing, great numbers of greasy men arrive in hulking hydraulic machines, thirsty to steadily drink down the marsh until only a modest creek remains to trickle across and then eventually alongside Temple Avenue until being driven into submission under the soil. They tip the groundwater table up and down all along Temple Avenue as holes are poked and things are buried.

The Los Angeles Country Club golf course opened to game-starved club members in August 1921. Today's roster promises remarkable matches on this virgin emerald fairway, where you'll remember a shallow lake once was. If you stand near that ruddy trench separating the jockeys from lackies, you'll spy a silver sliver sipping daylight before digging back under the cover of freshly plotted sod. The golfers, junior Jesuses, every last one, are essentially walking on water. After a heated match, a formal dinner on a tented lawn is held near the Clubhouse. 400 guests eat and dance. The entire event is filmed.

It is October 18, 1922, opening night of Sid Grauman's Egyptian Theatre on Hollywood Boulevard ::: NOW SHOWING ::: *Douglas Fairbanks in Robin Hood.* Grauman hired designers Meyer & Holler only several months back to dream up a Mediterranean-themed interior, but, for reasons unknown, the décor duo made an eleventh-hour executive decision to change the entire design—from floor to ceiling, projection booth to restroom stall—to an ancient Egyptian ruin, complete with plaster pillars and polystyrene gods. And wouldn't you know it, by a dumb stroke of blind luck, Meyer and Holler's stupidly optimistic moment of design intervention is validated five weeks later, when on the afternoon of November 26, 1922, archeologist Howard Carter discovers the nearly completely intact tomb of King Tutankhamun. Carter had searched the Valley of the Kings for three years before uncovering the find of the century. Tut's bougie booty sets off a North American facelift—*Egyptmania*, it's called. Boring, flat urban apartment spiced up their facades by affixing all kinds of Egyptian thingees over entryways and arches. Where once Spanish tile greeted tenants, now instead is a cartoonishly carved winged disk with a Sumerian god zooming around in the salad bowl. Bodega owners rub doorknobs down with scented oils. Movie stars are mummified in celluloid, embalmed by the plastic arts. All this ancient ballyhoo and this theatre well ahead of the culture curve; how very fortuitous for Sid Grauman.

We have driven two hours north to arrive at the Guadalupe-Nipomo Dunes in San Luis Obispo. Miles and miles of the coastline are rimmed with rolling mounds of silica. It is here in 1923 that Cecil DeMille utilized the desolate desert to construct the biggest film set ever for *The Ten Commandments*; Paul Irbe's art direction required the enormous efforts of 600 craftsmen. Half a million feet of lumber filled the space, plastered over with 250 tonnes of white minerals. It's been a rough shoot, and this desert getaway didn't work out quite like he intended. The desert sun has turned DeMille's brain to mush over the prolonged shoot, and now after principal photography has wrapped, and full-blown paranoia has set-in, he has but one commandment of his own; dynamite the entire 800-foot wide, 110-foot tall set to molecules—assuring beyond any shadow of doubt, that not one of those two-bit, wannabe talentless goons looking to steal his every creative fart—tucked into the smokey back booth of Musso and Franks—not a single one of them will get the chance to rob DeMille of his greatest acheievment, nor to reduce his trademark to a fad. And so it was, the *City of the Pharaoh* was blasted to smithereens, leaving men and diggers to shovel tonnes of sand over dismembered plaster pharaohs, chalk pillars, and papier mache hieroglyphs. From a loma off the highway, a perched spy documents the processional, transcribing coordinates and computations onto the sleeve of his dress shirt. He backs off into the darkness, moving soft-footed and undetected as a mynx on a bed of pine needles.

Tinsel Town's population exploded tenfold in the first decade, growing to over 60,000 residents, and in 20 years, over 1.5 million souls call Los Angeles home. The motion picture industry thrives here and has advanced in both technology and social value, with the eighth art evolving from the world of two-reelers and penny arcades into features and movie palaces. Overnight growth leads to the west portion of Temple Avenue gaining its own identity: Beverly Avenue. (*Beverly*, Old English; *a beaver stream.*) A crew of surveyors lines the new avenue, moving in unison like a flock of pigeons in search of abandoned fried mozzarella sticks. Each surveyor falls in line behind the last; the leader sets out ahead. The trailing tribe inputs measurements and data, and the leader shouts back at them as he shakes dowsing rods, witching away in search of Mother Nature's mainline. At this rate, if they continue due east, they'll find it quickly swaps identities first with a small segment of Virgil Avenue, before forking into Temple Street and Silver Lake Boulevard. Walking the paved path would effectively demonstrate that many Los Angeles streets are shaped and vibrate as a silk ribbon dropped on the floor, lying atop the natural flow of rivulets. All avenues and boulevards feed into the Los Angeles River, seeping into the Pacific Ocean at a spot the natives called Balona Bay. The ontology of the word *balona* is little more than mythos. Gabreilinos and Tongva's stories point to the spill-out being a port for beluga whales, a rest stop along their 3,000-mile journey to new waters.

In May of 1927, there it is, written clear as crystal in the *Los Angeles Times* for hooch-mover-cum-wireman E.L. Smith to read aloud at the breakfast table—*BEVERLY BLVD. Major cor. Beverly & La Cienega. Cor. Beverly & Laurel. Must be sold. Make offer, Mr. BENSON, WHitney 1138.* The paper crinkles loudly under Smith's thumb when he turns the page over to judge his family's reaction to his proposal. In mid-June, Smith submits an offer, and Mr. Benson accepts, and no sooner does the deed ink dry than Smith gets the jump on this landmark-making industry looming over SoCal. Smith submits plans to the city, illustrating his intent to erect the largest structure on Beverly Boulevard; a giant brick and steel chocolate box that will consume the northwest corner of Beverly and Laurel Avenues, a combination of retailers and hotel rooms, essentially two 55'x55' blocks flanked by an eight-foot-wide vestibule housing a set of stairs that lead up to a mezzanine. By midsummer, the Los Angeles Municipal greenlights Smith's schematics (which fail to incorporate the wireman's intention to add four stories soon before evolving city codes circumcise any skyward ambition—a three-story cap is to be placed on all structures, preventing the growing Hollywood cityscape from blocking views of Mount Wilson and criss-crossing arclights).

DEPARTMENT OF BUILDING AND SAFETY

Application for the Erection of Buildings
CLASS "C"

Lot No......*352*......No. of Rooms......No. of Families...........

Purpose of Building...*Store*...+...*Hotel*...............................

Owner's name........*E.L.Smith*..

Owner's address.......*2708*......*So*...*Vermont*........................

Architect's name........*Eric*....*Black*...................................

Contractor's name.......*E*...*L*...*Smith*.................................

TOTAL VALUATION OF BUILDING $....*37,500*..............

Size of proposed building....*55.48*.....x.*118.6*.................feet

Lot size..*56*x*120*...No. of stories...*2*...Highest point...*31.6"*...

Foundation...*Concrete*.....Floors.....*wood*....Roof...*compo*........

Material of exterior walls.......*Brick*.... interior walls...*plaster*.

PERMIT NO.

22788 [crayon check mark]

APPROVED!

America dried up like an old maid seven years ago, and now stricken with the itch, Smith is off to the races building his Hollywood speakeasy cake-topper. After two weeks of construction, Smith makes several amendments to the municipality-approved schematics, petitioning for a *basement enlargement* for a basement that, by all accounts, doesn't exist. This sub-structure has not been officially recognized in any building documents. The floor rests eleven feet below street level; the plans indicate expanding the floor plan with a five-foot-by-seven-foot addition and a small shower area. SoCal builders are not in the habit of building such subterranean quarters, much less one in the footprint of a swelling rivulet displaced by a country club up the road. We've already discussed at length the unique situation Los Angeles finds itself in; no matter how much paving one does, dino pee pee is forever. Anyway, *enlarge basement. Install sidewalk door. Substitute stud partition for brick.* In July of 1927, dry agents from the Venice sheriff's office blitzed a roadhouse in that county. Flasks and bottles vaporize, but twenty not-so-magical whisky runners get busted for illegal *transportation*. E.L. Smith is among the unfortunate bootleggers caught red-legged. The D.A.'s office confiscated Smith's automobile, and he will likely spend a handful of days in pokey, all for selling three pints nearly a decade into Prohibition. Before the big shakedown ended, officers kicked over hundreds of gallons of hooch, spilling alcohol rivulettes out, quenching the dirt.

At the start of 1928, after months of schematic amendments and hooch runnin' run-ins, fragments of a structure pull together to form a stucco box that eclipses the northwest intersection of Beverly and Laurel avenues. The build is two stories; 21 rooms are allocated for use as a workshop, hotel, and stores, with a footprint on land and in the air totaling 13,446 square feet. At its core it is reinforced brick, skimmed with a flawless stucco job—tinted in the fashionable colors popular around the affluent and beauty-conscious neighborhood—soft pinks, greens, blues, and yellows—Once, I received a postcard from an ugly cousin; the front was a gouache painting of a canoe rowing upriver to a Spanish colonial mud hotel with tall, warm, show-through windows lining the second floor, everything overlooking the busy waterway below. One might be struck with the same sentiment standing across the beaver stream, taking in the myriad colors washing over the building as beams of setting sunlight graze it unobstructed, turning the evening pastels neon in the twilight. Smith is far from finished and decides to convert a few closets into a hallway and install a shower and toilet for use by men only, of course. Oh, and there's that little matter of marking skylights in place on plans that already have stamped approval. I hope this will not be an issue in a few decades …

Some peculiarities surround the physical mailing address. Its facade runs 55 feet down Beverly Boulevard, with two entrances; the main center gate is 8053 and accounts for the entire second floor. 8055 is at the farthest-west corner of the building and is a partitioned single unit. The east wall of the building runs from the corner of Beverly Boulevard, down Laurel Avenue 118 feet, which exposes five entrances; 8051 Beverly Blvd. takes up a significant portion of the first floor, and then four doors trail leading to similar but smaller units; 301, 303, 305, 307 of Laurel Avenue. Turning the corner down the alley, the building's rear is latticed with a fire escape system staggering from the rooftop down to a single large reinforced door at the west end of the wall, a steel gateway leading from the alley directly underground, where most of our second part is to take place, but let's not put the cart before the horse:

Application checked and found O. K. *1/16/28*

HOTEL

Purpose of Building presently? *STORE & APT BLDG*

HOTEL

Purpose of Building hereafter? *STORE & APT BLDG*

STATE EXACTLY WHAT ALTERATIONS WILL BE MADE TO THIS BUILDING: *ADDITION OF WORKROOM ON LOWER ROOF. AND ELEVATOR ROOM ON UPPER ROOF.* **Addition size?** *35 x 26* **Application checked and found O.K.** *1/28/28*

> Apr. 14—$100,000 WAS SPENT ON THIS NEW BEVERLY BUILDING—The new E.L. Smith Building at Beverly and Laurel is said to be the largest business structure on the boulevard west of Melrose. With the announcement that the new Smith Building, erected for $100,000 and located at the corner of Beverly boulevard and Laurel avenue, is completed, E.L. Smith & Sons, owners and builders, and electrical contractors formerly of Huntington Park, are planning to occupy their new home on May 1. The new Smith Building is one of the most unique in Southern California; it is a class-A structure, reinforced brick with stucco covering, tinted in various rainbow colors in keeping with the beauty of the elaborate residences of the fashionable Beverly district. Plans were drawn up by Eric Black, architect, with the view of making the building one of the finest structures, with facilities and space for offices, businesses, and apartments combined, departing abruptly from the usual type of building. Erected on the property, which affords the structure with floor space of 7000 square feet on each of its three floors, the Smith Building will undergo a few changes when the builder adds several more floors to the top. Smith intends to make the addition within the next two years with the view of having a limit-height building.

On the first day of May, the Smiths move into their new home at 317 N. Laurel Ave., which sits mere yards directly behind their $100,000 crown jewel. E.L., as proud as he is of his architectural achievement, is eager to see a return on his sizeable investment. Until asses occupy rooms, it might as well be a pile of cow patties. Pressures from outside are coming to Smith about getting his literal underground speakeasy down and running.

higher.

The fog

and

higher,

rises higher, and

H lly od is blot ed out west of where Beverly Avenue and Fairfax Avenue conjoin.

BOOK | ONE

I found something so repulsive in this idea—*let's look deep into yourself or myself.* If you look deep into any person, you will discover shit; dirty dreams, horrible things. I like appearances; MASKS. I think the only way to do something great is to have an obviously false, wrong! idea about yourself and to follow it to the end. Already, in real life, we are not who we are. We are *acting* in the sense that we identify with a certain image of ourselves. I am totally opposed to authenticity because authenticity presupposes that behind all the games you are playing, you have some deep identity—*the real yourself.* Maybe there is something like this, but I prefer not to know about it. It's horrible, a nightmare. This is the lesson of psychoanalysis, not to *become who you truly are.* The lesson of psychoanalysis is just to briefly confront that horror so that you may again acquire distance from it—SLAVOJ ŽIŽEK

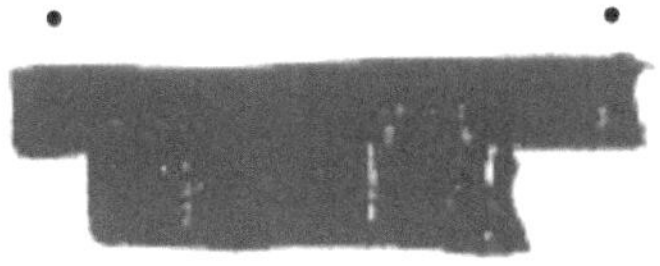

TIPPY-TOP SECRET

July 7, 1965

MEMORANDUM FOR

V.I.R.U.S. Director, PROONE GHEISTWHITES

SUBJECT: Classification review of PHASES ONE (1) and TWO (2) of the PONSONBY COMMISSION REPORT.

gent Siouxx and I have successfully obtained

a ssion currently the opening

P NCHON has been

COMMISSION

th

th

FB thering

PHASE I

VITO—Latin: *life-giving*, from the ancient German word *wido*, meaning *wood*. Wido is further bastardized into the derogatory American slang term *guido*, referring to an urban working-class, aggressive, macho Italian-American, usually one of questionable character. Verb: *to avoid, shun, or evade.*

Vito Paulekas, 22, "Sanpaku, Sanpakme" from *The Boston Globe* (1936)

• •

BANANA OIL SPECIALIST—May 9, 1928; 11a. We rock aboard the *SS Karlsruhe* of the North German Lloyd, anchored temporarily in Commonwealth Pier in Boston. The last American Pagan, Vitantas Alphonse Paulekas, or simply VITO, as he will come to be known to the world, is a secondary school dropout condemned to work for nearly a year as a Western Union bicycle courier. Vito lives in a small brownstone at Pacific House, 71 Oak St., in Somerville, MA, with his father, Jonas, a manufacturing operative, his sister, Albena, 4, and a handful of familial immigrant transplants from Lithuania; Mama Rose wrangles the rejects. Vito was born under the Taurus' charge on May 20, 1913. At the age of four, Vito learned wood carving from his grandfather, a master craftsman and sculptor in the Paulekas' homeland of Lithuania. At the age of six, Vito entered grammar school and learned to speak English, having previously spoken only Russian with his family and Sicilian with his neighborhood gangs. The Boston Red Scare and the 1920 trial of Sacco and Vanzetti made a profound impression on the seven-year-old. That same year, Father Jonas's brother, Julius Paulekas, moved his wife and three-year-old daughter, Eva *Bobo* Paulekas, back to Lithuania, where he bought a farm for $3,000. But, when the Cabinet of Lithuania required age-eligible male citizens to patrol their neighborhood streets at nightime in the name of national security, Julius paid the $50 fine, sold the farm at a $1,000 loss, and booked the family back to the US, settling down in Noblestown, PA, 590 miles southwest of Boston. At age 12, Vito fell in with a rough crowd, leading to his enrollment at the Massachusetts Reformatory in Concord, MA. He *attended* the school for a year and a half before returning to Cambridge to enroll at Rindge Technical High School. By September 1927, the 14-year-old had crested his personal limit for restructuring, reforming, or correcting of any sort, exhibiting little authorship. Vito is heading for the same fate as the doomed Italian duo whom he so admired. He has been called cunning; the kid's a natural, and he knows it, realizing at the exact right moment that his major asset is his mouth. With an emotional governance over intellect, Vito drops out of school, opting for street-level adventures more akin to those had by Huck Finn than those of Alex Bell, filling his days by exploring Bean Town backstreets as a Western Union *trotter*—learning to navigate the dingy urban grid with ease.

But, today, aboard the *SS Karlsruhe* tethered in Boston's Commonwealth Pier, Vito is 15 years old; his pudgy, inescapably Baltic frame snakes down maritime corridors like a tiny hungry shrew, working his way from one cabin to the next, methodically rummaging, quickly inventorying items in the rooms to pocket. This felt-tip marking pen, which Vito has only heard of, will have to do, and it fits nicely into the slip between his pomaded hair and messenger's cap. He carries on in the same fashion to the next cabin, and then the next cabin, moving through steel arches, working his way down into the hull. It is hard to make out, but Vito ignores the final checks and last calls just before a brutal jolt as the enormous turbines erupt to life, pushing the ship from harbor to sea.

Tomorrow, on May 10, 1928, this hull-jacking stowaway makes page one of the *Boston Globe* morning edition:

> MESSENGER NEARLY GOT A FREE TRIP TO EUROPE—BOY, AN OCEAN LINER FOR FIRST TIME, DID NOT THINK ABOUT THE SAILING HOUR—Vito Paulekas, 15-year-old Western Union messenger boy, just missed getting a nice, long, free ride to Europe yesterday afternoon, it became known this morning. Instead, he got a lecture from his "boss" when he showed up to go to work today. It seems that yesterday forenoon at 11, the steamship Karisruhe of the North German Lloyd was scheduled to sail from Commonwealth Pier. The office af the line, at 65 State st, had a last-minute message to send to the purser of the steamer, and they called for a messenger. Vito was the boy

they got. Vito went aboard the liner. He didn't know where to find the purser. He had never been on a big steamer before; in fact, he had never been in anything bigger than a rowboat. He went "downstairs," looked around a bit, found the purser, and delivered the message. Then he let his interest wander a bit. He roamed over the steamer into the smoking rooms, through the corridors, and everywhere. After a time, he came "upstairs" again and hit the deck. He looked around, and lo and behold, the pier had vanished. Vito hadn't known the line had started, so smooth was the motion, and there he was.

"PRETTY TOSSY OUT THERE"—"How did you feel then?" he was asked this morning. "I got a thrill," he answered. He knew, in a general way, that the ship was going to Europe, but he didn't know where exactly. He was a bit flabbergasted, but before he had time to think about it very much, an officer found him and escorted him to Capt Filsinger. The skipper, thinking he was a stowaway, let loose upon him a torrent of harsh language. It was mostly wasted, because it was all in German, and Vito didn't understand a word of it. Finally, the skipper made him understand, "What are you doing here?" Vito managed to explain, and the skipper's ire abated at once. Just then, the pilot boat Liberty was getting ready to take off the pilot from the Karisruhe. The pilot went over the side, and then they fastened a rope around Vito's middle and lowered him into a small boat. "It was pretty tossy out there," Vito says. Once aboard the Liberty, Vito was royally entertained. The crew gave him a big feed and gave him the run of the craft. "Then I began to get groggy, sea-sick," continues Vito's story. "When I'd feel sick, I'd go up on deck, where it was cold, and then I'd go downstairs again."

OFF BOSTON LIGHT ALL AFTERNOON—The pilot boat loitered around off Boston Light all afternoon, and no opportunity offered to put the passenger ashore. Meanwhile, the Western Union people were having a nervous fit, to put it mildly. They sent radiograms to the Kardsrhue, and they communicated with Vito's mother, Mrs. John Paulekas of 381 Portman St., Cambridge. They were all hot and bothered. "Where is he?" they all wondered. Then, along about 5 in the afternoon, a fishing schooner came along, inbound. Vito was transferred to it in another small boat and

> came into Commercial Wharf. He reported to the company's office at 6:30 pm. That was all until this morning, when Vito reported at the North German Lloyd office. "I delivered your message, sir," he said, and presented the receipt, signed by the purser of the Karlsruhe. And then Vito's own supervisor, the Big Boss, sent for him and gave him a lecture. It doesn't appear that it was anybody's fault, particularly that Vito got a ride on a liner, but probably the worry he caused had to be unloaded somewhere. Anyway, his spirits do not seem at all lowered today. He likes his job, for it keeps him out in the open air and provides plenty of exercise. He went to Rindge Technical High in Cambridge until about nine months ago. He has been wearing his yachtman's cap and uniform ever since leaving school. He is of Lithuanian descent.

Vito's not just all hold-ups and sticky fingers, though. An insatiable interest in art, music, performance, social politics, and scheming has festered in him ever since he cracked his lupine eyes open to the third dimension. In fact, during the summer of 1928, Vito toured with a traveling amateur vaudeville troupe, performing in Somerville, Lowell, Medford, Fitchburg, and several other cities that kiss Greater Boston's borders.

BOVRIL

IS A GOOD DEFENCE AGAINST

INFLUENZA

•　　　　　　　•

TO THE SHITMEN GO THE SPOILS—May 16, 1929, Fontana, CA. A cargo train pulling a string of gondolas grinds to a stop near Fontana Farms, its massive cars spilling over with slop intended to be shoveled into a dugout that stretches 30 yards of ballast. Ten-foot-wide mud trenches lead down to an enormous pen lined with troughs, where farmhands sift through the dumped riches, separating the inedible materials from the *food.* A pile of discarded silverware accumulates at one hand's feet. A fella can certainly bring home the bacon peddling this crap to fools to melt into knick-knacks and tchotchkes for tourists and dreamers. Fox Movietone News and Paramount News Service film crews are on site to document the world's largest hog ranch, home to 2,000 low-squealers until it isn't. In the most prominent building, the one with—P R O C E S S I N G—painted in giant black block letters across a pale blue corrugated roof; that's where the swine are slaughtered. By the time their pink and fleshy squeals reach the film crews, they have morphed into the tensile waves of an orchestra tuning —*SEE WHAT ALL THE SQUEALING IS ABOUT THIS SEPTEMBER, ONLY ON THE BIG SCREEN!*—It can be stated with certainty that this will not be the last time that swine take over the talkies. When the cargo train makes its return run one hour east to Los Angeles tonight, the free world's favorite hypokrites of the day soirée in the Blossom Room of the Roosevelt Hotel, gathering for the first Academy Awards ceremony. Take a look-see at these faces—some from this esteemed bunch will go home with a golden trinket, a metal homunculus; the Academy Award of Merit, manifested by the world-famous George Maitland Stanley, nicknamed by him simply as *Oscar*. Stanley makes no guarantee that his Oscar isn't comprised of semi-precious pigslop.

• •

Christmastime, 1929—The Paulekas tribe moves to 381 Portland St. in Cambridge on the very block where 53 years earlier, Alexander Graham Bell made the first-ever telephone call via a two-mile wire woven precariously through these streets two miles to Thomas Watson in Boston proper. But, Vito will not come to give two shits about this fact, and perhaps neither should you. Vito has gained siblings and ditched immigrant family members since we last checked in with the household count. Vito's older sister, Albena, is now 20, and his brothers, Bronsilo, is 14, and John, 9. Americans don't know it just yet, but the Great Depression looms over the horizon. 16-year-old Vito works as a dishwasher and busboy at a Cambridge hotel that has become a favorite meeting spot for organized crime goons; for example, crime boss and owner of Messina & Co. grocers, Gaspare Messina—who recently moved his family less than one mile east of the Paulekas's—occasionally employs Vito and other trotters to perform small-time fencing gigs in exchange for mad money. Vito's father, Jonas, is a sausage linker for The Boston Sausage & Provisions Company at 168 Blackstone St. in Boston; his fingers flat and broad, perfectly shaped for this line of work, but Vito needs fingers for fighting & fucking, not stuffing sausages. In the evening, Vito performs with a local theatre troupe in an unheated theatre.

1930. New Year's Day. Two and a half miles west of Vito's home, officers graze Daniel Callahan's ransacked Cambridge apartment at 1423 Cambridge St. Callahan discovers that thirty dollars in cash is missing from his telephone table. A detective announces to everyone in the hallway that a set of wax keys had been jammed into the locks to gain entry. Maggie With A Limp from across the hall, is interviewed by detectives and describes a short, hatted young man entering the unit quietly and quickly.

Midget Golf has swept the nation. Over the last decade, 25,000 courses have been installed across the country, constructed from secondhand materials, waste, anything people could get their impoverished mitts on. Movie theatre owners are pulling all kinds of stunts to drive asses off those janky links and into their *comfortable* seats. Cleo Short has bet against the theatres and found course-building in Maine to be a lucrative business. He leveled his sights on making it big in Boston and relocated his wife, Phoebe, and their four young daughters, Elizabeth, Nony, Joan, and Muriel, 107 miles south from Portland to Boston at 49 Evans St.

• •

January 11, 1930. After one year of public service, the anticipated thoroughfare, Beverly Avenue, is christened Beverly Boulevard, cutting commuters between downtown and Beverly Hills. The Greater Beverly Boulevard Association celebrates that their *most optimistic anticipations* were exceeded. Cars and cars and people and more cars and more people, all day; every day chugging past the pastel stucco box that eats up the corner. The three opposing corner lots at the quadrant of Beverly and Laurel are cleared and posted for sale.

> *The Los Angeles Times.* BEAUTY parlor, good location. See Dentist, Beverly Blvd. at Laruel, or DRUG store for rent, new. 8051 Beverly Blvd., cor. Laurel. See Dentist

Over the next two months, Smith's suite 203 tenant at 8053 Beverly Blvd.—dentist Dr. DeMonoco—sets in LA's three major newspaper outlets a springtime honey trap to collect specimens for an *experimental psychological study group* ... for *dentists.*

> DIFFERENT—INTERESTING—HELPFUL. Dr. De Monoco's System of Experimental Psychology. Phone or write for details. 8053 Beverly Blvd. 203, OX-6200.

> INTENSELY INTERESTING EXCLUSIVE—My lectures or instruction in EXPERIMENTAL PSYCHOLOGY will appeal strongly to women of individualistic tendencies, refinement, and good intellectual and educational backgrounds. In other words, I wish unusual women attend not because the study is most fascinating but because a good mentality is a necessary prelude for the student to gain the full measure of benefits. No matter what the extent of your knowledge and experience. I believe you will contact here something different. Bearing these qualifications in mind, for details, call in person or write Room 203, 8053 Beverly Blvd., at Laurel Av.

BUSINESS PERSONALS—EVERYBODY Even YOU like to meet the REAL thing. You, Miss or Mrs. Intelligent Woman, are invited to call. Will you? Instruction in EXPERIMENTAL Psychology (Personal and Lectures) Benefit yourself. Suite 203. 8053 Beverly Blvd.

Intensely Interesting—Lectures and individual instructions for intelligent women based on the natural laws of Experimental Psychology. You will find that this unique system will give you a new confidence in yourself and your potentialities and an aim to strive for in your life, no matter in what field you may be interested in. Call in person or write for details. Room 203, 8053 Beverly Blvd. A STUDY GROUP for Doctors and Dentists is being organized.

2 YOUNG or mid. aged women to introduce Dr. De Monoco's System of Experimental Psychology. New, different, interesting. Excellent earnings possible. All or part time. Call 11 a.m. to 8 p.m. Suite 203, 8053 Beverly Blvd.

CLASS in Experimental Psychology now forming. Limited number. Interesting, helpful & different. Write immediately for details, Suite 203, 8053 Beverly Blvd.

2 YOUNG ladies for refined, dignified, interesting work, pertaining to appointments relative to Experimental Psychology. Room 203, 8053 Beverly Blvd., at Laurel.

PURSE lost, lady's green leather, cont' letter addressed to England. Reward. 8053 Beverly Blvd., Rm. 203.

•   •

TIMED MACHINES—As the stroke of midnight nears in the Midwest, eleven couples are left swaying on the dance floor, after relying on a comatose partner's support for the last 130 hours (14 days) of pushing their mental and physical endurance to its breaking point. The risks may be high, but 500 big ones are on the line. A talking machine is unceremoniously rolled onto the stage to let the orchestra take five. A lanky dancer smashes to the boards, bringing down along with him his somnambulist partner—OUT!

At 1:45a, ten couples remain. The promoter switches OFF the music machine to announce that the marathon committee is in the red and cannot afford to complete the event, let alone pay the winners, but thanks for coming. The big brooms emerge and sweep the stick-it-out kids and tired housewives through the doors. At the 2:00a buzzer, the arena has been cleared, the double doors chained, and the public barred. Endurance challenges of all kinds fall out of fashion across the states as the newspapers marginalize US citizens, calling them *insane* for wanting to participate in, or worse, view these public displays of destitution distraction. Vito trades his scuffed oxfords for a nickel barrel and pharmacy-grade domino mask before seeking out Fantömas to momentarily take control of the harbor streets by knocking over a string of retailers, nabbing autos, and robbing outdoor lovers.

> June 21—*The Boston Globe*, YOUTH HOLDS UP DORCHESTER STORE—Vincent White was closing his drugstore at 798 Washington st, Dorchester, at 10 o'clock last night when an 18-year-old boy walked in and demanded the contents of the cash register. To emphasize his demand, he pointed a long-barreled pistol at White's head. "Let me have the money right away, or I will shoot," the boy announced. White argued for a moment, but he did not like the look of determination in the boy's eyes, so he turned over to him five $1 bills, all that was in the cash register. Then, the boy

> insisted on being taken to a rear door through which he disappeared. The boy was about 5 feet 5 inches tall, White told the police, wore a gray cap and a gray mixed suit, and has a flesh-colored mole on the left side of his nose.

Vito is 18 years old and 5 feet 4 inches tall. Then, three weeks later, only a mile and a half south:

> July 10—*The Boston Globe*, YOUTH HOLDS UP STORE MANAGER—Escaped With $73.17 After Holdup in Ashmont —John Featherstone, manager of the First National Store at 1668 Dorchester av. Ashmont was robbed of $73.17 this afternoon by a young man who entered the store while he was alone. The youth disappeared in an automobile parked just below the store. Featherstone told the police that the man accosted him at the counter and asked for a package of cigarettes. When he faced his "customer" with the package, he said, he was staring into the muzzle of a revolver and was met with a demand for the money in the cash register. His only alternative was to comply with the request, he told the police. He said the man was about 5 feet tall, weighed about 160 pounds, and wore a soft gray hat and gray suit. The description of the man was teletyped to all the police stations.

Cleo Short's once-thriving miniature golf course building business has turned a hole-in-none and forced him to rotate through a series of remedial jobs. When spring 1930 arrives, time is up for a personal loan payment. The summer of 1930 was spent dodging debt collectors and knee-breakers until a piecrust promise caught up with him in the fall. Phoebe, scared and outraged that the family is in the crosshairs, demands that Cleo concoct a solution quickly. Cleo will fake his death and disappear, and Phoebe will collect on his life insurance policy. Soon after, the knee-breakers return to New England with news of being forever unable to collect, and so forth, the dominoes falling accordingly. Then, Cleo will shuffle the family to the sunny West Coast, where they will, of course, all live happily ever after. The parents work out the details, settling on suicide by drowning; Cleo leaping to his death from the Washington Street Bridge that stretches over the Charles River. It's an awful way to go, and perfect.

On October 12, 1930, at 11:30p, Cleo positions his sedan just right on a bank of the Charles River. If he stands on tiptoes to gaze to the southwest, away from the Charles River N. Washington Street bank, Cleo could likely spy the Paulekas house. Reading the note one last time before placing it on the front seat, Cleo has trouble keeping his lips pulled down over that big 'ol toothy Flatbush cemetery grin as the plan falls easily into place.

> Oct. 15—*The Boston Globe*, TWO YOUTHS HOLD UP HARVARD STUDENT, GET $4—Two youths, one carrying a revolver, late last evening held up Herbere Olds, a Harvard student residing in James Smith Hall, on Dunster st, Cambridge, relieving him of $4 and his wallet. Olds told the police that the holdup pair were only about 18 years old. In the past week, two youths answering a similar description were successful in three other holdups.

In Boston, a school bus carrying Vito's 15-year-old brother Benjamin collides with a large delivery truck. Benjamin walks away unscathed, but several students are injured. One child dies.

> Dec. 27—*The Boston Globe*, DANCE CONTEST—Danny Duggan, former champion ballroom dancer of the United States, will conduct an inter-city dance contest at the Bowdoin Square Theatre next week. Contestants are requested to hand in their names and addresses at the box office of the theatre this week. The preliminary contests will be held nightly at 9 o'clock, with the final contest on Saturday night. Any kind of dancing is included, including Highland fling, Irish jig, the Blackbottom, waltz, ballet, and eccentric dances. The prize includes three engraved silver trophies, and the winner of the first prize will be given a week's engagement at the Bowdoin Square Theatre.

Vito is gonna win this if it kills him.

He scours his usual back alley sources for a try-out partner, and finds a seemingly formidable contender, but his choice proves a poor one, and Vito is cut from the roster.

SHORT-ARM INSPECTION—After 1931 finally manages to roll out of bed and wander into America's living room, it finds that most of its inhabitants continue to suffer in one capacity or another from economic hardship. Relief from desperation reaches an apex, leading many citizens to willingly push their food sacks well past their physical and mental limits simply for a fair shake at staying on this rock.

Widow Short moves herself and four daughters into a modest apartment at 115 Salem Street in Medford, only one half mile due east of the Paulekas home. Phoebe finds steady work as a bookkeeper. The collectors have stopped coming by, and Cleo's insurance checks, small as they are, help close the financial gap. Phoebe hasn't heard so much as a peep from Cleo. Maybe he did get it in the end.

A new automobile stolen from Medford, and another from 16 Highland Avenue, Cambridge, were found abandoned on the West Side, two and a half miles west of Vito's home. Chief of Police Rogers and patrolman O'Connell arrive on the Cambridge streets armed with riot guns, prepared for the worst. On February 25, 1931, *The Barre Daily Times* reports that the robbery of a Sommerville filling station by two youths went tits-up after the attendant was shot and critically wounded, a little flub that gets Vito's partner taken off captor duty come March 4 when they rob a store in Malden. Vito muscles the store owner and his wife to the back of the shop while the partner rifles through the till for a $60 take before firing up their small getaway car and splitting. Two weeks later, while William Burke and Mary Griffin are seated in a parked car in Somerville, they are seized and ordered by Vito, Joey Mikowski, and Tony Evanofsky to exit the vehicle. Burke is jacked for $30 and his machine. In another week, three masked robbers enter a Revere chain store brandishing nickel-plated pistols. One toughie charges the cashier and demands access to the register—*The first, about 5 feet 3 inches tall, wore a black leather jacket and a brown soft hat*—Another thug blocks the exit, demands that the manager and customers line up along the wall, and lets the third toughie tie their hands behind their backs—*the second, with blue glasses and of dark complexion, was about 5 feet 6 inches and wore a black overcoat and a brown soft hat, and the third, about 5 feet 5 inches, was of slim build and wore a black overcoat and brown soft hat*—So it goes: the hold-up develops as smoothly as any good criminal could wish. Their take is 85 smackers and a shiny watch from the manager. The short fella got an armful of cigarette cartons as a consolation prize. Moving over one county, to a store in Everett:

> March 26—*The Boston Globe*, Cool to the point of even waiting upon a customer who chanced in before they had completed their work, three young men, all under 24, held up the drugstore of Francis Buckley at 52 Nichols st, East Everett, tonight and made off in an automobile with a total of $82. Menaced by pistols, Buckley and his sister, Miss Elanor Buckley of 45 Wolcott st, were forced into the cellar after Buckley was made to give over his gold watch and his wallet, containing $11. The youths took $71 from the till and 12 packages of cigarettes. They had backed Buckley and his sister into a rear room when a customer came into the store. Two of the men jammed their pistols at the Buckleys while the third youth went into the front and calmly waited upon the customer, who left without suspecting a holdup was in progress. SEARCH REVERE CUSTOMER — These descriptions were given to the police: The first about 5 feet 3 inches tall, wore a black leather jacket and a brown soft hat: the second, with blue glasses and of dark complexion, was about 5 feet 6 inches and wore a black overcoat and a brown soft hat, and the third, about 5 feet 5 inches, was of slim build and wore a black overcoat and brown soft hat.

All three related incidents appear in the next morning's edition of the *Boston Globe*. Vito is getting good ink.

April 7, 1931. Vito eats dinner with the family at their cramped kitchen table. The radio plays loudly, trying to overpower a heated argument Jonas and Vito are having in Lithuanian. Jonas wants his 17-year-old, unemployed son to join him at The Boston Sausage & Provisions Company and earn a good, honest wage, achieving social stability. Yet, Vito remains unwavering, refusing to compromise. Big sister Alberta contributes, working as a hairdresser. Brother Benjamin has his foot in the door of law enforcement, working at Jonas's place of employment as a security guard. Later that night, Vito suffers a mild change of heart when he reads the *oh-shit* news splashed across the front page of the *Boston Globe* evening edition:

> MIKOWSKI AND EVANOFSKY ARE HELD IN $10,000 BAIL—Joseph Mikowski, 17, of 8 Elm st, Somerville, and Anthony Evanofsky, 18, of 55 Harding st, Cambridge, pleaded not guilty to robbery while armed when arraigned in the Somerville District Court yesterday. Their cases went over until Thursday for trial. They were held for $10,000 each until that time. They were arrested Sunday in connection with the holdup of William E. Burke and Miss Mary Griffin as they were seated in a parked car in front of 74 Walnut st, Somerville, on March 19. Burke was robbed of $30 and his car, which was found abandoned the next day in Cambridge.

SWEET EGGS, $10,000! These two had better omertà their asses off, keep those fucking traps zipped, but before sunup, police descend upon 381 Portland St. and take Vito Alphonse Paulekas into custody.

> PAULEKAS HELD IN $10,000—CAMBRIDGE YOUTH TAKEN IN SOMERVILLE CASE—The third youth, Vito Paulekas, the last of a trio wanted on charges made in connection with the holdup of William E. Burke of 43 Hobart st, Brighton, and Miss Mary Griffin of Somerville, as they were seated in a parked car in front of 74 Walnut st, Somerville, on the night of March 19, was arraigned in the Somerville District Court today.

ESTABROOK'S REACH—On the morning of April 9, Vito appears before the judge, who gives the usual run-down, punctuating the offensiveness of the acts while armed. CLANG! According to today's *Boston Globe*, Vito is freed after his public hearing *at the request of the Government*, then immediately re-arrested by Chief of Police Thomas Damery and Sergeant Inspector Daniel M. O'Connell. When it's all over, Vito is spared jail time but ordered to serve three months at one of President Roosevelt's developing Civilian Conservation Corps camps headquartered in a boys' corrections facility in Concord, NH, and Albany, NY. The experimental program has Vito building and mending outdoor structures and parks throughout rural communities in New England. In late June, Vito returns to 381 Portland St. with 15 bucks in his pocket—$75 has already been delivered to his parents. Vito is worse off than ever, but if being enrolled in a criminal summer camp is the worst hand he could be dealt, he'll gladly take his chances. Jonas and Rose lack the appreciation of how deep-seated Vito's addiction is and expect their son to *go straight* from here on out, but Vito's need to thrill his balls all the way to notoriety, preferably using public print as his megaphone, is taking priority.

On a muggy July morning, Vito and his new partner dig in their heels and perform five consecutive successful auto holdups. *Boston Globe* reports:

> The thieves took 25 cents from Skillings, $2 from Riley, and $2 from Benson. The armed youths were described as being about 18 years of age and hatless. According to the police, Skillings was the first to be held up. He was driving a car on Grove st, near the Medford line, when suddenly, the two youths jumped from a clump of bushes to the side of the car and leveled a revolver at him, ordering him to stop the car. They forced the couple from the car and then jumped in the car themselves and drove away. Less than 75 feet away, they forced to the curb another car driven by Riley. They forced Riley and a girl to leave the car, and after taking $2 from Riley, abandoned the car operated by Skillings and sped away

> in Riley's machine. Riley and his companion got in the abandoned car and drove to the Winchester Police Station, telling their story to Lieut John A. Harrold. Skillings and his companion arrived at the police station soon afterward and had a similar story for the lieutenant, who immediately ordered a thorough search of the district. In the meantime, the youths had staged another holdup in the same section. The victim this time was Benson, from whom they took $2. Sergt Edward W. O'Connell was assigned to the case and, accompanied by patrolman Dolan, he searched the section but was unable to locate anyone. The police learned later that the youths had staged two other holdups in Cambridge and East Cambridge.

The heat is coming down on Vito, his house visited by detectives looking to connect him to the recent rash of machine thefts. Vito may be daring, but he stocked patience in spades. He and the new partner cool their patent leather wide-balls for a spell. When fall arrives, Vito's nest egg has thinned translucent. Time to get back to work; time to lap up more of that good, good ink. Say *ah!*:

> Nov. 3—*The Boston Globe*, LYNN STOREKEEPER ROBBED OF $100 BY BOLD THIEVES—LYNN, Nov. 2—Police were notified by Joseph Savoy of 137 Franklin st, proprietor of a variety store, that he had been held up and robbed of $100 by three men shortly before midnight tonight. Savoy told police that the three men entered his store, and one of them asked for a package of cigarettes. As Savoy turned to get the cigarettes, another man pointed a pistol and ordered him to throw up his hands. The other then ransacked the cash register and warned Savoy that if he called the police, they would return and shoot him. As soon as they left the store, Savoy saw them run down Franklin st in the direction of Saugus. He then notified police and gave a good description of the holdup men.

1932. KING DODO—Half of the United States' 30 million citizens are unemployed and desperately seek refuge from the colorless day-to-day reality. Once, whacking a ball into a licked-clean olive tin fit the bill, but midget golf has now gone bust. Americans desire getting swept away in wild adventures, and the exploration of alien worlds in pulp fiction, *Buck Rogers*, *Doc Savage*, *Thrilling Detective*, and, most popular of all, *Fantômas*.

The movie industry pushes a particular interest in theatres as the new places of worship, enforcing Depression-era feed-and-fucks smear campaigns across the nation, encouraging citizens to sit their starving asses down in air-conditioned theatres, and avoid those social credit demerits altogether. The city of Finchburg feels differently and gives the finger to local governments by hosting an endurance dance. An ad in *The Finchburg Sentinel* offers a special rate bus line that will make the 60-mile round trip to White City Park in Shrewsbury, MA.

Vito arrives in Finchburg on a packed chartered bus and registers for the heavily promoted contest. Jitterbuggers and lindyhoppers spill out and into the quasi-amusement park property, cooling off and pigging out on the free food. Vito dances for days. Then three weeks. Before he knows it, five months have passed, and the event suddenly ends. He's just woken up from a long, deep slumber, his overachieving dick swollen and shades of purple after endless seaside conquests during the mandatory 45-minute breaks. Weeks of synchronizing his heartbeat and circulation with the Foxtrot have left him with his stamina, and that's about it.

He can American Smooth and fuck for hours on end.

s l o w s l o w | quickquick

s l o w s l o w | quickquick

s l o w s l o w | quickquick

s l o w s l o w | quickquick

Vito is left to roam White City Park. Hobos chug wine from coffee mugs as if visiting Beowulf at Mead Hall. Armed with little more than fleeting thought forms of pretty faces down and round asses up—but little good those elicit memories do him now with unraveling, holey pockets full of nothin'. No matter, he hadn't the bus fare home to start.
It's all becoming clear again: he must do what must be done.

Vito forges a relationship with a small Shrewsbury criminal enterprise, simultaneously entering a romantic entanglement with a fellow gang member's mother, Planchette Palinka. Vito crashes with the middle-aged, widowed dancer for a few weeks. Palinka feeds the little lover-boy and nurses him back to health—she is part mama eagle, part cum bucket; a powdered and oiled stack of curves and creases and folds, pounded by filtered coastal-east morning sun—*If you dream it*, she told Vito sitting backwards in his rigid lap, *you can probably fuck it*— Although she lacked confidence in her summation, Vito found Palinka's philosophy concise and correct. They share a moment of visiting Valhalla when Palinka wrapped Vito's flat fingers around her fragile, frigid neck—throttling her ligaments and straps until she climaxes; blood rushing in to fill the whole of Palinka's neck to warm Vito's meaty palms.

On May 24, the gruesome threesome targets the Fenmore cafeteria, and then the American Gas & Oil Company filling station in Fitchburg at the end of June ... $50 here, $35 there ...

It's time to return to Cambridge, but before leaving, Vito sculpts his soup-can-dick out of a bar of soap and leaves it behind as a reminder for the widow.

He cashes in his chips and bails on the Fitchburg operation, and hitches a ride back to Boston with a bundle of filthy bills weighing down his britches—his head is loaded and cocked with tall tales of marathon wins. Although the *Boston Globe* reports a possible alternative source of Vito's mad money:

> July 6. FORCE CAMBRIDGE CLERK TO OPEN SAFE; GET $75—Two armed men calmly walked into the Emma Jettick shoe store at 5640 Massachusetts av in the heart of Central st. Cambridge, at noon today, tried on several pairs of shoes and then held up the clerk and robbed the store of $75 and a pair of shoes. The two men forced the clerk, Francis Lee, 25, of 25 Highland av, Arlington, to open the safe and turn over to them the $75 in cash. The men then shoved Lee into the basement of the store and fled. Lee told police inspectors who are investigating the holdup that the men walked into the store and asked for a pair of shoes. He said one of the men, after trying on several shoes, decided to purchase a pair, and as soon as he had the shoes tied up, they held him up. He described one as wearing a sweater and the other as a pugilist. The manager of the store, Otto Nelson, was out for lunch at the time of the holdup.

> JANITOR HELD UP AND ROBBED OF $10—Geneo Calaforto, 50, janitor of the building at 145 Homestead st, Roxbury, reported to the police early this morning that he had been held up there about midnight and robbed of $10.55. He was in the basement of the building, he said, when two young men entered, and one of them pointed a pistol at him while the other took his money. They went away, he said, in a large automobile. It is believed by the police that the youths were using a stolen car.

Loew's Orpheum Theatre at the intersection of Washington Street and Hamilton Place reinstates its dancing girls contest after taking a ten-year hiatus. Poverty seems to have left many seeking solace in long legs and stretched necks.

19-year-old Vito watches Sophie Tucker's raucous performance, the mistress of ceremonies doing THIS, and THAT, and then a little more and more of THIS before handing out a cache of door prizes to a lucky contender.

What a life, that of a performer.

> Oct. 24—*Fitchburg Sentinel*, TWO YOUTHS HOLD UP CAFETERIA; GET $150—BOSTON. Two youths, armed with revolvers and wearing handkerchiefs as masks, early today held up five customers and the proprietor of the Fenmore cafeteria in the Back Bay section and robbed the cash register of $150. Manuel Gavallas, owner of the cafeteria, was closing for the night when the youths entered. One of the robbers ordered the customers and Gavallas to "line up against the wall." The other took the cash from the register. The five patrons, all men, were not molested, although all of them were carrying considerable amounts of money on their persons. The youths jumped into an automobile and got away.

June 1, 1933—The Loew's Orpheum runs an advert on page 22 of *The Boston Globe—Air conditioning. Girls. Hell Below. John Barrymore. Friday morning, Public Rehearsal*—President Roosevelt approves one of his New Deal programs, the Civilian Conservation Corps, which is put into practice after the experimental criminal youth program Vito participated in a year earlier proved successful. Roosevelt hopes this government intervention will dampen the growing number of unemployed and left-tracking young American men. As a side effect, a Manchurian Candidate or two might saddle up to George Estabrook's mesmerization program.

• •

ONE BIG AMERICAN WET DREAM—Prohibition is murdered three weeks shy of Jesus's 1934th birthday party. Drunks claw out of holes and shuffle into any number of booze slinging clubs that hide from the sun. Some of the pastel shimmer has drained from the Smith Building. After seven years of ownership, the once-promising and successful speakeasy has gone dark since the bootleggers retired. E.L. Smith has lost all direction, and prepares his family for a beaver stream exodus from the cold stucco and steel shadow:

> *Los Angeles Times,* MORTGAGES, TRUSTS, DEEDS—$2800 BEAUTIFUL 7-rm. owner's home, Beverly & Laurel ave. Rose. UN.2553.
>
> FURNITURE AT AUCTION 346—AUCTION—EXTRAORDINARY FURNISHINGS MONDAY, MARCH 11, 11 A. M. 8055 BEVERLY BLVD. Partial list: Florentine console & mirror, pair needlepoint love seats, massive gilded cabinet—handsomely carved, lamps with porcelain & onyx bases, Venetian side chairs, carved walnut table & fireside bench, radio bar, coffee tables, bric-a-brac, marble statues, beautiful living, dining, bedrm, suites, oriental rugs, fine Brunswick Balke billiard table, equipt., elec. refrigerators, ranges, reducing machine, athletic equip., office fixtures & many other high-grade items. Come prepared to buy. Owners leaving city. Every piece must be sold, rain or shine. W. DWIGHT HAMMOND AUCTIONEER. EX. 0444.

1935. Christmastime on the East Coast. Vito, 22, Charles Malkewicz, 23, and George Stockman, 23, trade stories in the fashion of Dick Tracy criminals meeting in a secret lair. One by one, they recount the criminal endeavors they have successfully executed this year, securing their rent and keeping the conveyor of ladies moving. Vito spends much of his alone time as a horny juvenile detective, explaining that he has developed an insatiable fancy for following women home—dancers are of particular interest. He obsesses over watching their bodies ripple on stage or studying them from a distance, learning exactly how those elegant padded skeletons move on life's stage, such as walking the dog or checking the mail. Not to be shown up, Malkewicz chimes in, blathering about his fascination with stubby, round girls with crooked noses and the close-set eyes of Midwesterners. The thugs take thuggy digs at one another, then argue about the correct way to reassemble a shorted-out shortwave radio that has been dismantled into a thousand electrical trinkets and dusted across the coffee table. Stockman consults the current issue of *Shortwave Notes* and slowly puts the miserable thing back together, before plugging it in and melting their portal to the local present into a bubbling plastic pool.

Elizabeth Short, 10, lives with her mother and sisters in Medford, a mere four miles north of Vito's home at 406 Columbia St., Cambridge.

1936. Feb. 23—Charles Malkewicz sits alone in a restaurant across the street from the RKO Boston Theater (co-owned by Joseph Kennedy), eating a modest lunch alone while peering out the window for several long spells, drinking in the image of the film house—He daydreams about the robbery of the theatre at gunpoint yesterday with George and Vito—Charlie finishes breakfast, pays, and exits, but before he scales the landing, several officers swoop in. One of them shouts *Charles Malkewicz!*, but before Charlie spits out a wisecrack, he's on the ground with silver cuffs and black socks blocking his view. Blue boys toss Malkewicz's bedroom at his family's South Boston Tudor Street home. Another explains callously to Mr. and Mrs. Malkewicz that their deadbeat son, as well as his deadbeat, good-for-nuthin' *best friend*, George Stockman, are held downtown on indictments of armed robbery and carrying weapons deemed in collusion with last night's hold-up of the RKO Boston Theater in which five people were tied up by three assailants who stole nearly $13,000 by brute force—*Aha!*—An officer digs out $4500 in bills from behind a radio console. Mama Malkewicz bawls hysterically—*!BOLO¡*—The banditos have fractured, but the loyal boys refuse to give Vito up, and so the little Lithuanian escapes apprehension—for now, but he has some damage control to run to keep it that way.

Vito tails a 19-year-old girl from her home to a corner store, where she uses their phone to contact the police, telling detectives she knows all the details of the case and agrees to come down to the station and spill it all to help *clean up*. The shop owner watches as the caller appears to recognize a short, young man who watches her from across the street, then drops the receiver and hurriedly exits. The following day, Vito calls the station after the girl fails to make her appointment and convincingly spins a yarn, portraying the girl in question as a totally and completely unreliable *drug addict*. Page one of the *Boston Globe* reports:

> JURORS INDICT TWO IN HOLDUP—THEATRE ROBBERY LAID TO SOUTH BOSTON PAIR—Indictments in the $12,800 robbery at the R. K. O. Boston Theatre were returned against two South Boston young men today by the Suffolk County Grand Jury. Charles Malkewicz, 23, and George H. Stockman were indicted on charges of armed robbery of Arthur Zinn, assistant manager of the theatre, and carrying weapons. A third youth is still being sought in connection with the holdup, which occurred in the cashier's office of the theatre at 9 o'clock the night of Feb 23 while about 300 persons were watching the show. Three men held up Zinn, Miss Norine Curtin, a stenographer, and two other men who were in the office at the time.

Vito followed RKO cashier Norine Curtin around town all day, spying on her going to and from the theatre, eating dinner with her family, and playing with a kid brother in the backyard. Vito needs to tie up a loose end, so on March 3, Vito calls Norine at her home. At first, he attempts to mimic a female voice. He threatens Norine about her upcoming testimony at trial for the February 23 robbery, making it clear *she ain't know nothing.* For the next week, a special service police officer picks Norine up in the morning and drives her home from the RKO Theatre each night.

> March 11. *The Boston Globe,* JURORS INDICT TWO IN HOLDUP—THEATRE ROBBERY LAID TO SOUTH BOSTON PAIR—Indictments in the $12,800 robbery at the R. K. O. Boston Theatre were returned against two South Boston young men today by the Suffolk County Grand Jury. Charles Malkewicz, 23, whose pink cheeks led to his arrest, and his best friend, George H. Stockman, were indicted on charges of armed robbery of Arthur Zinn, assistant manager of the theatre, and with carrying weapons. An additional charge of receiving stolen goods was returned against Malkewicz in whose home, Tudor st, South Boston, police claim to have found almost $4500 of the stolen currency. A third youth is still being sought in connection with the holdup, which occurred in the cashier's office of the theatre at 9 o'clock the night of Feb 23 while about 3000 persons were watching the show. Three men held up Zinn, Miss Norine Curtin, a stenographer, and two other men who were in the office at the time. The following day Malkewicz was taken into custody and he was issuing from a restaurant almost directly across the street from the theatre. Arraigned this afternoon before Judge John M. Gibbs, Malkewicz and Stockman pleaded not guilty. They were held in the same bail as set by the lower court, $24,000, with two sureties, for Malkweciz and $22,000, with two sureties, for Stockman. No date was set for trial but it is believed the cases will be called in May.

• •

SHOW ME YOUR WADS OF CASH—After nearly a decade of dominating the northwest corner of Beverly Boulevard and Laurel Avenue, E.L. Smith releases his worn pastel beast:

> March 29—*Los Angeles Times,* ARE you looking for a dependable business income with a real future and at a low foreclosure price? Drive by the N.W. corner of BEVERLY $ LAUREL. (8051 BEVERLY BLVD. 2 blocks West of Fairfax.) Here is a property you will be proud to own. Income $4000, which will double with business revival. One of the best-looking, best-built Stores, Office & Apt. Bldgs. in town. Brick & Steel construction, steel windows, high-grade appointments. Cost over $75,000. Foreclosure price is $37,500 and will take part in clear local exchange. Here is a property you can be proud to own. Drive by and see it (don't disturb tenants.) Call J. R. BANKS—GL. 3012.

But DO disturb the tenants if you're in the market for ten frogs:

> March 29—*Los Angeles Times,* FROG RAISING—FROG BREEDERS (Rana Catesbiana) $3.50 pair. Instructions with order 5 pairs or more. SEQUOIA FROG FARM. Office—8053 Beverly Blvd., Los Angeles, ORegon 0211

Or a low-mileage Chevrolet:

> March. 31—*Los Angeles Times,* CHEV. '35 coach, prvt party, 8000 mi. 8053 Beverly Blvd. WY. 0019 HO. 2911

• •

FRIENDS ARE ONLY GOOD FOR ALIBIS—It's Holy Weekend of April 1936. Malkewicz and Stockman are arraigned and awaiting trial in May. It has been eight weeks since their capture. If they had squealed, Vito would be in there with them by now, but he is instead left all by his lonesome on the outside. Despite the setback, he is not in the least bit deterred from plotting his next heist—another theatre, solo this time. Vito hedges his bets, having learned a thing or two over the past decade about proper assault procedures and etiquette. For instance, he has already dedicated the last three weeks to cold runs to and from the Loews Orpheum Theatre. He has religiously followed the cashier, Kay Lovely, in her daily routines at work and at home. This method worked like a charm with the last wannabe police informant, the cashier. Vito has computed thousands of mental notes about Lovely's graceful, delicate way of leaning into a doorway or carrying a healthy deposit to the office safe. Vito's criminality is fusing with his sexual conquest; the subversive behaviour itself is becoming increasingly erotic.

April 26—Using a grease pencil and theatre wax, Vito procures a fleshy scar that stretches across his right cheek from his temple to jawbone, a kind of *reminder wound* a teenaged Vito witnessed grown men accept for their complacency or inability to pay-up in the eleventh hour; the type of injury Cleophus Short likely faced had he hung back Medford and gulped his medicine (Lest not lose track of dat sot).

THE BOSTON DAILY GLOBE

THEATRE HOLDUP MAN CAUGHT

Robber Ties Up Five and Takes $3009 at Orpheum

Two Employees Make Capture

April 27—*The Boston Globe*, CAMBRIDGE MAN HELD IN $25,000—Police Say Amateur Actor Admits Orpheum Theatre Robbery—Vito Paulekas, 22-year-old amateur actor of Cambridge who, in vaudeville parlance, "laid and egg" whe he allegedly attempted a hold-up in disguise in Loew's Orpheum Theatre last night, was ordered held in $25,000 today when he appeared before Municipal Court Judge Michael J. Murray. A second Cambridge man whom police sought to implicate in the $3009 holdup was exonerated and released after Paulekas, taking all the blame upon himself, forced theatre employees to admit that they saw no one with him in the theatre. Paulekas waived examination on a charge of armed robbery and five charges of assault. Police produced in court a nickel-plated .38-caliber revolver which they alleged Paulekas concealed under a newspaper.—Wax Scar on Cheek—When captured in the theatre lobby following the holdup, in which five Orpheum employees were tied up, Paulekas, said by police to be an ex-convict, was disguised in actors' makeup, with an artificial three-inch wax scar affixed to his right cheek. Police say that in the lineup at headquarters, the youth admitted the holdup, disclosing that he had planned it for three weeks in advance. Members of the Special Service Squad, with the cooperation of Cambridge police, searched the suspect's home on Columbia st, Cambridge, and brought to the police station for questioning a man they found there. Later, Paulekas satisfied police that the second man was ignorant of the holdup. In the Paulekas home the officers say they found three black masks, three pairs of goggles and a makeup box as well as a short-wave radio.—Holdup in Theatre Lobby—The holdup occurred shortly after 10 o'clock last night. Paulekas intercepted the cashier, Miss Kay Lovely, and her escort of three employees in the lobby. It is the custom of the theatre to have the cashier guarded by several employees. Last night, Miss Lovely was escorted by Joseph Dervin, treasurer, Thomas Brock, and George Gileo, doormen. Just as the last of the party were entering the treasurer's office, Paulekas started to follow them and was halted by Al Charmichael, an usher, who became suspicious. Paulekas allegedly trained a gun, hidden beneath a newspaper, on Brock and Charmichael and forced them into the treasurer's office ahead of him. There, according to police, he tied them up with looped sections of clothesline, which he had brought with him. He took the money from the safe, but was captured before he left the Washington-st lobby. —Usher Gives Warning—Gerald Pelrin, 36, of 123 Atlantic st, North Quincy, an usher, became suspicious when he saw Brock and Carmichael being shoved into the treasurer's office by the treasurer. Telling his story, Pelrin said: "When I saw that, I called Arthur Tuohy, the assistant manager, and he sounded a citizens' alarm. At the same time, he called to Vaughn O'Neil, an assistant manager, and Frederick Perry, the head usher, and they rushed over to the treasurer's office door as the man fled," said Pelrin. "They followed him into the lobby and hopped on him just as he got a few yards down the lobby toward the Washington-st exit. As he fell, his pistol fell from his hand. They then held him until the police arrived."

April 28—*The Boston Globe*, BAIL SET AT $25,000 IN THEATRE ROBBERY—Actor Seized by Police Absolves Second Man—Vito Paulekas, 22-year-old amateur actor of Cambridge captured Sunday night in an attempted holdup of Loew's Orpheum Theatre, was ordered held in $25,000 bail yesterday when he was arraigned before Judge Michael J. Murray in Municipal Court on a charge of armed robbery and five charges of assault. A second Cambridge man, whom police found in the home of Paulekas and whom they sought to implicate in the $3009 holdup, was exonerated and released after Paulekas, taking all the blame upon himself, forced theatre employees to admit that they saw no one with him in the theatre. A nickel-plated .38-caliber revolver, which

> Paulekos allegedly concealed under a newspaper, was produced by the police at the arraignment. Paulekos waived examination. When captured in the theatre lobby following the holdup, in which five Orpheum employees were tied up, Paulekas, said by police to be an ex-convict, was disguised in actors' makeup, with an artificial three-inch scar affixed to his right cheek. Police say that in the lineup at headquarters that he planned the holdup for three weeks in advance. In the Paulekas home, the officers say they found three black masks, three pairs of goggles and a makeup box, as well as a shortwave radio.

One week after his botched holdup, Vito shares the front page of the *Boston Evening Globe* with the doomed airship:

SPEEDING ZEPP NEARS N. E. COAST

THE BOSTON EVENING GLOBE

Cambridge Actor-Robber Gets 25 Yrs

The Hindenburg hovers over a montage of areas as it approaches the East Coast. A 12-year-old Edward Davis Wood, Jr. captures the helium-filled zeppelin on 8mm film as it passes slowly over the Hudson River at Poughkeepsie. On May 6, the Lakehurst landing grounds in New Jersey are flooded with men. Upwards of 500 day laborers spill out of buses, having shown up for little more than a promise of a mighty dollar or two in exchange for taming the tethered blimp when it arrives several hours from now. Keep your head on a swivel, get a 360 field pan of this yard full of inmates on the outside; see it polka-dotted with wandering dirty souls. This place wasn't always relegated to a common landing strip. Right here on this very spot at Lakehurst, the US military carried out munitions testing of various Russkiyes artillery. At one time, sheep freckled the land (as the convicts do today), their tight, matted curls blown to Purgatory by state-of-the-art Russian shells. On other occasions, the little curly buggers were set free to graze over a field of experimental land mines. Food rations may have been in effect, but one thing this base was never short on was entertainment. Today's weather shifts quickly out of favor, and the Hindenburg is struck by lightning and ignites. Documentary crews and spectators watch helplessly as tens of thousands of pounds of steel, cables, canvas, and good china and crystal shower down on the landing strip. What remains of the violent egg (that which hasn't vaporized) is shoveled deep into the day workers' trouser pockets, the warm debris to become future artifacts. Some unfortunate dirt-poor souls get too close and join the piles of smoldering things.

> May 8—*The Boston Globe*, ADMITS HOLDUP AT ORPHEUM —Vito Paulekas Sentenced for $3000 Robbery—A sentence of 20 to 25 years in State Prison was meted out this morning to Vito Paulekas, Cambridge amateur actor, when he pleaded guilty in Suffolk Superior Court before Judge John M. Gibbs to robbery of the cashier's office at Loew's Orpheum, on the night of April 26. Paulekas had been indicted on three counts. On a count of assault and battery with a dangerous weapon, he was given a concurrent sentence of 5 to 7 years, and on a third count of carrying a weapon, an additional concurrent sentence of three to five years. Paulekas, who is 22 years old, used his actor's greasepaint and make-up to disguise his appearance when he undertook the single-handed holdup of the Washington-st theatre. His disguise included a faked scar applied to one cheek. He had previously studied the layout and cashier's routine on visits to the theatre, and on the night of April 26, fell in behind the cashier, Miss Kay Lovely, as the treasurer and two doormen escorted her with the cash from the box office to the manager's office. Paulekas herded the girl and four men into the treasurer's office and tied them up with loops of clothesline he had prepared in advance to be used one-handed while he trained his gun on them with the other. He took $3000 from the theatre funds and started out, but was tackled in the lobby by Asst Manager Arthur Tuohy, Vaughn O'Neil, and Frederick Perry, who had been warned by usher Gerald Pelrin that a suspicious-looking man had gone into the treasurer's office.

• •

TEMPLES ON TAR—At the end of October 1936, another vacancy needs filling, so if you or anybody you know is looking for a three-room apartment, this one will set you back $22.50 a month (water included). You must, though, supply your own time machine to redeem.

Keeping long-term tenants has proven more difficult than Smith first anticipated. Throughout February and March of 1937, Smith attempts to offload his beautiful hunk of junk for $37,500, nearly half its original construction cost. Still, it will take another five months before Smith gets a bite on his proposition.

On September 10, 1937, the Smith Building gets a new owner, Orrel Philip *O.P.* Reed, whose wealth hails from San Diego. He immediately submits for amendments to the existing 23'x30' (690 sq. ft.) penthouse. Across the lines dedicated to a *Certificated Architect, Licensed Engineer, and Contractor,* Reed has confidently scrawled the word; *None*. When asked to describe briefly and fully all proposed construction and work:

> *Install complete bath, change electric wiring, cut two windows, put in partitions, plaster, and stucco all walls and ceilings.*
>
> *NO STRUCTURAL CHANGE* — APPROVED!

Just as soon as the alterations are completed, brothers Harvey and Dale Easton will open Easton Gym on the second floor of 8053 Beverly Blvd. Harvey is a champion bodybuilder; Dale, 23, is a boxer and bit-part actor. Both were born D'Orr but later adopted their stepfather's name, pulp fiction author Walter Easton. As Dale rises in the Hollywood ranks as a Western movie actor, he is encouraged to use the stage name Greg McClure.

The brothers Easton post an ad in *The Oakland Tribune*:

> BELLA VISTA PARK: Aerial wizards and acrobats, take note! A group of "Muni" stunt-men who have merged to give this department its first announcement of a Horizontal Bar Team, so help me, follows through with this challenge to wit: "We are ready to take on any team from any playground in the city." Signed Ed Estrella, Jack Weber, David Davies, Harvey Easton, and Dale Easton.

Pazuzu blows through LA County on February 27, 1938. What starts as a mist originating in Siberia rapidly develops over the next three days into a violent storm. By March 3, the winter deluge had dumped 30 inches of rain and caused extensive damage throughout LA. Water management becomes the city council's priority again. If you thought their 1917 water displacement solutions were impressive, buckle up for the most significant build-up, expansion, and population boom in LA's meager history.

John G. Bradley, director of the Motion Pictures and Sound Recordings division of the National Archives, tests sealed film vault cabinets which he designed to withstand 1500 degrees of direct heat, protecting the nitrate reels inside. On July 9 of last year, a massive fire at the Fox Vault Fire in Little Ferry, NJ, destroyed 40,000 nitrate reels during a three-hour five-alarm blaze.

Congress establishes the House Un-American Activities Committee (HUAC) to deal with Phase One of hearing the names of those wascally Wuskies walking amongst the good and decent, moral folks of Hollywood.

Hollywood's first movie studio, Nestor Studios, was built in 1911 at the junction of Sunset Boulevard and Gower Avenue, but has since been converted into the CBS Radio Studios and renamed Columbia Square. Before the angora-sweatered-soda-fountain fantasy took hold, the idea of being discovered belonged to a dangerous crowd of drifters that seemed magnetically drawn to the wild, westernized corner of

Sunset Boulevard and Gower Avenue, which had adopted the nickname Gower Gulch. A plump mother sets the circular table with pepperoni pizzas and paper sack Frito pies. Kool-Aid flows freely from a cracked earthenware pitcher. In the foyer, a real-life OK Corral plays out after a cowboy's main squeeze is stolen away from him. Outside, through the kitchen window, we can make out several cowboys pacing around an OOPA lying at their boots in the dirt.

Oh, damn it all, yells one of them. The bravest (or dumbest) risks everything and caresses the sides of the object as though he expected a genie to squirm out... *Tha hell you find this ageen?*

On that lot. Out behind ch'alls talkies factory. Some of da heifers we loans 'em was lickin' it ... Like this. The dusty weirdo gets on all fours and licks the object, sending him immediately straight and stern, convulsing violently; vibrating into the oncoming traffic speeding down Sunset Boulevard. He is hit and run over by a Pacific Electric Railway bus, leaving a pair of chaps and a tin of chaw at the point of impact.

• •

YOURS IS THE EARTH AND EVERYTHING THAT'S IN IT—September 20, 1938. A category-three hurricane makes landfall in New England, pummeling Massachusetts. Suffolk County State Prison floods, forcing its inmates (including Vito) to be temporarily displaced and shuffled to higher ground on the prison estate. It's madness as the possibility of a critical mass jailbreak hangs thick in the autumn solstice air. Almost six weeks later, on Halloween night, CBS broadcasts Mercury Theatre's *War of the Worlds* as a blizzard blows outside Suffolk County State Prison. Life for 25-year-old Vito Paulekas is cold and sticky brown; yellow and grueling. He has learned to play the violin and fiddle and performs with the pokey orchestra, playing for incoming inmates or the lucky few deemed *corrected* and released.

During Holy Week, Vito and a handpicked prison theatre troupe perform to the overwhelming praise of the administration and the inmates. It is a satire of a Russian Gulag Labour Camp performance that reeks of Jarry's obscene nineteenth-century play, *Ubu Roi.* The epic journey is full of sex and shitter jokes and scandals—that kind of rhetoric that gets a baby killer to put on a dress and braid his pony:

> *He Will Come in Turkish Armour (If the Wind Blows Just Right)* —1844—A fable of feldsher Kesti Anion; the barber-surgeon who uses social mobility to thrust himself into life behind the royal gates, who wants not to be king but the *true changer of times who whispers in the king's ear,* hidden and obscured from ridicule. But Kesti Anion is disgraced before he gets the chance, committed to a monastery after he claims to have discovered on his property the skeleton of a giant with six digits on each hand and foot. He is found mad by a jury of bipedal dogs and sentenced to serve as janitor at the mountaintop monastery. While mopping friar overspray, the holy shack is taken over by a boisterous gypsy artist and his court of bohemian muses, which he has collected from various houses of ill repute all along the five-mile trek up the

> mountain. The bohemians make themselves at home and squat in the dilapidated monastery. They agree to do remedial work around the grounds and maintain the livestock. But they instead create a bunch of erotic art with all of the holy relics and materials the monks have collected to ration. A song the nymphs (the prettiest and most alopeciaed of cell block D, in this case) sing in the rhythm of:
>
> Come se, come sa
> Come kill my pa
> For he will surely smite ya
>
> Suddenly, the bohemians disappear, leaving behind their pornographic sculptures and paintings, which Anion, in a moment of absolute necessity, decided to eat, and enters a euphoric state that sends him on a 6,771-mile pilgrimage to an area not yet known as Los Angeles, but still there all the same. Anion is befriended by *natives* who have just annihilated another *native* tribe and taken over their village. When Anion shows them how to eat art and trip balls, he is seated in the tribal council as plastic shaman. As a community, they freak in unison and receive a singular transmission from an unseen world, which gives them the exact earth grid coordinates of where to burrow into the earth to start anew with the six-fingered, six-toed giants.

During the play's finale, an inmate makes a break for it, but he is shot and killed in front of the spectators. Without skipping a beat, the moment is incorporated into the play. The Warden's head mutates into a steam whistle and blows his cap off his head, blasting a human-sized hole in the wall, and suddenly it's a jailbreak.

1939. Christmastime. The rest of the Paulekas family lives modestly at 381 Portland St. in Cambridge, four miles due south of the Short girls at 115 Salem St., Medford. Benjamin Paulekas, 25, registers for the military, listing Mama Rose as the person who will *always know his address*. He continues working at The Boston Sausage & Provisions Co. in Boston with Jonas.

IF THE BROWN EYE WINKS, THE WORMHOLE STINKS—The Suffolk County inmates trade handmade gifts that they have conjured over the last year. Vito returned to the forgotten art of soap carving, and he's accumulated a substantial Lever Bros. bars booty. He's already completed a pair of *Joan Blidell Breastfeeding Our Saviour*, and now he's attempting to sculpt the buxom debutante who put him up during the marathon days from memory. Vito has great difficulty recalling the length of Palinka's hair or whether her shoulders were broad or delicate. He does, though, with some ease, massage the amorphous blob into the shining, clear image of her bent over the kitchen table, gazing back, with both her slit and hole working together to form a perfect lower case *i*, the kind you stroked on lined and dotted primary school workbook sheets; a proud, tall line that cuts a glistening path north like a rocket splittting the air, pointing your soul toward a swollen cave suspended in the heavens …

UGGHHHH!!! THIS STATE ADMINISTERED ABSTINENCE IS DRIVING HIM FUCKING MAD! Vito is struck down to the lowest of lows, ripe with a case of second-degree cobalt balls that have turned full-tilt anquished purple. In a moment of blinding-white horny rage, Vito recalls the hidden pleasures of dough. He draws up in his mind a day a decade previous, a day in May of 1928—The skyline and planned city streets of his free Cambridge days pull together in his mind's eye, signaling droves of greyed men to pace the cobbled streets toward the Lever Brothers facility somewhere out there beyond the visible horizon.

The workers threaten to strike at the factory today, and Jonas knows this could spell trouble if Gotlieb's bakery falls behind. Jonas expects Vito to arrive at any moment, as today, Vito will be training as an apprentice (though more of a ward). Upon Vito's arrival, Jonas wastes no time in beginning the first lesson; *neatsilikti* he warns and then forms a generous mound of general-purpose flour, fingering it from the peak out to force a gaping wound into the center; a womb to which next receives and cradles several eggs that are spilled into it. Jonas rakes his sausage-link fingers through the ingredients, kneading the simple mixture into a sticky dough. Now comes the *necessary abuse*—Jonas punches and pushes the blob, flipping it, spinning it, stretching it, melting the dough between his digits as condensed energy escapes wildly through his hands, causing, as Vito remembers, a slight vapor to rise from the dough. Jonas rolls the dough out onto a slab, letting it rest for a moment before transferring it into a large woven basket lined with muslin, covering it, and then filling it into a cool, dark pantry at the rear. Jonas takes a smoke break in the back alley. As the blue sun peeks, Jonas sees that a handful of workers have turned back to walk in the direction of Gotlieb's, stopping on the sidewalk to form cliques of four to eight men each. Jonas heads back inside to get a jump on linking hundreds of sausages with Vito—*Atsiimkite duonos krepšelius*—Jonas demands of Vito. After proving for two hours, the dough has tripled in size, taking on the billowing characteristics of a padded, full-bodied woman, like the neighborhood marms. Jonas kneads the sticky pillow, pushing and pulling it, aerating it to create a smooth, alluring dome. Jonas bisects the dough torso into a smallish and larger diatome, from which several uniform bricks are garroted and displaced on the slab before him. With a controlled, gentile touch of his dense hands, Jonas refines the mini-blobs before tossing them into shallow, floured woven baskets. Jonas tasks Vito with hatching the bread. Jonas slashes first, careful not to cut too deep or too shallow. Vito is mesmerized by how the yeast loaf reacts under the pressure of a straight razor, erupting open before coming to rest with a wispy sigh. Jonas returns to the second half, splitting it up the center, then braids the soft tentacles until the loaf resembles hefty thighs intertwined in a kind of thick-legged orgy. Jonas slides the loaves of Challah dough they just molested into an oven. Jonas reaches his stride and operates like a machine, a convecting conveyor dusted in flour, stuffed with herbs, and slathered in oil. Now, it's Vito's go; but suddenly, the reality of being cold and locked-up, fah-fah away from yeast and eggs, overwhelms him, and for perhaps the first time in his life, as best he can, Vito musters something recognizable as a prayer:

DEAR

LORD

PLEASE PLEASE
PLEASE LET ME

FUCK

GIRLS

AGAIN

By the time the incantation leaves his lips, he realizes the crucifix has a nice shape to it; kinda all wide-hipped and shoulders to match …

• •

1940. REFINING VESSELS—On the precipice of the Second Great War, the United States military is in desperate need of a blood substitute to aid with battlefield injuries.

> Plasma is the liquid of blood separated from its cellular elements and to which an anticoagulant has been added; plasma can be stored in liquid or dried form for much longer than whole blood.
>
> Serum is the liquid separated from clotted blood. (Serum lacks fibrinogen, which is present in plasma)

Bleeders in the first war quickly and inevitably became piles of dead. Coconut water is nearly identical to human plasma, but early transfusions to human test subjects are traumatizing, and the substitution is quickly nixed.

> Feb. 8—*The Times-Dispatch*, BLOOD SERUM TRANSFUSION FOUND USEFUL—CHICAGO—Evidence that blood serum, the colorless liquid part of blood, has the possibility of being the first effective "blood substitute" in transfusions was announced yesterday. Three Chicago physicians reported in the Journal of the American Medical Association that the serum was found to have life-saving benefits when used on dogs and that similar results were noted in a limited number of human cases. It even has some practical advantages over blood, they said, because the serum can be given in massive amounts, doesn't require preliminary "typing," and can be stored without refrigeration "Human serum, as a blood substitute, should find wide use not only in civil emergencies, but particularly in time of war at the battlefront,": they said. The physicians, Drs. Sidney O. Levinson, Frank Newuwelt, and Heinrich Necheles concluded: "If serum transfusion proved to be as effective in treating hemorrhage and subsequent shock in man as it appears to be in the dog, it

would be a valuable and effective blood substitute." The serum consists of the clear liquid part of blood separated from its fibrin (a whitish protein) and corpuscles. "There is an urgent need for an effective blood substitute," the three men stated. "Even in large hospitals and in large cities where blood can be secured with relative promptness, there are situations in which immediate availability and injection of a good blood substitute would improve treatment and enhance the outlook from massive hemorrhage ... "Although whole blood is the best restorative fluid in massive hemorrhage, our investigations have demonstrated that serum overcomes all the effects of hemorrhage in dogs except the loss of red blood cells (this loss, as we have seen, may be quite extensive without serious effects) ... "Use of serums," they said, should "remove the need for 'emergency' transfusions and the necessity for hasty blood typing and compatibility tests." Another advantage, the large amounts that can be given, was emphasized by pointing out that it has been customary to give not more than a quart of whole blood from a donor, even though severe hemorrhages sometimes warrant from two to three times that amount.

PHASE II

V.I.T.O.—The alchemical motto: *Visita Interiora Terrae Occultum* (Visit the Interior of the Earth and Thou Shalt Find What is Hidden).

• •

1941. June. In the middle of the Mojave Desert, film archival technicians test the effectiveness of a sprinkler system that they have rigged to rain down over the levels of nitrate film reels enclosed in a tall cabinet, extinguishing a rager before it explodes. The experiment runs amok—the sprinkler system instead spreads the fire throughout the facility, superficially wounding several technicians.

Aug. 28—It's hot and muggy. The soil that cradles the Smith Building has swelled under the relentless rain, turning into a concrete bladder primed for pissing. From the stucco walls, water leaks. The floor is covered with a half-inch of stale seepage. Above ground, directly across the street tonight at 8056 Beverly Blvd., the Laurel Theatre is celebrating its grand opening, showing *I Wanted Wings,* starring Ray Milland, and *She Knew All the Answers,* with Joan Bennett.

In September, a giant swastika shape was patterned on the ground just feet from the Stevenson Cross (aka Cahuenga Cross, aka Hollywood Cross, aka Hollywood Pilgimage Memorial Monument) using sacks of lye. There is debate over whether Theosophists placed the symbol, or whether it was the work of a stateside Nazi organization. In Bob Pool's *LA Times* article, *History and Reverence Illuminate a Hilltop Icon,* the writer refers to the perpetrators as *apparent Hitler sympathizers.* Before Hitler adopted the swastika, this symbol was used throughout Madame Helena Petrova Blavatsky's Theosophical teachings onward from 1895, referencing the Eastern philosophies that inspired her.

• • • • ••• • • • ••• • • • • •

YANKEE WHITE or THE THIRD TEMPLE—In the spring of 1912, Albert Powell Warrington became the new US representative for the American Theosophical Society (ATS), and his first order of business, per ATS President Annie Besant's command, was to find a place to establish their utopian community KROTONA. Warrington found what he believed to be the perfect fifteen acres of land in a city patterned with groves and trees: Hollywood, CA, specifically a parcel once part of Charles Hastings Ranch. Warrington wrote Besant of his findings:

> The trolley comes within one long block of our site ... one can be in the business center of the city in 30 minutes. On the other hand, twenty minutes walk up the canyon will put one entirely outside all building improvements, and tucked in between charmingly wild canyons, one is as if in the wildest and most far-off mountain retreat. I have never known such an extraordinary combination of favorable conditions ... We can make the spot a veritable Garden of Eden.

September 29, 1912—The *LA Times* prints Arthur S. Heineman's depiction of Warrington's proposed community in the hills. By the spring of 1913, the well-established San Diego architectural firm Meade & Requa designed the spiritual hub of the Moorish/Egyptian-influenced TSA structures, Krotona Court, which housed a lecture hall and institute. The facility also operated as the Krotona Inn, the stateside home of the organization's newly anointed Maitreya, 17-year-old Jiddu Krishnamurti. This ambitious project was funded by Augustus Francis Knudsen (son of Kaua'i, Hawaii's Kekaha Sugar Company Baroness, Annie Sinclair McHutcheson Knudsen). In 1914, Architects Arthur & Alfred Heineman completed Krotona's Grand Temple of the Rosy Cross. The structure featured a 350-seat auditorium and a basement where Dr. Strong was free to conduct his complex *human body aura experiments*. Architect/Freemason/reverend Elmer C. Andrus completed the five-bedroom Tuttle Bungalow, which was soon followed by the Hieneman mega-structure, The Ternary.

By 1916, The Little Theatre Movement began; the race is on to find the North American Athens. Philadelphia's Plays and Players Club founder (and daughter of zinc magnate Samuel Price Wetherill), CHRISTINE WETHERILL STEVENSON (henceforth CWS, SHE, HER, and MOTHER), steps down as president, citing differing opinions on club aims. A conflicting opinion will become a personality type of CWS's. Childhood acquaintance and cousin, Mrs. Kenneth J. McCarthy, recalled:

> Christine Wetherill was always an unusual child. She never cared to play with other children or to enter into their games and amusements. Her one delight was to dress up. She loved to act and was never so happy as when she could induce her little companions to act with her. With all the qualifications of a born leader, it was as natural that she should direct as for them to follow and carry out her dramatic plans. She arranged her own plays, rehearsed them, and took part in them.

CWS made HER way to Los Angeles and used HER modest theatre clout (plus daddy's money) to produce Shakespeare's *Julius Caesar* at the first natural outdoor theatre in America, the Beachwood Park Natural Amphitheater in KROTONA. *Julius Caesar* plays to an audience of 40,000 and rakes in $2,500, reportedly donated to the Actors' Fund. Many of the 5,000 extras were students recruited from Hollywood High School. The *Santa Monica Bay Outlook* reports one venue-related death: an elderly lady fell from exhaustion, fracturing her skull. Despite this, the spectacle's smashing success bolstered CWS's goal of creating an outdoor arts venue. HER search is on for the perfect location—JUMP TWO YEARS AHEAD, to July 1918—CWS commissioned a modest production of Sir Edward Arnold's epic poem recounting the life of Gautama Buddha, *The Light of Asia*. The temporary 800-seat wooden amphitheater, Kratona Stadium, was little more than a converted section of the Italian Gardens that ran along one side of the massive Ternary. Although SHE was heavily involved in its production, CWS's name was curiously absent from the playbill. *The Light of Asia* is a smash hit, performed 35 times in three weeks to such distinguished spectators as LA's Mayor Frederic T. Woodman, and the Japanese consul Chiune Sugihara (who, in WWII, will issue thousands of visas to Jews, allowing them to escape occupied Poland and LITHUANIA), as well as many prominent motion picture producers and stars. The *LA Times* declared: *RICH ORIENTAL SCENES—WONDERFUL NATURAL SETTING.* After CWS's homebred theatrical success, SHE was keen to spearhead the construction of a permanent outdoor venue *for the seven arts of the theatre: acting, music, dancing, painting, literature, sculpture, and architecture.* Several joined HER in forming Theatre Arts Alliance, Inc., with each founder noted as having donated $1,000. In the Autumn of 1918, a trio of oddly dressed folks from elsewhere wandered around the rolling lomas and tepes of preemie-Hollywood, surveying on behalf of CWS, who, feeling the pressures of privilege, had charged these nomads with sniffing out the perfect location for a southern California outdoor amphitheatre. They sang, and clapped, and yelled, testing the acoustics of the rocky landscape. Near cragged hills east of the Cahuenga Pass, they stumbled upon their divine patch. Much excitement stirred up as they set to committing plots on a scroll, marking it—HOME OF THE HOLLYWOOD BOWL—On November 11, 1918, The Theatre Arts Alliance Inc. voiced concern over CWS's aggressive Theosophical convictions after SHE proposed productions of religious persuasion ONLY. Six months later, in the summer of 1919, CWS changed the title of HER masterwork to *The Life of Christ* before settling on *The Pilgrimage Play*. SHE compiled a new playbook derived from all four Francis Bacon-translated gospels of the King James Version of the Bible, restructuring the story into 12 zodiacal episodes. In July, architect Louis Christian Mullgardt was invited to survey the future site of the Hollywood Bowl and offer suggestions. After CWS found Mullgardt's ideas *too pretentious* for the natural landscape, he responded to the TAA:

> Mrs. Stevenson is considered a type of genius by some of her followers. It would be for the good of Society to cage that type with the other zoo exhibits at the expense of the Commonwealth so as to escape the destructive claws which their thin, virtuous Cloaks conceal. Surely the original purpose of the Theatre Arts Alliance were totally different in their sublime purpose, from those which Mrs.Stevenson's perversions have led to.

CWS blurbbed in *Hollywood Weekly Citizen* that *there is no movement that includes all the arts as does the modern theatre movement.* Yet, it was HER obsessive dedication to upholding traditional Theosophical ideals that conflicted with the other members, who wished to offer a broader range of entertainment. The general opinion of HER among spiritualists (particularly Theosophists) was waning. It became glaringly evident, even to HER, after giving a public talk at the future site of the Hollywood Bowl, describing *The Pilgrimage Play* as best SHE could to 2,000 eager attendees. HER anxiety took over, and the presentation garnered little if any interest.

1920. In April, with little to no support from AP Warrington, the TSA, or even the Krotona Administration, and amid increasing creative differences with the Theatre Arts Alliance, Inc. (TAA), CWS was forced to leave the Hollywood Bowl organization that SHE founded. HER $21,000 contribution toward the land claim was reimbursed, which SHE used to purchase 29 acres on the east side of Cahuenga Avenue to build HER Pilgrimage Theatre directly across from the chosen Hollywood Bowl site. SHE was finally free to perform any ascended master saga HER tiny, strained Theosophical heart so desired. CWS persuaded a handful of Bowl members to bail and join HER theatre mission: The Pilgrimage Theatre (aka El Camino Real Theatre, aka Obermmangau Theatre, aka Pilgrimage Bowl). Architects and theatre-arts enthusiasts Bernard Ralph

Maybeck and Rollin Germain Hubby quickly designed and built a natural amphitheatre at 2580 Cahuenga Blvd. East in El Camino Real Canyon out of wood and stone—*A more perfect natural amphitheater could hardly be imagined*—CWS has constructed the ultimate North American tarmac in preparation for the Second Coming. Even the entrance pylons were uncannily Mishqui Gate-esque (aka The Gate of God, aka Babylon, which protects the ancient holy biblical city of Nineveh).

The *Pilgrimage Play* was performed for the first time in the crude wooden canyon theatre. One thousand five hundred seats looked out over the star-filled sky and mountain-trimmed backdrop. Situated 100 feet above the stage, amidst the yucca (Spanish: *LORD's candle*) plant, was perched the massive cathedral pipe organ, orchestra, and choir chambers. Winding pathways cut down the hill to spill the performers out onto the stage through entrances and exits tunneled with bushes and flowers. Henry Herbert portrayed Jesus Christ for the first four weeks before returning to New York (replaced by understudy Reginald Poel, aka Pole, nephew of Shakespearean actor William Poel).

On August 8, 1920, CWS extended a 30-day option to buy out HER portion of the Daisy Dell property, a chunk of land SHE originally purchased for $21,000, but SHE was now asking the remaining members of the TAA $100,000 for it. Until this transaction takes place (or CWS deeds HER property), the building of the Hollywood Bowl could not legally commence, relegating the land to little more than a few benches and a scrapped barbecue pit. At the end of September, CWS extended HER original buyout offer by ten days, adding the stipulation that the TAA must have raised at least $90,000 by the original date. The downtown businessmen filled in the $10,000 deficit overnight, allowing the TAA to play catch-up. CWS visited Palestine in the Fall, presumably collecting more artifacts for the production's third run. SHE spent nearly a year in the Holy Land selecting artifacts and authentic textiles, some very valuable, such as a 2,000-year-old weave, adding instant authenticity and proprietaryship. While CWS was away, in an effort to sever itself from the Theosophical Society (or any spiritual community), and especially CWS, the TAA dissolved and immediately coalesced into the Community Park and Arts Association (CPAA). In December, the CPAA purchased CWS's Bowl share at a reduced price of $67,000, buying HER out entirely.

1921. Amateur architect, Marie Russak-Hotchener, completes Moorcrest at the intersection of Temple Hill Dr. and Helios Street. Summer. In July, *The Pilgrimage Play* entered its second run, slightly more polished but still lacking the authenticity CWS desired. Henry Herbert returned from NY to portray Christus. Nov. 14—CWS's mother-in-law, world-renowned Egyptologist, museum curator/author/ scientist, 74-year-old Sara Yorke Stevenson, died in Philadelphia, PA. Her personal estate was reported in the newspapers to be valued at $63,000.

1922. Jan. 22—CWS and associates have formed The Pilgrimage Play Association, Inc. On April 10 (aka The Great and Holy Monday of Lent), CWS's husband and son of Sara Yorke Stevenson, 45-year-old socialite William Yorke Stevenson, died at his in-law's Philadelphia estate. While summering in Palm Springs, widowed CWS rewrote the role of Mary Magdalene, bulking up the character's dramatic impact. On July 10, the third season begins and continues nightly (except for Sundays) for the next eight weeks. After several taxing years and significant script alterations, CWS produced *The Pilgrimage Play* to HER own satisfaction, considering it *the achievement of her life*. Henry Herbert reprised his role as Jesus for a hat trick, having *devoted a part of the summer to study and special research in connection with the play*. After two years of constant tinkering by technical experts, the stage lighting effects were reported to be the best achieved at an outdoor venue. Thousands of spectators were expected to travel from all over the country to witness *America's Passion Play*.

On November 11, 1922, CWS was overwhelmed with emotion, stricken, they said, while visiting NYC, and developed a weak heart attributed to the innumerable stresses endured while producing and perfecting HER life's work. HER illness was not considered severe enough to prevent HER from traveling, but only one week later, CWS suffered a collapse due to exhaustion, and HER condition worsened considerably. SHE was transported to HER sister Isabelle's home in Media, PA, on the outskirts of Philadelphia. In three more days, at age 44, CHRISTINE WETHERILL STEVENSON died suddenly *due to hemorrhages* [sic] *of change of life.*

> Nov 21—PHILADELPHIA. ARTISTIC LEADER PASSES AWAY WHEN HEART WEAKENED BY STRAIN FAILS HER. —Modeling an American passion play is believed to have cut short her career.

(CWS's cause of death was later attributed to pernicious anemia)

1923. *Los Angeles Times* owner and real estate mogul Harry Chandler acquired from CWS's estate the 29 acres in Bolton Canyon, as well as the public performance rights to *The Pilgrimage Play*, which commenced its summer run for the first season without MOTHER waiting in the wings. (This schedule will continue for the next five years until a massive brush fire burns the theatre to the ground in October of 1929.) On July 8, the Pilgrimage Play Association paid $200 for The Stevenson Cross (aka The Cross on Cahuenga, aka The Hollywood Pilgrimage Memorial Monument, aka The Hollywood Cross) to be hoisted high atop the hill where it will overlook Chandler's newly deeded attraction. Only two weeks later, on July 23, Harry Chandler's real estate group, Hollywoodland, dedicated their $21,000 giant hillside promotion erected by Thomas Fisk Goff's Crescent Sign Company. Dec. 4—*The 10 Commandments* premieres at the Egyptian Theatre.

1924. To Buddhists, Hollywood was, for a long while, Earth's throat chakra, but it had recently moved north toward Ojai, a move suggesting that perhaps a spiritual upchuck was to follow not too far behind. To Theosophists tucked away in Beechwood Canyon's KROTONA for the last twelve years, Hollywood was a cultural center ripe for the collision of religions, sciences, and self. Still, overcrowding, noise, and modernity forced the TSA to abandon the bulk of its ambitious efforts and split for a defunct 118-acre almond tree farm on the outskirts of Ojai, CA. The majority of the 500 continuing TSA members moved their spiritual operation three hours north to the esoteric lot that Annie Besant purchased on behalf of the organization, calling it ... wait for it ... KROTONA II.

Come Pilgrimage season, Chandler's *Los Angeles Times* advocated that people from all places should make a *Pilgrimage®* of their own to the hills of Hollywood.

1925. Lucile Vasconcellos Langhanke (better known to the movie-going public as Mary Astor) moved into KROTONA's abandoned Moorcrest after her parents (who were not Theosophists but friends with the home's builders, the Hotcheners, who themselves were high-ranking Theosophists) purchased it with the money the eighteen-year-old silver-screen sensation earned. Astor's parents were known to spend lavishly and invest poorly. When Astor was 17, she embarked on a sordid love affair with her married *Beau Brummel* co-star, 42-year-old John Barrymore. Her controlling parents held Astor virtually captive in Moorcrest until 1928, when she married Howard Hawks' brother, Kenneth.

• • • • • • • • • • • • • •

RETURNING TO 1941, sometime in mid-October, say one of those Theosophists or Friends of the Pilgrimage Play we just met, was perched on the shaky wooden cross, leering down at the Hollywood Bowl from the Cahuenga Pass, they would easily spy the *Sculpture of the Muse of Music, Dance, and Drama* by George Maitland Stanley, of *Oscar* statuette fame. *Muse* puts Stanley's little gold man to shame, the WPA Federal Art Project—one of their last—is designed in the streamlined modern style, and measures in at 22'x200'. She appears at the entrance to the amphitheatre, the granite giant poised to welcome patrons of the Hollywood Bowl, and cost American taxpayers $100,000.

Oct. 17, 1941—32 acres of land just west of the HOLLYWOODLAND sign, a parcel which includes the Pilgrimage Theatre and the Stevenson Cross on Cahuenga, are deeded to Los Angeles County by The Pilgrimage Play Association. A 99-year lease is extended to the established Hollywood Bowl Association, allowing them to continue with the *Pilgrimage Play* summer performances.

Dec. 7—Japanese fighter pilots attack Pearl Harbor. Parts of Los Feliz and Griffith Park are used as Japanese internment camps. Two-thirds of the Japanese interned in the ten camps in southern California were born in America.

Near Christmas, the corner first-floor unit under Easton Gym is reincarnated as the chocolate box it was perhaps always meant to be:

> Dec. 15—*Los Angeles Evening Citizen News*. NEW ADDITION TO CANDY STORE CHAIN OPENED HERE—Awful Fresh MacFarlane today announced the opening of another of his candy stores. This store, which is the ninth unit in the rapidly growing MacFarlane chain, is situated at 8051 Beverly Blvd., three blocks west of Fairfax. According to "Awful Fresh MacFarlane," over 200 varieties of candy and nuts will be carried in stock at all times. Donald L. MacFarlane opened his first candy store in 1933 with a slogan of "Taste B-4-U Buy." This confectioner opened its first store in Southern California in October of last year.

1942. There is a sudden nationwide halt in the production of fine art pottery and dinnerware ceramics. All five major potteries in California pivot to instead manufacture industrial clay pipes and fittings. *DownBeat Magazine* reports that the American Musician Association goes on strike:

B Y
O R D E R
O F A . M . A .
NO RECORDINGS
SHALL BE MADE!
Play live in clubs — OKAY!
Play live on radio — OKAY!
DO NOT
DOCUMENT
or your ass is
O U T
for
L I F E,
fucker.
ARE WE CLEAR,
SCAB?

Feb. 6—*Menasha Record,* ARTIFICIAL BLOOD FROM CITRUS FRUIT PECTIN—Discovery of an "artificial blood" made from citrus fruit pectin, which is expected to supplant blood transfusions in the treatment of shock, has been announced by physicians in Henry Ford Hospital laboratories in Detroit. Because it is easily and inexpensively prepared, the substitute is hailed as particularly important to war areas. The pectin is extracted from the skin of ordinary grapefruit or lemon and affords a shock treatment at probably one-tenth the cost of a blood transfusion. Dr. Frank W. Hartman, head of the Henry Ford Hospital research laboratories, and Drs. Victor Schelling, H. N. Harkins, and Brock Brush of the same laboratories are credited with the discovery. It has been used on 25 Ford hospital patients with excellent results, Doctor Hartman said. British military authorities have already consulted Doctor Hartman about his find and are expected to put it into use soon. Civilians suffering from shock are also expected to find it a life and money saver. Surgeons are using artificial blood as they would a blood transfusion to prevent shock during a long operative procedure. "This pectin solution can be used in every case where a blood transfusion is now given for shock," Doctor Hartman explained. Only in cases of uncontrollable hemorrhage is it unsuccessful.

LIGHTING FIXTURES
For Remodeling Homes
Special Setup
Offered by
E. L. SMITH & SONS
Lighting Fixture Specialists
at 141-143 N. La Brea Ave.
Phone WYoming 8887.
Improve Your Home Atmosphere Now!

Independence Day, 1942. Near White Sands, NM—In the clear morning light, a military bomber circles low over tin roofs, searching for a place to land. It's in trouble. A strip of unpaved road is cleared for landing, but as the giant plane touches down, it explodes into a furious ball of fire that singes the heavens.

• •

> During mass, the priest drinks wine, which has become the blood of Christ through transubstantiation, and the congregation eats the bread or flesh of Christ, who is thus sacrificed to God anew. The gospel, according to St. John, holds a passage that would well apply to the vampire mixing its blood with that of its victim. "Accept, ye eateth the flesh of the son of man and drinketh his blood. He had no life in him. So eateth my flesh and drinketh my blood, hath eternal life, and I will raise him up on the last day." Clearly aware of bearing a total curse. The ever-constant desire for life and renewal, coupled with a horrible wish to destroy human beings to maintain his own existence.

Vito suffers through a routine prison health check and is informed that he has been selected, along with 63 inmates of the state, for participation in a military medical study. They play the patriot angle on Vito, and Vito bites the bait. Anything for that sweet, sweet freedom—Freedom equals pussy, and he will wave that freedom flag until his arms break off if it's his only stab at getting at it—Ask and he shall receive—In August of 1942, Vito becomes a guinea pig state-sanctioned embracement sponsored by the US Navy and Harvard University biochemist Edward Cohn, 64 Bostonian prisoners are injected with bovine serum albumin (BSA). The procedure takes place in a make-shift medical ward in a prison room. THINGS GO HORRIBLY WRONG. This *synthetic* transfusion causes immediate aches and pains to surge through the body. Some inmates describe a *jolt of electricity* or a severe sensation of repeated internal *blowing up and exploding,* or they simply enter a *dreamy, half-drunk* state before collapsing. In many cases, the patients would go on to *suffer intermittent effects throughout the remainder of their lives*—SOME MEN ARE TORTURED. ONE DIES IN THE APARATUS.

Cohn's disastrous program was dismantled, and the results were classified. Documents were destroyed or scattered. Looks like it's back to the old drawing board for Dr. Acula. It wasn't all in vain, though; a Liberty battleship was christened in the name of St. Germain, (supposedly) honoring the legacy of the unfortunate inmate whose human pulmonary system was overwhelmed with bovine blood and kicked it.

UNDER CUNNING FOLK—Under the supervision of a Naval psych doctor, a post-experiment interview is administered to the recipients. A young female stenographer transcribes the following conversation between Vito and a nurse. A distorted series of pops and clicks stretches the air before the data collection begins with a series of straightforward questions. The nurse's voice crackles in:

... State your full name and age.

... Vitantas Alphonse Paulekas, er, Vito ... 28.

... Inmate's weight has increased from 140 to 155 pounds since his last examination. No changes in height: five feet, four inches. Shoe size, U.S. 5. Inmate Paulekas, you may begin your statement at any time ...

It went something like this: An immediate delirium washed over Vito as he initiated the inaugural energy exchange; his virginal vampiric communion. He recalls going to a plane where Vito helped his old friend—the newborn baby, Hermes—to fit boots over the hooves of the fimftigiwiz livestock that he had just stolen from Big Bro Apollo. Vito claims to have died during the transfusion, even if only for that slivered moment between heartbeats, but it was a sure death all the same, and at the hands of our Government—*make no bones about that!* Vito witnessed his FIRST DEATH: THE OBLITERATION OF THE FOOD SACK—the painful division of the etheric body—watching helplessly as his ASTRAL SELF, shown to him as a blurred, blobby, soft, shapeless, boneless thing, drifted into the dense surrounding jungle. Then the SWOON brought Vito back to life, minus that part of him.

WOMEN WANTED

23 TO 45 YRS. OF AGE.

Residents of Hollywood
and Beverly Hills
who desire to work in
Safeway Stores

No Experience Necessary

CALL IN PERSON

Rm. 204, 8053 Beverly Bl.,

Rm. 207, 1505 N. Western

BETWEEN 8:30 AND 9:30 A.M.
WED., THURS., OR FRI.

• •

December 1942. Cleophus Short, now 55, is a broke-down drunk living in Weymouth, MA, at 4 King Cove Rd., just 45 minutes to the south of the family he abandoned ten years ago. He reaches out to Phoebe and finds her understandably upset, telling Cleo never to call again. Cheques have stopped coming in when he got stupid in September of last year and fucked everything up when he applied for social security services with his Christian name and revealed to a watching Government that he was alive; this was all explained to Phoebe during a visit from a Medford social worker who told her the jig is up. Cleo insists on sending Elizabeth money, but Phoebe refuses to accept it. Cleo sends some dough anyhow.

1943. March 9—The United States military complex completes construction of Camp Detrick in Frederick, MD, a 92-acre facility employing nearly 500 scientists who work to create biological weapons and develop defensive measures against them. Camp Detrick's main objectives include investigating whether diseases are transmitted by inhalation, digestion, or through skin absorption. One of these procedures is blood transfusion using animal or plant-derived plasma components. These experiments relied heavily on human subjects.

In March of 1943, SOME HEMORRHOIDS MUST LEARN TO LIVE ON THE OUTSIDE—Vito Paulekas is released from Boston State Prison, Suffolk ... *Convicted guinea pigs, along with the non-injected volunteers, were soon released from prison under Chapter 222, a commonwealth statute referred to as the Clearly Act, which was enacted to aid the defense efforts by prematurely releasing convicts for essential military activities.*

WANTED
WOMEN

23 to 45 years of age
Married or Single for

RETAIL GROCERY
STORE WORK
DAYTIME — NO
SUNDAY WORK

Experience Is Unnecessary
You are paid while you take
valuable course of training.

STEADY WORK FOR
THOSE WHO QUALIFY

We can probably place you in
a store near your residence.

GOOD PAY
WITH OPPORTUNITY
FOR ADVANCEMENT

Apply in person, 8 :30 to 9 :30
A.M. on Tuesday, Wednesday,
Thursday or Friday at Room 207,
1505 N Western Avenue or at
Room 204, 8053 Beverly Blvd.
or, if it is more convenient at

SAFEWAY STORES

• •

GET YOURSELF SOME SLOW CLOTHES—June 3, 1943. What came to be known as the Zoot Suit riots surged throughout Los Angeles. The OUTPOST sign behind Graumann's is fully dismantled for repurposing in war efforts.

July—Vito visits Hollywood and meets with 30-year-old jazz trumpeter Syd Zaid. Zaid and his wife, Leola C. (née Gerson), a 22-year-old dancer at the Florentine Gardens, moved into a tiny Hollywood bungalow at 552 N. Windsor Blvd. after marrying in Chicago last November. Just days before Vito's arrival, Leola shipped out on the *USS Republic,* en route from San Francisco to Hawaii. Her name appears on a *Confidential List* of *Civilian Employees* of the *War Department.* The two ladykillers are left alone in Hollywood to fend for themselves. According to both men's military records, they are nearly physically identical:

VITO PAULEKAS: b.5.20.1913 | *white or light-skinned, blue eyes, light brown hair, medium build, 5'5", 155 lbs.*

SYD ZAID: b.3.22.1914 | *white or fair-skinned, grey-eyed, brown-haired, medium build, 5'5", 155 lbs.*

Syd has been a stateside Jew by way of Canada for ten years. He ran with a rough crowd in Chicago and is currently affiliated with the Communist Party. (Muhammad's traveling partner and scribe was an Islamic prophet named—wait for it ... SA'ID ZAYD) Zaid takes Vito out on the town, ingratiating him into Hollywood's underbelly jazz scene. Vito really lets his hair down on the dance floor, performing the kind of whacky shit that would get him court-martialed at the VA, but out here in La La Land amidst the remnants of the wild, wild west, these negros let him go whole-hog. Hell, they encourage Vito, affectionately calling him *the crazy Mexican.* Vito smokes lots and lots of weed and feels welcomed and right at home with this black Southland lifestyle.

In August 1943, Syd's application for US naturalization was denied; the reason cited was that Syd had moved to California from Chicago after filing. Two of Syd's friends back home signed the petition, listing as *Witness and Reference* fellow musician David Cunningham (remember this tidbit for later), and hotel bellhop Eugene Light.

> Aug. 18—*Los Angeles Times,* LOS ANGELES MAN REPORTED DEAD IN EAST—New York City police identified as Raymond George, Beverly Blvd. real estate dealer, a man who fell dead yesterday in the Pennsylvania Station shortly after he stepped from a train from Washington, D.C. They said papers in his pockets gave his business address as 8053 Beverly Blvd. and his residence as 1270 S. Hauser Blvd., the same as listed in directories here. The man was described as about 60 years old, 6 feet tall, weighing about 300 pounds, brown eyed with a small scar above the left eye. Documents in his pockets indicate he had been commandant and chief of staff, Department of California, Marine Corps League and public relations officer of the Ex-Marine Guards. Neighbors of the Hauser St. address said they had heard that George had gone east recently and said the description from New York corresponded with that of George except for weight and age. They estimated his age at 50 and weight over 200 pounds.

New England homes blackout their windows throughout September nights. Boston enforces a mandatory dimout at 5:45p—a pair of young lovebirds sit on the roof of their single-story colonial, watching over the coastline as tanker ships twenty miles offshore are torpedoed. The couple gets a little torpedoing of their own accomplished as maritime moans and groans echo underwater.

Oct. 5—After 15 weeks of service on the *USS President Monroe*, Leola Zaid arrives home to Syd, fresh from Honolulu. Vito split last week for Cambridge, detoxing by dancing before heading back.

RANK AND VILE—Nov. 27—Elizabeth celebrates Thanksgiving with her mom and sisters at 115 Salem Street in Medford. Elizabeth has been home for several weeks, and so has Vito, only four miles to the south in Cambridge at 406 Columbia St.

On Nov. 30, Vito and his mother, Rose, travel to Portland, ME, to enlist in the US Merchant Marines. Mama Rose signs as Vito's witness. Back home, brother Benjamin is employed by Lever Brothers as a guard at their Cambridge factory. Father Jonas takes the Longfellow Bridge to and from work at a Boston bakery. John Jr., like Mama Rose, does not work.

GOOD PAYING JOBS
IN AN ESSENTIAL INDUSTRY

Many excellent positions are now open
for both men and women with Safeway Stores.
Good pay and permanent, full-time jobs,
under pleasant working conditions
are offered those who can qualify.
Experience is unnecessary.

Now is the time to get into the food distribution industry

• • •

Essential in peace-time as well as in war-time.

FOR RETAIL STORE WORK,
CALL IN PERSON AT ONE
OF THE FOLLOWING LOCATIONS:

HOLLYWOOD:
8053 Beverly Blvd., Room 205,
between 8:30 and 10:00 A. M.
Monday, Tuesday and Wednesday.

• •

1944. May 26—Vito fills out his draft card, indicating that he works at the Lally Column Corporation, headquartered in Franklin, MA, on Erie and Albany Street. Upon completing his Naval registration, Vito is ordered to report for basic merchant service training in precisely one month. The merchant services took orders from naval officers, though they were formally considered volunteers.

June 6—American troops storm the Normandy coast; by day's end, nearly half a million soldiers, from both sides combined, are dead. Vito is called to duty earlier than anticipated and will report for basic training at Sheepshead Bay, NY, by mid-June. Out-at-sea training takes place at the state maritime facility, the Massachusetts Maritime Academy in Hyannis, near Cape Cod. (Two years earlier, state-controlled Maritime facilities such as the MMA relinquished operational control to the federal government, which then quickly developed and implemented much more rigorous and questionable training techniques.) Military life quickly becomes just a different type of prison, another process intended to instill reformations, but instead survives much more comfortably as a beacon for nefariums, the infirm, and the *wronged* to find one another. Future life as a maritime grunt sets in, and the odds of imminent death skyrocket. Some MMs are trained in munitions and arms use, but most Merchant Marines were recognized and treated as disposable grunts. Many of them join with criminal reputations, as part-time commies, or as bottom-feeders; whatever the symptom is that keeps them just left of the National Maritime Union. Surviving hooligans will be compensated extremely well for completing these *suicide missions,* making it a win-win for Vito: adventure + moola.

Fearing a return attack of the prison blue balls, Vito embarks on a major conquest to wet his member again and again in sunny Los Angeles.

Oct. 12, 1944—On Columbus Day, a loony dancer searches for his bobby soxer and finds her working at the Hollywood Canteen as a hostess. The next day, Georgette Elise Bauerdorf is found murdered in her West Hollywood apartment on Fountain. Avenue. Her body is face down in her bathtub, most likely sexually assaulted. A cloth has been wedged down her windpipe. The hankie (*made of foreign materials*) led detectives to believe they were looking for a well-traveled, pervy perp. A witness describes a soldier, a *swarthy mad dancer*, who appeared infatuated with Bauerdorf, cutting in on nearly every dance last night. Detectives scour USO centers and hot spots but turn up little, and then, out of the blue, a man claiming to be the *swarthy mad dancer* contacts law officials. He is questioned and subsequently exonerated of any involvement; his identity withheld.

WHEAT GERMS—In early fall, 31-year-old Vito hooks up with 27-year-old Margaret *Mary* Anne Coffin, and they are soon pregnant with a child. They wed in Cambridge in November and take up residency in a tiny house on the United States Marine Corps base in Danvers, MA. Their home was built on the site of a village at the heart of the 1692 Salem Witch Trials. Twenty humans were executed here, five of the deaths attributed to the year-long trials of four adolescent girls who suffer tantrums described by my witnessing ministers as *far beyond the power of epileptic fits or natural disease.* By May of 1692, the literal witch-hunt reached a fever-pitch, and in December, the *Act Against Conjuration, Witchcraft, and Dealing With Evil and Wicked Spirits* was passed by the General Courts. Maybe there is no better plot on this earth for the Neo-Pagan to come home to roost.

Elizabeth celebrates Thanksgiving with her mother and sisters in Medford when Vito signs on as a utility man aboard the Bert Williams, and his military service officially begins. As a utility man, he was charged with loading and unloading materials and other general grunt work. Vito's face-value mission: deliver a hullful of supplies to allied forces in the United Kingdom—departing today from Portland, ME. Orders will rain down from naval officers.

THEIR'S NOT TO REASON WHY, THEIR'S BUT TO DO AND DIE—January 15, 1945. After serving six weeks at sea, Vito and company depart Southampton, England, for a stop at Cherbourg, France, completing the circle by docking at Castle Garden in NYC. During the voyage, Vito is promoted from mop to slop and serves as a *messman* on the three-week tour. He is more than willing to make his way up the grunt ranks as long as it gets him what he has been promised: a chance to murder Mussolini—for his country, of course. Vito swaps ships in March, taking the *US Thomas Bradlee* to Antwerp, Belgium, where he will spend the next month at port before leaving in mid-April to return to NYC. At sea, news comes to Vito that on April 25, the Sawdust Caesar was captured and executed in the public square. Mussolini's corpse, along with several other fascists, was strung up by his ankles. Passersby paid their last disrespects, spitting and pissing on the brutalized corpses dangling out there in the city square like Christmas tree ornaments.

On May 2, Vito is given a health check-up before his discharge—*64 inches, 145 pounds. Status: Unremarkable*—The little Baltic bastard is cleared, but he feels robbed, jipped after his promised stab at Mussolini vaporized. Vito buses it back to Boston with the other grunts, some of them maimed and bandaged, some of them brimming with paranoia and shell-shock. Vito's military prospects have narrowed, and his necessity has been called into question. He boards the *USA Sweepstakes*, bound for service in Le Havre, France. To salt his wounds, Vito has circled back to a utility man. Preggers Mary, back in witchy Danvers, plays the part of the military bride beautifully. Thirteen miles away, Elizabeth works as a waitress at St. Clare's Restaurant in Boston.

The *All Hands* naval magazine features a line-up of eight bathing beauties walking arm-in-arm toward the camera, showcasing their long legs and tiny painted toes peeking out from furry slippers. Captioned—*LOOK FAMILIAR? "Psycho-analysts" in the pay of a movie studio know you boys erect the tallest flag poles for these girls, most*—Charlie, baby, Christ! Your babies look great, baby!

June 16, 1945—*Vitantis A. Paulekas* departs Le Havre on the *USA Sweepstakes* bound for NYC to drop anchor at Castle Garden after a ten-day voyage home. Vito doesn't know it yet, but he is a first-time father, back in Danvers; Mary gave birth to their son, Mark.

July 7—The US District Court of Los Angeles issues 31-year-old Sydney Zaid a certificate of naturalization. Both he and Leola register as Democrats.

BO[M]B'S YER UNCLE—On August 6, Hiroshima is nuked to fucking hell, and then three days later, Nagasaki is obliterated. The culmination of both detonations effectively ended the Second World War and unlocked the gates to an altogether different kind of era of terror. 3,049 Massachusetts-based Merchant Marines have died—*casualties in the United States area or as a result of disease, homicide, or suicide in any location are not included.* This number is likely modest when compared with reality. Nearly 10,000 of the 215,000 total Merchant Marines that served died, awarding their miserable military branch the highest casualty rate. This means that even though 1 in 24 grunts risked slipping into oblivion, somehow this small Bostonian that bled his way out of prison rolled the dice (repeatedly) and made it out.

Sep. 1—Elizabeth gets news of the suicide of her fiancé, Major Matthew Gordon Jr., who nose-dived his fighter plane somewhere over West Bengal, India, just four days before America's victory over Japan. Elizabeth quits St. Clare's Restaurant and heads northwest ten miles to begin a new job at Schrafft's Tea Room Restaurant in the neighboring town of Belmont. She works there with a rough-around-the-edges woman named Marjorie Cameron, who grew up and currently lives in Cambridge at 65 Winthrop St., only one and a half miles from the Paulekas family home at 406 Columbia St.

On September 5, 1945, three days after the war officially ended, 32-year-old Vito boards the *SS Edward Paine* in Providence, RI, on a high-risk mercenary mission; a Lend/Lease cleanup. Vito and the others were little more than cattle, efficiently grazing the leftover hazardous-material canisters. Married hooligans pull in even more dough, and Vito isn't one to be against fast cash, despite the inherent risks; maybe even because of them. Missions such as these often took place on ships without radar or sonar, and satellite navigation was not nearly as advanced as it is today. Payday, should he make it till then, is a guaranteed windfall, and considering that Vito has a ten-week-old's belly to keep full, he has discovered the perfect cover for getting his balls drained of thrill-juice.

MISTAKEN IDEN-TITTY

[line drawing of a Hirohito with a tit-shaped head]

SIR: In the interest of accuracy, I should like to distinguish that the image on p.28 of May's issue identified as a nut is actually a boob.—V.A.P., MM

You are right, of course.—Ed.

Nov. 22—The Hollywood Canteen at 1451 North Cahuenga Blvd. closes after a 25-month run, during which time the restaurant hosted over 3,000,000 patrons. Thousands of unemployed actors and down-on-my-luck servicemen are supplied with a place to stay for a night or two. It is less than 1.5 miles from The Smith Building.

1946. Near last Christmas of '45, Vito returned to the States from his first Lend/Lease mission, having dumped thousands upon thousands of gallons of chemical warfare waste, as well as millions of pounds of steel and rivets, into the Pacific Ocean near Australia. He is, no doubt, changed—suddenly aware with brilliant clarity of his role as an expendable cog in this machine. At the end of January, according to *The Los Gatos Times-Saratoga Observer,* Vito is stationed in Los Gatos, CA, while still enlisted with the USMS. He attends the first meeting of the *Darn It Club*, a veterans' organization that meets in high school theatres and at members' homes. Today we're at Mrs. Everett Shaffer's home, where friends have gathered *to form a sewing club and to renew old acquaintances and friendships. The next meeting will be at Mrs. Nicholson's home on February 5th at 2 p.m.* Vito is highly active in the many workers' unions along Cannery Row in Monterey, 60 miles to the south. Mary Paulekas and her seven-month-old son, Mark, remain in Danvers for the time being, 3,100 miles to the north-east.

February—Elizabeth Short, 21, makes her way back to 115 Salem St. in Medford, where mom and the four sisters still live, four miles as the crow flies north of the Paulekas family home. Elizabeth finds remedial work at a movie theatre and several restaurants between Medford and Cambridge, inching closer to the circle of opportunity.

• •

July 13, 1946—*Los Angeles Evening Citizen News,* WANT room, apt., house? Price open. HO-8053

At the end of August 1946, Elizabeth Short desperately tracks down Marjorie Graham to Pig Stand No·21 in East Hollywood, where Graham works. Graham gets an abbreviated sob story from Elizabeth—she needs a place to stay. Graham tells Elizabeth that she's got a pretty young thing who pulls in her portion of their week's rent in a single day—posing for photo enthusiasts—she's a nudie juvie runaway by way of Long Beach, calling herself Lynn Martin. Elizabeth is welcome to room with them at the Hawthorne Hotel, and she does, but the relationship between the three is rocky from the jump; Elizabeth, with her upscale needs and stories of her hoity-toity Boston blueblood family, is in the habit of misrepresenting others' stories as her own. Those life elements that Elizabeth considers identity-forming, most people would call lying. She is regarded by most around her as a *nice girl* with her fair share of nasty habits, like biting her fingernails to the quick, or neglecting her oral hygiene to the point that she travels with white taper candles, using the soft wax to fill in the blackest of cavities in her rotting bite. It's fucking with her self-confidence. Elizabeth does, though, control her wardrobe with ire, dressing with as much care as she can muster. She will not, under any circumstances, share one single shred of clothing with any roommate, so don't even ask. It's a personal restriction that often results in kerfluffles and scratching. Elizabeth seems to find the funds for rent and groceries, and new clothes, despite not holding down a job of any kind. Graham makes no bones about drinking hard and expelling a lot of hot air. Elizabeth, the sober beast, is having great difficulty dealing with Graham. Martin, the runaway, behaves in this way and is constantly at odds with the *grown women.*

After staying at the Hawthorne Hotel for a week, management requires Elizabeth to register as a *tenant.*

> Sep. 13—*West Los Angeles Independent,* Girl, to learn to be a Dental Technician. Paid while learning. Must have driver's lic. Marti Dental Studio, 8053 Beverly bld.

Sep. 13 to 15—7:30p, Vito is one of 15 violinists in the Los Gatos Pageant Orchestra, performing *The Cat Pageant* at the bowl. He has been stationed in Los Gatos since January. Mary and Mark remain in Danvers awaiting Daddy's discharge, but it will be a while longer, since Vito was offered and has accepted a hazardous duty pay mission that requires shipping out at the end of October. No soldiers, just merchants. Upon return from what is described as a *retrieval and wiping mission* in the South Pacific, his obligation to the Merchan Marine Services will be fulfilled.

Sep. 20—Constant squabbling gets Elizabeth, Graham, and Martin kicked out of the Hawthorne Hotel. Martin is a two-time runaway, leaving the two Bostonian broads to duke it out all the way to the Figueroa Hotel in downtown LA at 939 S. Figueroa St. Without Martin's steady modeling income, these two are broke as jokes. They spend a long week downtown until desperation forces Graham to put in a call to a loose, wild acquaintance—*a nutty musician of questionable character.* This guy's married, but Graham bargains for the two women to stay a couple of nights at the Hollywood home of Syd Zaid. Syd retrieves the girls from downtown and brings them home to 562 N. Windsor Blvd. (less than 3 miles due east on Beverly Boulevard to the Smith Building).

On October 1, 1946, the girls had been at the Zaid's house for a day when the trouble began. Graham sucked every bottle in the house bone-dry. Elizabeth shot her mouth off, complaining about the tiny accommodations that she would *never put up with* back in Boston—you know, given the pedigree of her family and all. Leola can't stand these walking messes that Syd dragged in, finally snapping after Elizabeth rages that last night, Syd drunkenly fumbled his way into the living room and tried to rape her. Under Leola's threat, Syd dumps the nasty meanies off at his buddy Mark Hansen's hoochie stable; a boarding house of sorts at 6024 Carlos Ave. that Hansen (who is co-owner of the Florentine Gardens Club) has set up for young down-and-out ladies to stay a week or two while getting back on their feet—sometimes literally—as many graduates join his roster of Florentine dancers. Not so long ago, Leola was employed by Hansen.

• •

The brain of man, like that of all animals, is double, being parted down its center by a thin membrane. For this reason, pain is not always felt in the same part of the head, but sometimes on one side, sometimes on the other, and occasionally all over.—Hippocrates.

BLACKBIRDING IN THE DEAD OF NIGHT—Vito's ship has been docked at the Russell Islands for three weeks. Soldiers who returned from the Guadalcanal theatre called this place *the island of death.* And what's with all of these blonde-headed black kids running around? The threat of blue balls taking hold looms. Everything on the islands is becoming sexualized and violent.

HIBAKUSHAS—Several lucid visions came to Vito while at sea for two weeks. He wrote Mary of a stowaway coyote that stalked their liner, making a mess of the mess hall. He wrote that this mission is the longest period of his short life, longer than prison, and by far. He told her that they arrived during a shit storm of rain rarely seen by human beings, and how coming ashore was of little relief. Everything metal is patinaed. Each time before offloading onto the island, the crew is given a mandatory DDT dusting, a heavy pump of the nasty stuff down the collar and waistband, and a squirt in each appendage cuff. Neither men nor beasts—but pests—have domain over these islands. Fifty years ago, Professor Froggatt discovered that the invasive coconut rhinoceros beetle had horned onto the Solomon Islands, ravaging the coconuts of the Lever Brothers' palm oil plantation (a bit ironic, perhaps, since the Lever Bros. depleted the island of palm/coconut oil more than any insect). To fix this problem, Frogatt ships in thousands of alien parrots and releases them onto Guadalcanal Island to devour the beetles. Their plan backfires, and the sqwaking birds take over the island, eventually rendering it uninhabitable to all but the Japanese military, who built and operated these bombed-out compounds that haunt the perimeter of a makeshift tarmac. Vito's damned ship crew is there to clean up the mess left behind the Pacific theatre's Guadalcanal Campaign from 1942 to 1945, charged with retrieving bouncing Bettys and land mines, and with loading retrieved drums of unused mustard gas onto ships to be dumped into the deep South Pacific during transport. *True patriotism*, as they were told, *is being absolutely prepared to do horrible things in the name of your homeland*, but the truth is that these men will likely become Taxman clean-burns. The Solomon Islands have maintained a rich history of bargain-basement labor. In 1914, a series of letters between one of the founding brothers of the soapmaking dynasty, W. Hulme Lever, and Dr. Horn in Brussels, made a strong case for the utilitarian and financial benefits inherent in employing bushmen and cattle to plow their coconut plantations—*Working bullocks live on grass only, and therefore do as much "feeding" as a cow, so they cost nothing, and we get their work free ... They are just what we want, and we must take some risks of loss to try to secure cattle. It is impossible to exaggerate the value of cattle in pioneer work in the Tropics*—Lever writes back a follow-up letter in March of 1914, responing to the Aborigines Protection Society's demands—*I am sorry we cannot accede to any proposal that appears likely to give us a lobour for the Solomons, but certainly to take a thousand natives out to the Solomons at an expense of £15,000 and then only half of their time and no security for the return of any of the £15,000 cost of transportation, and to have the native a free man to work half his time with the Lever Bros. or with some other planter, is altogether impractical. I return the papers herewith*—Dang, son, Lever Bros. ain't agreeing to move shit. Decades later, the labour topic arose again on April 19, 1924—*In reading a book recently on travels, I came across a description of Barbadees and reference was made that they were in difficulties with the increasing Negro population, which was now excluded from the United States, where previously the surplus Negro population, I understand, used to emigrate. Have you considered that we could recruit whole families, as I do not like indentured labour, to emigrate to the Solomon Islands and take up with coconut planting, and that they would be good labour? I might mention that to Mr. Thomas. The article said the rate of wages was 1 cent per day. There would be no difficulty in paying this in the Solomon Islands.*

The heat and junk of these island jungles create their own world entirely, one that began its mutation 30 years earlier and continues with each appearance of the sun and moon. What has become of the 7,000 missing Japanese soldiers? Did the Nips desert their posts to retreat into the overgrown forest only for the humidity to fester and bubble their pale bodies into beetle food? Did they start a new colony, one without conflict? Are They tracking the Gaijins from treetops or riding on the backs of enormous parrots? Or have the forever-soldiers instead opted for a life of conflict, clashing daily with the man-eating reptilian giants that local legends rumor to slumber throughout the cave systems?

Vito did not mail the letters to Mary.

• •

> *Los Angeles Eastside Journal*, CERTIFICATE OF BUSINESS FICTITIOUS FIRM NAME—The undersigned does hereby certify that they are conducting a Machine Shop business at 8053 Beverly Blvd., The City of Los Angeles, County of Los Angeles, State of California, under the fictitious firm name of Bake Engineering Company, and that said firm is composed of the following persons, whose names and addresses are as follows, to wit: Jacker Bader, 105 South Mathews Street, Chester Schiffman, 1440-4 Via Francisca Avenue. Witness our hands this 28 day of October. 1946.

HANG ON TO YOUR BRIEF—Before Vito receives his final pay and discharge papers, he is briefed in a meeting with several Naval brass who are rather impressed with Vito's attention to his assignments and with his ability to carry out those duties despite significant dangers. Vito tells the staff he can milk a bull, which is exactly what they want to hear. They remind Vito that he's been afforded the rare treat of seeing much of the world over; how would Vito like release from military services a decade earlier than first promised?

—I'm listening…

There is a building in Los Angeles, Hollywood, a big white box that was a portal for whisky runners during Prohibition, but now it is a suspected commie recruitment center. The building was recently purchased by a first-generation Ruskie named Kubernick. Commie mark and Easton Gym co-owner, Dale Easton (aka Greg McClure), has been on Government's radar for hosting Workers' Party meetings at his home. Back in June of 1945, Dale Easton's chance at leading-man stardom suffered a major blow when he was drafted into the US Military and shipped off to war shortly after his breakout role in *The Great John L.* Dale's bodybuilder brother, Harvey, is left by himself to manage their increasingly popular gym that occupies the second floor of the Smith Building at 8053 Beverly Blvd. When Dale returned, questions arose as to whether he and the Russian, Kubernick, were passthroughs for the Soviet intelligence community. Vito's assignment is simple compared to his years in lock-up and his MM tour—become a beacon, then a filing cabinet. Vito is to watch and report on these two cogs (Easton & Kubernick), as well as any other dirty Red bastard passing through shitting sickles and golden stars in their wake—*If you're unsure of their allegience, smell their breath*—Vito came to their attention when he linked up with that wannabe half-commie jazz hornist, Syd Zaid, whom they had their sights on at first, but will no longer cut the mustard. Vito is for sale, and he's got the goods they're looking for. Vito easily plays both sides of the camp; he is cosmopolitan, charming, and good-looking when necessary, while remaining incapable of maintaining a real, legal business venture (one that can be dissolved when needed). He is the absolute perfect creature to be swallowed up whole by the Intelligence Nations. THE BUSINESS: Vito is to procure a ceramic lamp manufacturer in the basement of a popular gymnasium on Beverly Boulevard, and get those celebrities patronizing Easton's gym (directly above his basement factory) talking about their crummy commie schemes. He has until January 14, 1947, to get his ass out there and set up shop if he so chooses to take on this task—all for Lady Liberty, of course.

—Where do I sign?

On November 20, 1946, the fictitious lamp-making business Lamparts was established to lend credibility to the Smith Building basement in the heart of Hollywood.

Dec. 29—CARGO CULT COMES HOME—*Vitantas Alphonse Paulekas* makes landfall in Portland, OR, aboard the *Edward Paine*. Fresh off a mission in the South Pacific near the uninhabitable Parrot Island in the Solomon/Russel Island cluster, the hemophiliac, lupine-eyed 32-year-old merchant marine is discharged, released from his service to be returned to the custody of average civilians. He has only his issued haversack with him. Vito looks neat and well-kept; his veiny, strong build bursts through his single-stripe wool sweater. He lived it up last night, dipping deep into his hefty Navy stipend. Into his custody was made an official-looking inter-office envelope filled with per diem and bus transfers ending in Los Angeles, but, instead, Vito sells the travel package and hitches a ride with a carload of twenty-somethings making their way to San Francisco for a New Year's Eve gala. They can take him as far as the Bay Area, and he is, of course, invited to join them at the party. Vito's mind wanders to the temptation of holding them all hostage, tying them up, and stealing their wheels. These kids wouldn't know what hit them; they wouldn't see this devil coming until it's too late, but he talks himself out of acting on the impulse, and this pre-Beat jazz freak starts philosophizing about his Hollywood ceramics studio to the stars. While Vito spins a tale, a whisp of smoke rises from his haversack. He pulls from it a smoldering Retina that bursts into flames as Vito launches it from the speeding car, where it most likely landed and melted on an otherwise peaceful stretch of asphalt that connects pine trees to a golden gate. After driving for a half hour, the teens stop off at a beach turnout to take pisses and pass around a much-needed (and much-deserved) fatty—*Pay attention to me, I'm only telling you this once*—Vito repeats to himself that as long as they swap stories around the campfire, he can keep the hungry monster at bay. He opens with a tale about his retrieval of toxic containers filled with mustard gas and ST. ANTHONY'S FIRE. Vito watched as a shipmate's arm dissolved into a toothpick when a barrel of Government sludge doused it. Another mate gets turned to a pink mist—he should have been looking down—but no matter, suddenly that problem, along with every other he had, was a problem no longer. Some MMs caved after exposure to a cocktail of noxious vapors. Others went mad from the incessant parrot squawking—THEY WERE ALL subjected to hypnosis experiments, torture, really—hours of exposure to the squawking—but Vito had learned to use the cacophonic vibrations for meditation, reaching a state of grace under the jungle canopy where the huge tuning fork in the sky launched his consciousness into the cosmos. The incessant chirping presented the Akashic Records to Vito, and he was commanded to *add to the design of the world around him* and tasked with its *co-creation and beautification.* In simple terms: fuck and make art—eat occasionally; dance frequently—*Ever done that, you stupid fucking kids?*—he thought. Vito tries repeatedly to make it with the girls, any of them, but now that they are high and sharp, these girls are feeling some major freaky vibes from this old dude. Some of the girls tease Vito that he looks like a Mexican, and he probably wasn't even in the Merchant Marines. To double down, Vito recites an encounter he and his patrol had with the secret *wildman* society; the offering made to the wildman—a wild woman! That island tail couldn't get enough of him. Never had they been raptured such—*Still not enough?*—Well, then, on a stopover in Papua New Guinea, Vito witnessed the mummification of a tribal leader in which they smoked his corpse over white coals for days before hoisting his sanctified jerky up to a cliffside perch where he will sit, staring down at them, in perpetuity. There, too, was the tribal hit job in which Vito was hired by a council Elder to lure a Japanese stowaway out from a cursed cave, so that he may stand trial for serial impregnation. Natives believe that this cave is home to a *half-human, half-giant flying rodent that glows in the dark.* Vito and his clan got stoned on some cannabis and kava before searching the cave a mile in, but turned up nothing. One night on the main island, the MMs were living it up in the village when three aboriginal headhunters, the Australian Kurdaitchas, arrived unnoticed at first on the island in their feather and blood slippers. Their years-long search for a plantation worker who has been fingered guilty in a dying man's confession has led them here to this cabana. The Kurdaitcha pointed its bone at the prey, and the natives went nuts. The MMs got carried away in the performance of it all and poked fun at the ritual, but several days later, when the accused rapidly sickened and died, their laughing stopped, and the Rosaries got passed around. Vito had seen grown men cut down, turned into pulpy purple and yellow ribbons, but what those psychic hitmen did was simply inconceivable even to his bullblooded, freaky mind. Coming down off their high, the kids are freaked-the-fuck-out when they load back into the car. Sixty miles from San Francisco, they abandon Vito outside of a diner.

1947—HAPPY NEW YEAR! Tens of thousands of maligned American Jesuses have returned home, many having written the *Achilles* chapter in their communal bildungsroman. But what wartime killed in them, primetime will numb. Over one million American households own television sets, piping in a steady stream of distractionary crowd pleasers: *Hopalong Cassidy*, *The Ed Sullivan Show, Juvenile Jury*, etc. The televised broadcast era emerges from a dialated cathode, its EMF static afterbirth floods American living rooms. One who renders a message or propaganda that needs endorsement, then consider this hyper-evolving delivery method of tell-a-vision. Those Angelenos not resting their haunches at home, sucking from the boob-tube instead, peruse their choice of nightclubs.

Vito has made his way to the Government-issued maildrop at 1925 Vestal Ave., a preselected place where he, the *asset,* as they called him, will not be disturbed while he's doing his thing at Lamparts; the future Freak art salon in the belly of Jewish Hollywood—JD Kubernick gives Vito an introductory tour of the basement lair waiting in the mud swaddled by the groundwater and tar. Step underground, and you instantly go off-grid, disconnecting completely from street lamps and sunlight. The basement currently serves as a storage room for paperwork and large machines. There are spools of electrical wire and lighting fixture parts left behind by the builder, E.L. Smith. One only has to tilt their head to compute that a basement pottery studio is a goddamn great cover. There is a shallow hole near the middle of the basement's concrete floor, which feeds into an underground creek. It is perpetually swollen with water. Vito is warned that *on rainy days, that fucker rises.*

A shower and kitchenette were installed during its early Speakeasy years, and Kubernick has chosen to keep them operational, hoping to register the basement as a *finished living quarters* soon. He'll have to add a toilet and outside window access, which will provide its own set of challenges, as being underground, surrounded by super-saturated soil, doesn't exactly offer a hot view for real estate agents to pitch—*You won't mind it down here?—Not one bit* … The building reminds Vito of a Spanish armory he once crashed in. Good observation, notes Kubernick, since, from what he understands, that was the building's original intention (but we know differently). He said a train used to pull right up to the front door and load and offload munitions, ranging from cap-gun rings to 675-round count cases of 12-gauge shells. Kubernick then sells hard the bomb shelter ontology; in the event of an above-ground attack on movie land. Either way, as far as the city is concerned, this place, just like Vito, does not really exist. Despite their different approaches, Kubernick and Vito hit it off. Kubernick adds that if things go well, and should Vito need an above-ground storefront, one might soon open up. Vito will never be sought here, smack dab in the middle of the city, underground and unacknowledged by the Los Angeles Municipality.

Jan. 7—POWDERED AND PAINTED. Heading nine miles to the northeast, we arrive at Gladding McBean & Co.'s 280-artist, 45-acre facility at 2901 Los Feliz Blvd. in Glendale. The company churns out pottery for top-tier celebrities and dignitaries at a time when most other ceramists and potters have shifted sharply from producing art and craft pieces to manufacturing utilitarian items, such as plumbing fixtures and pipes.

Vito has spent the last four days categorizing his studio, planning a layout, and taking inventory of his tools owned versus needed:

sharpened stick shapers + finishers
clay wire /garrote loops
knifes ribs
brushes scrapers
brayer

On the final day of creation, Vito dedicates his time to constructing a small kiln tucked in the damp back corner of the basement. A kiln is the potter's ritual pit, the witch's clay cauldron. Vito intends to use some of the fifty-pound sacks of concrete and vermiculite (a material mixed into a slurry for screed coating the basement floor, providing moderate protection against the swelling groundwater) left behind to reinforce his kiln. The word *kiln* was originally pronounced as *KILL*.

Tingle-balls & scrotum suck-up, Vito senses something big is on the horizon.

• •

January 9, 1947, 12:20p, Elizabeth and an awkward ginger gent have just checked out of the Mecca Hotel in San Diego, CA, after spending a platonic night together. This young Southland native, called *Red* Manley, has agreed to give Elizabeth a ride back to LA in his black Studebaker, where he has a house in Southgate that he shares with his new wife and baby. Elizabeth spins a yarn for Red about all the trivial decisions that have brought them together. Red realizes within a handful of sentences that Elizabeth is a habitual liar. She shows her age by reacting to obstacles as if it were her first day of school, and everyone else got a handbook on life; they know exactly what to do and where to go, but Elizabeth, alas, is always left behind. She tells Red that this drunk Graham got her in this mess, and then bailed on her last October 22, splitting back to her childhood home in Cambridge, MA. Elizabeth bounced couches, bargaining one dinner date with lonely Hollywood playboys after another. She wasn't willing to give up on Hollywood like that bully Graham. Hansen let Elizabeth move back into his dancer stable, but after two weeks there, she and a *real floozy* got into a nasty brawl. This *new tramp* thought she could waltz in and usurp Elizabeth, so Elizabeth made Hansen choose between that piece of trash blowing through or herself—and Hansen booted Elizabeth!—*Can you believe such nonsense, Red?* By ALMIGHTY's grace, one of Hansen's dancers (and Elizabeth's only *real friend*), Ann Toth, borrowed one of Hansen's extra cars without his blessing, and spirited Elizabeth three miles west on Hollywood Boulevard to the Chancellor Hotel at 1842 N. Cherokee Ave. Toth, ever the angel, even paid Elizabeth's first week of rent for a tiny fifth-floor room that she shared with eight roommates.

Elizabeth's logorrhea drifts over the next few hours of the road trip, covering a variety of inane subjects. Still, doubly-dumb Red refuses to accept the mistake he's made, and eats it all up with a spoon, nodding with the occasional—*uh-huh*—interjected. Elizabeth never says why she was in San Diego, but Red doesn't give a shit; he's just happy to have a pretty-ish sack of XX chromosomes accompanying him on the long haul home.

At 5:00p, the pair arrived in Los Angeles. Red drops Elizabeth off at the Greyhound bus depot near the Union Pacific Station. Her story was that she planned to meet her sister visiting from Oakland for drinks in the Biltmore lounge—*Whatever, just get out of my car already*—Red thinks, tipping his dunce cap to Elizabeth, bidding her a good life as he watched her okay-figure fade into the winter evening that swallowed the Biltmore Hotel.

• •

A portrait is a likeness in which there is something wrong about the mouth—JOHN SINGER SARGENT

RESPONSE TO IMPACT—On the early morning of January 15, 1947, both halves of a discarded body had been displayed near the curb of 3825 Norton Ave. Betty Bersinger made the discovery, stumbling upon the remains while strolling through Leimert (French; *to levitate*) Park with her pram. Bersinger tells a neighbor to call the police; she has just seen a mannequin in a vacant lot and does not want anyone else to share in her alarm. When authorities arrive on scene, they find not a vinyl-and-foam or plastic model, but something that was once a living, breathing, connected human organism.

This victim, clearly of foul play, is a female. She has been divided into two, bisected between the second and third lumbar along her spinal column—the torsos placed about 18" apart. Her intestines have spilled out, coming to rest under the buttocks. Her arms are stretched above her head. Her legs spread apart, creating an inverted V. (15th-century Romanian ruler of Wallachia, Vlad Tepes, was rumored to have cut a lover in half just north of the waist, displaying her publicly so his subjects could see *what he had been inside* and where he *deposited his seed.*)

Look well to the spine for the cause of disease—HIPPOCRATES

January 16, 1947. A HEMATOLAGNIAN'S PORTRAIT OF A DANCER—The autopsy has been completed. The victim's mouth has been slashed from both corners, outward about three inches toward each ear. A very sharp instrument was used to make those, as well as the tiny cuts along her upper lip. Her forehead and the bridge of her nose are gashed, bruised severely, and battered by a blunt object. A wedge of flesh was removed from the left breast, and the right breast has been skinned. A square plug of flesh was cut from her thigh; later to be found inserted into the lower torso orifice. The piece of thigh had markings of a rose tattoo clearly visible.—Vito's mother is named Rose—was this a moment not unlike those in pre-code movies, when just before making love to the vamp, the cleft-chinned Lead turned mama's framed 8x10 to face the wall? Was that image alone, one of a rose, enough to be a trigger? The victim's pubic area is hatch-marked with multiple lacerations. Several pubic hairs have been meticulously plucked. Centered directly above the hatches is a four-inch horizontal incision. The specimen's neck, wrists, and ankles show signs of having been bound with restraints. The remains have been exsanguinated and thoroughly washed. Decedent's teeth are in significantly poor condition.

Total weight of remains: 115 lbs. Estimated age: 18 to 25

According to LAPD Forensics Specialist, Ray Pinker, the subject died at 2:00a at the latest. Pinker found the postmortem discolorization of the face most likely happened from being transported belly down. Rough coconut fibers were found scattered about the body (possibly deposited by a coir brush during the rigorous scrubbing). Immediately before or just after disposal, both halves were wiped down with an abrasive astringent such as gasoline, acetone, or turpentine. The pieces of the corpse are positively identified as 22-year-old ELIZABETH SHORT of Medford, MA, after matching her fingerprints with those on file from her job at Camp Cooke's Post Exchange. The *Herald-Express* picks up the rest of the story in the afternoon edition:

WEREWOLVES LEAVE TRAIL OF WOMEN MURDERS IN LA

A heavily edited photograph of the dump scene appears for the first time, publicly, on the front page of the *Los Angeles Herald Examiner*. Nothing seen that day could have been printed in any media source at the time, but that isn't to say that this was an uncommon crime scene for the seasoned homicide detectives crouching down that morning for a better smell. LA has an illustrious, albeit nasty, history of unsolved or cold public mutilations. How many people encounter a work of art in their lifetime that actually changes their worldview? Was Elizabeth used as propaganda, a kind of WW Bonds poster—a symbol of what the word *no* gets you post-War? Elizabeth now served as a Jungian Archetype. Maybe even our collective psychoid or the American fetish—POP!—she was created by the zeitgeist. What is she the stand-in for? Is it something psychosexual, or something else entirely? The staging of her corpse is not unlike that of ancient Roman art. Was Elizabeth intended to represent the ETERNAL HULA DANCER, the ones popularized on occidental bound postcards and television lamp poles?—Even the gap created when her torsos were divided reveals to the observer a patch of land, conjuring the faint idea of a grass skirt.

• •

LAPD detective Finis Brown states—*Of course, it's a sex crime, and we're looking for a pervert.*—On the evening of January 17, 1947, a paper bag was found in the alley behind 8223 Beverly Blvd. containing a pair of female size seven red sandals and a pair of black shoes, a green wool knit dress, red silk halter, and four pairs of silk stockings. This unusual bounty was dropped only 300 yards from Vito's basement, due west down the same alley shared with the Smith Building.

Jan. 18—Homicide detectives track Cleophus Short down to 1020 South Kinglsley Ave., a beat-down apartment leftover from Egyptmania that sand-blasted the country 20 years previously. The two pillar pylons flanking the arched stucco entrance are crested with an Egyptian winged disk zipping about, piloted by Uraeus (representing the falcon-headed Horus, and later the sun disc deity Ra)—Aleister Crowley felt compelled by this same ancient symbol to emboss it onto the cover of *The Book of the Law-Thelema* (93). Detectives fail to pull any info from the drunk, aside from the fact that he works at a refrigeration repair shop east of Fairfax Avenue. Cleo has totally abandoned his family—*I didn't want anything to do with her or any of the rest of the family then. I was through. I want nothing to do with this*—and just like that, the father of a bisected, exanguinated young woman is left alone to sort out his bitter life.

> Jan. 19—*Los Angeles Times*, HUGE BIRDS KILL WHALE WITH BEAKS—MANTEO (NC)—Coast Guardsmen who rushed through fog and rough seas to the rescue of what was first reported to be an "overturned ship with survivors clinging to it" today were given ringside seats to a losing battle for its life between a floundered monster whale and a flock of sea vultures. The whale, described by Coast Guardsmen as the largest ever sighted off these shores, was wallowing in shallow water, helpless to defend itself against the flesh-ripping beaks of the huge birds. Shore station

> lookouts kept track of the drifting behemoth, driven before a stiff northerly gale, all during the afternoon. Tonight at high tide, it washed ashore eight miles south of here, only a short distance from where the wreckage of a yacht, which was breached by another storm this month, was.

Jan. 22, 1947—At 10:30a, a formal inquest is held at the LA Hall of Justice to discuss Elizabeth Short's autopsy findings. Detective Lieutenant Jesse W. Haskins testifies to—*finding blood down this driveway, which leads from where the body was found to the street there was a tire track right up against the curbing, and there was what appeared to be a possible bloody heel mark in this tire mark, and down the curbing, which is very low, there was one spot of blood, and there was an empty paper cement sack lying in the driveway and it also had a spot of blood on it ... It had been brought there from some other location.*

> Jan. 23—*Siskiyou Daily News*, POLICE SEEK BLACK DAHLIA DEATH ROOM—LOS ANGELES, Two score uniformed policemen today began a house-to-house hunt in the neighborhood where the mutilated body of "Black Dahlia" Elizabeth Short was found January 15, announcing they hoped to find a "torture chamber" where she was slain. Det. Lt. P. P. Freestone said a squad of 40 patrolmen would make the search. "We hope to find someone who saw her during the blank period preceding her death, or who might have heard screams when she was being tortured," Freestone said. "The police are in uniform so that housewives won't refuse to answer their ring." He said it was believed that a house or room in the vicinity was used by the slayer to cut Miss Short's body in two. Other officers quizzed women friends of Miss Short. Lynn Martin, 15, former roommate of the girl, told police that Edward P. (Duke) Wellington, whom she described as a former suitor, failed to return after telling her he was going to make a telephone call. Police said they wanted to question Wellington. They greying Wellington, reportedly a dapper dresser, left a note advising Miss Martin to surrender, police said. Police attention also swung to "Apartment 501" in a Hollywood building, where Paul Simone, a painting contractor, told officers he overheard a

> bitter quarrel between a girl he believed to be Miss Short and another woman. "It was pretty hard language," said Simone, and was broken off with the exclamation "Oh, nuts to you" from the other woman as he approached.

A person self-identifying as *BD Avenger* contacts *Examiner* editor Jimmy Richardson and expresses his disapproval of the media and law enforcement's handling of the murder thus far, before offering to make available some of Elizabeth's personal effects. Could the ontology of the writer's moniker have been lifted from the 1944 Jack the Ripper-based film, *The Lodger*, in which the antagonistic killer calls himself *Avenger*? According to *The Oxford English Dictionary*:

> AVENGE: to take vengeance for or on behalf of. 2: to exact satisfaction for (a wrong) by punishing the wrongdoer.
>
> AVENGER: A person who exacts punishment or inflicts harm in return for an injury or wrong.

The caller clearly feels just in their actions, selecting a descriptor that paints themselves as the original and actual victim, simply righting a perceived wrong. On January 24, as promised, Richardson receives an anonymous package containing some of Elizabeth's belongings: her original birth certificate, a handful of business cards, candid snapshots of her enjoying life, and a brown leather address book with *1937* embossed on its cover in gold typeface. Over 75 contacts are scribbled in it, but as many as 50 pages have been ripped out. The loot is turned over to LA detectives, who call in both cleared men, Red Manley and Mark Hansen, to confirm the items' authenticity.

On the following day, Elizabeth's remains are laid to rest at Mountainview Cemetery in Oakland, CA. During the service, detectives respond to a call about one of Elizabeth's handbags and her shoes having been discovered in a dumpster at 1819 East 25th St., a few miles from her drop site.

The handbag and its contents had been, like her remains, soaked with a *gasoline-like chemical,* erasing all but one smudged-but-unidentifiable fingerprint. Dr. Joseph de River weighs in:

> We are dealing with a homicidal maniac who craves attention for his crime and may come forward in a bold and spectacular manner for his curtain call after he has wrung out the last drop of drama from his deed.

Handwriting expert Henry Silver examines the original parcel note and postcards and determines:

> The sender is an egomaniac and possibly a musician. The fluctuating baseline of the writing reveals the writer to be affected by extreme fluctuations of mood, dropping to melancholy. The writer suffers from mental conflict growing out of resentment or hatred due to frustration with sex urges. Because the last letters of many words are larger, it reveals extreme frankness. The writer is telling the truth. Furthermore, he can't keep his secret and feeds his ego by telling. There is a fine sense of rhythm present, showing the penman to be either a musician or possibly a dancer. He is calculating and methodical.

A musician or *possibly a dancer* ... Hmmm ... Captain Donahoe adds:

> It appears impossible that the Short girl was murdered in the city. We are forced to this conclusion by the failure of anyone to report a possible place where she was killed within the city limits. If she was slain in a house or a room or a motel in the city, it seems impossible that some trace has not been reported or found. This leads to the conclusion that she was killed outside the city. The killer could not have emerged from the place in clothing worn when the murder was committed and the body drained of blood. He could have been too easily detected, and stains would have attracted attention.

This is true, unless someone has access to, say, a basement … Perhaps one under a busy, loud gymnasium that could easily mask distress calls; an undocumented, underground lair with a machined hole in the floor which feeds directly into the city's groundwater table. At the end of January, some crude notes and postcards were delivered to both the *LA Times* and LAPD. They are examined for connective characteristics:

> Feb. 3—*Evening Vanguard,* Mysterious 'Black Dahlia' Note Received by Police Here—Note Indicates Musician May Be Involved—Culver City stepped into the "Black Dahlia" murder last night after a crude postcard was received at the Culver City police department, giving an address on Watseka Ave., indicating that the murderer might be hiding or residing at that address. Investigating that street number, Det. Sgt. Charles Lugo reported that although he found a magazine in the mailbox, such as a musician might subscribe to, he placed little faith in the validity of the mysterious postcard. Hints at Musician—The postcard contained newspaper clippings, one of which quoted a handwriting analyst who had been called into the "Black Dahlia" case. His analysis of a previous postcard indicated that the writer was a musician.

• •

THE WAR ON WOMEN—At 2:00a, on February 10, 1947, while working his shift at the Pan American Bar at 11155 West Washington Place, bartender Joseph Nesco witnessed Jeanne French (aka Jeanne Axford Thomas), 47, sitting beside a *medium build, swarthy-complexioned male*. At 2:30a, French leaves quarreling with the stranger. At 8:30a, French's beaten corpse is discovered on Mountain View Avenue in West Hollywood, dumped face up at a spot in the weeds with her clothes piled on top of her nude body. She is positioned 100 yards north of Indianapolis Street with her feet pointed toward Grand View Avenue. Her pocketbook was some ten feet from her body. French's shoes are found in a field with 60 feet between them. The coroner estimates that she was murdered at another location, half an hour before her discovery. Across French's lower torso, the messages—*FUCK YOU BD* and *TEX*—are scrawled in lipstick (the applicator later found when French is rolled over). The coroner notes that she was beaten about the head with a blunt metal instrument, probably utilitarian, like a pipe or wrench. Death came to her slowly from bleeding internally after her lungs and liver were punctured by fractured ribs while being *danced on… her body bludgeoned and covered with heel marks made by a small man's size 6 or 7 shoes*—leading to the culprit's height estimated between 5'4" and 5'7". Vito, as documented in his military records, stands at exactly 5'4" …

Congress takes precautions right up to the edge when deviant crimes in the greater Los Angeles reach a fever pitch. Government steps in, leveling higher *legislative efforts to curb California crimes, particularly those of a sadistic nature, such as the "Black Dahlia" case*. The Los Angeles City Council agrees that the streets of LA must be made safe for women and girls again and pledges to combat the rising body count and victim rap with street lamps and plenty more of 'em. The DA's office suggests a measure that *would require the registration of all known sexual perverts* and sponsors a bill *permitting the sterilization of perverts and feeble-minded persons, but only after a full hearing in Superior Court and after their discharge from an institution.* Elizabeth Short's murder helped make a case for state-sanctioned sterilization—after due process, of course.

March 1—Impeccable timing. The essay *The Engineering of Consent* by former theatre agent Edward Bernays was published in *The Annals of the American Academy of Political and Social Science, Volume 250, Issue 01.*

A letter to the editor on page 38 of the March 2 *Fresno Bee*:

> Bible Reference—Editor of The Bee—Sir: I would like for the Public Thinks letter writer who signs herself A Wife, condemning the Black Dahlia, to read Matthew 12:36-37. Fresno. M. G. ROBINSON.

The above-mentioned, in accordance with the KJV:

> 36: But I say unto you, That every idle word that men shall speak, they shall give account thereof in the day of judgment.
> 37: For by thy words thou shalt be justified, and by thy words thou shalt be condemned.

FREAK CENTRAL—On March 11, 1947, the beaten corpse of 42-year-old former Paramount Pictures legal department secretary Evelyn Winters (aka Victoria Windham) is found next to railroad tracks two miles outside of downtown LA. Winters's undergarments and shoes are discovered one block away near Center Street. Formerly of 115 Burton Street (two miles from 43-year-old Vito's Vestal Avenue house in South Gate), Winters had been homeless for at least four months, spending days barhopping around downtown's Hill and Figueroa streets. She is dressed in a bathrobe, and a skirt has been wrapped around her neck, posthumously. Winters's left eye was stabbed, nearly removed, but death came to her by way of strangulation, ala LAMP CORD. Detectives discovered a bag of her belongings at a nearby liquor store she was known to frequent. Among the items was *a book on metaphysics with the dead woman's name inscribed on a leaf.* 28-year-old railroad section hand George Wickliffe is subsequently jailed after questioning and admitting to kissing Winters on the lips as *she lay in death*, but he denied stabbing Winters's eye. Four days later, a steep increase in Los Angeles crimes causes Chief of Police C.B. Horall to add 250 patrol officers to his force, implementing tactics not all too different from the Gestapo, whom many of these boys in blue had just returned from killing. Some push-back is anticipated:

> March 15—*Redwood City Tribune*, In Los Angeles alone, the police record showed that for the last twenty-four-hour period, there had been sixty-eight thefts, forty-one burglaries, seven assaults with deadly weapons, one murder, twenty stolen automobiles, two attempted attacks on women, twelve robberies, and one morals offense. Seven late-night street blockades in efforts to crush a crime wave that started with the mutilation killing of Elizabeth (Black Dahlia). Surprised motorists stopped last night as police teams halted and checked all automobiles. Uniformed patrolmen, radio cars, and motorcycle officers worked in teams while detectives stood by at stations. Any suspicious cars or occupants were detained for further investigation. Innocent motorists were permitted to proceed with the least inconvenience, Reed said. The roadblock system, first tried here in 1923 and revived briefly in the 1930s, will be used periodically at varying intersections, Reed added. Results of the first night's roadblock roundup included 35 men booked on suspicion of robbery, two on suspicion of burglary, seven juveniles nabbed for curfew violation, and an assortment of pistols, knives, and clubs found in cars or on persons "shaken down."

Then, on March 25, 1947, 200 coppers-on-loan performed the same dance, nearly doubling the number of arrests, taking in 71 persons on a litany of charges—49 are picked up on robbery suspicion after guns and knives are turned up in their vehicles. Crime prevention stats show a 27 percent increase in rape cases in LA from 1944-45. In the first month, after Short's discovery, the LAPD claims to have picked up, questioned, processed, and eliminated approximately 75 potential suspects in connection with Short's murder. The FBI asks for help in narrowing down their interrogation list of California medical students, a task due in large part to Detective Harry Hansen's offhand remark that the perpetrator required near-expert medical skills to properly bisect Ms. Short in the manner in which she was. That contentious tidbit was picked up instantly by the media, propagated by law enforcement, and absorbed by the populace like melted butter on bread. But, wouldn't anybody with even the slightest understanding of organ placement and an average knowledge of skeletal structures, say, an artist or sculptor, not find the obvious path of least resistance? It is the only section of the spine not obstructed by the ribcage and protected organs.

April 9—*Los Angeles Times* runs an ad for Harry Lowitz's furniture, radio, and appliance mart located at 303 N. Laurel Ave., calling itself *Out of the Way—Worth Finding!*

May 26—Just three months after joining the hunt for the BD Avenger, the FBI issues a memo warning of the communist undertones in Frank Capra's *It's a Wonderful Life*. This fax comes across the desk of the California Film Commissioner while the corpses of violated women across the Sunshine State's landscape pile up:

> With regard to the picture "It's A Wonderful Life". [REDACTED] stated in substance that the film represented a rather obvious attempt to discredit bankers by casting Lionel Barrymore as a "Scrooge-type" so that he would be the most hated man in the picture. This, according to these sources, is a common trick used by Communists. [In] addition, [REDACTED] stated that, in his opinion, this picture deliberately maligned the upper class, attempting to show the people who had money were mean and despicable characters.

At the heart of the movie, we have the impact of one man on his community, something philosopher Ayn Rand calls Objectivism: *The concept of man as a heroic being, with his happiness as the moral purpose of his life, with productive achievement as his noblest activity, and reason as his only absolute.* The film's mantra—*No Man Is A Failure Who Has Friends* —borrows from 16th-century English poet John Donne's sentiment in that *No man is an island, entire from itself.* He felt strongly that *human beings do not thrive when isolated from others.* There are several interesting hat tips to Theosophy in Capra's film adaptation of the Phillip Van Doren Stern short story, *The Greatest Gift.* For example, the protagonist's surname was inexplicably changed from Pratt in the short story to Bailey in the film; perhaps a reference to New Theosophy's modern matron, Alice Bailey. This bolsters the FBI's reasoning; you have to keep a close watch on these creative commies. Capra and Barrymore are both staunch Republicans, wholly consumed with the bottom line and how to avoid it. Both elephants HATE paying taxes. But, tonight, in the back booth of Musso & Frank's, Capra's concern isn't coin, it's the clap, and how to kick it and keep from catching it again. Barrymore suggests Capra look into having an adult circumcision, and in sheer desperation to keep his dick wet (not spotted), the first-generation Sicilian goes in for a trim; but he gets a hack-job, and his once beautiful minchia is forever mangled—*and therefore never send to know for whom the bell tolls; it tolls for thee.*

July 2, 1947—A New Mexican thunderstorm southeast of Corona calls pastorals to their porches, watching out across the barren land as the rain system trawls in, calculating which ranch is getting the good stuff, and for how long. Five days later, at 1:30p, an army base mortician puts in a call to the local Chaves County mortician, hoping to get his hands on a set of the smallest hermetically sealed, ready-off-the-shelf coffins—something around 3'6". The caller launches questions: *Now let's say you want to preserve a specimen for later testing … like a hog! What's the procedure for something like that?*

Well, you'll want to give it a 24-hour formaldehyde and water bath first to allow deep tissue punctures and cavities to aspirate with fluids if there are any ruptures. Then, give it a lye and sawdust jacket before storing it. When the mortician offers to personally take care of the caller's needs, he is reassured that the inquiries come from a place of preparation and that the scenarios are purely hypothetical. Before disconnecting, one final question: *What does one do, or should not do, to preserve the integrity of the biological sample?* Before the mortician can twitch his lips, the caller excuses themself, and the line goes dead.

July 8, 1947—20-year-old Rosenda Josephine Mondragon (Spanish; *mount of the dragon*) is murdered—strangled—tossed from a moving vehicle at 129 East Elmyra St. in downtown near City Hall; only one mile from the Winters crime scene. Mondragon's right breast, like Short's, has been slashed.

July 30—In Hollywood, at the Coronet Theatre at 366 North La Cienega Blvd. (less than a mile west of the Smith Building), a paranoid Charles Laughton is backstage preparing to perform as Galileo in Brecht's *The Life of Galileo*. Immediately following the final curtain, dubious and tenacious Coronet curator, Raymond Rouhauer, premieres 20-year-old Kenneth Anger's short film, *Fireworks*. It is at this screening that famed sexologist Dr. Alfred Kinsey befriends Anger, buying a print of *Fireworks* to donate to the Institute in Indiana, where Kinsey teaches. (Anger also networks with and gains admiration from established directors James Whale and Robert Florey.)

Back three years, in 1944, Kenneth Robert Anglemyer and his family moved in with their Hollywood costume mistress grandmother, *Big Bertha* Coler. Not long after doing so, Coler died, bequeathing her silk robes and vintage costume collection to the then 16-year-old Kenneth. While attending Beverly Hills High School, Kenneth discovered the Rosicrucian philosophies littered throughout Theosophist Frank L. Baum's *Oz* collection. He became a student of the occult, studying the works of Eliphas Levi and, especially, Aleister Crowley. Kenneth befriended BHHS classmate Marilyn Granas (aka Maxine Peterson, aka Shirley Temple's stand-in), and he asked her to appear in his occult-themed film, *Demigods* (later re-titled *Escape*

Episode). Granas accepted, and Kenneth shot the 35-minute silent love story in a *spooky old castle* in Hollywood. Anger considers this an apprentice film, describing it as a *boy-meets-girl seaside yarn, a free rendering of the Andromeda myth*. The girl is imprisoned in a castle by her clairvoyant aunt, who uses the girl as a stooge in a fake séance. During a secret rendezvous with her new friend, the girl plans to escape, which she accomplishes in the final reel. In September of 1945, the Ballard Film Society joined the American Contemporary Gallery in Hollywood for the premiere of young Kenneth Anglemyer's *Escape Episode* in the auditorium of an apartment building at 7021 Hollywood Blvd. Screening art and experimental pieces in public living quarters, lobbies —even stairwells—was a common practice at the time; this isn't your standard multiplex fare, remember. Kenneth shaved eight minutes off *Escape Episode*, cutting it to a slim 27 minutes, while adding sound effects, narration, and Theosophist Alexander Scriabin's *Poem of Ecstasy* as the score. Kenneth screens the fresh cut at Barbara Cecil's The Great Film Society of Beverly Hills (The modernist hub soon comes under attack by the Tenney Committee after an investigation exposes their hand-in-hand association with the People's Educational Center). It wasn't until the summer of 1946 that Kenneth Anglemyer mutated his surname to *Anger*.

On the Fall Solstice of 1947, Universal Pictures technicians drove two truckloads stocked chock-full of nitrate film reels to the desert. The new Universal archival facilities are threatened with sky-high insurance premiums if the temperamental nitrate film stocks are to remain on site, so the liability reels are burned and buried, leaving behind two more coastal dunes than they found. A documentary crew films the plastic and oil sacrifice from a safe distance.

October—Working in clay has become a *thing*, and behind every good *thing* will forever follow sell-ebrities. Look! Here comes one now:

> Oct. 23—*Wilmington Daily Press Journal,* HOLLYWOOD FILM SHOP—Henry Fonda, actor and sculptor, looked over a gallery of his own statuary today and said there wasn't a Hollywood head among them because Hollywood takes the character out of a woman's face. Girls in Hollywood are good-looking, he admitted, but all in the same plastered way. "They get slick, brittle, and stereotyped after they've been here six months," he said. "They don't make good subjects for sculpture." He said the ideal American faces were those bent over a soda at the small-town drugstore or behind the piano at the church social. "Small-town girls are American womanhood at its best," Fonda said. "They have individuality and character. Their beauty reflects their lives instead of conforming to a standard of so-called glamor. "As soon as they migrate to Hollywood, they get that unfortunate Hollywood gloss." The star's convictions are backed up by the impressive line of modeled heads that stand in his own gallery of statuary. There isn't a star's head among them. They are all non-famous, simple, beautiful American types. "One of the things that I like about working with director John Ford is the fact that it means getting into rural areas, where I like to shoot," Fonda said. "It gives me a chance to make sketches of types more beautiful than anything I see in Hollywood. When I get back home, I have a chance to develop them in clay." Fonda made "The Fugitive" with Ford in Old Mexico and took another location trip with him to the Rocky Mountain states for Argosy Pictures' "War Party." "The eye of the sculpture [sic] sees differently from the eye of a camera," Fonda said. "The camera sees a rough mouth and shiny nylons, but the sculpture [sic] sees the arch of a nose and the wave of hair." And the best place to see them, he added, is on Main Street.

October—Curtis Harrington announces in *The Hollywood Quarterly* that he and Kenneth Anger have formed the Experimental Film Society, producing their own films and distributing them through Creative Film Associates. According to Robert Pike, this independent separation ensures the *film artist's impact well beyond the standard private screenings or house parties.*

Oct. 24—Walter Elias Disney and actor Ronald Reagan testify before the House Un-American Activities Committee (HUAC), resulting in LA County requiring its 20,000 employees to sign affidavits indicating that they do not advocate the overthrow of the Government by violence, nor do they have any affiliation with the approximately 140 designated communist organizations. The Hollywood Ten are used as an example of this procedure—*DO NOT FUCK WITH US UNLESS YOU WANT TO FIND OUT*—Many cities in metropolitan California adopted this practice. Film director John Huston and others quickly formed the Committee for the First Amendment in retaliation, citing their industry's unfair singling out by the Feds. On the same day, at her Los Feliz apartment on Fountain Avenue, 73-year-old Jane Wolfe receives a Western Union telegram from Thelema's new Outer Head of the Order, Karl Germer: *Aleister died Monday noon peacefully please notify everybody love = = KARL.* Aleister Crowley, 72, died in Hastings, East Sussex, financially destitute and severely addicted to amphetamines.

1948. Kenneth Anger's new benefactor, Dr. Alfred Charles Kinsey, publishes his report *Sexual Behavior in the Human Male,* postulating that a large percentage of American males have had non-heterosexual relations at least one time in their lives.

On the first anniversary of Elizabeth Short's murder, nearly 200 persons of interest have been connected to the case. LA judge Kaufman has had enough of the *confessing Willies* and makes an example of the sixteenth and most recent *offender,* Charles Lynch, 23, sentencing him to 60 days in jail.

NOT ALL ABOUT EVA—These next two doozies share the *Daily News*'s On February 15 front page: 1:30a, two days before, 36-year-old Viola Norton is abducted from an Alhambra sidewalk by two men, 16 miles outside of downtown. Norton was beaten with a tire iron about the head and face, before being driven to Leimert Park, dumped for dead, only blocks from the spot Short made infamous. Then, soon after midnight, Vito's first cousin Eva Paul (aka Barbara *Bobo* Paulckiute, aka Jievute Paulckiute, aka Eva Paulekas) marries for the second time, trading up from a Sears to a Rockefeller—Winthrop III, grandson of Standard Oil magnate John D. Rockefeller and nephew to the incumbent Vice-President Nelson Rockefeller. Eva and Winthrop's wedding took place at the Palm Beach estate of sportsman Winston Guest. The Duke and Duchess of Windsor are in attendance. *Time Magazine* tells us—*Bobo's mother and stepfather, who were unable to attend the ceremony because they were making a batch of Lithuanian cheese on their Indiana farm, both announced that they were happy for Bobo*—Eva's biological, estranged father, Julius Paulekas (Jonas's bro), according to print, at least, is delighted for his moody daughter, but clarifies that *too much money is no good for me.* And, then, on Valentine's Day morning, real estate agent Gladys Kern is stabbed to death in the kitchen of a vacant house she was scheduled to show at 4217 Cromwell Ave. in Los Feliz, CA, less than half a mile west of where trusted HUAC-loyalist Walt Disney and his family rest their noggins et neigh. When Walt reads in the paper about all these killings in his backyard, he goes next door to a house identical to his own, where brother Roy and his family live, lamenting: *Time to get the hell outta here, buddy-boy!*

April—22-year-old Helen L. Sweet is a Government stenographer, a resident of 1829 Stockton Ave., and a registered Republican. Vito (as he is a card-carrying Communist at this time) is not listed on this year's Voter Registration, choosing instead to lie low during Red Scare: Phase One. His (legal) wife, Mary, on the other hand, is a registered Democrat and resides with their son, Mark, in their 576-square-foot, one-bedroom Silverlake house at 1925 Vestal Ave.

• •

May 14, 1948—Syd and Leola Zaid have lived at 552 N. Windsor Ave. for three years. Leola is a registered Democrat; Syd is voting IP for the new Progressive Party, whose representative, Henry Wallace, is preparing to dissolve the impending HUAC regime. Syd's connection with Elizabeth and Graham in October of 1946 drew negative and unwanted attention to their home. Hansen had blabbed to the detectives that Syd had been playing chaperone to the girls, even giving them a place to stay. Leola's husband is acting peculiar. Last year, after the Zionist state of Israel was quarantined from the Jewish Palestine sector, Syd was consumed by going all-in with support for the Holy Landers. Leola has difficulty with Syd's sudden allegiance, and their relationship is severely strained. Leola wanders into the waiting arms of another man, and she is impregnated with said lover's child, and the Zaids move to Splitsville. Leola moves back in with family in her hometown of University City near St. Louis, MO; Syd remains at the Hollywood bungalow. Did Leola have good reason to fear Syd? To answer that, we must travel five years back to August 1943:

• • • • ••• • • • ••• • • • • •

Zaid's Naturalization petition to the US Courts was denied because he had moved to California from Chicago after submitting his form. This submitted, notarized document was signed by two *witnesses* and *references* vouching for Syd's newfound national loyalty. One of the signatures belongs to Eugene Light, a hotel bellhop who resides at 943 Eastwood Ave. in Chicago. The other fella, a musician named David Cunningham, lives at 5340 Kenmore Ave., Edgewater, IL.

You'll recall that Syd reportedly ran with a rough crowd in his days as a Chicago musician. Syd was in the company of wolves, not just jazz bohos and helpful bellboys.

On June 5, 1945, in a Chicago suburb just one and three-quarters miles due south of David Cunningham's house, 43-year-old Josephine Ross was found dead in her apartment at 4108 N. Kenmore Ave. Ross had been stabbed in the throat; her entire body was covered with tiny slices. A skirt had been placed over her face. The killer washed Ross and attempted to close her lacerations with cello tape. Her corpse was posed on the bed where she was later discovered.

Six months after Ross' murder, on December 11, 1945, in apartment 611 of 3941 N. Pine Grove (two miles due south of David Cunningham's 5340 N. Kenmore Ave. house), Frances Brown's body is found in her bathroom, shot twice, and, like Ross, stabbed clean through the neck, this time with a butcher's knife. Brown's head was wrapped in an unsubststantiated article of clothing (like Ross's). Brown, too, was stripped and washed and left slumped over the bathtub wall in a kind of sculptural pose. The killer had taken extra time to scribe a message across the living room wall, in lipstick no less:

> For heaven's sake catch me before I kill more I cannot control myself.

Less than one month later, at 3:00a on January 7, 1946 (Eastern Orthodox Feast Day/Saint John's Day), it is assumed the killer again makes their phantom presence known, kidnapping six-year-old Suzanne Degnan from her family home, the historic Colvin House, at 5943 N. Kenmore Ave. (Cunningham lives less than one mile due south of the Degnan home.)

The takers have left behind a narrow sliver of paper with a clumsily scrawled ransom written across its face:

Get$20,000
ReAdy &

WAITe
foR woRd

do NoT NoTify
FBI or
Police

Bills in 5's&
10's

Within hours of her disappearance, detectives discovered a blood-soaked laundry room at 5901 N. Winthrop Ave. (three-quarters of a mile due south of Cunningham), leading them to believe that the worst possible outcome to this kidnapping is likely ahead, a worry soon confirmed when a dismembered torso (identified as Suzanne's) is located in nearby sewers.

If you're keeping tally, you'll know already that this marks the third sadistic murder to happen within two miles of David Cunningham's home address; Cunningham, a musician friend of Syd Zaid's who was close enough to the Canadian commie to vouch for Syd's right to US citizenship. Could the chances really be so great? Are we to rationalize that with 1 in 150,000,000 statistical odds that these two men, Zaid and Cunningham, could not only be linked by loyalty and friendship, BUT ALSO by the almost inconceivable chance that both can be easily and intimately linked to two media-obsessed, nationally-charged sex/mutilation crimes? It is also worth mentioning that in the decades since

Short's murder, a lore has developed, seemingly out of nowhere, that in the year leading to Short's demise, she was fascinated with the Degnan murder, even visiting the area during one of her many visits to the Chicago area.

Police Commissioner Prendergast orders a search of every catch basin and storm drain within a block of the Degnan's fashionable North Side manor. By 8:00p, the little girl's decapitated head is found in a catch basin at the corner of Thorndale Avenue and—you guessed it—Kenmore Avenue. This intersection is only one half-mile (2,640 feet) due north of Cunningham on the same street. Suzanne's left leg turns up in another drain, and then later that night, her right leg in yet another. National newspapers turn the screw on the police department, demanding that they account for these murders by the person the media now deems: *The Lipstick Killer.*

> KIDNAPED GIRL, 6, DISMEMBERED; LYNCH MOB GATHERS IN CHICAGO—Neighborhood Terrorized; Bar Doors, Lock Windows—Fear Maniac at Large; Find Head, Torso in Sewer.

January 11, 1946—3,000 people attend Suzanne Degnan's funeral at Chicago's St. Gertrude's Church. When she is laid to rest, both of her arms are still unaccounted for and are not discovered until February 20, nearly six weeks after her murder, when a city electrician found them in a sewer drain (just three blocks from the Degnan home).

•• • • • • • • • • • ••

RETURNING TO 1948:

> May 15—*Los Angeles Evening Citizen,* ARTISTS WANT TO EAT, TOO—MASS-PRODUCTION STATUES PLANNED TO

AID SCULPTORS—CHICAGO. A man spends ten years chipping away at a ton of rock, and what does he get? Nothing but a statue. He is a sculptor. Anybody knows he is not supposed to be paid, Maurice Milford, a Chicago businessman, said today. A sculptor is the kind of guy who lives in an unheated flat, dreams wild dreams, and doesn't eat, Milford said. But now, this time-honored tradition may have exploded. Milford said he's going to make statues—masterpieces created by the nation's top sculptor—as common as ashtrays. He hopes to employ mass production methods to put bankrupt sculptors on a paying basis. The "Swinging Tree" or "Monkey in the State of Repose" will enter American homes at prices anybody can afford to pay. "There aren't more than 1000 practicing sculptors in the country today," Milford declared. "They chip on a mountain of granite for a couple of years, haul their work to an exhibition, and then look for a janitor's job when they learn nobody can pay what they have to ask." Under Milford's plan, stone chiselers would not only be able to cash in on their originals but on hundreds and maybe thousands of stone reproductions as well. Here's how it works, he said: "A 'Stripped Gear' or 'Reclining Nude' statue, for example, is copied in plaster. Then, pulverized stone is poured into the plaster mold and 'out comes a reproduction that looks almost as good as the original." Some of the country's best sculptors have joined in Milford's plan and will exhibit their first mass-produced statues here next week. There will be Alexander Archipenko's "Standing Torso," Humbert Albrizio's "Winking Girl," Hugo Weber's "Many Faces," Gwenlux's "Male Torso," Pego Waring's "Head of a Horse," and many others. Some of the originals of these works sell for $1200, but the reproductions will go for a flat $75. "Maybe sculptors will be eating steaks pretty soon," said Milford.

Syd Zaid begins working steadily as a band leader:

June 30—*Los Angeles Evening Citizen News*, Supper Party For Juniors—The 3528 W. Adams Blvd. home of Dr. and Mrs. Guy Van Buskirk was setting for the Jate Crutcher Juniors' cocktail and supper party. Ballroom and terrace dancing highlighted the evening, with Sydney Zaid and his orchestra setting the mood.

One-time Easton Gym co-owner Greg McClure is poking around for another cash cow since being outted by the industry because of his supposed Red ties:

> July 4—*Desert News*, Neck Stretcher—Strong man Greg McClure of "Lulu Belle" has invented and patented a rubber and plaster device that stretches a person's neck muscles. Greg claims that the device can cure a stiff neck in two hours.

> Aug. 16—*Los Angeles Times*, DEALERS-Collectors. Exceptional values, fine prints, etchings, bric-a-brac. Write Van Frankfort, 8053 Beverly Blvd. Phone WE-0914

Marti's Dental Lab occupies the second floor of 8053 Beverly Blvd., having spent most of 1948 gathering a staff of technicians and receptionists.

> Sep. 9—*Los Angeles Times,* DENTAL lab. representative, exper. Oppor. for right man. Salary & com. Marti's Dental Lab, 8053 Beverly.

> Sep. 11—*Los Angeles Times,* DENTAL technicians, high grade, fixed bridge & plastic. Don't phone. Marti's Dental Lab, 8053 Beverly.

Sep. 11—Syd Zaid is the special musical guest at the Festival of Music at the Shrine Auditorium, sponsored by the Central Jewish Committee and Westside Division for the Benefit of the Los Angeles Sanatorium. Prizes will be awarded, including stoves and combination radios.

October 1948—Paul Ballard's Film Society changes its name to The Hollywood Film Society, finding a permanent home at the Coronet Theatre at 366 North La Cienega Blvd. (3/4 of a mile due west of the Smith Building). Ballard hopes to promote film as a formidable art form by screening the experimental works of Curtis Harrington, Maya Deren, Kenneth Anger, etc. Ballard screens Anger's re-cut 1944 *Escape Episode.*

> Oct. 5—*New York Daily News,* PAULEKAS, PAULEKIUTE—Queens: Why should the Winthrop Rockefellers handicap their baby boy with the feminine middle name of Paulekiute? Why didn't they use the male form—Paulekas? MRS. J. NAGLE.

On the same day, another classic name gets mangled:

The

HOLLYWOODLAND

sign loses

LAND

> Nov. 25—*Valley Times,* Jewish Groups Sponsor Dance—"Aid to Israel" will be sought by a dance Saturday at 8 p.m., sponsored jointly by the Burbank Lodge B'nai B'rith and Burbank Jewish Community Council at the Burbank Jewish Community Center. Music will be by Sydney Zaid and his Moody Melodies in Music. Door prizes will be offered.

• •

In January of 1949, two years into the Black Dahlia case, an LA Grand Jury convened to, among other things, litigate alleged police misconduct during the ongoing investigation. Detective Harry Hansen testifies that a *medical man* committed the torture killing—*I've seen many horrible mutilation cases, many of them, and if any of you ladies and gentlemen had ever seen a case like that, and would see the pictures of this Elizabeth Short case, you could detect the difference immediately.*

> Jan. 28—*Los Angeles Times,* CHILDREN'S shop, estab. 5 yrs. Branded mdse. Good living for couple. 8051 BEVERLY BLVD.

Lowitz's appliance repair shop moves from 303 Laurel Ave., into the much larger unit—8051 Beverly Blvd.—allowing Vito to barter a deal with Kubernick and snatch up 303 to be used as a storefront for his lamps and growing collection of fine art sculptures. Vito and Mary's marriage is strained, to say the least.

> March 6—*Los Angeles Times,* EXPLOSIVE WATER TOPS ARRAY OF ODD SUBJECTS AT CALTECH—NATURE FREAKS PAY DIVIDENDS IN SECRET WORK BY WILLIAM BARTON—Explosive water, water that makes steam without heat, and water that chews up iron as easily as soap—these are among the freaks of nature being studied at the world's outstanding hydrodynamics laboratory on the California Institute of Technology campus. As a result of fundamental studies sponsored by the Navy, revolutionary yet secret methods of propelling ships, submarines, torpedoes, and even automobiles are in the offing. Also, because of the similarities between water and airwaves and the fact that water waves are easier to see, the laboratory has contributed to the design of rockets, airplane-launched torpedoes, and echo-free auditoriums. By improving the efficiency of pumps, millions of dollars have been saved for the consumers of Colorado River water.

ONLY LABORATORY OF KIND The only laboratory of its kind in the country is directed by Dr. Robert T. Knapp, assisted by Dr. Vito Vanoni and 70 researchers and technicians. Some of the recently installed apparatus features might as well have been located on another planet for all that the average layman can make of it in a quick tour. Located below ground level (where no spies can peer into windows) are huge water tunnels that serve the same purpose as wind tunnels in aircraft design. In the high-velocity tunnel, water travels a 340-foot path and whizzes through the section where models are placed at 70 miles per hour. This is the fastest flow ever attained in a tunnel, and the feat becomes more impressive when you realize water weighs 800 times as much as air. An 11-foot-diameter tank, sunk 85 feet beneath the laboratory sub-basement or as far below ground as a 6-story building is above it, is an important part of the high-speed tunnel.

"SHOOTING GALLERY" The laboratory's "shooting gallery" intrigues visitors. Its purpose is to simulate the release from speeding planes of super-speed torpedoes into harbors and the sea to destroy shipping. A spinning wheel (its front edge toward the tank of water or other target) serves as a gun to shoot 2-inch-diameter torpedoes. At present, the tiny torpedoes are hurled off the wheel at 80 m.p.h., speeds which are to be stepped up to 160 m.p.h. in a few weeks. To test the flight path accuracy of torpedoes of various shapes, the missiles are hurled from the wheel at a "bull's eye" consisting of a 2 1/2-inch hole in a screen. Two batteries of motion picture cameras are used to photograph the torpedoes' behavior, eight cameras in all. They take 3000 pictures per second and can be used for studies of simulated underwater bomb blasts. If it were not for an elaborate optical analyzing system that requires a special room for projecting the thousands of pictures on mathematically divided screens, it would take years of study to make the pictures mean anything.

Melody Johns was born to Leola Zaid in March 1949. Leola has separated from Syd, moved back to her home state, Missouri, and changed her last name to Johns, despite not being officially divorced or remarried. Is she in hiding?

April—Helen Louise Sweet, 22, is a typist for the Compton Water Department. She shares an apartment at 1829 Stockton Ave. with her elderly father, William C. Sweet.

> May 13—*Los Angeles Mirror,* CLUE LETTERS—METHOD PROTECTS CITIZENS—Anyone offering information under The Mirror Citizen Witness Plan is guaranteed complete secrecy by the simple 15-point method to be followed in claiming a $5000 reward. Possibly reading these words is someone who knows the key clue to the Black Dahlia mystery but has kept silent out of fear of the publicity attending any big crime. Perhaps he has personal reasons for not wanting it known that he was at a certain place at a certain time. Under The Mirror Citizen Witness Plan, he can keep it secret forever and still collect a reward. If you—anyone living anywhere—know something that might lead to the identity and conviction of the Black Dahlia murderer, follow this simple method:
>
> 1. Write down all you know about the crime, giving names, dates, and times.
> 2. Use plain paper.
> 3. Typewrite, or else print by hand—use no handwriting.
> 4. Do not sign your information.
> 5. Pick out any two letters of the alphabet and any four figures.
> 6. Write this code (Example: AX1856) at the bottom of your information sheet in the center of the page. (See illustration)
> 7. Tear off a small corner of the page in a jagged line.
> 8. On this piece you have torn off, write again the same code letters and number you have written on the letter.
> 9. Keep the torn bit safe somewhere. Its code letters and numbers must match those on your information sheet; its torn edge matches the missing corner of your sheet.
> 10. Mail your letter to P.O. Box 1313, Los Angeles 53. Nothing will be paid for information phoned in.
> 11. If you have information on more than one murder, write separate information sheets on each one.
> 12. All letters on the 20 murders must be postmarked before

midnight July 13, 1949, to qualify for a reward.
13. In case of duplicate information, the reward will be paid to the person whose information is received first.
14. To collect, you or your agent need only present the "code corner" of your letter to *The Mirror* city editor after the code signature has been published in *The Mirror*.
15. Read *The Mirror* daily for fact outlines on the 20 unsolved murders.
All information received will be checked and then turned over to the police. *The Mirror* will remain the sole judgment in all matters arising out of this reward offer.

The Mirror Citizen witness plan will have to make an amendment when their 20 murders tally ticks up to 21 on June 13, 1949—Louise Margaret Springer, 28, is found dead in her car in a downtown LA parking lot at 126 West 38th St. Springer has been strangled with a white sash cord. The perpetrator(s) broke off a 1-inch-thick, 14-inch-long tree branch inside Springer's vaginal canal.

• •

BYE-BYE DOMESTIC TRANQUILITY, HELLO DEBUTANTES!—Vito Paulekas is in demand these days, Rasputinizing himself into a successful (underground) fine art sculptor with the help of the (above-ground) elite's mullah. Vito has established a street-level art salon—The Clay Workshop—at 303 Laurel Ave., wallowing in the ancient tars, timing his takeover just so—He's teaching sculpting classes and selling custom pieces to the bored Jewish neighborhood debutantes.

> Aug. 8—*Los Angeles Daily News,* WEEK'S ART CALENDAR... MONDAY: OPENING: Paintings by Edith Tuchman and Modern Sculpture by Vito Paulekas; Albin Van Horn Studio, 8953 Sunset Blvd.

> Aug. 13—*Los Angeles Evening Citizen News*, On exhibition: At Tis-Say's, competent landscapes and character studies in oil, by Marcelle. At the Albin Van Horn Studio, 8953 Sunset Blvd., capable oils by Edith Tuchman and fantastically conceived sculptures by Vito Paulekas. At 1631 N. Las Palmas Ave., oils of what impressed Roy C. Grimes during his service in the Pacific War.

> Aug. 14—*Los Angeles Times,* ARTISTS OF CALIFORNIA AND EAST GIVEN SHOW—PAULEKAS-TUCHMAN SHOW—Max Brand, Phil Paradise, Jessie Arms Botke, Dean Fausset, Phil Dike, Sol Wilson, George Picken and Emil J. Kosa Jr. are among those whose pictures are familiar in their present setting. A sculptor from Boston with a humorous eye for bodily rhythms and a Los Angeles painter with a rare affection for significant detail have a joint exhibition at Albin Van Horn's 8953 Sunset Blvd. They are Vito Paulekas, sculptor, and Edith Tuchman, painter. Open today through Aug. 31.

PHONE FOR THE FISH KNIVES, NORMAN—August 16, 1949—48-year-old *vivacious brunette* dowager Mimi Boomhower serves barbecue beef and a salad at her Bel-Air mansion house party at 701 Nimes Rd. Two days later, on Thursday evening at around seven o'clock, Boomhower telephoned a friend, and then changed her outfit, discarding the first dress on the bed before leaving. A week later, delivery men take notice of Boomhower's mail and packages piling up:

> Aug. 24—*Los Angeles Evening Citizen News*, Socialite Missing; Kidnapping Feared—Bel Air Woman Hunted by Police—Feat that wealthy Mrs. Mimi Boomhower, 48, was kidnapped from her fashionable Bel-Air home was voiced today by friends of the missing socialite widow, while police scoured the city for clues in her mysterious disappearance. Mrs. Boomhower vanished from her home late Thursday night or early Friday, police disclosed. Detectives, informed of the disappearance Sunday morning, raced out to her home at 701 Nimes Rd. to find the lights burning and Mrs. Boomhower's car still in the garage. She is the widow of Novice Boomhower, sportsman and linoleum tycoon. A noted big-game hunter, Boomhower had assembled one of the world's largest trophy collections, valued at $300,000. The hint that Mrs. Boomhower might have been kidnapped from her home was offered by Helen Tyler, a long-time friend of the widow, who was the last known person to talk to her before the bizarre disappearance. Miss Tyler said she spoke to Mrs. Boomhower over the telephone "from about 7 to 8 o'clock" Thursday night. "She seemed gay and cheerful," Miss Tyler said. "We discussed everything, and she apparently wasn't in any hurry to get off the phone. I received the impression that she was going to remain home, alone, all night." Miss Tyler offered the theory that a prowler might have entered the grounds shortly afterward. "Why else would she have turned on all the lights in the house? She must have been awfully frightened." Possible motive for a kidnapping might be the fact that Mrs. Boomhower wore "well in excess of $10,000" in jewelry, Miss Tyler suggested. Among the gems, she said, was an expensive diamond watch. Miss Tyler's theory was borne out by another friend of the widow, Robert Howe, 1261 Stone Canyon Rd. Howe pointed out that Mrs. Boomhower cancelled only one of her many appointments scheduled from Friday on. "If she planned to go away—of her own free will—she'd have notified her friends." Howe said,

> "That was her nature. Also, when she leaves for the evening, she leaves only the patio light on." Police received permission to enter the grounds of the Boomhower estate from Mrs. Olga L. Herman, of Hewlett, L.I., sister of the missing woman. Mrs. Herman, on learning ot the disappearance, telephoned Harry Kem, Beverly Hills, real estate broker, authorizing officers to search the house in quest of evidence. But there was no evidence to be found. Detectives checked taxicab companies in the hope that a cab driver might have picked her up at her home. Her business manager, Carl Manaugh, 915 N. Highland Ave., who spoke to Mrs. Boomhower Thursday afternoon, told reporters, "Maybe she has gone off to get married—I hope," but declined to elaborate on the statement. Police doubted this possibility, pointing to the floodlighted house and the widow's failure to cancel appointments. A missing persons report broadcast by police this morning described the woman as five feet, four inches in height; 175 pounds; heavy build; black hair; dark complexion, with a medium nose and chin. Manaugh said Mrs. Boomhower told him she had an appointment with a man on Thursday evening, but did not state the person's name or address. Mrs. Boomhower had several films on game hunting, which she was attempting to sell to a television station, Manaugh said. Police also learned she had not kept a social engagement with Mr. and Mrs. J. Fred McCulloch, 3709 Wilshire Blvd.

Aug. 25—Boomhower's handbag is discovered in a supermarket telephone booth at 9331 Wilshire Boulevard. Written across the face of the calfskin tote in ballpoint pen ink is the message:

Police Dept.—We found this at the beach Thursday night.

Lifeguards search the coastline for Boomhower's body, and detectives hunt in Los Angeles. A phone tip comes in to the LAPD from an anonymous caller pointing the finger at a notorious Las Vegas high-roller with whom Boomhower was seen shortly before her disappearance. Detective Sergeant Jack Ferges isn't sure if this is just an elaborate hoax at this point or if there is a serious reason for concern.

September—Five weeks later, the LAPD is no better off with leads. Sgt. Jack Ferges states:

> She just vanished into thin air ... We've tracked down every possible lead, and we still don't know any more than we did at the start. It's one of the most baffling cases I've ever heard of ... Mrs. Boomhower must have had more friends than anybody else in the world ... We've questioned about 75 so far, and they all have a different idea about what happened. Some say suicide, some say it was foul play, some say she ran away to get married, and some say she was kidnapped. Stir them up and take your pick.

Boomhower was last seen in public at The Cheesebox—8033 Sunset Blvd.—1.4 miles northeast on exactly the same boulevard where Vito Paulekas's sculptures were being exhibited at Van Horn Studios—8953 Sunset Blvd. Her night of disappearance coincides with the opening night of Vito's show, inching their social circles closer to lensing.

September—Mary Paulekas is pregnant with her and Vito's second child. Vito appears to be going straight, or at least creating the illusion of commitment and stability. In reality, most of his time is devoted to the 303 storefront and basement art classes, leaving preggers Mary and little Mark to fend for themselves at 1925 Vestal Ave.

> Sep. 29—*Lodi News-Sentinel*, WIDOW DECLARED "DEAD" LOS ANGELES—A judge today declared vivacious Mrs. Mimi Boomhower, 48, legally dead just six weeks after she disappeared from her Bel-Air home. Despite the action of probate court judge Newcomb Condee, West Los Angeles police said the plump widow still was being carried on their records as a missing person.

At 2:30a, October 6, 1949, 26-year-old Earl Carroll Theatre dancer, Jean Elizabeth Spangler, reportedly gets into a spat with a *30 or 35-year-old clean-cut fellow* sitting in a booth at a Sunset Strip restaurant.

Spangler goes missing after patronizing the Sunset Strip with a pair of dark-haired men. The Clay Workshop is less than three-quarters of a mile to the northwest of Spangler's apartment. Syd Zaid's ex-wife, Leola, was also a dancer at the Earl Carroll Theatre during her Hollywood days. Spangler, like Mimi Boomhower, *vanished into thin air.* In three days, Spangler's purse is found by grounds attendant Henry Anger ten feet from Fern Dell's Los Feliz Boulevard entrance. Two hundred officers arrive on site, suspecting Spangler may have been buried somewhere in the sprawling city park. They scour the trickling man-made creek for a fresh grave, search under low palms, lily pads, and ancient stag horns, but turn up nothing.

Vito and Mary's marriage isn't the only Paulekas union facing uncertainty—Barbara *Bobo* Eva, and hubby Winthrop Rockefeller are still legally wedded on paper, though the two reside in separate residences. It's only a matter of time before it's official … or rather, unofficial.

December 9, 1949—35-year-old Sydney Zaid weds 32-year-old Annetta P. Lee in LA. Annetta and her 8-year-old son, David, moved into the 552 N. Windsor Blvd. bungalow, where Syd's elderly parents, Salomon and Sarah, already live. Syd is the sole breadwinner and bacon bringer, providing for the household as an orchestra bandleader. His political allegiance has migrated from *Communist* to *Democrat.*

> Dec. 13—*The Fresno Bee,* Mimi Boomhower is Adjudged Still Alive—LOS ANGELES, Superior Judge Newcomb Condee ruled Mrs. Mimi Boomhower, 48, who disappeared three months ago, still is alive in the eyes of the law. Judge Condee pronounced her legally dead on September 30, but later there was no proof. He made the ruling in naming attorney M.M. Holman trustee for the $45,000 estate of the widow of Novice E. Boomhower, floor covering inventor. Mrs. Boomhower was declared only "a missing person."

Dec. 18—*Los Angeles Times,* APPLETONS OPEN HOUSE—Original and lovely decorations will mark the decor planned for the open house this afternoon from 4 to 7 p.m. for 200 guests at the home of Mr. and Mrs. Harold G. Appleton, 25 Laguna Place. Assisting the hosts will be Dr. and Mrs. Milton Van Dyke, Messrs. and Mmes. William Mead, Robert Ritner, Clarence Miller, Vail Young, Tell Tuffli, and Dillon Stevens of Los Angeles. Among the guests invited will be Vito Paulekas, a distinguished sculptor, one of whose works of sculpture is owned by the Appletons, and Maj. and Mrs. Harry Hart of Santiago, Chile. In the living room, a pink smoke tree with pink feathers blown over it will be featured. On the dining room table, a dramatic white tree arrangement will be hung with golden swirls and Christmas baubles with turquoise and raspberry net draped at the base. A large Christmas drip candle in tones of gold, turquoise, and raspberry will adorn the credenza.

Two hundred guests (likely made up of mostly strangers) pass through the Appletons' home. Did Boomhower and the Appletons ever connect through the art collector world?

1950. Raymond Rohauer takes over programming at the Coronet Theatre and curates a hodgepodge of exploitation and art films. Rohauer begins an aggressive daily playbill that author David E. James calls—*a unique oasis where [he] educated the generations of cineastes who came to their maturity in the next decades ... Nothing like it since has existed in Los Angeles.*

Jan. 21—The Musicians' Association of Los Angeles dedicates their new structure with a star-studded program. Syd Zaid is slated to perform a solo session from 5:00p-6:00p in Rehearsal Hall No. 1.

> Jan. 30—*Los Angeles Times,* Drapery, and Lamp Shows Bring Crowds of Buyers—Thousands of buyers from all over the nation were in Los Angeles yesterday for the opening of two exhibits sponsored by the Chamber of Commerce. Showing California-made items were the California Lamp Show at the Biltmore and the sixth annual Curtain and Drapery Show at the Alexandria. The lamp show, first ever held on the West Coast, featured more than 15,000 lamps and shades, including a television lamp with a transformer designed to cut out static interference ... Both shows, held under the direction of the chamber's Los Angeles Trade Fair, Inc., will run through Wednesday.

Vito's four-year-old son, Mark, lives with Mama Mary at 1925 Vestal Ave. Mary is listed as *separated* from Vito, who, at 36, has acquired a new mail drop address two miles away at the rear unit at 424 1/2 North Bonnie Brae St. Vito's occupation is listed as a *Sculptor* in a *Lamp Factory,* where he puts in *40 hours a week.* 23-year-old Helen Louise Sweet is a *Medical Secretary* for a *private practice physician* in Los Angeles. The independent, never-been-married *head of house* has made her way from Arkansas to a Hollywood apartment #102 at 7270 1/2 Melrose Ave., very near Paramount Pictures studio, before moving to 680 S. Westlake Ave. Her political party affiliation has changed from Republican to *IP*. Vito and Sweet went from living five miles apart to less than half a mile between them, two mesely blocks really. No Government documents, city census, or federal certificate discloses Vito's political registration.

> Feb. 13—*Los Angeles Times,* $79.50—5 rm. studio liv. qts. 2nd floor. Beverly & Laurel. OL.3-7193

Feb. 16—*Los Angeles Mirror News* publishes that *Margaret C. Paulekas* has filed a divorce suit against *Vito A. Paulekas.* Vito is shocked when Mary's attorney (ironically, Vito's close friend), Mendel H. Lieberman, amends the suit to separation maintenance. Vito denounces Lieberman's character when the counsel sought to usurp Vito's loyalty to protect his client.

• •

THE SEVEN-YEAR [B]ITCH—February 27, 1950. At the time of their first divorce hearing, Mary Paulekas—32, homemaker—is seven months pregnant with her and Vito's second child.

March 14—*APPLICATION TO ALTER, REPAIR, OR DEMOLISH*—Jacob Kubernick is on the hook for another $1000 in repairs to the Smith Building. Harvey Easton has taken the business lead, running the gym, ever since his brother Dale's acting career reached its stride five years ago. Brother Harvey proposes that Kubernick change the Smith Building's structure description from *stores and offices* to *stores and GYM*. But to do this, the City first requires Kubernick to:

a) *Remove partitions specified by dotted lines and run a header (diagonal lines) to carry the req. load.*

b) *Close three existing doors and open one new door.*

c) *Remove existing tile in bathroom and replace with new tile.*

APPROVED!

April 9—*Los Angeles Times,* DENTAL technician, plaster, polishing, packing. Must be expd. & fast. Marti Dental Lab, 8053 Beverly Bl.

The Burbank Junior Chamber of Commerce

Once Again...Proudly Presents

THE 1950

MISS BURBANK

SELECTION

AND

DANCE

SATURDAY, APRIL 29TH

SELECTION STARTS 7:00 P.M. — DANCING 'TIL 12:00

MUSIC BY SID ZAID AND ORCHESTRA

111 WEST OLIVE AVE.

ADMISSION 50c INCLUDING TAX

May 2—Mary Paulekas gives birth to a daughter whom she names Ann after her own middle name. Mary and Vito's next divorce hearing is scheduled for two weeks from Ann's birth date.

> May 12—*Los Angeles Times,* DENTAL TECHNICIAN Chrome finisher & polisher Exper, Marti Dental Labs., 8053 Beverly Bl.

Aug. 2—At the Los Angeles Courthouse, Vito and Mary Paulekas attend their second divorce hearing. Vito is served with the judge's ruling on August 8:

> Appellant [V. Paulekas] called on Lieberman and was served with a copy of the decree. He thereupon read the decree and stated that he had no questions, that he understood it fully, but 'of course' he would not make these payments; that if he paid as much as he could, 'they can't do anything to me.' He expressed no 'anger, surprise, doubt, or bewilderment.' He thanked the lawyer 'for everything'.

The CBS Radio broadcast *Somebody Knows* replaced the regularly scheduled *Suspense* while it was on summer hiatus. Tonight's show promises a $5,000 reward to anyone supplying information that leads directly to the arrest and conviction of the person(s) involved in the three-year-old Black Dahlia murder case.

> Oct. 20—*Whittier News,* NEW DESIGNS IN TELEVISION LAMPS—One field that has supplied an enormous impetus to ingenuity in designing not new lamps but new lighting forms is television, according to Retailing Daily. Though special television lamps appeared six months or more ago, they have burst forth in profusion this season. The most common form that they have taken is the vase of metal, pottery, or even wood with the bulb placed inside to shoot all light straight upward and allow direct light. Design-wise, some consist of no more than a table-sized adaptation of a metal reflector torchiere design. Others, particularly pottery styles, are adorned with all sorts of sculpted or painted decorations.

> Primitive designs on lamp bases are appearing in much greater numbers and variety. Most commonly, these are seen as small etched or graffito designs of people and animals in a primitive style on square, cylindrical, or cone-shaped pottery bases. Also, they appear in the form of small African figurines or masks in wood, pottery, and metal.

Nov. 10—Bit-part actor Max Handler confesses to Elizabeth Short's murder. He is interviewed by detectives and released, doing little more than adding his name to the growing list of false confessors. It is worth noting that Handler's apartment is located at 1360 N. Laurel Ave.—a mere 1.5 miles north as the crow flies from The Clay Workshop. Now, the same alley PLUS! the same street on which Vito lives, works, and parties have been evidentially linked to the Elizabeth Short murder investigation.

> Nov. 27—*Los Angeles Times,* FRIGIDAIRE. 5 CU. FT. $54.95 8051 BEVERLY BLVD. WY-3176

1951 arrives. Richard *Dick* Bock is the music director at the popular jazz club, The Haig, at 638 South Kenmore Ave. near Wilshire Boulevard, directly across the street from The Ambassador Hotel. Despite its tiny footprint and impossible-to-park-in parking lot, jazz heavyweights such as Chico Hamilton, Chet Baker, Stan Getz, and others make The Haig a hot spot.

> March 4—*Los Angeles Times,* PACKARD BELL SALES HOLLYWOOD WEST—HARRY LOWITZ 8051 Beverly Blvd.

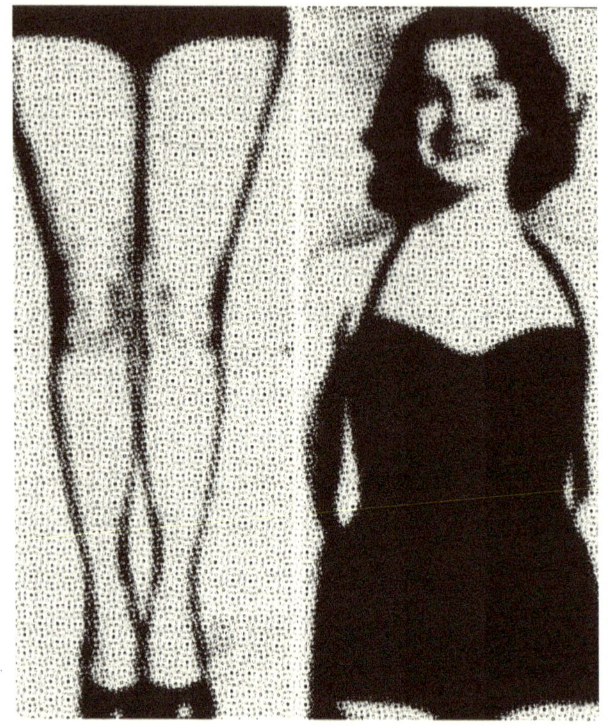

March 22—*Santa Cruz Sentinel,* Her Legs Are Perfect—John Vogel, a portrait painter who says he's searched 20 years for a perfect pair of feminine legs, thinks those pictured at left are the most perfect in America. They belong to Hollywood Movie Actress Julia Adams. For the rest of Julia, see picture above. Artist Vogel, a brave man, says, "90 percent of American women are either knock-kneed or bow-legged, and that goes for Hollywood, too."

March 28—*Los Angeles Times,* BOY WITH MOTORCYCLE & saddle bag for pickup & delivery. Marti Dental Lab., 8053 Beverly Bl.

SONS OF THE COVENANT—The Red Scare: Hollywood Edition. Many show business employers and employees are named. While some are soon cleared of false allegations, an unlucky few, deemed the *Hollywood Ten,* are convicted and sentenced to prison terms. Dale

Easton (aka Greg McClure, aka the rising Western star, aka co-owner of Easton Gym) is publicly outed during these hearings for suspected Red sympathies, accused of hosting meetings at his Silverlake home. At the end of April, Dale's brother, Harvey, runs damage control after Dale's bust. Harvey applies to have a 10'5" sheet metal sign fabricated and hung 16 feet off the ground on the facade of the Smith Building—the Free Market demands you gotta spend money to make money, and not many commies are buying American-made steel signs—*wink, wink.*

Less than one mile due east of The Clay Workshop, the popular 20-year-old LA eatery, El Coyote Cafe, has relocated to 7312 Beverly Blvd. from its original tiny location at First Street and La Brea Avenue.

> May 14—*Los Angeles Times,* DENTAL TECHNICIAN A-1 technician for Denture Dept. 8053 BEVERLY BLVD.

> Sep. 1—*Evening Vanguard,* Hawaii Theme Planned for Fall Dance—"A Night in Hawaii" will be the theme of the seventh annual fall dance being planned by the Leimert Park B'nai B'rith for Saturday evening, Sept. 15. The setting for this outstanding event will be the lovely Mayfair Room of the Beverly Wilshire Hotel and popular dance music will be featured by Syd Zaid and his orchestra.

Pulling some tenant clout in the Smith Building, Lowitz scales back his *LA Times* ad to include ONLY his business name, leaving readers to speculate just what the hell it is that Lowitz does.

> Dec. 9—HOLLYWOOD-WEST—HARRY LOWITZ 8051 Beverly Blvd. WY. 3176.

> Dec. 26—*Los Angeles Times,* ISLANDER HAS NEW IMPROVEMENTS—The "Islander" will have the benefit of the latest improvements developed by present-day builders. For instance, the acoustical problem in the restaurant was solved by the use of Zonolite. Ben Falgren, Los Angeles Lathing and Plastering Contractor, said the use of this lightweight aggregate embodies all the recent major

> developments in the plastering industry. He pointed out that the fireproofing qualities far exceed City requirements, plus the fact that the use of Zonolite decreases the weight of the building. The last word in scientific lighting was ingeniously accomplished by E.L. Smith & Sons, Electrical Contractors, under the supervision of Grant Lockhart.

1952. February—Typed too soon; Harry Lowitz can't cut it on the ground floor of 8051, and after several months of struggling, he vacates the storeroom and is quickly replaced with the booze & 'bacco outlet A+D Liquor, which made a very short move here from 8075 Beverly Blvd.

> Feb. 23. *Los Angeles Times,* $42.50—48x36 ft. basement, gd. for print, assembly, lite mfg., storage, or whatever you wish. 8053 Beverly Blvd. WE-0850.

Vito smells a big rat and swaps out communism for bohemianism, renting the other half of the basement to have dominion over the entire underground unit. He spends much of the day locked away in his Babylonian hanging garden, maintaining a safe distance from Redhunters. Many of the great artists preceding him squatted in their laboratory at one time or forever. Vito is living as one of his ancestral Lithuanian refugees had, as an escapee of the Great Purge—lying low, waiting out the witch hunt from the confines of a clay tomb, learning to hunt as Gauguin had from the natives: *jump on backs if they get any closer!*

Vito maintains his mail drop address at 424 1/2 Bonnie Brae St.

July—Richard *Dick* Bock and jazz drummer Roy Harte open the Pacific Jazz Records studio in Hollywood at 6124 Santa Monica Blvd.

July 17—National Neon Products moves A+D Liquor's old 200-lb. lighted sign from their previous location, and affixes it to the exterior northeast corner of 8051 Beverly Blvd. Not even a week later—not one to be outstaged—Harvey Easton wants a *projected* neon sign of his own and files an *Application for Permit to Erect or Alter Electric Signs* ...

APPROVED! National Neon Products is called upon once more to build and install the protruding metal beast. The Smith Building's de-evolution is afoot.

By November of 1952, Helen L. Sweet, 24, moved to 1829 Stockton Ave. and changed her voter registration to *Republican*. Barbara Eva *Bobo* (Paulekas-Sears) Rockefeller and Winthrop Rockefeller split up.

1953. The abstract expressionism boom takes root in Hollywood's buried marshland. *Fine art* galleries pop up all along La Cienega Boulevard. This is excellent timing for Vito, who is strategically placed three-quarters of a mile from the epicenter near the crossing of Fairfax. The temporary leader, Ferus Gallery, was founded by Walter Hopps, a biochemist turned zine editor and a self-proclaimed *art explorer* who, at times, reports back his discoveries to the First World. Before Ferus Gallery, Hopps had opened both the Syndell Gallery and Now Gallery.

> Jan. 16—*Los Angeles Mirror*, Shapely brunette Mara Corday, one of the top West Coast models, will make her starring movie debut in the title role of "The Black Dahlia Case." Producer Brooks Randell is readying the famous murder case as a semi-documentary. John Ireland has been signed on for the role of the criminal investigator on the film, which is to get an early start date. The Black Dahlia character, incidentally, will be considerably toned down in moral character from her real-life counterpart. And the ending will be left up in the air, in the same place as the official investigation after all these years.

> Feb. 15—*Los Angeles Times,* $85 mo. 2nd flr. corner. 1200 sq. ft. Will remodel for offices or 2-bdrm. apt. 8053 Beverly. Kahan, WE-8050.

> Feb. 17—*Los Angeles Times*, CORNER SUITE, 4 lg. ofcs. Beverly & Laurel. $85 mo. Kahan, WE-0850

March 4—Jacob D. Kubernick registers his business, Ideal Paper Company, with the proper Los Angeles municipalities, indicating that the business will operate out of a warehouse at 350 S. Anderson St.

> March 9—*Los Angeles Times,* $62.50. 3-rm. apt., living or business., 8053 Beverly., Kahan. WE-0850

March 27—Vito, dissatisfied with the divorce ruling from three years previous, which requires him to pay Mary $175 each month in alimony, appeals the court's decision:

> Docket No. 18674. APPEAL from a judgment of the Superior Court of Los Angeles County and from an order denying the motion to set aside defaults. Clarence M. Hanson and William B. McKesson, Judges. Affirmed. Vito A. Paulekas, in pro. per., for Appellant. Mendel H. Lieberman for Respondent.

> April 23—*Los Angeles Evening Citizen News*, $77.50. 5 rms. bus. & liv. 2nd. flr. 8053 Beverly at Laruel. WE-0850

An identical ad is placed in the *Los Angeles Times* the very next day, and then on the subsequent three days. Kubernick struggles to fill the space after nearly four months of relentlessly advertising reduced rates.

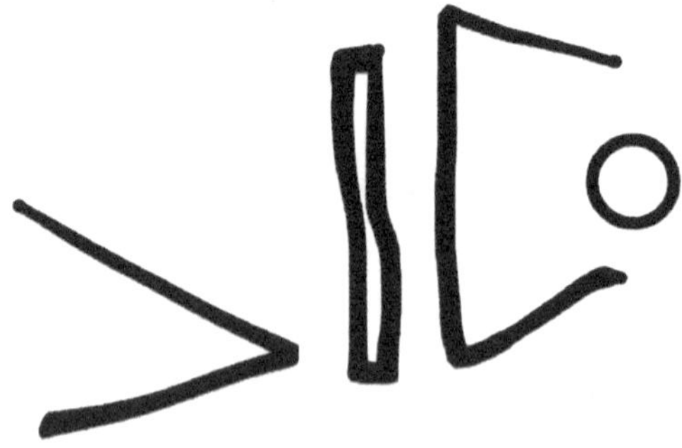

ILL – 54

18.

LUCY

I know just what you need, Mr. Grant. -- Uh… Eddie?

EDDIE

What?

LUCY

How would you like to have a beautiful girl to take you around and show you the town and go dancing?

RICKY

Uh, Lucy, leave Eddie alone -- Eddie, Fred tells me that your uncle was in show business with him.

EDDIE

Yeah --

LUCY

Oh, speaking of show business, you'll want to see all of the big Broadway shows, and it would be just ridiculous if you went alone. Now, wouldn't you like someone to share all that fun with you?

EDDIE

Well --

RICKY

Lucy, that'll be enough. Uh, Eddie, what kind of an act did your uncle have?

EDDIE

He did a magic act -- Sawed a woman in half.

RICKY

No kidding?

EDDIE PANTOMIMES A SAWING ACTION.

LUCY

Have you ever stopped to think how nice it would be to have a woman of your own to saw in half?

RICKY SQUIRMS IN HIS SEAT.

RICKY

No, but I have!

LUCY BACKS OFF QUESTIONING EDDIE JUST AS FRED BUSTS INTO THE ROOM.

• •

Aug. 3—*Los Angeles Evening News,* $10 Reward contents tan valise lost cor. Heliotrope-Monroe July 30. No questions. Dan Smiderman, 8053 Beverly Bl. WE-85697

Oct. 13—National newspapers report that the divorcing Rockefellers—Winthrop and Bobo—have reached a settlement agreement, with an award of 5.5 million dollars going to Bobo. But Bobo and her attorney, Nizer, refuse the conditions and instead ask for twice that prize. My, my, there surely isn't much under our sun that the other freshly-divorced Paulekas wouldn't do for that kind of parting coin.

1954. The US Government issues the Communist Control Act, stripping card-carrying communists of all rights and rendering them wholly un-American. Vito has had his fill of this Intelligence gambit and wants to focus on becoming a legitimate sculptor. His Cold War-crushing efforts have been exhausted, and he's primed to rejoin his previous art life and the American pursuit of a slice of the Reserve. Not to mention, Vito wants to smoke weed by the boatload, and most of all—fuck.

Freely.

Amen.

• •

DEALING WITH ROUGH CONDITIONS—In February of 1954, Vito Paulekas appeared on Groucho Marx's television program, *You Bet Your Life*. Vito stands beside a portly woman to his right. Both of them face Groucho as he fires questions at them from behind a lectern like a jacked-up Peter at the Pearlies.

The archival clip begins with Groucho addressing Vito first:

GROUCHO: Are you from Mars, or are you just from outer space?

Vito rumples his slept-in-sheets face, crafting a suitable answer:

VITO: Uhhh ....

GROUCHO: Now, you say you were sent here to see our president?

Vito glances over at the woman. She smiles back with equal concern. Calmly, with a smile on his face and a tinge of annoyance, Vito says, in his best raspy Bostonian voice:

VITO: Not exactly, Groucho.

Groucho addresses the rotund female contestant.

GROUCHO: I'll get around to you shortly, Shorty. I think we'd better make it gradual, eh?

VITO: Okay.

GROUCHO: My doctor says I have to avoid shock. Well, how would you know if I had any talent?

VITO: Well, uh, first of all, to expose you to the medium, I would make accessible to you a lump of clay and ...

GROUCHO: What about this live model you have?

VITO: Uh ... We could arrange for a live model present, too.

GROUCHO: That'd be good.

VITO: We could find some clay for you and a sharpened stick, and, uh ... after ...

GROUCHO: You give me a stick and a live model, and I'll do my own business.

[*audience roars*]

Beat Hell out of her ...

Vito smiles blankly out at the unseen-but-heard watchers, his lupine eyes carrying a message that cuts through the black and white broadcast—'Stay in your lane, funny man.'

• •

Mar. 17 & 23—*Los Angeles Evening Citizen News,* $200—
Beaut. 7 rm. Lse. Beverly & Laurel. YO-7466 A.M.

June 19—After some very public divorce hearings, Bobo Paulekas is awarded and accepts a nearly six-million-dollar settlement. This is terrific news for Bobo, as she has been living on the $30,000 she earned by pawning her wedding ring three years ago. Bobo tells the Associated Press that *when she was separated from her husband, Mrs. Rockefeller had a fail-safe tactic for striking a good bargain. When a merchant demanded a price she considered too high, she would simply respond, "Who do you think I am, a Rockefeller?*

THE CROWNING BEAUTY
TO ANY TV SET

Beautiful CERAMIC
TELEVISION LAMP
REG. 7.95

Created by one of Hollywood's outstanding lamp designers. A beautiful selection of graceful and decorative designs and colors.

ON THE LEVEL—November, 1954. Miss Helen L. Sweet's mother, Edna, moves into her daughter's LA apartment at 1829 E. Stockton Ave. Helen attends Vito's Clay Workshop, and the two forge a fast courtship, one that Edna disapproves of, sending Helen into Vito's waiting arms at 303 Laurel Ave. Syd Zaid, his wife Annetta, and her son, David, have moved from their longtime East Hollywood home to 12455 Hortense St. in Studio City.

1955. *Father of Spin,* Edward Bernays, publishes an extended book-length version of his 1947 essay, *The Engineering Consent.* Bernays is one of eight contributors to the volume.

> Jan. 31—*Los Angeles Evening Citizen News,* PROBLEM DOG? FREE OBEDIENCE Lessons, Friday, Feb. 4—7:30 8055 Beverly Blvd. Demonstrated by Larry Ackley, expert obedience trainer.

> Feb. 4—*Los Angeles Evening Citizen News,* An exhibition of sculptures produced by members of the Clay Workshop will be held at 8 p.m. Sunday at 464 N. Western Ave. The cooperative group has been meeting at 303 N. Laurel Ave. for five years.

March 5—At the height of the Red Scare, 41-year-old Vito Paulekas and his 28-year-old girlfriend/roommate Louise Helen Sweet depart from Brooklyn, NY, aboard the *SS Giacomo C,* bound for the port of Genoa, Italy. The passenger sign-on list is limited but reveals a certain truth about Vito's position within the States. He is listed under his military travel name, *Vitauyas A. Paulekas,* and noted simply as born in the *USA.* Both female passengers specify their place of birth by city and state, something indicated at the bottom of the document as being *required for international travel* ... just not for Vito, apparently. The lovebirds plan to live in Italy for one year while Vito studies sculpture at the Accademia di Belle Arti di Roma. Vito played his cards right, making arrangements to return to the Smith Building at the end of the sabbatical. Most Americans, let alone a stenographer and TV lamp sculptor, hardly have enough disposable income to take a year-long hiatus, while also retaining a studio and storefront back home in the States. The funds that financed this trip are ALWAYS (by Vito himself, usually) attributed to winnings from *You Bet Your Life*, but this is improbable, if not impossible, as only $500 was ever awarded in any one episode. Is it likely that Vito guessed Graucho's *secret word* on ten separate occasions?

> March 27—*Los Angeles Times,* $71.50. 4 rms. 2 bdrs. 2nd flr.
> 8053 Beverly at Fairfax WE-89601

•　　　　　•

GIURIN GIURELLO—For the summer of 1955, we take a trip to Italy and bob in the filthy canals of Venice. Observe the decayed, rotting plaster softening under sea water licks. Moving on to Rome, it takes us a minute to register just exactly where we are. The rolling golden hills are specked with low green patches. Coca-Cola advertisements are painted on nearly every rural wall. Forgotten, faded half-sheets hang in shop windows, artifacts left over from Rome's preparations for the 1940 Olympic Games, which were cancelled due to World War II. Ancient Rome is also home to the Russian/Soviet Embassy. In Italy, Vito lives freely above ground. He learns centuries-old sculpting techniques at the Accademia di Belle Arti di Roma. He is especially fond of the Scuola Libera del Nudo (Free School of the Nude), which has taught human form *appreciation* since 1754.

An outbreak of dancing mania, aptly named—*Tarantism*—sweeps over a tiny Italian village, just as it is rumored to have done so every year for the past five centuries, at least:

> The Dancing Plague of 1518: Over 400 people (mostly women) joined a fervently dancing townsperson, Mrs. Troffea, as she danced erratically down the streets of Strasbourg for a month, resulting in heart attacks, strokes, and exhaustion, causing up to fifteen deaths per day at its height. The plague was marked by what nobles and local physicians described as "hot blood," and it was a 'natural disease' that should not be bled out but danced out. Modern theories point to a wheat grain (such as rye) that has produced a toxin called ergot fungi, which causes similar effects to lysergic acid diethylamide (LSD-25) as it is chemically structurally similar. This fungus is also considered responsible for contaminating the wheat used in bread-making before and during the Salem Witch Trials, perhaps originally causing the afflictions.

Vito and Sweet travel to Sicily to spend the summer months working on a very special project. In June, Kenneth Anger arrives on the tiny Sicilian island of Palermo, having made a personal pilgrimage to Aleister Crowley's abandoned Abbey of Thelema, a kind of 20th-century sex-cult chateau cum-monestary. Anger has rented the dilapidated structure for the next three months, and is hell-bent on restoring and documenting Crowley's colorful hand-painted frescos of *dogmen* and *negresses* that once adorned the abbey walls before Mussolini ordered their whitewashing 22 years ago.

• • • • ••• • • • ••• • • • • •

THE ABBEY OF THELEMA—On April 2, 1920, Aleister Crowley arrived at the small Sicilian fishing community of Villa Santa Barbara from Paris, with his devoted Concubine No.1 (aka Leah Hirsig) and her newborn daughter, Anne *Poupee* Leah. Crowley rented the old farmworker's cottage overlooking a cliff-side rock formation known by locals as Rocca di Cefalu. Within that aging structure, Crowley installed his Abbey of Thelema. Crowley originally intended to construct the Collegium Ad Spiritum Sanctum—*A College Toward the Holy Spirit*—on that very *rock head*—but the Italian government prohibited him from doing so. Crowley established this anti-monastery epicenter to promote and teach his newly created religion of *will*: Thelema. Concubine No.2 (aka Ninette Shumway) joins the pair, but the combination of women sparks instant disdain for each other. Historically, their vicious arguments drove Crowley away on Parisian getaways to calm his nerves, trips which usually ended up with the Great Beast getting loaded on his drugs of choice: heroin and nose candy.

In July 1920, after two years of correspondence with Crowley, 45-year-old actress and one-time Theosophist, Sarah Jane Wolfe (aka Soror Estai, aka Neophyte number 516, The Manifestation of Horus as Genius and the Light in the Realms of the World of Matter) leaves Hollywood to join the squatting Thelemites in Sicily, for a life in the dark arts. Wolfe quickly rises in ranks, becoming Crowley's secretary, adopting the intriguing moniker: *Red Flame.*

In October 1920, Leah Hirsig's newborn daughter, *Poupee*, dies from exposure to the abbey's unsanitary conditions. Wild, diseased animals were allowed to enter the building and wander about—Crowley is content with this; it's his *idea of Heaven.* Only weeks later, Crowley's newest child, Astarte Lulu Panthea, is born to Concubine Nº·2. Both concubines have moved in and set up shop, presiding over the occasional all-ages Gnostic Mass, and then spending the remainder of their day exploring their many interests. Crowley adorns his bedroom (which he now calls *La Chambre des Cauchemars ... The Room of Nightmares*) from floor to ceiling with explicit erotic frescoes depicting men, women, and hermaphroditic beasts in flagrante delicto. It is here within these exclusive quarters that Crowley carried out his most intense, psychoactive-induced nighttime initiations. In February of 1923, devout Thelemite Raoul Loveday (aka Frederick Charles Loveday) died at the Abbey of Thelema from typhoid fever after drinking from a polluted stream out back and developing a severe liver infection. Loveday's widow, Betty May, returned to London, England, on March 24, seething with a deep detest for Crowley. She made some wild claims to the *London Sunday Times* publication, *John Bull.* For instance, May claimed that the *Wickedest Man in the World* once forced her husband to drink the blood of a sacrificed cat, and that Crowley forbade his pupils from using the universal ego pronoun, *I,* unless they desired a punishment of razor lashings. By April, reports surface of unruly, disobedient mistresses being trussed to the Rocca di Cefalu to be ravaged by violent night storms or to suffer sun exhaustion by day. Sicily's fascist authorities are warned of the goings-on at the abbey, resulting in Crowley receiving a deportation notice from Benito Mussolini. After three years of abbey rule, Crowley abandoned the abbey, fleeing Italy just as the Knights Templar were driven from France by Philip the Fair. By order of Mussolini, the abbey is immediately whitewashed and vandalized by angry Sicilian villagers who were blinded by the moral incomprehensibility of the sordid tales and of animal sacrifices and ritualistic sex orgies. In October 1927, Jane Wolf ditched the *Red Flame* character and left Europe for good. Destitute and in ill health, Wolf made her way back to Hollywood, CA.

•• • • • • • • • • • ••

RETURING TO SUMMER, 1955: Anger doesn't know the first thing about stone art restoration, so Vito is absolutely instrumental in walking Anger through the proper nondestructive removal techniques:

> To cook up this soap solution, you will need soda ash and a bar of laundry soap. Pour three gallons of warmed water into a bucket, and into it dissolve five tablespoons of soda ash, plus two tablespoons of finely grated laundry soap. Apply to the infected area and gently abrade to help saturate the whitewash. Then, simply wash off the chalkiness with a sponge soaked in the solution. Scrape off as necessary.

WIZARD WHILE YOU WORK—Vito tells Anger of a 1933 memo from Musollini in which the fascist bragged of having captured a crashed UFO that went down in Lombardy in northern Italy. June 1933—Special Research 33 stores the detained disc in Magenta, Italy, near Milan. When reports flooded the local military from all over northern Italy about cylindrical objects zipping and floating in the skies on August 22, 1936, Musollini circulated this memo:

SHUT UP OR DIE, ON PERSONAL ORDER OF IL DUCE [STOPPA]

At the end of the war, a rogue band of American troops captured the fallen object from the Italians and shipped it back to the States.

By mid-July 1955, after two months of restoration, the La Chambres Des Cauchemar and the mass room of the abbey are exposed just in time for biologist Dr. Kinsey's visit and tour of the newly exposed freaksexaglyphs. Kinsey interprets their possible meanings, decoding the ontology of the transgender negress painted on the back of one door, and the spying dog people who watched over Crowley's mattress that once sat bare on the floor. Dr. Kinsey spins a yarn about the strong interest in Paul Gauguin, both himself and his art, that Crowley often referenced. Crowley stated in a 1921 entry into his diary:

> 11:40 P.M. I feel easier but over-excited. Gauguin literally torments me; I feel as if by my own choice of exile rather than toleration of the bourgeois, I am invoking him, and this painting of my house seems a sort of religious-magical rite, like the Egyptian embalmers', but of necromancy. I would he might come forth "his pleasure on the earth to do among the living." I gladly offer my body to his Manes if he needs a vehicle of flesh for new expression. I could never have done quite that for any other spirit—I have been faithful to my own Genius. It is maddening to think that I might have known him in the flesh; he died in 1903, MAY 8, eleven months before the First day of the Writing of the book of the Law. Just six months after I had met Rodin. I feel very specially that I should consecrate my house to him, not to Beardsley***, a quite inferior type deriving from pifflers like Burne-Jones and the over-elaborate school of Japanese, while he sniveled and recanted disgustingly when his health gave way. So, by the Power and Authority invested in Me, I Baphomet 729 ordain the insertion of the name of Paul Gauguin among the More Memorable Saints in the Gnostic Mass.

***On March 7, 1898, having converted to Roman Catholicism one year earlier, the tuberculosis-ravaged 25-year-old illustrator Aubrey Beardsley comes to terms with his imminent death, making a final request to both his close friend Herbert Charles Pollitt and long-time publisher Leonard Smithers:

> Jesus is our Lord and judge.
> Dear Friend,
> I implore you to destroy all copies of Lysistrata and bad drawings.
> By all that is holy, all obscene drawings.
> Aubrey Beardsley
> In my death agony.

Oct. 25—*Vitautas Paulekas* and 29-year-old *Louise Sweet* board the *SS Federico Costa* in Naples, Italy, bound for the port of the Polynesian island of Norfolk, an island covered with pine trees that would have made Osiris hard; an island of peoples colonized by the British in 1788—the same year that the continent of Australia relegated itself to a remote penal settlement.

On November 1, 1955, while on the water, the Second Indochina War (aka The Resistance War Against America, aka The Vietnam War) began after several conflicts in Laos, Cambodia, and Vietnam.

Nov. 12—Vito and Sweet dock at Newport News, VA aboard the *SS Federico Costa.*

SUN BEAT LEAVES / / GRAZING SAND

August of 1965. Thomas Jr., or Tad—or, since we shall *obliterate the name of the exalted,* henceforth known only as T-d—is in the throes of a chapter of one of the four books he is writing simultaneously, strung out on junk food and what's left of the PANAMA RED pot, that which hasn't gone to dust. He landed here in Manhattan Beach, CA, after bailing on a sequestered life in Mexico, first stopping off in Houston, TX, where T-d shacked up with married friends Fred & Phyllis Gebauer, before they decided to blow the humid southern oil fields for the fat, busting burritos slung on the west coast. The Gebauers found a place in Westwood. T-d stayed with them for weeks before finally moving to his own place, a tiny first-floor bachelor's apartment directly behind his landlord's beachfront duplex on 30th Street. T-d quickly moved three streets over to another property owned by his landlord. It's another ground-level spread, this one situated a short saunter east to what became his favorite dive, The Fractured Cow on Highland Avenue.

T-d sat alone at a booth in the Fractured Cow, disguised as how he thought a longshore fisherman looked, a turtleneck and eye patch, his body contorted in the vinyl booth in such a manner that his cheek floated an inch above a plate of something called The Lumberjack. On rare occasions, today being one, T-d dips into his dwindling advance to treat himself to foods in excess of the nourishment found in popsicles and tortillas. *If I wasn't wearing this toboggan and ratty sweater, I might have gone unnoticed,* he thought, forking a lump of perfectly hard-scrambled eggs and jam into the waiting pocket hidden under his overgrown stache. How fortunate for agents SIOUXX and COAK—who are expected at any moment—that T-d is stuck perpetually with this stubborn, onry delightful disposition. *It's hard to believe,* thinking again as he lapped up blueberry syrup, or what he's almost certain is blueberry syrup, *that I was hired only a year ago*; a time in that strange void before pot strangled his life and gave it meaning and direction. Anyway, like he was thinking: *ONE YEAR OF LIFE, that was the cost, that's all, and there's only a bit longer to go before it's time for all parties to make good on their agreement,* so *keep it straight, T-d, keep it straight—Those idiots had better get here soon.* When OCTAVIA LISTENS slithered in like a burglar between the foam seal of the closed glass doors, a vicious string of expletives overwhelmed T-d's senses—*Christ!*—VIA always complained about some aspect of their current set-up, no matter the case or quality. She had de-evolved over the last three years into a cosmopolitan bohemian—a *COBO*—the worst of the ilk. VIA, like T-d, is technically minded; sharp as a tack, but consumed wholly by lust and desire for sexual dalliances, and the insatiable need for admiration as a *true artist's muse*—as if she's Oona O'Neill, ha! This brainy COBO loves reminding T-d that artists have needs—deep, emotional, spiritual needs—something HE wouldn't know anything about being a writer. HE is living proof of her theory. Conversely, T-d is proud of his frugality, particularly his ability to have stretched Lippincott's advance to the last red cent. The plain and simple atomic truth is that HE and VIA were damned for all times. It was never, ever going to work.

"Oh, there you are," and "ha, figures!" were her boothside pick-up lines when she found him trying to duck out of view.

"Hey there, hun; you coming to the beach or not?" VIA took note of T-d's practically translucent skin; so whitely deficient of vitamin D that the maroon vinyl booth cushion shone through where a face should be —his exposed ankles and wrists revealed soft pine streaks and scuffed linoleum squares. Once VIA's big brown doe eyes shook back to life, she muttered something in the ghost's direction before dumping a short stack of delivered mail under his chin. She took a sip of his coffee and a single big bite from his last bacon strip, and then vanished out the way she arrived, missing the late agents by seconds in classic Marx Brothers fashion—and a good thing that, too, for they hate VIA with a passion—condemning her as a fully functioning, honest-ta-gawd witch. SIOUXX and COAK pick at T-d like meddling parents trying to persuade their child to see that the mate they've selected is not up to snuff. They constantly leverage their little power, hoping for the green light to make VIA … uh … vanish. T-d need only whisper the order, and it's lift-off, baby! The crowd goes wild when VAL SIOUXX and LEVIS COAK order one coffee and one tea; they'll work out who will drink which later—it's hardly important. Perhaps. These two are in relatively pleasant moods and come bearing notes from DIVISION DIRECTOR PROONE GHEISTWHITES, who is, for the most part, over the moon with T-d's constructed NARRATIVE thus far. However, GHEISTWHITES has a few *PAULEKAS points* that need tweaking, as well as details that are imperative to be worked into the THIRD AND FINAL PHASE. COAK produces a memo for T-d's review:

> PHASE III IS TO BE COMPLETED IN NO MORE THAN ONE YEAR FROM TODAY'S DATE, AT WHICH TIME YOUR CONTRACT WILL BE CONSIDERED FULFILLED [STOP]
>
> ARE YOU UP FOR IT [STOP]
>
> CIRCLE ONE [STOP]
>
> NO PROBLEMO [STOP]
>
> NO WAY JOSE [STOP]
>
> D.P. GHEISTWHITES [STOP]

Fuck Salinger, T-d thought as his hand hovered for a millisecond above the declination, and then he drew a big, hard ellipse around the answer that's going to ensure his riddled opus gets published at the House of HIS choosing, no questions asked, and with changes behest HIS wishes only.

THE BOPSEY TWINS AT THE SHORE—The unlikely trio made their way out onto the beach, and flew a kite and chain-smoked cigarettes until the sun disappeared further out to sea.

From behind a boulder, T-d spied PETER YARROW putting his predictable, pathetic moves on VIA, but she didn't bite—DAMMIT—It looks as though another easy-out for T-d gets foiled. He will have to remain patient. Surely another lug-head will blunder along soon; they always do.

While COAK and SIOUXX packed up and shook the sand from their blazers and tuxedo shoes, T-d used his long, bony fingers to rake a pentagram in the sand around them, scooping up hundreds of butts that had been burned down to their filters. And then, with absolutely no provocation (but certainly for good measure), SIOUXX and COAK roughed up T-d, driving home the dire reality of the situation; to demonstrate the inherent stresses which temporarily own T-d, those which HE agreed upon involvement with (contractually speaking, of course). HE should consider this beat-down a reminder. It's nothing personal (or not *too* personal). Their shallow, slow punches and light heel digs were, in fact, secretly connected to the novelist having made them travel to MEXICO one year ago.

They both get a few more jabs in before propping T-d against the softest boulder they could find.

T-d felt the warmth of photons scattering across the bridge of his nose and cheekbones in the final dying moments before the deep blue puffings set in.

TOPPEST-SECRET

6

M

S

O

S

J

• •

PHASE III

VITAUS—Spanish: an Andalusian style of music and dance, such as *Saint Vitaus Dance Craze,* which became known as *dancing mania.* Related names: *Vito*

• •

HOLY WÖD HUNKY PUNK or HIDING FROM RADU THE HANDSOME IS COMPLICATED—1956. Attendance diminishes at many of the once negro-rich Hollywood nightclubs. Over the last twelve years, the art scene has exploded, and big money has filtered into some unexpected hands. The *art world* exists outside of traditional regulations and oversights as the last vestige of the American Wild West—California's newest gold rush—with pedigree and ideals mined rather than precious metals. 15 to 20 exhibitions open on La Cienega Boulevard alone every Monday night.

When Vito and Sweet arrived back stateside last November, Kubernick had made arrangements for Vito to keep the basement and to move his Lamparts storefront from 303 Laurel Ave. (which Vito occupied from 1950 to 1955) next door into 301 Laurel Ave., 15 feet to the south in the Smith Building. By the spring of 1956, Vito, having gone full-blast Bacchanalian, had learned to navigate both the underground bohemian dives and the gilded drawing rooms. He dismantled Lamparts entirely, refining his identity by reinventing his sculptor's hut into an American hounfor; his very own Yellow House, Maison de Pleasures, or Abbey of Thelema. The once Egyptianesque tomb, with its soppy cave walls, has mutated into a hidden Mayan ch'ul na, or some kind of potion castle for Tinseltown witches. Framed under stuccoed arches and whirling belts, from street level, one would hardly suspect that such an institution could exist among Hollywood, let alone in its belly, and thrive. Vito's ex, Mary, 38, remains in the Southgate house at 1925 Vestal Ave. She has full custody of both children.

DILATED TIME, HYPERVIGILANCE—May 1956. Dick Bock's World Pacific Jazz Records reissues *The Chico Hamilton Quintet in Hi-Fi*. Vito is featured on the cover with one of his sculptures. This is part of Dick Bock's Pacific Jazz *West Coast Artist Series*:

WEST COAST ARTIST SERIES **5**

Our cover photograph (by William Claxton) of the Los Angeles sculptor, Vito, illustrates the climax of an exciting afternoon at the sculptor's studio where the Hamilton Quintet performed, entertained and inspired an energetic group of students of Vito's Clay Workshop.

Since its founding in 1947, the Clay Workshop students can boast of having won four first awards in sculpture in various exhibitions in Los Angeles.

Although Vito's work can be described for the most part as semi-abstract, he is a well-known portraitist and commercial sculptor in the literal-classical concept of interpretation. Vito has just returned from a year's study in Europe to begin work on his ambition to establish a center of endeavor in the arts – for both adults and children – embracing sculpture, painting, dance, and the theatre arts in Los Angeles.

Out of all the approachable, destitute modern artists living and working in Los Angeles—particularly fine-art-saturated Hollywood—how did Vito Paulekas (an obscure artist compared to the others selected for Bock's series) find his way to being photographed by William Claxton and Gordon Parks? Were these pics selected for publication in an April issue of *Life Magazine* because Vito Paulekas was so entrenched in the jazz scene and integral to the fusion of music and art? For the LP cover image, Claxton has caught Vito refining a sculpture titled *Counterpoints*:

> *Counterpoint*: derived from fifteenth-century Middle French: a) One or more independent melodies added above or below a given melody. It is also the combination of two or more independent melodies into a single harmonic texture in which each retains its linear character: polyphony, or the art or technique of setting, writing, or playing a melody or melodies in conjunction with another. b) According to fixed rules or an argument, an idea or theme is used to create a contrast with the main element.

Vito most likely chose this particular piece as the cover art since its title applies directly to jazz musicality, or perhaps he meant counterpoint, as in—*a testimony in court to the contrary*—as evidenced in his lengthy divorce from Mary. Besides, the word *contrary* plays right into Vito's contentious attitude toward authority, oversights, and agencies. Vito appears committed to perfecting the Jungian/Neitzche's posture of circular time, a symbol of unification and rebirth: The Wheel of the Year.

The Sicilian flag, designed in 1282 during the Rebellion of the Sicilian Vespers: Three legs, representing the three points of Sicily, circle Medusa's noggin. Trinacria—*having three headlands*—was the original name of the island. The three spinning ears of wheat commemorate Sicily's seat as a superior and reliable Italian granaio:

The augmented Greecian teras illustration on the Sicilian flag mirrors the tenth spirit of the 72 *daemons*, Buer, the mythological teacher of *Moral and Natural Philosophy*, depicted as a lion's head encircled by a wild mane and five clockwise-running, hooved & hairy beast legs. Buer appears in the *Ars Goetia* section of *The Lesser Keys of Solomon*, a 14th-century document that Crowley confessed to being obsessed with; literature which he considered a cornerstone in the formation of his Thelema:

During Vito's recent Italian travels, he, without doubt, encountered both the Sicilian flag and learned of the 72 Keys from either (or both) Anger or Kinsey.

> May 13—*The Los Angeles Times*, Vito and his students, sculpture. Clay Workshop, 301 N. Laurel Ave., 4 to 10 p.m. today only.

Aug. 25—One year after visiting Anger in Sicily, 62-year-old Alfred Charles Kinsey dies in Bloomington, IN, of heart failure set off by pneumonia. In his absence, protigè Anger enters an abysmal phase, and his productivity slows to a crawl.

Nov. 6—Miss Helen Louise Sweet is listed as residing at 301 Laurel Ave. with Vito Paulekas. This time, on her party affiliation registration, Sweet *declines to state*. Five days later, Sweet embarks from Honolulu, Hawaii (where she's been for the last five weeks) for San Francisco, CA. When she returns to LA soon after, Sweet moves out of 301 and into 340 B West Magnolia St. in Compton. As far as Vito is concerned, Sweet's gone radical, registering as a Republican—and she's out.

> Dec. 16—*The Los Angeles Times*, Students' mosaics. Clay Workshop, 301 N. Laurel Ave., 2 to 9 p.m. today only.

1957.

> Jan. 27—*Los Angeles Times,* S t u d e n t sculpture. Clay Workshop, 301 N Laurel Ave., 2 to 9 p.m. today only.

Feb. 10—At 3:00a, 50 firefighters battle a two-alarm fire raging through Easton's Gym on the second floor of the Smith Building, causing in excess of $10,000 in damage. By some stroke of luck, the building's structural integrity was not compromised, but three responding firefighters required hospitalization. Ten days later, Kubernick files an *APPLICATION TO REPAIR* and shells out $3,000.

> May 12—*Los Angeles Times,* Student's mosaics, Clay Workshop, 301 N. Laurel, 2 to 7:30 today only.

May 14—*APPLICATION TO ALTER, REPAIR, DEMOLISH*—Kubernick wants to knock *four openings through the interior stud walls on the second floor only. REF File X6321 ... APPROVED!*

June 9, 1957—Ferus Gallery gets plugged in the *LA Times*:

> WALLACE BERMAN, oils, sculpture, a first one-man show. Ferus Gallery, current through July 3.

A week later, a couple of Intelligence Officers dressed like hep cats check out Ferus Gallery at 736 A North La Cienega Blvd., and soon thereafter, the LAPD raid the gallery dedicating probable cause to an *offensive* sculptural piece by Wallace Berman, a sculpture titled *Temple*—a collection of objects, one of which is a small illustration, *Peyote Vision*, depicting a female on all fours getting yahooed from behind by a daemon. The drawing is not by Berman, but by his close friend and fellow subversive artist, the Scarlet Woman—Marjorie Cameron. Berman is arrested on paper and charged with obscenity (later found guilty of *OBSCENITY*, but eventually acquitted).

Ferus Gallery contributor and artist Burt Shonberg takes a dose of LSD and has his first of many dramatic experiences *beyond the limits of so-called everyday consciousness.*

On June 21, Midsummer/Summer Solstice, the night of the Wheel of the Year, at 8:00p, 37-year-old buxom ginger nurse Geneva *Jean* Hilliker Ellroy arrives at the Desert Inn bar at 1721 Valley Blvd. in El Monte, CA. Ellroy is soon joined by a couple that neither the Desert Inn staff nor the Regulars recall having ever seen before. Patron Michael Whitaker downed a few drinks barside the three unknowns and claimed that the *swarthy man* told him his name, but alcohol has hazed the details, and he has since forgotten. Other patrons reported seeing the odd trio leave together, telling detectives that the MALE UNSUB is:

about 5'6"—Vito is 5'4".

about 40-45 years of age—Vito 44.

thin—Vito is ... well, you get the picture.

White... No, Mexican. No, white ... with a swarthy complexion

As a point of reference, to best describe how Vito looks to somebody not in the know, if you've ever seen Charles Dennis Buchinsky (aka Charles Bronson), you could paint a portrait of Vito; they could have easily passed as blood brothers. Buchinsky, just like Vito, is of Lithuanian descent, specifically from the ancient Lipka Tartars who braved the mud flood and clay rain. Buchinsky's exotic look often led to his portrayal of Mexican and American Indian characters in film and television throughout his career. Both similarly looking Lithuanians were easily and frequently mistaken for adjacent heritages. The MALE UNSUB, with whom Ellroy left the Desert Inn bar, was *accompanied by a blonde woman, white, maybe 30 years old*, her hair pulled back in a ponytail (perhaps just as a dancer or sculptor with long hair is known to do). When waitress Lavon Chambers was questioned, she so accurately described Ellroy's dress and fake pearl necklace that detectives singled her out as the mouthpiece witness, and she told them the trio left in a dark green 1955 or 1956 Oldsmobile. When presented with the police artist sketch of the *swarthy man*, Chambers agrees that it's a fair likeness, but the man was *definitely white, not Latin.*

At 10:20p, Ellroy and the unknown man enter Stan's Drive-in, talking very animatedly. The blonde 30-something-year-old female is not with them. The man drinks a coffee, and Ellroy eats a cheese toast sandwich.

At 1:00a, now June 22, 1957, Ellroy and the *swarthy man* leave Stan's, only to return in one hour, their moods tanked, gone sullen. The man reprises his coffee order.

At 2:45a, they leave for good.

Near 9:00a, Geneva Ellroy's body is discovered on Kings Row near

Lower Azusa Road. She has been strangled, garroted with a clothesline or sash cord, and then dragged and dumped near Arroyo High School. Ellroy's house at 756 Maple Ave. is located ten miles southwest of here in El Monte. Like many of the other LA victims, her shoes and purse are missing. Ellroy attempted to fight off her assailant, catching skin cells and bloody beard hairs under her fingernails. Her car was abandoned behind the Desert Inn. Ellroy leaves behind a ten-year-old son, Lee, who lives with his 60-year-old alcoholic accountant father, Armand Lee Ellroy, at 4980 Beverly Blvd. (2.5 miles due east of Vito's Clay Workshop on the same boulevard.)

July 17—The LAPD struggles to pin promising suspects for the recent sex murders, and instead resorts to blaming society's *moral indecency* for the *Werewolf Murders*. In a sweeping attempt to restore the moral center to Los Angeles, the blueboys crack down on the establishment, issuing this memo that justifies a state-wide violation of the First Amendment:

> THE STATE OF CALIFORNIA PROCLAIMS—Obscene literature consists of any writing, or printed matter, picture, image, drawing, figure, photograph, or other pictorial representation that is unrelated to science, art, or scientific study and taken as a whole is indecent, lewd, lascivious, and has the effect of inciting to lewdness or sexual crime. Whoever sells, lends, distributes, exhibits, gives away, or shows or offers to sell, lend, distribute, exhibit, or give away or show or has in his possession with intent to sell, lend, distribute or give away or to show, or knowingly advertises in any manner, any obscene literature or lewd, lascivious, filthy, indecent or disgusting book, magazine, pamphlet, newspaper, story paper, paper, writing, drawing, photograph, figure or image, or any written or printed matter of an indecent character, or any article or instrument of indecent or immoral use on purporting to be for indecent or immoral use or purpose, or whoever designs copies, draws, photographs, prints, utters, publishes, or in any manner manufactures or prepares any such book, picture, drawing, magazine, pamphlet, newspaper, storypaper, paper, writing, figure,

image, matter, article or thing, or whoever writes, prints, publishes or utters, or causes to be printed, published or uttered, any advertisement or notice of any kind giving information, directly or indirectly, stating or purporting to do so, where, how, of whom, or by what means any, or what purports to be, any obscene, lewd, lascivious, filthy, disgusting or indecent book, picture, writing, paper, figure, image, matter, article or thing named in this section can be purchased, obtained or had, or whoever prints, utters, publishes, sells, lends, gives away, or shows, or has in his possession with intent to sell, lend, give away, or show, or otherwise offers for sale, loan or gift, or distribution, any pamphlet, magazine, newspaper or other printed paper devoted to the publication and principally made up of criminal news, police reports or accounts of criminal deeds, or pictures of stories of deeds of bloodshed, lust or crime, or whoever hires, employs, uses or permits any minor or child to do or assist in doing any act or thing mentioned in this section, is guilty of a felony, and upon conviciton, shall be sentenced to imprisonment not exceeding two (2) years, or to pay a fine not exceeding two thousand dollars ($2000), or both. As amended 1957, July 17, P.L. 973, § 1.

July 15—In the Arts section of *The Los Angeles Times*:

the massa gallery

SCULPTURES

by

VITO PAULEKAS

"Joining"

THE CURRENT GROUP SHOW

748 N. La Ciénega Bl.

One hundred and twenty-one feet of La Cienega Boulevard's pavement separates the Massa and Ferus Galleries. Vito and Burt Shonberg meet and become fast friends. At this time, Shonberg and Marjorie Cameron —who now goes simply by Cameron—are an item, and an odd item at that.

> Sep. 29—*Los Angeles Times,* Student sculpture, mosaics, paintings. Clay Workshop, 301 N Laurel Ave., 2 to 9 p.m. today only.

1958. Dick Bock expands the World Pacific Records catalog well beyond jazz and bebop recordings, releasing *India's Master Musician*, introducing Ravi Shankar and Eastern music to the masses in the West. Although Shankar's eastern sound is not an immediate success, rising-star musicians take notice and borrow from Shankar's arrangements accordingly. Jay Carter England works for Bock as a studio technician. England, 37, is a tenor saxophonist first, and a well-read history junkie a close second. He and Vito, 45, talk for hours on end in the studio, swapping wartime stories as England, too, served in the US Marine Corps for three years. Vito has few peers of England's capacity, and the two men enjoy each other's company. England even occasionally pokes around The Clay Workshop.

Movies are out, G_d is in. Please read the menu closely, as many intentions have changed or been discontinued. The condemned Laurel Avenue Theatre, directly across the street from Vito's at 8056 Beverly Blvd., was converted into a synagogue after 12 years of screenings.

January 30, Kubernick hires E.O. Smith, son of Smith Building original builder, E.L. Smith, to contract for the addition of a *Parapet corridor along Beverly Blvd. and Laurel and rear alley.* It costs old Küb a cool $2,000.

> Feb. 23—*Los Angeles Times*, PRICES LOW—Getting a public showing for their work is often a difficult problem for young artists. To help ease this situation locally, Joseph Massa last week opened extensive galleries bearing his name at 746 N La Cienega Blvd. Massa believes that many people will enjoy owning young artists' works if prices are kept low. His initial show represents a dozen or so painters who work in styles ranging from traditional to abstract, and one sculptor, Vito Paulekas...Average age of his exhibitors, Massa says, is 25 years.

Tonight's television broadcast of CBS's *Mr. Adam and Eve*, April 1, 1958, features exterior and interior shots of the Smith Building, and it isn't a pretty picture. Kubernick flies into a tizzy when he sees his baby depicted in such a dim light. Mary Paulekas, 40, remains at 1925 Vestal Ave. with son Mark, 13, and daughter Ann, 8. Mary has resided here for a decade. Helen Louise Sweet remains at 340 B West Magnolia St. while working for the Compton Police Department in a clerical capacity. She has stayed a firmly registered Republican since leaving Vito two years ago.

April 2—The term *beatnik* is coined in a *San Francisco Chronicle* article by Herb Caen, referring to the current youth generation who are clinging to the aging Beat propaganda:

> Beatnik: a) a diminutive of *Beats*. b) less than a *Beat*, a *baby Beat*.

> April 22—*Los Angeles Evening Citizen News*, CITY SEEKS TO EXPAND STORM DRAIN PLANS—The city may obtain funds to construct 39 extra storm drains in addition to 74 drains included in the proposed $216,743,000 country-wide storm drain bond issue, it was reported today. City Engineer Lyall A. Pardee said the needed $15,705,000 may be available from a $25,000,000 included in the bond issue to cover possible rising construction costs. Should construction costs not require the entire sum, it will be used to build additional drains, Pardee said. He said if none of the $25,000,000

> earmarked for price increases is required, the city will construct the extra 39 drains. If some of the money is used to meet anticipated price hikes, the county and the city will divide the remainder proportionately. The 39 "reserve" storm drain projects are apportioned geographically, including Council District 5—Beverly Blvd. from Laurel Ave. to Kings Rd. at a budgeted cost of $170,000.

Council District 5 plans to fix the problem, starting directly under The Clay Workshop.

April 29—*APPLICATION TO ALTER, REPAIR, DEMOLISH*—Kubernick pays $500 to *bring stairs up to code, move non-bearing walls, enlarge windows, and make corrections per file 6321. ... APPROVED!*

May 22—*APPLICATION TO ALTER, REPAIR, DEMOLISH—8051-8053-8055 Beverly Blvd. owner* Kubernick coughs up $150 for engineer R. Hall to *remove non-bearing wall. ... APPROVED!*

> Aug. 5—*Long Beach Independent,* 'MR. ADAMS, EVE' SUED FOR $900,000—LOS ANGELES. A $900,000 Superior Court suit was filed Tuesday against the Columbia Broadcasting System over the April 1 showing of the "Mr. Adams and Eve" television show. Harvey Easton, owner of Easton's Gym at 8053 Beverly Blvd., charged in his complaint filed through Atty. Floyd H. Schenk that on April 1, without his consent, station KNXT showed filmed episodes of the exterior and interior of the gym. The gym owner contends the establishment caters to select clientele consisting largely of business and professional people. THE SUIT CHARGED the TV show filmed the interior of the gym as being "run down, old, shabby and a place frequented by rude, rough, tough and ill-mannered persons." Easton, according to the suit, demanded a retraction on May 2, but it was refused. Also named in the suit were Television station KNXT, Bridget Production; Four Star Films Inc., R. J. Reynolds Tobacco Co., and Ida Lupino and Howard Duff, stars of the comedy show.

BEVERLY WILSHIRE ART GALLERIES

Auction De Luxe

Magnificent Furniture — Valuable Paintings
Distinctive Decorations — Art Property

Rare Persian rugs, fine furnishings and Ojbects d'Art from the Palm Drive Beverly Hills residence of Mr. E. L. Smith. Direct importations—estate matters and consignments by various owners.

PUBLIC SALE

TODAY — Afternoon only at 1:30

TOMORROW — Evening only at 8 o'clock

Superb antique Royal Bokhara (priceless example of museum quality). Mason square piano in old Rosewood case. Salon oil painting by A. Wilkow "The Old Mill in Winter." "Boulevard of Paris" by Amedio (French Modern). Antique Royal Vienna China Roast Set. Magnificent Capo-diMonte urn (mounted as lamp). Custom-made period suites and occasional pieces. Superb Persian and Chinese carpets and rugs. Imported Chinese contemporary furniture, lacquers, ivories, screens, bronzes and porcelains. Sheffield and sterling silver. Tiffany crystal drinking glasses, Continental porcelains, mirrors, lamps and paintings by artists of note. Chandeliers and electrical appliances.

"Attend These Gallery Auctions for Fine Bargains"

CONDUCTED BY

Z. N. BAIDA & PAUL CURTIS

• •

LA-based visual artist Burt Shonberg licks all his postage after becoming fascinated with LSD and how it *expands* his creativity. Shonberg, Doug Myres, and *Star Trek* teleplay writer, George Clayton Johnson, partner to open the ultimate California counterculture coffeehouse in Laguna Beach—Cafe Frankenstein at 860 S. Pacific Coast Highway. At first, the shop is hounded by local law, but it soon becomes the Blueboy's actual hangout after finding that, contrary to their beliefs, the coffee house serves coffee. Lord Buckley, a personal favorite comedian of Vito's, performs regularly at Cafe Frankenstein.

> 1958. Nov. 30—*The Los Angeles Times*, Burt Shonberg, paintings, and drawings, through January, Coffee House Positano, 19453 Pacific Coast Highway, Malibu.

1959. I WISH I HAD SOME REASON TO BELIEVE YOU—The Clay Workshop completes its transmutation into Clay Vito (aka Chez Vito), dedicating itself to becoming a Hollywood cultural landmark, a destination art salon for all walks of life—but the sexier and richer the walk, the better. Shop shelves once lined with TV lamps are now covered with statement pieces facing out of 301's bay windows. Vito has begun weaponizing his art. His new sculptural pieces have taken on a primitive, island-borne aesthetic; long, tall, extruded figures with lived-in faces, the ghouls frequently sneaking up on somebody.

Vito tapped into the desperate debutantes market, looking for those local unicorns—lonely housewives who bring their teenage daughters along to *class*. Actress Doris Day's 16-year-old son, Terry Melcher, attends Vito's basement art classes with the simple, red-blooded, blue-balled hope of seeing some of those beautiful naked women he's heard about from his Fairfax High buddies. Melcher said—*Vito was an art instructor. When I was in high school, we'd go to his art studio because he had naked models … I'd just pop in and say, 'Hi, I'm thinking of taking some art lessons.* Souanne Shaffer, another Fairfax High School student, hears about Vito and his wild basement studio happenings less than a mile from campus, and she, too, falls prey to curiosity and attends one of Vito's evening sculpting classes with some of her girlfriends. Sue, as she is known, is barely 16 years old, a cheerleader and competition roller skater, and, like many teenagers of her persuasion, eager to challenge her (land developer) parents' authority. Were Melcher and Shaffer friends before simultaneously arriving at Vito's? Did Melcher introduce Sue to Vito? Sue and her friends were into low-budget films and the unusual & unique; all roads would have likely led her to Vito, eventually, per the Universal death-drive. Sue and Vito (30 years her senior) meet and begin a courtship almost immediately.

The first edition of Kenneth Anger's *Hollywood Babylon* was published in France by Jean-Jacques Pauvert. On a double-page splash across pages 128 and 129, as well as a single full page on 133, un-edited photographs of Elizabeth Short's divided corpse are published for the first time, ANYWHERE.

March 3—Thomas John *Jay* Kummer adopts the Sebring surname (for his love of cars) before opening Sebring International at 725 North Fairfax Ave. with his 19-year-old business partner and fellow hairstylist, Lawrence *Larry* Geller. The shop is three-quarters of a mile due north of Clay Vito. Club owner/producer Lou Adler is an early investor in the shop. Sebring is romantically involved with actress Barbara Luna, who appears regularly on *Star Trek* and *Zorro*. The shop struggles financially at first, charging $50 for a men's haircut when most barbers would trim a fellow up for a buck. Everything changes after Luna brings celebrity crooner Vic Damone in for the Sebring treatment. Damone is so deeply moved, as if he had *never had a haircut before,* that he is compelled to introduce Sebring to Sands Hotel co-owner and head of entertainment, Jack Entratter, who reciprocates the praise and tells other heavyweights, who tell others, and so forth. Sebring and Geller rake in the dough.

On May 26, 1959, the Mosaic Exhibition and lectures were held at 8104 Beverly Blvd. Clay Vito Studios is among those exhibiting:

> Southern California leads the way in the flourishing revival of mosaics, an art which until recently was almost lost in a tradition of more than 1,000 years," said Georgia Haley, exhibit director. "We are presenting the artists who lend new excitement to an ancient art in our largest and most representative collection of mosaics to date."

In June, Burt Shonberg creates artworks to accompany Elizabeth Case's book of anti-war poetry, *Pax and Dig*. Shonberg's relationship with Cameron is wildly complicated and always strained. Frankenstein's Monster and the Scarlet Woman sell their artworks at various street bazaars and fairs in San Francisco and Los Angeles. Shonberg gives an interview to *The Desert Sun*, citing his new paintings currently on show at the Left Bank Cafe:

> He says that he places "no limitations" on his brushes, abides by "no academic rules"—although he knows them—and simply strives to "explore the unknown—my unknown. The three other paintings I did at the Left Bank don't depict anything; They're really expressions—extensions of myself." ... "In a way, they're me—or me as I was at the time I painted them," Shonberg admits that such spontaneity in paintings has its drawbacks. "It's difficult to communicate with people when you paint like this," he sighed. "People are looking for a label they can attach to everything. When they fail to find it, the object gets the only label they have—bad. In reality, the only thing that counts in painting is quality and validity. Like I said before, I'm not concerned with the viewer.

Syd Zaid is back; he and wifey Annette file a $150,000 emotional damages lawsuit against Warner Bros. after a popular song is released by the label, which features the Zaids' Studio City residential and business telephone number. *Valley Times*, page one, explains:

> Aug. 21—AND THE PHONE RINGS ON—"No, you can't borrow my comb!" cries orchestra leader Sydney Zaid to the caller, interrupting business conversation as his wife Annette reaches for another ringing telephone. The Zaids, whose tele-number can be reached by people dialing the number recited by Edd "Kookie" Byrnes on record "Like I Love You," have averaged more than 100 calls a day from persons trying to reach either "Kookie" or "Marcia," his girlfriend on record.

Sep. 7—33-year-old Helen Louise Sweet arrives back in LA, fresh from Mexico aboard World Atlantic Airlines #626. Sweet does a great impression of a yo-yo, moving, once again, this time to 1021 S. La Cienega Ave. in Hollywood, only two miles southwest of Clay Vito.

In mid-September of 1959, celebrity athlete Jack LaLanne celebrated his 45th birthday by *executing 1,000 perfect push-ups and 1,000 faultless chin-ups at the chrome-plated sinew-mill over on Beverly Blvd. in Hollywood—Easton's Gym.* Kubernick badly needs good press, and this type of celebrity slop will do nicely.

1960. AMERICAN MERCURIAL—Marijuana is temporarily decriminalized for terminally ill patients. Some cancer patients receive a monthly supply of 80 joints delivered in a coffee tin. Following the delivery driver from one neighborhood to the next, each becomes more diverse than the last, until we arrive in Hollywood, where Chief of Police Parker has packed the boulevards with 200 cops shipped in from Sacramento to shut down the teen hangouts plaguing the city. For the first time, the Sunset Strip goes dark.

May 20—On Vito Paulekas's 47th birthday, he appeared on CBS's *On the Go,* followed by *The Joe Pyne Show* with guest author Elisha Gerald *Jerry* Hopkins. Vito and Hopkins meet during this taping (although, later, Hopkins will remember it differently).

Mary Paulekas has relocated herself, son Mark, 16, and daughter Ann, 10, to Palo Alto, CA. Mark attends Cubberley High School and is pictured in the yearbook playing cello in the school orchestra. He is the same age as many of the girls seeking culture and direction from his estranged father, who's bagging that juvie tail like groceries.

> June 12—*Independent Press-Telegram*, Today at 9:30 p.m.—channel two—ON THE GO: Jack Linkletter visits Vito Paulekas' art studio.

> June 16—*The Boston Globe*, Today on TV—High Spots—ON THE GO: Jack Linkletter visits with artist Vito Paulekas: 10:30.

Clay Vito suffers a steady stream of celebrities taking a keen interest in Vito's subversive evening sculpting classes; showfolk like Steve Allen and his hairstylist—*the* stylist to the stars—Jay Sebring, actors Joe de Santis, Jonathan Winters, Mickey Rooney, countless freshmen & sophomores from Fairfax High and Immaculate Heart in Los Feliz. 27-year-old Beverly Hills hair stylist, Sheldon Jaman, is there a lot, becoming one of Vito's original Freak dancers.

Saturday, June 18, 1960—Vito throws a benefit dance bash down in the basement studio:

> Room at the Bottom. Music, dancing, and entertainment will highlight Wonderland Youth Center's fund-raising bash, "Room at the Bottom," at 7:30 p.m. next Saturday at Vito's Basement Studio, 303 N. Laurel Ave. Actresses Sheree North and Nita Talbot are slated to attend. Proceeds will be used for the center's building fund and summer program.

Shonberg completes several oil portraits to appear on-camera in Roger Corman's upcoming Vincent Price flick, *House of Usher*. Shonberg is stoned hard on some good grass and describes a painting he's working on, one depicting an encounter between himself, Vito, and an extremely tall, lanky male being with shoulder-length hair. This Giant, as Shonberg understood him to be, has a massive schlong that drags on the ground behind him as he walks. Three virgins are required around the clock to hoist this protracted pecker onto their dainty shoulders, draping it flacidly over as if it were linked pyramids of wheat —and do this they must, day in, day out, following the Giant down every corridor and through every window. One of the girls interrupts Shonberg's story, wanting to make it real, and she does. Oh yeah, Shonberg remembers that the Giant came to earth to teach us all the proper way of fucking. *For far too long, you humans have been doing it all wrong. In fact, for all times. Ya'll put that over here, when it's supposta go into that ...*

Several parents arrive at Clay Vito the following morning to pick up their underage daughters, who have not yet returned home. Sometimes they find their kid crashed out in the studio, sometimes they don't—Vito doesn't give a shit.

Aug. 3—*Ocean's Eleven* premieres in Las Vegas, NV. The film stars five of the Rat-Packers and features Entratter's Sands Hotel heavily. The screenplay was written by Cafe Frankenstein co-owner/*Star Trek* writer/Shonberg's roommate, George Clayton Johnson.

Oct. 10—On Jay Sebring's 27th birthday, he and 17-year-old print model Bonnie Lee Marple wed in Las Vegas, with Vic Damone presiding as best man and supplying The Sands for the reception party. Sebring christens his new bride—*Cami*—a Hebrew name meaning, *virginal* or *unblemished.* The newlyweds share an apartment above Sebring's shop at 725 North Fairfax Ave., less than one mile north as the crow flies from Clay Vito.

Late in 1960, Burt Shonberg answered a newspaper ad seeking artist participants in a program overseen by LA-based psychiatrist Dr. Oscar Janiger, to whom the US Federal Government had commissioned to administer LSD-25 to willing subjects for research on its effects on the human creative process. Shonberg takes the acid, the looney tunes, and trips balls. He paints, and loves it, repeating the examination frequently, concluding quickly that LSD must be the source of his creativity. His muse finally arrives, and she's wearing stripes.

January 1961. At the CBS television studios at 7800 Beverly Blvd., near Fairfax Avenue, Vito and several of his students are welcomed onto the backlot loading dock, allowed to riffle through a mess of outdated Baroque and Victorian costumes that the wardrobe department has deemed dusty and threadbare and decided to chuck. The Freaks fill Vito's VW bus, having to open all 17 windows to make enough room for their take. As the bus takes off, making the short 1,800-foot drive west on Beverly Boulevard back to Clay Vito, black air and bloomers and frilly knickers spew from its rear.

ANOTHER CLUB—February. A massive diesel freight train plows down the middle of Santa Monica Boulevard, blazing its midnight Route 66 trail first directly out in front of the Troubadour club, and then PJ's at 8151 Santa Monica Blvd. PJ's holds the distinct honor of being LA's first discotheque.

Feb. 18—The Bay of Pigs invasion.

Vito adds—Art Gallery—to the résumé of 303. The April 28 edition of *The Los Angeles Citizen News* reports that sculptures by artist Hungarian immigrant Steffan Kolati will be shown at Clay Vito on May 7, for one day only, from 2:00p to 9:00p.

Today, on July 7, Sue Shaffer becomes an adult, and as one, she and 48-year-old Vito are finally free to elope, and they do just that. When Sue's father arrives at Clay Vito to retrieve his daughter on the morning of her birthday, it is made crystal clear to the land developer that his little girl is all grown up. She is a wife now and will be living at the Smith Building with Vito from here on out.

Jay Sebring is a guest on the November 15, 1961, broadcast of *The New Steve Allen Show,* which films inside a retired Vaudeville theatre at 1228 North Vine St., 3.4 miles northeast of Clay Vito. Vito's acquaintance, talent coordinator/writer/co-producer, Jerry Hopkins, has arranged for Sebring to appear on the show.

Nov. 17 through 19—Nelson Rockefeller's fifth child, 23-year-old Michael Rockefeller, disappears in the Asmat district of the Netherlands New Guinea after his canoe and that of Dutch anthropologist Rene Wassing's get stuck 12 miles offshore. Wassing is rescued on the 18th, but Michael is nowhere to be found. When rescue efforts are called off, it's clear his disappearance may remain just that—forever.

1962. Over the next year, more than 30 galleries will open, lining both the north and south sides of La Cienega Boulevard. A troupe of Freaks calling themselves the La Cienega Group crawls from one Monday night opening to the next along the boulevard. Tonight, July 9, 1962, the La Cienega Group attends the reception for Andy Warhol's Campbell Soup can exhibition at Ferus Gallery. Vito finds the artworks' lack of beauty shocking, and later mocks so-called *modern art* and its makers.

SCARE THE MUD OUTTA THEM—Karl Orentes Franzoni resides in Redwood City/Menlo Park/North Beach in the Bay Area with his brother John. Franzoni claims his mother is a countess and his father a stone carver from Rutland, VT. He says the Franzonis arrived from the quarries of northern Italy, and cut the stones that make up many of the United States' founding monuments. Franzoni studied photography at the San Francisco Art Institute under Imogen Cunningham, who was then in her mid-eighties and considered a master of the craft. Franzoni bartends at a San Francisco dive on Broadway, directly across from The Peppermint Tree dancehall at 660 Broadway. It is here that Franzoni meets Cecilia de Steffano, a married woman with whom he begins an illicit affair. When Franzoni's co-worker Joe Dana puts the question to him—*Do you wanna get into a business*?—Franzoni answers *yes* and convinces De Staffano to divorce her husband of 11 years, sell the house, and hand over the monies to he and his new business partners (The Brothers Biali and Sid Weinstein) allowing their MAIL-ORDER-ONLY breast pump business, *Cecilia de Steffano of Hollywood*, to get off the ground. De Steffano's two young boys stay behind in San Francisco with Dad, and she and her seven-year-old daughter dump the Bay Area, moving into a lovely Hollywood apartment on Third Street. The Bay Area transplants sell the atomizer-driven breast pump out of an office on Melrose Avenue, just west of Fairfax. This sucker is guaranteed to perk those puppies. Franzoni, Cecilia, her daughter, along with Joe Scallaci & his wife, all live together as a single, mutating organism, moving frequently from one Los Angeles County apartment to another.

> Sep. 13—*Los Angeles Evening Citizen News*, Gunman Robs Liquor Store—An unshaven gunman wearing dark glasses escaped with $121 during the night after robbing a Beverly Boulevard liquor store, police said today. Officers reported the bandit walked into the F & R Liquor Store, 8051 Beverly Blvd., shortly after 10 o'clock and purchased a package of cigarettes from owner Felix Rogen, 60, produced a revolver, and ordered the owner away from the cash register. After scooping $101 in currency and $20 in coins from the register, the gunman fled from the store on foot.

Sep. 16—Vito's mother, Rose, dies in Cambridge, MA, at age 74.

STRUGGLE MEAL // LEARNING TO SPEAK VIOLENCE

October 22, 1962. T-d boards a bus in Redding, CA, bound for San Francisco, where he will transfer to a smaller, stinkier charter bus to Mexico. As T-d steps onto the bus with a thermos of cold coffee, President Kennedy addresses Americans with a terrifying speech about the United States' sudden involvement, today, in the Cuban Missile Crisis.

The bus takes off, T-d watches the bouncing landscape for three whole hours. By the time he pulls into the San Fran depot, the entire metropolis of 740,000 citizens is on a quasi-mandatory lockdown. The bus offloads riders, spilling them out onto the dead, empty streets, and announces that all bus service is postponed until further notice. Only a local beer barn and a drug store remained open, but T-d lacked a need for either. The undetermined layover mixed with the final cold sips of coffee sends our man, as it would any curious being, on a journey.

T-d is waved over across the street toward a vacant toy store smack dab in the middle of an outdoor strip mall. The waving arm is attached to a hobo, one of two who quickly introduce themselves and dump their life stories on T-d, begging for self-worth assurance even if their shoes are family-size tin tuna cans with the lid curled back over the key for a tongue.

MILT JAFFERS, according to himself, hails from a well-seated Motorcity legacy, but was excommunicated after he lost his father's best Sunday boots during the 1942 Guadalcanal Campaign, learning later that they were spotted in an elephant's trunk in Adyar, Chennai. Until recently his line was that of a gagman for Jay Ward Production "right here in the U—S—fucking A, man," until a bunch of "Mexicans" who were "pulled off the street—stole" Jaffer's job in 1959 when General Mills' agency of record, Dancer Fitzgerald Sample, out-sourced all their animation productions to a cardboard cut-out studio in Mexico City—GAMMA PRODUCTIONS (formerly VAL-MAR).

"Tha fuck do Mexicans know about cartoons? SERIOUSLY? Name one Taco-toon?"

"Speedy Gonzales ..."

"Damn you to Hell, HAZELNUTS, you know quite right what I meant."

SODY HAZELNUTS' story wasn't all that different from JAFFERS', though HAZELNUTS never had his boots turn up in India. And, he was never a gagman, but he did work for over a decade supervising classically trained painters at creating mile-long background scrolls and 12-field layouts—archaic rooms cluttered with time machines and trinkets, or a busy roundabout during a Budapest spring.

"Look how far I can turn my head," JAFFERS interrupted, going on to do what he just said.

"Get yer shit together," HAZELNUTS said, giving JAFFERS a swift kick to glüts, sending him back up on his feet.

The hobos have stacked full boxes of teddies and piggies against the wall, creating a clearing around the back loading dock door, where a pot of Mulligan stew simmers over a glowing compacted ball of polyfill. They have propped the door open with a tin fire truck, creating an easy escape route for the white smoke and themselves, if necessary.

"HAZELNUTS puts on an apron and turns into a culinary wizard," JAFFERS explained while serving T-d stew in an upside-down plastic novelty ball cap, then filling a mug made from a cored-out Louisville Slugger with homebrewed hooch that these weirdos called *Bull's Blood.*

The newfound friends slurped stew and got loaded on peace-water, all the while watching through the paned glass across the breezeway, a monolith of televisions in the Woolworth's main display window. The men have gone radio silent; the only sound is that of their smacking, bleeding gums. The repulsive waves bounced off the piles of Wham-O Superballs and the Etch-a-Sketch bunkers that engulfed them. Six eyes hang on each strobing image beamed into their brains at 30 fps.

JAFFERS was the first to snap out of the strobing spell, "Can you believe such rotten luck as this? All day it's been missiles this … crisis that … Is it asking too goddamn much for just one cartoon?" And then, after a gentle prodding, in an overwhelming instant, the Bull's Blood acted as a mild truth serum, sending our docile budding novelist into a logorrheic monster, expelling his poorly structured, loose babble-tale from 1953 when T-d was just another rowdy student of Cornell University, living in the Kline Road Dormitories. He remembered the housing facilities looking not unlike many of the concentration camp *houses* depicted in some propaganda he had recently seen. T-d described his move to Greenwich Village while awaiting the approval of the Ford Foundation Grant that never came. He licked his wounds by crashing through Ornette Coleman's deep cuts, and inadvertently falling in love with a striking young JAP, BECCA HEKSUM, whose father denounced T-d's uncircumcised, WASPy ways, refusing to allow his daughter's courting by a gentile, even if the gentile was a genius. T-d's agent wrangled him $500 of the $1500 book advance Lippincott promised. Depressed, lost, T-d moved his tall, pale ass to Seattle, WA (a city he grew to love, but loathed its residents more), settling in as the third wheel at the home of some married friends (a marriage T-d subsequently breaks up, running off with said wife—but, that's a story for a different dossier). Wifey—VIA—worked T-d into a position at Boeing, writing technical reports and data manuals—"You fellas ever heard of BOMARC or the Minuteman intercontinental ballistic missile?" … (crickets) … "What about ICBM?" … (crickets) … "Well, that's fine, no matter; after nearly two years of that interesting trite, last month my work there ended. Now, it's Mexico or bust, baby!" ...

"SSSSSSHHHHHUT UP POINDEXTER! LOOKEE THERE, HAZELNUTS!" JAFFERS barked over T-d's autobiography. Each of the three took turns rubbing the hell outta their eyes, and then blinked into focus the flickering stack of cathodic gods:

> A van with STATEHOOD FOR MOOSYLVANIA painted across the sides arrives at the gates of 1600 Pennsylvania Ave. It is covered from bumper to bumper with paisley swirls and daisies; a large Cheshire Cat-style smile on the front hood and bumper. Within seconds, the van is swarmed by the NATIONAL GUARD, who drag out two middle-aged men and a young woman and take them to Government pavement before feeding them a couple of green and tan knuckle sandwiches. Several soldiers clear the van first before commandeering it, driving it through the gates and out of view. YOUR COUNTRY THANKS YOU FOR YOUR DONATION.

"This is one helluva stew, HAZELNUTS," T-d muttered as he filled his cold coffee thermos to the threads with potion while the two hobos celebrated like a pair of unhinged madmen, shouting praises, pumping up T-d's adrenaline—"Go on, GET! TAKE THAT MEXICAN WORK, let's see how they like it!"—"¡Time to pack up la máquina de escribir de Nuño y Yáñez!"—"Lest not discount Azuela's departure!"—"Goodness, no, you idiot, Azuela died ten years back, last March!" T-d faints. The hobos picked T-d up by his lanky, powdered limbs—like a jumprope—JAFFERS manning the wrists, HAZELNUTS cinching the translucent ankles. "It's your turn, now, baby! Let's get you on that bus!"

And they did.

• •

1963. RIDE THE GOD CANDLE AND BE FRUITFUL—The first cycle of American music recordings established in 1932 has come to a close, and a new 30-year cycle begins. Nobody knows it yet, but the Brits are rowing up to the coast. They will be fought off tooth and nail with electrified American folk diddies. Wannabe musicians Roger McGuinn, David Crosby, and Gene Clark met in Greenwich Village, NYC, and soon formed the first incarnation of what would become the Byrds: The Jet Set.

CONSTANT MOVEMENT, CONSTANT STILLNESS—Vito implements the terms *freaks* to describe his body-painted tribe and their new techniques of self-imaging—and *freak-out*: their form of ecstatic dancing long before the greater media latches onto the subdued moniker, *hippies*. Vito philosophizes that through dance, one's blood is cleansed. Controlled breathing forces cells through the body's pulmonary system, giving you a natural high. Some dancers, like marathon runners, suffer syncope, or fainting, when at rest, due to a reduction in blood supply to the brain. Ravi Shankar pays a visit to Clay Vito. Until trading dancing glory for citar fame in 1938, Shankar was in a troupe with his brother that toured India. He is a natural fit for Clay Vito, and like many celebrities, wildly interested in Vito's happenings.

January 28, 1963—Sebring is a contestant on *To Tell The Truth.* The panel correctly identifies him. Sebring's celebrity status—a rarity for a men's hairstylist—facilitated the purchase of 9820 Easton Drive, a 1920s prohibition-era Swiss chalet built into a Benedict Canyon mountainside. The mansion features many hidden chambers and secret rooms. There is a bar hidden behind a bookcase. Another room hides a temple. Despite these peculiarities, the first thing Sebring shows off to his business partner, Larry Geller, is the upstairs bathroom doorway where Paul Bern shot himself dead. Sebring uses his finger to outline

Bern's imaginary corpse, driving home the impact on Geller. On September 5, 1932, 42-year-old film producer Paul Bern was found dead from a *self-inflicted* gunshot wound right here in this mansion that he shared with his bride of only two months, mega-starlet Jean Harlow. A suicide note written on a page torn from a journal was left on a small table just feet from the body:

> Dearest dear, unfortunately, this is the only way to make good the frightful wrong I have done you and to wipe out my abject humiliation, I love you. Paul, you understand that last night was only a comedy.

Jan. 30—Speaking of comedies, Timothy Carey's low-budget epic, *The World's Greatest Sinner*, establishes the concept of the *rock god* at a Wednesday night premier at the Vista Theatre in Hollywood, carried out in Carey's notorious grand fashion. Carey, who wrote, directed, and starred in the film as God Hilliard, is the night's master of ceremonies. From his greasy hair to his suede slippers, Carey was swathed in a silver lamé suit with *GOD* stitched on the sleeves. He initiates the screening by firing .38 into the air. A year and a half earlier, in June of 1961, you'll remember that Carey hired 21-year-old Frank V. Zappa to compose the soundtrack. The following November, Zappa enlisted eight musicians to record the rock-and-roll numbers for the film, and then, in mid-December, a 55-piece orchestra joined to record the score. Zappa tells Pomona's *Progress-Bulletin* that—*the score is unique ... in that it uses every type of music*—As the film is released to theatres, Zappa initially makes a good pitch-kid. Carey appreciates the promotion, but Zappa quickly bitters, feeling that his work for the *dirt-cheap* fee of $2,500 would have fetched any other film composer five times that amount on average.

In February 1963, Sicilians Leno and Rosemary LaBianca moved into Walt Disney's former Los Feliz mansion at 4053 Woking Way. Rosemary is co-owner of the Boutique Carriage dress shop at 2625 N. Figueroa St. Leno manages the Gateway Ranch Market at 2619 N.

Figueroa St., situated at the opposite end of the same plaza. Antonio LaBianca (Leno's father) and Antonio's brother-in-law, Peter DeSantis, have owned Gateway Ranch Markets since 1952. Franzoni and company exist at the Gershwin Hotel at the corner of Western Avenue and Hollywood Boulevard, where he, in his own words—*watches television all day long, learning what LA is all about*—It is sticking like glue to this strict methodology that gives Franzoni his first glimpse into Vito's underground world of the beautiful Freaks: Vito appears on *The Steve Allen Show* over five consecutive broadcasts, sculpting a bust of the host as Allen interviews a string of guests. Two episodes were taped each day, making this a three-day gig. Upon completion of Allen's bust, Vito, Sue, and their trove of models—cloaked in Sue's sexy home-constructed bohemian *Freak* garments—are introduced on camera. The Paulekases seize the opportunity to plug their Freak boutique at 301 Laurel Ave., where cats can stop by and dig on Vito's far-out sculptures. Franzoni, watching this all on the boob tube, goes gaga.

March 4—*Steve Allen Show* talent coordinator Jerry Hopkins books a young, dapper, and suited Frank Zappa for his first television appearance. Allen interviews Zappa, who *plays a bicycle* and then publicly denounces Tim Carey and *TWGS*, the very thing that gave him even the slightest bit of musical clout beyond his sub-atomic influence in the sticks:

> I did the score for *The World's Greatest Sinner*. It's the world's worst movie, and I did the music for it. It's a Tim Carey production, Frenzy Productions. They shot it in El Monte. Tim Carey and a cast of a thousand people that he found down on Main St. someplace. We have a 55-piece orchestra, and we had a very unusual reed section, we had a contrabass clarinet, uh, two bassoons—no, four bassoons, uh, two oboes, English horn, four flutes and piccolo, uh, four trumpets, four horns, and four trombones and a tuba, and uh, I forget, there's a bunch of ... We recorded it in the Chaffey College Little Theater in Alta Loma, California. For twelve hours, we recorded it.

Carey watches it on television at home, has a breakdown, and goes *batshit* cray-cray, tearing his room apart and then crying in the arms of his wife, Doris. Vito, Hopkins, and Zappa all become pals during this taping. Two and a half weeks later, *The World's Greatest Sinner* threatens to come to a theatre in Zappa's hometown of Pomona. Local rag, *The Progress-Bulletin*, is more than happy to promote Pomona's legacy and fan the flames of vanity:

> Zappa studied music and art at Chaffey College. He wrote the score for *The World's Greatest Sinner*, a low-budget tale about a sacrilegious imposter who repents. Sinner premiered at Vista-Continental Theater, Hollywood, and opened Wednesday, March 20, 1963, at the Ken Theater, San Diego ... Zappa writes musical commercials for TV and radio. They are recorded at Pal Studio, Cucamonga.

March 21—Vito's father, Jonas, dies at 83 in Cambridge, MA, just six months after his wife, Rose. In spring, Steve Allen's art department installs a new set for the show. Vito's 13-year-old *unofficial show assistant,* Ken Patterson, is assigned to drive a pick-up truck full of discarded production materials to the dump. Patterson stops first at Vito's basement, where the Freaks dismantle the goods, adopting many of the materials for basement repairs and using others to build a raised rooftop stage. Within this mess, Patterson finds one of the original Maltese Falcon statues manufactured for the production by Century Props haphazardly piled under caked ashtrays and stained blotters. In both Dashiell Hammett's short story and John Huston's film adaptation of *The Maltese Falcon*, the bird of prey represents false wealth, enticing those greedy bastards who covet it to achieve that illusory social status by any nefarious means. The message is always the same: Those who seek it out will end up with less than nothing. Vito assists Patterson with molding the statuette, priming it for mass production (note: avians know a collection of falcons as a *cast* ... let that circular existance set in before continuing) Vito and Patterson procure a small set of replicas; the first of which went to Steve Allen (who proudly displayed the frozen bird on his on-air desk for years), and the rest were distributed as a limited series to local bookstores and private collectors. The falcon has long been the universal bird-headed sales rep for Horus.

Pacific Jazz Studio technician, tenor saxophonist, and Vito's pal, Jay Carter England, leaves LA to accept a Professor of History–Western Civilization position at NYU.

June 16—*Press-Telegram*, tonight at 11:15p, a repeat broadcast of the *Steve Allen Show with Dave Barry, Molly Bee, and sculptor Vito.*

In August of 1963, after three rocky years of marriage, Jay and *Cami* Sebring call it quits, get a divorce, and go their separate ways.

GALLOPING CANCER—Lee Harvey Oswald arrives in Jackson, Louisiana, in late September, and gets a haircut at a local barbershop on Main Street. He asks about finding work in the area and finds out that workers are always needed at the 9,000-acre potato farm that Jackson and Clinton border. Oswald is directed to go down to the Clinton Courthouse on Helena Street and register to vote. Oswald does just this, striking up a conversation with some of the negroes on line. Make no bones, Oswald is there to be seen. Oswald waits out several days until he receives the special delivery from confidante Judyth Baker, and makes for Mexico City on September 23 with the box o'bad cells, expecting to make the final exchange with a mysterious *Mr. B*, but when Hurricane Alma hits Cuba, Mr. B is unable to keep his appointment with Oswald.

John Fles curates a midnight screening of Stan Brakhage's *Dog Star Man* and Jack Smith's *Flaming Creatures.* An announcement for some comes by way of USPS mail:

> October 12, 471 years ago, Columbus discovered America. Today, you discover the New American Cinema!

This event, though not a commercial success, successfully bridges the social gap separating modern experimental films from mainstream films. Before this showing, art films were rarely screened outside of private salons, in apartment lobbies, and nightclubs.

On October 16, 1963, Lee Harvey Oswald was hired by the Texas School Book Depository Company, having applied the day before when *family friend* Ruth Paine set up an interview. Oswald earns the minimum wage of $1.25 an hour. After two weeks of filling orders under his belt, Oswald blows off steam at a Halloween party in Dallas, attending with anti-commie activist David Ferrie and a young woman (who is not Oswald's wife, Marina). Oswald's old buddy, Russian-born anti-communist George DeMohrenschildt, would have loved to have been there, but he was away on an unscheduled trip to Haiti.

A ZIPPER HIDDEN IN THE SLEEVE!—November 22, 1963. As the Presidential limo cuts through Dealey Plaza, making a wide berth onto Stemmons Freeway, the Nation will collectively transform into something that still appears human, but isn't. On the last production day of the *Gilligan's Island* pilot at Moloaa Bay in Kauai, HI, America's 35th president, John Fitzgerald Kennedy, is assassinated 3,680 miles to the east in Dallas, TX. Within 45 minutes, ex-Marine and TBD employee Lee Harvey Oswald is apprehended by Officer Nick McDonald at the Texas Theatre in the Oak Cliff neighborhood.

Nov. 25—Oswald is assassinated on live national television as he is led through the underground parking structure of the Dallas Municipal Court Building at 106 South Harwood St. Carousel Club owner Jacob Leon Rubenstein (aka Jack Ruby) is the gunman who shot Oswald point-blank in the torso with a .38mm snub-nosed revolver—the entire sacrafice was televised—Oswald is taken to Parkland Hospital, where Chief of Surgery Dr. Tom Shires opens Oswald's abdominal cavity. Surgeons McClelland and Perry assist Shires in clamping Oswald's vena cava and aorta closed. Oswald received 18 pints of type O-negative blood in a transfusion, but entered cardiac arrest mid-operation. Dr.

Perry opened Oswald's chest cavity, and he and Dr. McClelland took turns massaging Oswald's heart, doing so for nearly thirty minutes before the organ went *flabbier and flabbier.* Shires pronounces one Lee Harvey Oswald *DEAD* at 1:07p. The Cold War just got warmed up, and that nasty seven-letter word—*Communism*—is back on Americans' lips.

Kennedy had been dead for one week when on the first day of December, 1963, the New Age Harpocrates, the Magickal Egyptian Child God Horus!—GODO PAULEKAS—was born to Vito (Osiris) and Sue (Isis) in Los Angeles.

1964. THE BEGINNING OF THE END—The successful assassinations of Kennedy and Oswald, and their quick wrapping-up, proved that stovepiping is the way to go. Public celebrity deaths are both fashionable for the media and handy in invisible social manipulation. Many young Americans adjust to the paradigm shift just fine. (Edward Bernays published an abstraction of his seminal study, *Crystalizing Public Opinion*, in a 1923 medical journal detailing how his praxis as a public relations counselor helped *solve* various communal problems—Lithuania + Bernays = psych-reformation bedfellows):

> Promoting Lithuanian national identity by forming a Lithuanian National Council, disseminating information of interest respectively to intellectuals, politicians, sports fans, and other demographically profiled groups. Thus: "He reflected those communities whose crystallized opinion would be helpful in guiding other opinions, facts which gave them the basis for conclusions favorable to Lithuania.

Time may soon reveal that it will not be technology that does humanity in, nor the impending machine/human hybridization, nor the drag-race to the moon—but our total relinquish of FREE WILL—our opening of the door to Big Brother, and our invitation for them to enter, put a record on the hi-fi set, mix us a cocktail ... and then push us out of windows.

Michael Rockefeller is declared dead despite no remains ever being discovered. Some believe an alligator devoured Moneybags. Another tribe, the Asmats, claims they rowed up on the adventurer's corpse riverside, and then proceeded to eat him in a kind of roadkill-ritual-gone-wild. Some even consider that Michael survived and was taken in by a tribe, where he has lived quite comfortably ever since.

Artist Wallace Berman and his wife Shirley Morand bail on LA for good after Wallace is found guilty of obscenity charges for his *lewd* sculpture, *Temple.* Ferus Gallery owner Walter Hopps examines a sculpture that Berman gifted him before parting; inscribed on its back:

> Walter, it's a fast city.
>
> Love Wallace Berman, 1964.

NOT AS PRETTY AS YOUR PICTURE—At Ben Frank's on Sunset Boulevard, two miles from Clay Vito, Franzoni lunches with his business partner Joe Scallaci. Mary Mancini, a teacher at Immaculate Heart Catholic School in Los Feliz, catches Franzoni's horny eye. He puts his usual sticky moves on Mancini, and two days later, Franzoni and Scallaci visit Clay Vito dressed in suits like a couple of mafia goons. As instructed by Mancini, Franzoni uses a coin to tap on the window of 301 Laurel Ave. Sue Paulekas soon arrives to welcome Franzoni and Scallaci in, showing them the way down into the basement. Franzoni remembers having paid Mancini $350 for one of her paintings; the honeyfuggler hoped that his purchase counted as a down payment toward what he really wanted to take home and nail to the wall—but it didn't. Franzoni's first take on CLAY VITO—he described the basement as looking like the Texas Book Depository shown on the news at the top of every hour—its tall windows and a lofted top floor that overlooks a busy boulevard. It is the ideal sniper's nest, one that Simo Häyhä would have, well … killed for.

Franzoni meets Vito, and his interest in joining this scene is piqued.

For the next two months, Franzoni eases into the world of the Freak, first using his photographic skills to snap pics of baby Godo before attending Clay Vito's evening art classes. Franzoni suddenly finds himself surrounded by creative heavyweights like Richard Avedon, Valerie Porter, Joe DeSantis, Jack Nicholson, Dennis Hopper, Jonathan Winters, Mickey Rooney, and, of course, Burt Shonberg—students, trolls, Freaks, squares, etc., it's a diverse socialscape.

January 15, 1964—41-year-old, ex-corrupt Chicago cop aka *Captain's Man*, Elmer Valentine, uses $20,000 of his $55,000 PJ's buy-out to invest in and open the Whisky a Go Go (simply the Whisky from here on out) at 8901 Sunset Blvd. Johnny Rivers headlines a club full of dancing A-list celebs tonight.

March 7—During their raid of the Cinema Theatre on Western Avenue, the Hollywood Vice Squad seized Anger's 35mm print of *Scorpio Rising* after the film was deemed pornographic for including brief imagery of male genitalia. Vice was initially called out because of rowdy neo-Nazis who were protesting the portrayal of their flag in Anger's gay-centric short. The raid ends with film programmer Mike Getz being arrested, at least on paper, for *lewd exhibition*.

March—Vito teaches his dance class, *Can You Dig It?* in the upstairs studio of the Coronet Theatre on La Cienega Boulevard, less than one mile due west of Clay Vito. Franzoni is in attendance, claiming that famed choreographer David Winters (who portrayed A-Rab in 1961's *West Side Story*) and musician Tony Basil would sit at the back, watching the unique Freak style—and then borrowing *what they liked.* Franzoni has practiced dance with the Freaks at the Coronet for six months. Still, he stayed away from public dancing until the dancers migrated from a dancehall on Fairfax Avenue to the Trip at 8572 Sunset Blvd., near La Brea Avenue. Franzoni attempts to indoctrinate his new wife, Cecelia, into the Freak scene, but she is unwilling and uninterested and soon grows frustrated with Carl's insatiable Freak fascination. They divorce. Carl sells off the motorcycles Cecilia gifted him and ditches his bazooms-builder business to devote himself entirely to Vito's universe.

Franzoni dances his ass off among industry stars and entertainment producers at the Whisky, finding solace between the legs of a secretary and dancer named Lori Zimbal. Zimbal thinks Vito is a creep and refuses to dance with him. Vito was known to throw girls across the dance floor. Pamela DesBarres remembers keeping her distance from him out of fear of being launched without her consent.

> April 10—*San Pedro News-Pilot,* To Marvin Zeiler, the lovely models in the noon fashion show at the Tasman are just so many lines to be sketched on a pad. Zeiler is a student of cubistic art and is studying under the direction of Vito Clay in Los Angeles. Some of Zeiler's works are now being shown at the Lee-Verne Gallery in Beverly Hills.

April 16—31-year-old Franzoni marries 23-year-old Lori Zimbal.

May 7—In Hollywood, American jazz alto saxophonist Joe Maini (Hebrew; *bitter, rebellious*) *accidentally takes his life* by sucking on a pistol as a joke; the punchline—his brains on the ceiling. Vito, a long-time friend of Maini's, believes otherwise, insisting that one of his basement rats—Mary Mancini, the siren who first pointed Franzoni to the basement—was fatally attracted to and obsessed with the married musician, and it was Mancini who drove Maini to suicide—Vito alleges that Mancini harassed the musician by calling him at home at all hours.

Early May. GET ANTIZONKED, BABY. Vito and his studio are getting beacoup write-ups in local and national publications. The Freak lifestyle is depicted on television programs all over the world. The UK and its subsidiaries now have a master mould for their counter-culture takeover, just as soon as the other side of the pond is ready to be destroyed. In May, British journalist Alan Whicker of *Whicker's World* makes a trip for the BBC to interview Vito and Sue Paulekas at their Beverly Boulevard bunker. This is a perfect time for the Freaks to play it up for the world. Vito is immediately depicted as a cat-suited dance instructor choreographing a series of jerky, balletic steps, which his Freak Dance Troupe, of a dozen or so in tow, replicate as best they can. This is all for the TV crew, as Vito usually conducts dance class at the Coronet Theatre. Some familiar faces are present: Franzoni is positioned directly behind Vito. Hair stylist Sheldon Jaman is next to Franzoni. Sue is, of course, there, following intently:

> VITO: Left, right, left. Right, left, right. Now, really get fixed every time you bring your head back. Left, right, left ... Right, left, right ... Left, right, left ... Right, left, right ... Now we'll do it with a little jump. So its like this, and ... [whispering] Right, left, right ... and ... Right, left, right ... and ...
>
> WHICKER [V.O.]: This aging face upon a youthful body belongs to Vito, perhaps the oldest, most elusive hippie. A brilliant sculptor, he runs a Los Angeles troupe that gives Freak-out dance performances at happenings. His wife Sue, aged 25, awaits their second child. Like all hippies, they attack the middle-aged values of their land of milk and money, its worship of property, and questioning the acceptance of the quick buck and the ultimate achievement of a three-car garage. Conventionally unconventional, hippies repudiate most of society's uplifting moralities: the family, patriotism, chastity, the sanctity of marriage, and respect for the law. They deny the right and confidence of parents, schools, and governments to make decisions for everyone. A far-out arch hippie, but the only one I'd met who is also against LSD.

Though Whicker remains unseen for most of this interview, he is felt, leering off-screen; on occasion, appearing for a few frames, leaning in for a closer look at Vito's lived-in face. Vito holds court, lounging in his comfortable hole, filling the frame with a smiling intensity that holds the close-up shot for its entirety. Vito manages to keep it together, even knowing that his Frankenstein's Monster has strayed—the free lovers have soured, gone to bad seed and shit, and it's just the beginning:

VITO: I think of it as an escape from the good things that are happening around us and the bad things that are happening around us. Most of us need to get away from the bad things that are happening around us. I haven't any quarrels ... One of the kids, for example, a teenager, will come to me and say; *Hey Vito, you're gonna be bugged.* Bugged about what? He says; *I got loaded on some LSD last night. I got wasted on some LSD last night.* They say so themselves. Listen to them; they'll tell you what's happening behind that stuff. They use words like *wasted,* and *I fell out behind some LSD.* So I think that getting loaded behind any kind of junk like that is to evade your responsibilities as a human being. Listen, if you're loaded behind L.S.D. or some of those other hard, what I consider hard junk, you don't want to do anything except just sit back and contemplate, you know, something else. I have paintings around here by a guy who is a very dear friend of mine [BURT SHONBERG], and he's a groovy artist when he's straight, and he'll tell you if you ask him; hey, man, how 'bout you getting loaded behind some L.S.D.? And he'll say; *Oh, yeah, man ... I really found new kinds of things ...* And it isn't true because when he is loaded behind that stuff, he doesn't do anything. He just stands there looking into space, man. You know, you could push him, and he might fall down, but he isn't doing anything. People who are loaded behind that kind of thing don't do anything. This HEAVY KIND OF INSISTENCE every place you go...with all the media about; *WOW! Look at the colors! Look at the lights! Look at the strobe things blinking, man! ... You can really find a trip if you get loaded behind this stuff.* There's a lot of that kind of thing insisting that we become aware of it, that we become sensitive to it. And a lot of the young people are sensitive to it, and they become curious about it. So they say, *which of it is bad?* I say, man, ALL OF IT IS BAD! But if you HAVE TO HAVE IT ... If you need to relax, I'm not gonna put grass down. Marijuana isn't that bad. A girl stopped me not too long ago, and she had a bumper sticker that said, LET'S LEGALIZE MARIJUANA! She says, *Hey, you want this, Vito? Will you put this on your car?* Heheh! I'M NOT INTERESTED IN PROPAGANDIZING AND LEGALIZING MARIJUANA! THE WORLD IS FALLING DOWN AROUND US! PEOPLE ARE GOOFING AROUND WITH THAT ATOM BOMB BUTTON, AND SHE'S ASKING ME IF I AM INTERESTED IN LEGALIZING MARIJUANA! I'm not interested; it doesn't

> motivate me that way. I'm interested in so many other things. I'm interested in the jeopardy and the threat of this establishment where they're taking young people and slapping them into concentration camps that they call Army Camps, and those that they don't are slapped into a concentration camp like that are sent off to Vietnam to be killed or kill somebody else! And the ones that are left walking on the streets are being terrorized by the police! This is the culture, you know. The kid says; *NO, BABY, ARE YOU OUT OF YOUR MIND! Forget about it! I'm gonna find something that's gonna make me nice and rosey and zonk me out, and I'm gonna sit down on the floor somewhere where it's not too cold, and I'm just gonna get wiped out ... AND STAY WIPED OUT, BABY ... AND NOTHING'S GONNA GET THROUGH TO ME!*

In mid to late May 1964, Franzoni first met the then still-nobody, Frank Zappa, and the other Mothers, at Ben Frank's. They are a gang of hat-donning young baldies, hailing from the boonies. Just a few weeks back, on Mother's Day in fact, the Pomona-based R&B group, The Soul Giants, replaced saxophonist David Coronado with Zappa after a nasty dispute erupted between Coronado and lead vocalist, Ray Collins. The new line-up: Zappa and Ray Hunt are on guitar, Collins supplies vocals, Roy Estrada plays bass, and Jimmy Carl Black bangs the drums. While Vito has been working for decades, fine-tuning his outfit, exhausted from getting his Freak-on, this little Pomona punk, Zappa—who hasn't done shit but burn bridges that he didn't even build—makes the best decision of his short life. As the new head of operations, Zappa recommended they ditch the R&B covers grossly associated with their old incarnation, and instead inaugurate HIS original material—*Play my music, and I will make you all rich and famous—also, we're changing our name to Muthas.*

May 23—The *LA Free Press* (*FREEP* from here on out) publication appears for the first time as an eight-page tabloid sold during a KPFK fundraiser at the annual Los Angeles Renaissance Pleasure Faire and May Market.

June 1964—Vito and Sue become involved in the filming of Robert

Carl Cohen's pseudo-documentary/recruitment film, *Mondo Hollywood,* after Zappa's manager, NYC-based artist Mark Cheka (who already booked The Muthas for the film), recommends that Cohen consider exploiting the Paulekas's, his studio, and the Freaks. Principal photography begins on the Summer Solstice.

July—CWS's *The Pilgrimage Play* is performed for the last time after the Civil Liberties Union sought injunctions against LA County for spending taxpayers' money on religious-based performances. Using county-controlled venues on city-owned land is ruled in direct violation of the separation of church and state. Not entirely unrelated, there is a link to *The Pilgrimage Play*, Kenneth Anger, and his civil liberties violations—Anger tells the story that the 1949 Frank Stayer feature film version of the *Pilgrimage Play* (shot entirely at the Pilgrimage Play Theatre and surrounding Cahuenga hills standing in for Jerusalem) anonymously appeared on Anger's doorstep, and after its review, Anger felt a creative obligation to shoehorn this divine intervention into his most recent work, *Scorpio Rising*—resulting in sporatic segments of Nelson Leigh—as Christ, sometimes performing miracles, sometimes taking a late-nite donkey ride—intercut throughout the 28-minute film with radical hippie bikers as they prepare for critical mass. It was this exact smashing together of images that has since made *Scorpio Rising* the masthead in Art and Media's battle to protect the First Amendment.

Summer—Byrds manager Jim Dickson has the keys to Dick Bock's World Pacific Studios at 8715 West Third St.—one mile southeast of the Troubadour and one mile in the opposite direction to Clay Vito. Dickson is allowed to use the facility after hours for band rehearsals and demo tracking. This is the same studio that Ravi Shankar recorded his first American releases in the mid-1950s. The Byrds listened to some of Shankar's half-inch tape masters in the studio when recording their own demos. Clay Vito-patron-turned-record producer, Terry Melcher, takes an immediate interest in implementing Shankar's eastern dynamics into the Byrds' debut album.

BOLT-ACTION // ACROSS ALAMO ALLEY

Alas, we arrive at the intersection of time when this confounded task was first put to T-d in MEXICO in August of 1964. T-d has just been visited by a pair of CIA goons, and coerced into formulating their official PONSONBY COMMISSION REPORT narrative, a timeline intent on exposing a potential former FBI asset who wasn't properly burned, and so now the Agency needs a juicy ending before this artist-cum-dancer who has learned to make demands of his own, does some very real, very irreversible national security damage. The unlikely-but-legitimate offer loops in T-d's mind as he rummages through a footlocker in the cramped lobby del hotel. For a moment, his obsessive cycle is interrupted, switching to disappointment when he discovers that a return message he was expecting from a Seattle chum (one of the few) had not arrived. Despite most of us knowing T-d's eventual trajectory, you wouldn't look at this unremarkable American of settler blood, and immediately, or perhaps ever, think--"now, there goes a fella destined to enter the annals of post-modernists, seated at the right hands of Foucault, Barth and Eco,"—but alas ... T-d has been a Mexican refugee for nearly two years, holed up with his recently divorced lady-friend OCTAVIA LISTENS, wasting his days sleeping, and then most nights translating a private collector's archive of unpublished poems by Borges and Márquez.

Our MAN weaves the quiet Mexican streets toward his hogar on Colonia in Quintana Roo. He is nervous and jumpy, paranoid about the uncertainties wrapped up in his agreement, the one he is forbidden to blab about to VIA. He can't yet illustrate for her just how much this goes against his core philosophical and moral principles, but, eh … getting published, ain't just whistlin' Dixie. The question, put to any novelist worth a damn, would have been answered the same in a heartbeat, but, VIA, she could never comprehend how sweet the honey they slathered on his smokes was. It's his own fault, really; the success of his first novel, published one year ago in March of '63, put T-d not only on the national literary radar, but also on the adoring US Federal Government's. COAK's story went: the folks over at VIRUS were very impressed with the research skills that T-d exhibited in his debut novel. COAK read aloud a notation he made while interviewing former Boeing co-workers: "Subject is long-haired, mustachioed, and dresses drably. HE is distinguished not for his fashion sense, but for his meticulous and tireless research that is unmatched within the corporation ranks."

Okay, that's not horrible, definitely could have gone worse. And then it does—"I'm not finished … 'Subject is remembered as difficult, ornery, solitary, and very, very pale'."

Damn, those truths cut deep.

He'd put money on VIA going all Marina Oswald on the miserable writer, and he is having trouble enough. To think she dumped the good life for this, indicating with her turned-up chin that her dig comes straight from Snootsville, where she grew up and hopped a golden chariot to here, Mexico, just to torment him. She earned a degree in Engineering Physics and a Bachelor of Arts from Cornell—"don't forget". Well, how could he? T-d reminds VIA that he has one of those as well—"Then why do you write all night and sleep all day?"—He's devolved back to stapling black sheets over all the windows and doors and cracks. He's going vampirical and losing all concern for vitamin D. She can't be in here during the day. Besides, he neglects her. She just wants a good fuck. She hates this life, and the money coming in from book sales of his first novel is not nearly enough for them to live on. She moves on to a new theme, taking superficial potshots, like his drab dressing style, and he could have used some of that advance to get his Bugs Bunny grill aligned. Like, relax, lady! T-d bites his lip, itching to tell VIA everything, but no, no, no ... she's gonna have to wait to read about it in *The Times*, like everyone else.

Without noticing that his pace has slowed from a brisk plank-knee shuffle to a smooth stroll, T-d draws within a block of home. The last beams of twilight are absorbed into the impossibly deep blue night sky. And then, as if bumping into a primary schoolmate after years of dodging, T-d takes hyper-notice of a Ford Econoline van parked near the corner bodega. Throughout the past week, the out-of-place vehicle (OOPV) has flopped street sides several times, but maintained, always, that its fogged headlights face T-d's casa, drilling an invisible aural hole through the front door. Tonight, T-d will have to side-step the van since it has been pulled up on the sidewalk. As T-d passes, he makes note of the lack of plates and tags. Freshly painted across both side panels, in a wild typeface:

EL PROGRAMA DE SUPERCAN

PRESENTADO POR GENERAL MILLS BRAND CEREALS

— SÁBADO POR LA MAÑANA! —

At least a dozen times, T-d has witnessed dead drops of leaflets and postcards wedged under the van's windshield wiper blades. Larger items are tucked into the wheel cab. This whole thing is beginning to stink of the *Time Life Magazine* ambush that befell the 25-year-old last March at the Hotel Central in Guanajuato, only two weeks after Lippencott had published his bestseller. It was an ambush which T-d appropriately foiled and escaped photographic capture by bussing it to a small mountain village eight hours away, where he remained, lower than the red dirt, for eight weeks before returning to his trusted lookout-landlady's property. Obtaining exposure and intrigue and rock star status the world over is something NOBODY would accuse T-d of, much less assume that he possesses the necessary wiring for positive social interplay, or even starting a conversation.

Anyway, after latching the front door in place, T-d fingers the window shades, splitting them just enough to watch the van for a few moments longer. He makes a promise to himself that if it's still there when he awakens tomorrow evening, he's gonna make a stink about it.

Yes, sir, a right proper stink.

• •

September 18, 1964—The reworked Warren Commission is released nearly a year after Kennedy's murder, officially naming Lee Harvey Oswald as the lone assassin.

Oct. 1—Works by Vito and his students are featured in a sculpture exhibition at the Family Savings and Loan Association. An advertisement appears on page 45 of the *California Eagle*:

> SCULPTURE EXHIBIT—45 outstanding sculptured pieces will be in the Community Room throughout October for you to view. Works by prominent sculptors Vito Clay, Marvin Zeiler, Eva Lengyel, and Yolanda Lengyel. You'll enjoy this unique collection of sculptured pieces. Another exciting event for you from Family Savings.

In November of 1964, the Freak scene had been fairly established, and Vito's friends and their bands were nationally recognized, firmly stabilizing Vito's footing in attaining his dream of living as a full-time bohemian. Vito books a rock show at The Interlude club on Melrose Avenue. Now all he needs is a rock band to perform. He auditions many bands in the basement, but it's a surf-rock band, The Tarantulas, that gets the Freaks a'movin—the band's name is derived from the Italian choreomania that has swept the countryside for hundreds of years. Well, that's convenient, yes?—Right about then, Melcher approaches Vito asking a favor: he has this East Coast band, the Byrds, that are hard-up for a rehearsal space ... maybe Vito would let them use the basement? ... *Okay*, Vito agrees to give the band a shot, but they gotta pass muster. He's got a gig lined up; it will be the perfect opportunity for the Byrds to sharpen their beaks. Vito's only stipulation: do not be late. But, of course, the relationship gets off on a sprained wing when the band misses their first audition at Clay Vito. To scare the Greenwich boys into straightening up and flying right, Vito sends over Sam Hanna (another tenant in the Smith Building), a big, rough-and-tumble character actor who has appeared in *Naked City* in 1958 (and will soon appear in Russ Meyer's *Mudhoney*). Except for David Crosby and Jim McGuinn, the band members are dirt poor, barely existing in an above-the-garage apartment on the fringes of Beverly Hills near Doheny Drive. Vito's miniature psy-op works, and within a couple of days, the Byrds serenade devening patrons of Clay Vito, primarily sophomores and freshmen of Fairfax High.

November—It has been a good art year for Burt Shonberg, too. He has separated from the witch/artist Cameron and is garnering painting gigs aplenty, swathing the exteriors of LA and Bay Area clubs in purple and orange stripes and splotches. Public buildings, youth hangouts, and billboards become his new canvases. Shonberg paints a custom billboard ad on Sunset Boulevard and La Brea Avenue, and then he paints the exterior of *a very funky place right across the street from Ralph's.* He paints teen hangout favorite, Pandora's Box, lining the exterior walls with wide alternating lavender and lilac vertical stripes. He paints San Francisco's North Beach Beat, and one of Lenny Bruce's favorite spots to perform, The Purple Onion. Shonberg gives Bido Lito's in Hollywood's Cosmo Alley a facelift, and the Bastille and Seven Chefs, too. Shonberg executes a handful of magazine advertisements and record album sleeves.

1965. Clay Vito's rooftop theatre (like Voltaire's home Petit Theatre) employs guests as stagehands, and others are cast in parts ranging from heroes to villains. Vito and Freaks built the tiny stage and enclosure from leftover and reclaimed building materials collected over the years. Franzoni (illegally) lives in the defunct elevator room on the rooftop, near the makeshift stage, having quickly secured his position as Vice-Freak.

Jerry Hopkins buys into the hippie lifestyle, leaving behind his suit-and-tie work as a television producer/writer to open the first headshop in the Westwood district of Los Angeles, Hopkins' Headquarters. His head shop is one of only three operating nationwide. Shonberg is employed to paint the joint's exterior and floors, of course.

April 12. PROTEST AS PROFIT—The Byrds release their first single, produced by Melcher, *Mr. Tambourine Man.* The track is an immediate and enormous success, and Vito seizes his fortuitous position right now and gets the Byrds-ball rolling, renting out the upstairs comedy club of Elmer Valentine's new dancehall, The Trip. (The Trip replaced The Crescendo when the jazz club's owner ditched the nightlife industry to focus on producing albums for GNP Crescendo Records.) The comedy club above The Trip is another one of Bruce's favorite spots to kill at: The Interlude. Frequent headliners there included Chico Hamilton, Lord Buckley, and Clay Vito junkie Jonathan Winters. The Interlude's interior was designed to resemble a Catholic church. Vito plastered the faux-holy walls with thirty STOP THE WAR! signs, a kind of guerrilla activism-by-art long before anti-this & anti-that signage became commonplace at these types of venues.

On May 25, 1965, over 200 music-starved teens show up at the Interlude and fork over the $1.50 cover charge, of which a dollar from each finds its way to the band to be split; the leftover 50 cents goes directly into Vito's polyester-lined pockets. Franzoni recalls that the Byrds were *the first white rock and roll group with that kind of music and dance that they could relate to. They could have started their own church with the kind of music they were playing.* Thrilled with the night's success, Byrd's manager Jim Dickson invites Vito and his Freaks dancers to repeat their performance at Ciro's, booked for the next night.

On May 26, the Byrds perform in Ciro's giant 40'x25', all-red room, lined with leather booths. Attendees included: Sue Lyons, Sonny and Cher, Jack Nicholson, and Peter Fonda. Vito and Franzoni show up with 15 dancers, one of whom is 18-year-old Robert *Beatle Bob* Roberts; his lanky 6'6", 180 lbs. fame capped by a pageboy haircut, makes an impression difficult to forget.

Vito greedily tries a couple of weeks later to repeat his teen-dance triumph, but the police show up and shut the whole damn thing down, citing Vito for *holding an illegal dance party*; a charge he contests in court, but gets slapped with a suspended sentence and banned from ever hosting another *teen dance in Hollywood.*

Sebring's making the television rounds and feeling very comfortable in his unique celebrity. On June 21, Sebring is a guest on the half-hour morning variety program, the *Gypsy Rose Lee Show*, and then in nine more days, he appears on the show again, this time alongside comedian Paul Lynde.

July—Despite the judicial injunction against him, Vito forks over $400 to rent out Dave Hull's Hullaballoo; he's got another teen dance in the works.

Franzoni, *Beatle Bob* Roberts, and his barely-legal girlfriend, Karen, shadow the Byrds during their first two-week tour of the Bay Area. The dancers-on-loan often work the floor for three-hour stretches as the Byrds belt out half a dozen sets each night. Franzoni recounts that during performances of *Hey Joe,* the Freaks would go into the wildest, most primitive screaming fits, turning the club chaotic in an instant.

YOU CAN BE IN LOVE WITH ANYONE—In early August of 1965, Dickson approaches Franzoni, asking again for him and some Freak dancers to tag along for the band's *Mr. Tambourine Man* tour. Franzoni consults Vito about joining them this time, but the elder Freak declines as he has *business to take care of.* Franzoni and Roberts tagged along on a 30-day Midwest tour—beginning with them being dumped in Denver, CO, to then dance their way east by bus through Wyoming, Nebraska, Iowa, and Minnesota, keeping on starward to their hub—Chicago—before heading south to Ohio, Kentucky, Indiana, and Missouri. Early on, Franzoni and Roberts managed to collect five teenage girls as additional *dancers*. Byrds' roadie Bryan MacLean is young and talented, and wildly good with girls. He makes quite the impression, and by all logical accounts, is next in line to join the band should a mutiny arise.

The Byrds play to a crowd of 2,000 patrons who have yet to witness anything like this Freak show before. Barney Hoskyns credits—*the roving troupe of self-styled freaks led by ancient beatnik Vito Paulekas and his trusty, lusty sidekick Carl Franzoni*—with a great deal of the initial success of the Byrds. At the conclusion of the tour, Jim *Roger* McGuinn harbors concerns about the Freak dancers stealing the band's thunder and feels they are becoming reliant on their ancillary support. Franzoni felt burned by not being more involved in the performances, plus getting stiffed on all-you-can-eat free-lovin'. When Franzoni returned to LA and picked up his check, he was informed that his services would no longer be needed. And just like that, the Byrds' global success severed them from the Freaks. They went off to tour the planet, leaving the golden geese behind.

Broken clean away from the now world-famous Byrds, Vito and Franzoni search for another mainstay, settling for the time being on Arthur Lee's LA-based band, The Grass Roots, and according to Freak Dancer, Kim Fowley, The Grass Roots used Vito's basement studio as their exclusive practice space. Arthur Lee even lived in the Smith Building for a short while as the band evolved into its influential proto-interracial entity, Love. The band's biggest fan, a 17-year-old kouros named Bobby Beausoleil, was added to the line-up on rhythm guitar after Beausoleil accosted Lee following a performance. Beausoleil only lasted as the band's rhythm guitarist for three weeks, never making it to a recording session with Lee. Bryan MacLean has been a roadie for Arthur Lee ever since flying the Byrds alongside Franzoni. With the support of Vito and Franzoni, Beausoleil is removed from the band on account of *being too green for the scene* (or so says Beausoleil), and MacLean is folded in as rhythm guitarist. Lee expounds:

> People say I was a strict leader with Love. But a rhythm guitarist has no right to do anything but play rhythm guitar if that's all he knows how to do. I write, produce, sing, and play guitar, drums, and piano, and I wouldn't attempt to do

> anything I couldn't cut. If you're just a rhythm guitar player, don't tell me what to put in my song! ... I have everyone's part planned out. Some people disagree with their parts. But I want what I wrote. And if there's something wrong with that, then I'm strict. That's why I've changed groups so many times. I try to get cats who want to participate in things I've written.

Beausoleil claims that *in an effort to smooth things over,* Lee changed the band's name to—Love—in honor of Bobby's ridiculous and ill-fitting nickname, *Cupid.* Lee gives a very different reason for the new moniker; the Almighty itself instructed him—*Love on earth must be.* It also didn't help that another band named Grass Roots (sans the *The*) was already getting some groovy attention in LA. MacLean moves into an apartment in the Smith Building.

Sep. 2—The Doors record their first demo at Dick Bock's World Pacific Studios. Bock is responsible for making many seminal live jazz recordings available during the 1950s, before moving on to release mega-influential world music (namely Ravi Shankar). The studio is in yet another transitional state in response to the sudden upswing in rock and roll bands flooding the market.

Sep. 5—San Francisco journalist Michael Fallon coins the term—*hippie*—in his article, which focuses on the Blue Unicorn, a popular Bay Area meeting spot for counterculture groups, such as LEMAR and The Sexual Freedom League. *Hippie* was subsequently popularized in a *San Francisco Chronicle* article by Herb Caen, who had coined the term *beatnik* for the same publication just seven years earlier. Caen used *hippie* to describe the youth movement that clutches onto archaic *beatnik* propaganda; so he kinda scores coming or going. Despite Caen being a major proponent of Lenny Bruce, Vito undoubtedly harbors measurable animosity toward this label being blanket-applied to himself, his Freaks, and other innocent participants. Even Beausoleil never considered himself a hippie, but rather a bohemian. Arthur Lee claims the same. It's all semantics, but Vito is losing a grip on his social and professional identity, and he is beginning to feel used just as he did in the military and with special operations.

> Sep. 23—*Reno Evening Gazette*, Radio Interview Ends With Fight—LOS ANGELES—A fistfight broke up a radio program discussion last night between moderator Joe Pyne and actor-producer Timothy Carey. Carey, 36, was being interviewed about a controversial movie, *The World's Greatest Sinner*, in which he plays the part of a singer turned evangelist. Pyne, 39, who welcomes telephoned comments during his programs, asked Carey to leave, and Carey did not go. "Then about four or five strongarm guys pulled me up by the seat of my pants and flung me out bodily," Carey said. Pyne was struck in the chest by the receiver of a telephone. "I just used the telephone in self-defense," Carey said. A spokesman for the radio station KLAC said the clash came after an interview of more than 1 1/2 hours.

I'M MR. BLUE—Vito redirects his energies from sculpting clay into sculpting thought, beginning with the newly accepted and lucrative platform of Blue movie-making. Initially, Vito's contributions to the medium are purely aesthetic, providing a subterranean shooting location and sculptures to art departments.

Sep. 28—*The Beach Girls and the Monster* premieres. The creature-feature tells the story of a misunderstood, foreboding mad sculptor (go figure) who dresses up as a cave-dwelling monster and attacks random girls partying on the beach—clawing at their faces, killing them. The film depicts clay busts suffering brutal face-scratchings and on-camera destruction. Vito contributed pieces for use on screen as examples of the tormented sculptor's skills, but he goes uncredited. It is worth noting that Margo Lynn Sweet is one of the Whisky dancers *supplied* to American Academy Productions by Elmer Valentine. His dancers are the titular *Beach Girls* who get it throughout the B-movie.

On October 1, Timothy Carey is again interviewed about *The World's Greatest Sinner* (*TWGS*), but this time by *Freep,* which is not much more forgiving than Joe Pyne. (Lest we not forget that it's probably in the magazine's best interest not to bite the teat that nourishes the sucklings.) The public's ideal of what *rock gods* are is an ever-evolving concept, a moving goalpost that performers like Elvis Presley, once on the bleeding edge of cool, are now antiquated and sprinting to keep their beautiful fat asses up with it. Page nine of this same *Freep* issue features a sliver of an advertisement: Cinema Theatre is showing *TWGS*, *plus* Stanley Kubrick's *Lolita.* Of Kubrick's six features to date, Carey appears in two—*The Killing* + *Paths of Glory*—and in both instances as the most memorable supporting characters.

Tonight, the Byrds, Barry McGuire, and Grass Roots play The Trip. The Byrds are priming Los Angeles for an upcoming extended two-week run at The Trip, a venue they played long before the Whisky; a clear indicator of how the two clubs were aimed at different audiences, but Valentine (who owns both) is prepared to make significant changes in policies to maximize his influence, in accordance with the Stripture. Melcher remembers:

> The Byrds were the catalyst—they brought all the kids to the Strip ... They took the Dylan songs, we electrified 'em and rock 'n' rolled 'em, and kids came from everywhere. It just happened. One day, you couldn't drive anymore. It was, like, overnight—you couldn't drive on the Strip.

1966. BYE, BYE BYRD BRAINS—Like some modern-day Rasputin, our counterculture snake charmer from the loading docks, Vito Alphonse Paulekas, is lapped up by higher society, welcomed in with open wallets into places that this third-hand-clothes Freak always dreamed of infiltrating, but never expected to be the guest of honor! Celebs (or those on the up 'n up) pop in on Clay Vito on any given evening. Vito is becoming the barber, inching close enough to the king to whisper societal seeds into his ear. His Freak Dance Troupe now includes teenage vixen Pamela Miller and the highly coveted Rory Flynn, nymph daughter of promiscuous swashbuckler, Errol Flynn. Franzoni has taken to wearing a black cape to which he has embroidered a giant *F,* which he says stands for the *Fuck* in his new identity—*Captain Fuck.* Music manager and record producer Kim Fowley is still around, and so is Vito's oldest LA friend, Sheldon Jaman. Some visitors like Bob Roberts never leave. One anonymous young studio visitor remembers:

> My family had just moved to Los Angeles from the Midwest (in 1966). We moved to West Hollywood, Genesee near Beverly Blvd. A block from CBS TV Studios. One night, our friend Gene came by and asked if my brother Charlie and I wanted to see something interesting. We walked about 3 blocks to Laurel Ave., to the "sculpture & garment" shop, and entered the world of Vito and Szou. The first time I saw Szou, she was standing at the foot of the stairs wearing a beautiful macro-may dress with a see-through top. She was blonde, with short bangs. Utterly beautiful. She hardly paid attention to us as we made our way downstairs to the studio. Once downstairs, we noticed a sculpture studio filled with strange-looking pieces of sculpture, and an old man, Vito, talking animatedly with his hand gestures filling the air. There were many guests, both very straight-looking and those whose clothing suggested a bohemian lifestyle. We would sit on the rickety couch for hours, just watching. Every once in a while, Szou would come downstairs and wrap her arms around Vito. It looked odd. A guy in his 60s with a chick about 20. It was certainly not your ordinary couple. Their son Godot was a 2-year-old blonde moppet wandering around the studio, stark naked, and filthy as can be. Vito & Sue couldn't care less. One night, we were all down there, once again observing, and I saw Godot walk towards a chunk of gray potter clay. He began to stick it in his mouth. I ran over and pulled it away before he could swallow it. He began to cry. Suddenly, Szou looked over and, in a panic, began to scream at me. "What are you doing to my baby?" I told her that Godot was just about to eat the clay. She began screaming again, calling me a liar. A very strange, neurotic woman. I never saw her laugh or smile.

The Freaks outgrow Ben Frank's restaurant and migrate to Canter's Deli, which is struggling to pull in eaters. Overnight, the late-night Freak-eaters turn Canter's into *the* Hollywood wee-hours hot spot to spy a movie star sucking down lox and breaking matzo.

Arthur Lee has lived in the Smith Building with Vito for a while now, and they have developed a mutual admiration. Vito arranges a private Love show at Bido Lito (1608 Cosmo St., in East Hollywood) for Electra Records executive Jac Holzman. This venue has become so popular in recent years that both ends of the alley are closed, and a cover charge is in effect to listen to the performing bands from outside. Holzman signs Love, becoming the first rock act to join Elektra Records since the label's founding 16 years earlier.

Jan. 12—R.L. Frost's sexploitation mockumentary *Mondo Freudo* premieres. Margo Lynn Sweet, a Whisky dancer and one of the *beach girls* in *The Beach Girls and the Monster*, appears in the film as a topless Watusi dancer, serving drinks to businessmen on luncheons.

During January, the Freaks wail hell on the Whisky's newly renovated raised stage. The distinction between patrons and performers of Valentine's two venues couldn't be more different. The Byrds have moved on from the Whisky, and the Freaks, as a community, have ditched the Byrds.

Jan. 24 thru 27—Love records their debut self-titled album at Sunset Sound Recorders at 6650 Sunset Blvd., 3.2 miles east of Clay Vito. Holzman co-produces the album. One-time superfan and temporary rhythm guitarist, Bobby Beausoleil, is nowhere to be found during these sessions, having finally taken the hint to move on.

February 1, 1966—14-year-old El Monte, CA youth Steven Earl Parent is taken into LAPD custody as the prime suspect in a string of school vandalism and burglaries.

In tomorrow's edition of the *Los Angeles Times*:

> YOUTH, 14, HELD IN 6 SCHOOL BURGLARIES—EL MONTE. A 14-year-old El Monte youth was in custody Tuesday on suspicion of burglarizing one school and possibly six here. Police were called to investigate six-weekend school burglaries, ranging from theft of a $223 television set to undetermined amounts of change. Investigating officers said the television set was taken from a room at the Cogswell School, 11050 Fineview St. The room was also sprayed with red paint, which covered desks, the floor, and a blackboard, police said. At Arroyo High School, 4921 Cedar Ave., padlocks were pried from outdoor vending machines near the student activities building, and an undetermined amount of change was taken. A burglary at Mountain View High School, 2850 N. Mountain View Road, resulted in a loss of $10 in stamps from the attendance office. Theft of a stapler and benzene torch were reported from Columbia School, 3400 N. California Ave. An obscene message was written in chalk on one chalkboard, officers said. At the Baker School, 12043 Exline St., a burglar entered by taking the molding from an office window. The burglar then took $1 in change, $1 in stamps, a $5 stopwatch, and a dozen ice cream bars from a classroom and a cafeteria.

Lenny Bruce is the guest speaker at the UCLA campus on February 9. He produces an item from his pocket and holds it up to the audience as proof:

> I brought a picture out here. It says, "Support your local police." You probably have seen the picture. It's a picture of Southerners. And what a lot of people in the North aren't hip to is that Southerners are less sophisticated than Northerners, and they smile when they see a camera. So people in the north figure, well, uh, you know … they're being sort of surly when they're not. They're just shit-kickers, and that's the way they look, and uh … they're not being snotty at all. And not knowing about the geography in the south … that's happened to Melvin Belli, you know …

The February 11, 1966 edition of the *The Los Angeles Evening Citizen News* features a photo of a staunch Vito standing at the head of a crowd, draped in a shiny blouse that Sue do doubt procured; his strong, old left arm raised, his hand making the global symbol for—*GUN*—aiming his finger at the committee as if taking a practice shot:

> LEADERS GROPE FOR SOLUTION TO HOLLYWOOD JUVENILE CRIME—Among those attending were a group calling themselves "The Hands," led by controversial spokesman Vitantas Alphonse Paulekas, 53, who owns an artist school at 303 N. Laurel Ave., Hollywood. Handbills, signed "The Hands," reading "Stop Police Terror," were distributed in the area earlier this month. Paulekas blasted the panel of six during a five-minute speech from the floor in which he termed the activities of the police department "a conspiracy of terror." Told by moderator Capt. Charles Crumly said that he would have to confine his comments to the subject of what a community can do to aid in law enforcement. Paulekas and his 25 followers walked out of the meeting without incident.

Vito's enigmatic name for his clan—*The Hands*—may be a reference to Antonio Mirabito's Sicilian mafia extortion ring—*Black Hands*—who were HQed near Boston. Why is Vito telling the paper that he goes by *Vitantas Alphonse* after he has been constructing this singular VITO persona? Is this a Jekyll/Hyde distinction? Is he in a state of re-invention, or is he running ... or is he hiding in plain sight?

February 25 thru March 10—Love plays the Whisky with The Leaves.

March—Vito and his Freaks attend the *Mondo Hollywood* wrap party at director Robert Cohen's Talmadge Avenue rental in the beautiful former Gabrielinos/Tongvas village now called Los Feliz. Many celebrities are in attendance, and the Mothers perform as tonight's house band. Cohen films the entire party, intending to shoehorn as much as he can into his propaganda. Cohen hunkers down in his garage for the next several months to whittle down the 22 hours of silent footage he shot over the last two years. Cohen and Vito have become close acquaintances and pal around Hollywood on the regular during the construction of *Mondo Hollywood.*

March 8 thru 12—Record producer Tom Wilson signs the Mothers to Verve Records, enforcing the first of many stipulations—that Zappa adds *of Invention* to the tail of their name (henceforth MOI). It is around this time that long-time friend and manager Mark Cheka is succeeded by Herbie Cohen and his lawyer brother, Martin *Mutt* Cohen. MOI's debut album, *Freak Out!,* was recorded at TTG studios in Hollywood. From 2:00p to 5:00p on March 12, the final five songs are tracked. Both *Help I'm A Rock* and *Return of the Son of Monster Magnet* required the participation of Vito and a dozen of his Freaks that he brought along—one of whom is Bobby Beausoleil, who makes a second play at the Freak-life, finding Zappa's zaniness refreshing compared to that hard-ass, Lee:

> I knew Frank on a casual basis. When I was 16-17, I used to follow him around, haunting his early recording sessions with the Mothers and, when he would let me, hanging out at his apartment listening to the wild-ass tapes he made. I was in awe of his musical talent, ability to lead unruly musicians, and his musicians, vision as a composer. He also made me laugh a lot. As you note, I found a guitar and taught myself to play. When I knew Frank, he was just beginning to pick up the guitar. At that point, I was a better guitar player, but his musical knowledge was miles beyond what I knew. He wouldn't let me join the band—he said because I didn't know how to read music.

March 14—The Byrds release their single *Eight Miles High* to critical and popular acclaim, skyrocketing record sales, but founding member and golden-egg songwriter Gene Clark has had enough of Crosby and announces his resignation from the band. Clark is simply another human being who wants to either kill the fucking shit out of

David Crosby or take their chances going solo. To our chagrin, Clark chose the latter.

April—Love plays to a receptive crowd at the Whisky. The Doors play three clubs west at the much seedier dive, The London Fog. Doors drummer, John Densmore, is too broke to cover the admission charge to the Whisky, so he watched Lee and the boys through the gap between the front doors—*I really wanted to be in Love, but I was in the demon Doors.* Lee refuses to tour or play out beyond Los Angeles County, even though this means Love's new self-titled album on Elektra Records will have a challenging climb ahead to sell even a fraction of what *Eight Miles High* has. This is a heavy Freak Dance Troupe period. They attend every Love and Doors show possible. Densmore recalls watching his favorite Freak from the stage as he beat his skins—*I'd be playing and getting off on Rory Flynn in her sheer negligee, dancing ... And then I'd notice guys in suits trying to be cool and acting like they didn't see.*

April 4 thru 10—The Byrds headline a final week at the Trip, Modern Folk Quartet opens.

May—Armed with the kind of confidence that comes with instant success, producer Terry Melcher rents 10050 Cielo Dr. for him and his girlfriend—*Charlie's Little Sister,* Candice Bergen—to live at for a while. They share the property with Paul Revere and the Raiders frontman, Mark Lindsay. This estate is a rugged five-mile jaunt from Clay Vito.

During the first week of May 1966, the Doors are still destroying it at the London Fog when Valentine's promotional director, Ronnie Haran Mellen, wanders in. She is immediately taken in by *the poetry* of Morrison's words, claiming to have *never heard lyrics like that.* Mellen arranges for the Doors to audition privately for her boss, Elmer Valentine, at the Whisky on May 9. Valentine likes what he hears, and definitely digs what he sees, and he immediately books the Doors as the new Whisky in-house band.

May 10—An East Coast vs. West Coast feud bubbles up between Lou Reed and Frank Zappa after they get into it during a shared-bill show at the Trip. The sheriff's department is called out and shuts the show down. Three days later, the club closed its doors for good, barely making its first anniversary. Valentine has put all of his century eggs into one Whisky basket.

Zappa completes mixing *Freak-Out!* in mid-May, and then moves in with Pamela Zabrubica into her tiny Hollywood cottage at 8404 Kirkwood Dr.

May 23—Starting tonight and continuing for the next 12 weeks, the Doors will open for every single act that headlines the Whisky. Captain Beefheart and His Magic Band with Buffalo Springfield are the inaugural acts.

June—The Cinema Theatre at Western and Santa Monica avenues runs a weekend of programmed screenings featuring works by Kenneth Anger. The 800-seat venue has established a strong business bond with *Freep*, and the programming has gained enough counterculture clout that the opening of this sister theatre appears justified. Only a decade ago, the Vice Squad would have busted this kind of screening to pieces to protect fragile Angelenos' souls.

June 1, 1966—The Doors open at the Whisky for Love and Captain Beefheart & His Magic Band. Captain Beefheart's (aka Don Van Vliet) childhood buddy, Frank Zappa, sits in with them on guitar.

June 4—Vito exhibits his sculptures at the Independent Gallery at 744 1/2 N. La Cienega Blvd. The show runs until June 18.

• •

THANKS FOR THE MAMMORIES—Beautiful women are a part of the world's beauty; they just are. Their observation, idolization, etc., can itself become a force of nature—Lest THEY never underestimate the power of a great pair. Saul Resnick's *The Maidens of Fetish Street* (aka *The Girls of F Street*) premieres in San Francisco on June 10, 1966. A segment features a semi-disguised Vito sculpting a bust of a male in his dark, dank basement. This is a real turning point for Vito, now appearing on screen as a character, not just himself, even if the character is a lonely sculptor living in squalor near Angel Heights in downtown/Chinatown.

MAIDENS OF FETISH STREET

FROM THE SCREEN PLAY

THE DEGENERATES

There is, strangely, no writer listed, but They want you to know that a screenplay existed. It is very likely that this uncredited screenplay source —*The Degenerates*—is actually based on the unproduced screenplay—*The Degenerate*—co-written by Lenny Bruce with William Karl Thomas; one of three failed screenplay collaborations between the two, although its immaculate conception would make for a fine Bruce kind of thumb-in-the-eye. Perhaps Bruce didn't want his name to appear anywhere on it because he was restricted from receiving any monies over $20 to maintain Pauper Status in the state of California. And away we go!

— A MOVIOLA PLAY BY PLAY —

NICK NEEDS PUSSY—Nick patronizes a hootchy-kootchy parade at THE ARTTHEATRE. His conscience works on him while watching a buxom stripper roll across the stage, her bunched-up, wedgied thong occasionally peeking out from under dense, ungelating rolls. His blue balls send him speeding down fantasy lane, dreaming of a buxom blonde (henceforth: Sandra) as she arrives by carriage at a house she finds empty, and enters. Seconds later, Sandra descends a staircase in a robe and makes for the backyard pool area when she is violently disrobed by a brunette (henceforth Sweet, played by Whisky dancer, MARGO LYNN SWEET—whom you should remember was featured in both *The Beach Girls and the Monster* and *Mondo Freudo*). Sandra's figure is revealed, wrapped in a pure white one-piece. She dives into the pool for a quick swim, exiting at the other end to be ceremoniously toweled off by Sweet—BACK INSIDE FOR TEA AND CAKES—The two sit across from one another, silently, Sweet laying the *fuck-me-eyes* on thick as mud as Sandra nibbles a pastry, thinking: *Sandra, you've been here several times, but never before have you been so acutely aware of those weird, hungry, unnatural looks that almost defy description.* Sandra gets more come-on looks from Sweet, who has resorted to lip licking since Sandra can't seem to take a hint, and has gone back into her own head again: *Are you now becoming concerned for your safety? And why are you here? Or are you afraid to answer your true feelings?* Suddenly, Sweet rises from her chair and wanders across the room to arrive at an unfinished clay bust of a female, grotesquely rendered. Sandra remains seated in the background with her long Russian legs crossed. With her back to Sandra, Sweet retrieves a clay ball near the bust and kneads it with sensual clutches, tightening her grip, squeezing the clay, tearing it as she works to steady her heaving breaths. Sweet wedges the clay on the tabletop, nearly straddling it. She becomes aroused. Her breath is labored. Sandra, without prompting, rises from her seat and passes by Sweet to strike a pose in front of a set of French doors that lead to the pool area they came from. Sandra removes her black party dress, leaving her only in a black bra and panty set. Thunder rumbles over the tense strings soundtrack. Sweet is inspired to return to the clay bust, wetting her fingers in a pot of water, and then caressing the clay shoulders, cheeks, and breasts. Sweet checks back at her model, who is poised, arching her back against the glass doors, her now bare breasts scooping up and down as she fixes her hair. Sandra pulls her long arms up over her head and spins around for Sweet to take her in from every angle. The thunder keeps rolling—more ominous shots closing in on Sweet and her work. The film's contrast is high, the blacks are crushed, making Sweet's eyes look like black balls as she fondles the clay bust, running her hands over the neck and shoulders, squeezing gently along the way. When the thunder climaxes, we get a good view of the bust's globby face for the first time. It is glistening, wet, and workable as Sweeet increases in aggressiveness, moving the clay under the cheeks and eyes around, working her way down to two large mounds that will eventually be shaped into supple breasts. Sweet's hands slow for a moment and soften as they caress and refine the cleavage, and then the nipples. When we see Sweet's face again, she is shrouded almost entirely in darkness, except for her eyes and her hands, which are covered in dark, wet clay, running from them down her forearms. The camera pulls back, revealing Sandra, her body turned a quarter away from us. It is pouring outside the windows now, and we can hear the loud, layered trickles of rainfall. Sweet is in the foreground, giving the entire bust a significant rubdown; its shape has elongated to appear like a fountain with water running down the bust. Sweet checks over at Sandra, then gets to work refining the breasts. She works the right breast hard, defining the nipple by pulling clay from the underbelly of the bosom out to a point.

Tougher to reason with is why a one-inch long, deep stab wound has been intentionally sculpted onto the left clay breast above the nipple.

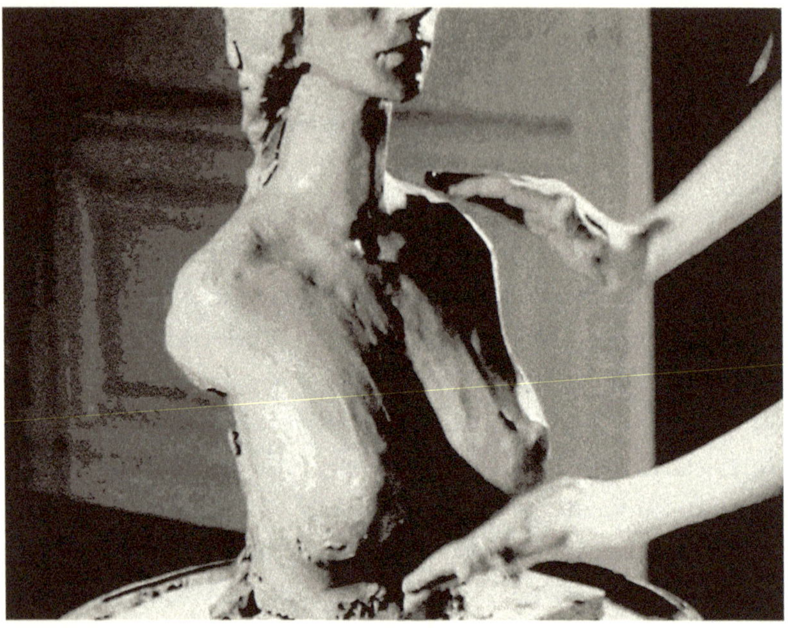

Sandra intensifies in her spinning, posing, and dancing. Sweet rubs, pushes, and pulls at the bust more and more. You know who gets lost in thought—*Your hips and hands move so that a more creative result will ensue. So you, of course, respond with fascinating, undulating hip gyrations. Strangely, this motivates unexpected excitement within you. A sensuality that had been dormant becomes more and more out there.* At this point, Sandra has taken to the floor, stretching out on her back with her arms raised in the air, her stockinged legs pulled up, her back arching in a slow, choreographed ecstasy. When Sandra stands in front of the French doors, she is completely naked. The rain pounds down as hard as ever. Sandra is in the zone; she pulls her arms up, glances over her shoulder at us, and waves her naked rump at Sweet, who is gently fingering the clay surrounding the breast incision, which now appears deeper and more obvious. Sandra freezes with her ass to us, her right hip kicked up with the prominent cheek glazed in tan lines, forming a perfect half sphere, her arms up, both hands hanging onto the door casing for dear life. Then Sandra shifts and thrusts her pelvis at the French doors, clenching her butt cheeks, clamping her pussy shut on some imaginary probe just in time. The camera, as if possessed, cannot help but push in on Sandra's amazing ass and hold on it for a while before traveling slowly up her back to end on her face, gazing at us sideways. She pants, her breasts and back heaving. Sweet works the left clay breast and then the right one, then moves on to the neck and chin—BUT THEN!—without any warning, CLAWS THE SHIT OUT OF THE BUST'S FACE (just as the mad sculptor in *The Beach Girls and the Monster* had). Sweet digs her nails in and curls away chunks of clay, disfiguring Sandra's likeness before her. The booming thunder is replaced by the sound of a jaguar's roar and growl. A JUMP CUT returns the bust to its unnamed condition. Sweet retrieves a bathrobe and seductively approaches a terrified Sandra while the jaguar growls grow. Sandra stands topless in the doorway, her arms held high over her head, her hands lazily clasped behind her back as if tied by a pair of invisible restraints. The jaguar, plus jungle sounds, swarm the soundtrack as the two women make eyes. Sandra accepts the robe from Sweet and dresses. A look of total satisfaction washes over Sweet's face. Sandra, on the other hand, looks as though she's been violated. The animal shrieks fall silent as the two embrace, showing the camera two very different reactions to what just went down. Sandra shoots Sweet a look of emptiness and death before they simply pull away from their embrace, floating out of frame, leaving only the image of rain beating down outside the French doors filling the screen—BACK TO ARTTHEATRE—The big girl struts her stuff on the stage, silhouetted in the spotlight. Nick heads down the street to Movieland, an all-night nudie stand with walls lined with photos & comics. Nick picks out a comic and then finds photo 106, which piques his desires—*Rhonda in Angeles Flight at the House of Fetish*—Nick makes his 32nd trip here. He has been coming to Hilda's boudoir for three years. Hilda is old. Hilda is gross. Nick is in bed with a jiggly brunette when the old woman, Hilda, clad in a leopard print dress and brandishing a whip, explodes with hate at the sight of the two, and Hilda attacks Nick, and they wrestle in bed before Hilda drives the girl out with the whip. Hilda puts on a 78rpm and forces the brunette do a striptease dance to the song in the bay window. Hilda keeps close watch of Nick's reaction; he licks his lips. The record plays on. The brunette's dancing intensifies. She jiggles a lot and twirls just as much. Hilda demands that Nick tries to make it with the jiggly brunette, but he is too shy, so Hilda whips at the brunette and calls her over. Hilda challenges Nick to watch over their "love nest" while she attends to personal matters. No wandering women are to enter. Nick agrees but becomes agitated and impatient, and suddenly Toni—oh Toni, Nick's wonder woman—arrives in all her ebony glory. They go upstairs, and as soon as the door closes behind them, Nick is on the fuckies attack. Toni fights Nick off and runs into the room, where she immediately goes into a topless striptease. Nick sits on the floor like a little boy watching television. The thunder returns as Toni peels off her stockings on the couch. She suddenly stops teasing Nick and walks out of the room into the hallway. Nick moves to the window; it's raining. Toni sinks into the tub in the bathroom at the end of the hall. Nick, thinking Toni has left, watches out the rainy window for her. Toni washes her face in the bath when Nick appears, soaping her back with a sponge. Toni is ecstatic. Nick squeezes soapy water down her neck and over her enormous, dangling breasts—Suddenly, we are on the staircase—Toni is at the top, dried and dressed. Nick tries to get at her breasts, which billow out of the dress, but he is launched backward and tumbles down the stairs. Toni laughs—Back in the room—Nick is bound and tied to a chair. Toni drizzles Blackstrap Molasses from a bottle over him and then retrieves a small ant farm. She is just about to dump the ants on sugary Nick when we—CUT BACK TO the bathtub—back to soaping. Both Nick and Toni appear to be having a good ol' time. Toni stands and towels off, her giant, flat, glistening black ass in Nick's face. He is frozen, holding the sponge-like his member—up and ready to launch into the abyss—but Toni abandons Nick to collect her unmentionables and follow her around like a needy little puppy dog. Nick watches Toni re-dress, and then the two mug down. As Toni climbs onto Nick's lap in the chair and kisses him passionately, Hilda descends the staircase and enters the room. The wild animal growls and roars overwhelm the soundtrack. Hilda throws a drink in Toni's face and then attacks her. Nick watches on, grinning. Then, the brunette dancer from earlier appears and helps Hilda subdue Toni by pinning her legs down. The three converge into a bony, jiggly flesh ball rolling on the ground. They fight and claw and growl, all while Nick joyfully watches on. Hilda wails on Toni's ass with hard slap after hard slap before crunching over to bite Toni's calf. The crazy animal squeals continue as the women fight, when Nick casually walks past them, out of the room, and up the stairs to Hilda's bedroom. Nick seems worried and lies down on the bed to have a hard think. Hilda bursts into her bedroom, whip in hand; the jaguar growls, announcing her presence. She climbs onto the bed slowly, and then she and Nick mug down hard. He gets hot and bothered with the old bag. Suddenly, it's all over—CUT TO—Nick makes the descent from Angel's Flight.

— THIS IS WHERE THINGS GO META —

Vito Paulekas, playing a version of himself (henceforth known as SCULPTOR), is shoe-horned into the strange film, which just got stranger, choosing to explore the mysterious, dangerous sculptor trope that Hollywood is currently so fond of. SCULPTOR rides the Angel's Flight incline car, offloading at the bottom of the course, carrying with him a folding chair and a cane—CUT TO—Inside SCULPTOR's showroom (which is actually 303 Laurel Ave., on loan). Marionettes line the hallways. Shelves backlit by leaded-stained-glass windows present tall, Pacific-inspired pieces. Over the sound of a ticking clock: *Is life with all of its infinite dilemmas and manifestations more real than these masks that repose so nervelessly? Perhaps these faces shaped and molded by human hands are relieved to permit life to relentlessly parade by into eternity.* We get a tour of SCULPTOR's (aka Vito) FOR SALE works. Most are grotesque. One life-sized piece depicts a man sneaking up behind a woman and stabbing her in the left breast with a chisel or some kind of sculpting tool; their faces are wickedly contorted with huge, exaggerated smiles. This SCULPTOR is into some grim shit:

We are suddenly down in SCULPTOR's dark studio (which is actually CLAY VITO, also on loan). The disembodied voice starts back in with some revealing purple prose (likely written in part by BRUCE) as SCULPTOR carves away furiously and exactly at the bust of an older male. SCULPTOR cuts and digs and scrapes, adding years to the face by clay subtraction. Just two feet behind the bust is a curious nude female figure, displayed lying on her side so that all of her glorious sculpted curves face VIT ... er ... SCULPTOR, motivating his artistic urgency. Her arms are raised over her head—*The young life breathes its initial existence; head erect, confident, supreme, issuing forth and accepting challenges from any source. No one and no thing can meet or defeat him, or he so truly determines. Eventually, before comprehension can take effect, the suffocating tentacles of the pulsating process slowly encircle its prey. The stifling and choking entwine its trapped victim. The defenseless hero becomes surrounded and engulfed by the ravages of the timeless deterioration that chips and cuts away with fearless abandon, ceaselessly, showing no mercy, until the total and complete destruction spells The End; The End bearing the cloak of mercy. The final, carefully dotted period punctuated by the slashing and gouging of the human claws, infested with its poisonous venom*—There is a moment of silence as we are forced to watch SCULPTOR quickly cut brow lines, shaping a grimace on the man's face. An ominous, OFF-SCREEN organ tubes in while SCULPTOR now uses both hands to refine the bust (we get a good look at Vito's strong hands and arms, doing his thing), in the short depth of field behind the bust, the lying woman's torso remains floating. SCULPTOR presses clay onto the eye hoods and cheeks and indents lines around the mouth. In the next succession of shots, it becomes obvious that VITO is sculpting a self-portrait. CUT TO a CLOSE UP: We pan the length of the lying clay female, starting at her outstreched arms, moving past her head and large breasts and cinched waist (with a strange dividing line carved into it), onto a set of wide hips and full legs—ending the pan on an EXTREME CLOSE UP of the OLD MAN BUST covering the whole of the frame, showing the SPECTATOR the contents of his mind. The next LONG SHOT reveals SCULPTOR's studio. In the background, we are introduced to two additional full-size sculptures just hanging around the studio; one is a standing woman, her arms also raised overhead. To her right stands the more peculiar of the pair. It is an upright human figure form with a white sheet or big bag pulled snuggly around its entirety, the wrap tightly bound where a human neck would be. In the foreground, with his back to us, SCULPTOR carves on.

A jump cut replaces VITO with SWEET, who feels all over the MALE BUST as a blind person might, before using both hands to CLAW ITS FACE:

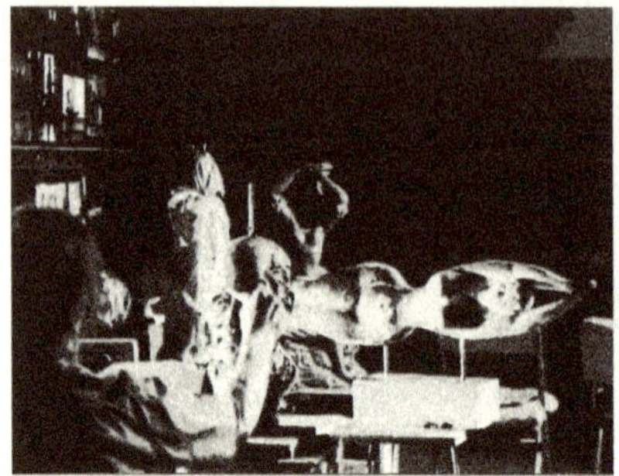
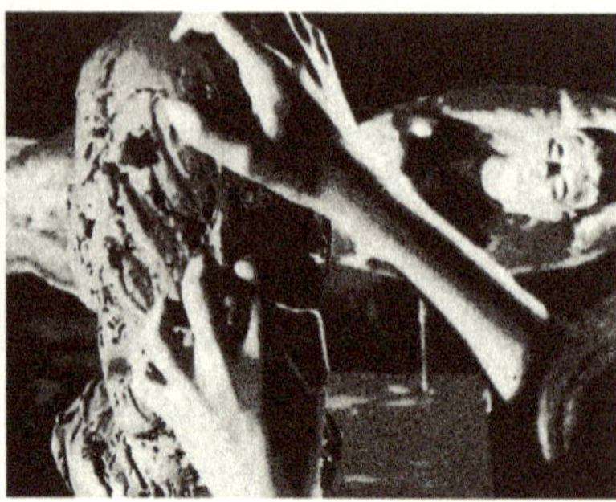

Vito's credit is succinct, and in no way highlights his ON-SCREEN appearance, nor his accidental/intentional portrayal of the Jungian Shadow:

THINK HORSE NOT ZEBRA // AGENTS IN 'DIS DRESS

June 7, 1966. SIOUXX and COAK drive through crowded downtown Los Angeles one-ways, complaining to each other about not being in Mexico.

"Remember the first time we talked to T-d? ... Or went to Mexico?"

"I'm not a goldfish, Valencia, of course I do." COAK also remembers that, while on that mission, essential components of their 16mm projection equipment, as well as their classified training film reels, were stolen from their unlocked, rented sports coup.

VALENCIA *VAL* SIOUXX and LEVITICUS *LEVIS* (like the American-made working-class denim) COAK (like the world-renowned fizzy caramel water) are barely low-ranking CIA mules, hanging on to Agency rank by their undies since both sex-addicts were recently knocked from *queer patrol* for Operation BUNDLESTIX, down to glorified custodial servers for Project VIRUS, or—VIRTUAL INFORMATION RETRIEVAL for the UNITED STATES—a classified government program within the CIA which federally compensates unnamed ghostwriters who contribute a particle to the official National Narrative which makes up our illusory zeitgeist.

Both MEN were initially recruited for political extortion purposes out of fear of public ridicule or familial humiliation for their own transgressions. In the short three years in debt to the government, these two goons have performed innumerable secret services in the name of life, liberty and the pursuit of hedonism, employed in *transforming* ranking lawmen and civic leaders into Agency assests, simply by shaking their gluts and luring desperate, horny lechers out from the discoteques, and into any one of the CIA's dozens of fully-stocked *Love Dens* spread eagle on the opposing coasts. It also didn't dim their numbers, given this pair just plain, flat-out loves fucking. They were tremendous agents in that regard. They've always been in it, life and work, for the sex. It has worked out gloriously for a while; it had been a helluva good run, but days once filled with figurative pencil-pushing turned to the literal sort, and at the dissolution of BUNDLESTIX required their reassignment as partners to GHEISTWHITES' newly formed VIRUS, being immediately put on T-duty.

Not long after that initial summer of '64 Mexico visit, things got supremely sketchy between the two. For as many senators and dog washers went down with only a wall separating their acts, SIOUXX and COAK never made a go at one another. It was on that long, hard drive back to the US field office when they stopped at a bodega for a nightcap some thirty miles shy of the border. The pair, just dying for a reason, were tricked by a strong bellboy into getting blasted on peyote, and then, after taking a kaleidoscopic detour, screamed across the electric blue agave hills with an afternoon thunderstorm tight on their ball sack, tickling their short and curlies the harder COAK toggled his throttle, melting them and the coup into the Mexiscape.

They pulled off at the nearest hacienda de rouge to wait out the storm, to lie low until the silence returned, but instead they wound up in a brothel on Vaseline Alley where they gave in to their burning lust, returning to their former glories; going all in, Crossing the Abyss, and they will tell you—NOBODY ... NOBODY! will fuck you harder than a friend.

With that romantic memory slipping out of COAK's ear, then sliding off the back windshield onto the rear bumper, before vaporizing on the sizzling asphalt of the JUICY JAMES HAMBURGERS ON THE STRAND parking strip. The agents arrived in HERMOSA BEACH at their usual pick-up spot, having agreed over the years to respect T-d's privacy at his Manhattan Beach pad. Also, VIA remains a roomie, at least for the time being, and the agents are not two to mince words; they hate the very G-ddamned sight of her. On more than one occasion, COAK and SIOUXX have accused VIA of practicing witchcraft, promising T-d to dedicate their best skills to *relocating* her should she need specialized *relocation*. To date, T-d has repeatedly declined their bid, but he does not want their massive chutzpahs to go unrecognized.

Peering in through the white burger box window, SIOUXX and COAK easily make out T-d's tall frame, pacing. A fucking fruit bat could see T-d's stoned off his rocker. T-d knows sure as all get-out that he's gone, gone far beyond, quite possibly the most stoned he, or any being to BC date for that matter, has been. He has taken this measure partially on purpose in preparation of releasing the final contracted PHASE from his paternal custody, something he figured would be no skin off his back, but after committing an additional two years to collecting and research, HE's grown attached and is already working through seperation anxiety; he is secondly stone cold stoned because his second novel, a much shorter short work than his first, has been published, and if you're willing to believe it, garnered still more literary and readership acclaim than his debut output. T-d is in an unlikely-but-lusted-after position for a young novelist to find themselves in, and despite it all, the turned-on college kids making pilgrimages to his beachfront apartment, or letters from fans in Japan who find just the correct-enough address to ensure their postcard finds its way to one of his many maildrops. He has maintained geographical anonymity and the enigmatic presence of a fruit fly somewhere in the same room with you. His ability to sustain a modest-to-comfortable existence in Manhattan Beach is due in no small part, and he knows this, to Lippencott's generous $10k advance for his *potboiler* (their words).

Today, T-d celebrates Independence Day a month early, waving goodbye to the impending graduation and liberation from PAULEKAS detail. Not to mention, he is chomping at the bit to cash in one hard-fought and federally sanctioned PUBLISHER's IOU.

The next one, the untamable novel that nobody will have any say in, the closest thing to a visual scan of his brain, that very thing everybody claims to be after, will be put to the public for future generations to scrutinize and pick and prod over each quarter of every sentence. He will sit in on college courses on campuses across the country dedicated to his prose. Joyce's ghost will mop up the saliva and cum trail leading to his balcony. It is getting close—Real close—But first —T-d comes down from his PANAMA RED-induced daymare; he's in the backseat of the coup, navigating SIOUXX by aid of a crude map which T-d has plotted in a rainbow of markers, all of which he now forgets the meanings of. The spot is 185 miles south in Jacumba, CA, 15 miles from the Mexican border, where a month ago he and PETER YARROW buried PHASE III somewhere under the Goat Canyon Tressle Bridge. When they get there, he'll remember the exact location.

On the three-hour drive, they split six hot dogs-on-a-stick, six cheeseburgers, and six strawberry milkshakes. The TRAVELING TRIO chow-down and discuss T-d's newest NOVEL. SIOUXX and COAK both enjoyed it, much more than T-d's first one. T-d is flattered that they had many insightful contributions to make. COAK and SIOUXX talk about T-d's future as if he's their kid going off to college. They feel like they've had a hand in raising T-d to this standard.

In the Anza-Borrego, under the bridge—the hand off. They enjoy the remainder of the day watching the sun die between the rungs and stilts and trusses suspending the pile of matches halfway to Heaven, casting long shadows as the boys climb around the rocky landscape. They are presented to us every bit like a lovely family on a summer holiday. SIOUXX and COAK are very proud of their version of T-d, and shower him with encouragement and praise, so much so that T-d questions if a double suicide might be on the horizon.

THE GREAT, WONDERFUL DAY.

ALL TIME IS LOCAL | COMPLICATED PIGMENTS

At midnight on December 27, 1888, Theo and Paul arrived in Paris by train after a twelve-hour journey from Arles. It has not been easy keeping the act up around Theo, driving the madman angle hard, convincing him that his troubled older brother has lost touch with reality entirely. Paul and Theo leave the train station, say *good night* to each other, and part ways, agreeing to reconvene later in the week to get business back to normal. Paul visits a local brothel and falls asleep there with his big, drunk head buried deep in the pillowy, rhomboid thighs of a pretty-ish night-laborer. Paul dreams of four days previous—The Winter Solstice of 1888, December 23, at 3 a.m.: Paul and Vincent huddle around a malfunctioning furnace centered in the indescribably cold quasi-art salon. The two weirdos have recently returned from one of their exhausting all-day *hygienic excursions*, but Vincent manages the energy to rant about Paul's abhorrent brothel behavior; his aggressive, rough & ready nature with the whores. Never has Vincent seen such pushing and pulling outside of a bullfight. That's it; Paul is more a matador than a painter at times! Paul changes the subject to what's really on his mind: murder. He says that the barmaid, Gaby, at Café de la Gare, mentioned that he and the damned criminal Prado share an uncanny likeness. She would know. Prado frequented the cafe, and Gaby would nearly always serve him. Could Vincent ever believe such a thing? Vincent attempts to recall if this Prado had indeed crossed their paths. Perhaps they've even met the condemned killer. Paul drinks more wine and goes on a philosophical rant about physical truths colliding, like how smoke makes our air temporarily visible. Without fire, we would always be blind. Paul folds the wheatpaste-soaked newspaper gently over his forearms. What do you think would happen if I just left this as it is, let it dry up? The pills have taken full effect, pushing Vincent to confide in his new friend that he is in love with the brothel maid, Gaby, the very cafe maiden Paul spoke of earlier. Paul tells Vincent he's gone mad, then. No sir, ARTISTS! must remain steadfastly immune to the implications and derangements associated with this *in-love* disease. Gaugin has six children to prove this theory. No. Vincent is destined to indulge limitlessly and endlessly. Paul feverishly attempts to fix the fire while Vincent prepares materials for their fieldwork planned for tomorrow. Paul is annoyed at having to make a last-minute change to a painting for Theo to ensure its sale. Vincent mixes a crushed Indian yellow pigment into an oil suspension, getting a bright, translucent yellow paint in answer. Yellow-based pigments have booned greatly from advancements in modern science, offering many more color variations and possibilities. Vincent has a major love affair with the color yellow. This ochre that Paul has brought here is magnificent. Vincent talks admirably of its deep emotional truth and how it shines as a symbol of the trifecta: sunlight, life, and GOD—GOD! Paul begins the origin tale of the rank golden brick, and GOD's intervention is perhaps the farthest thing from its ontology. : : : We are transported to a tiny northeastern Indian village in the Monghyr region of Bihar. It is 1883. Moving closer, still, we arrive at a farm spotted with dairy cattle, but it is not a dairy farm. Recently, their manufacturing methods have been called into question by the London-based Society of Art and the Royal Botanic Gardens, Kew. Paul pokes and prods and questions his way through the fabled production of unrefined Indian yellow pigment manufactured for painting and textile dyes. Paul is introduced to the cavalry of gwalas or *milkmen*. He questions the guide about the leather bindings suspending the cattle inches off the ground. He is sold a story of bovines historically kicking over bucketfuls of sona, and a farm of this stature cannot sustain such losses. The cows must be hand-fed. This maintains the safety of all creatures involved. The cows survive on a strict diet of adolescent mango leaves and water. Nothing else to ensure peak pee-pee pigmentation. A side effect of this diet often finds the cows afflicted with kidney stones, which requires the gwalas to massage the steer's genital region to coax out that precious pungent gold. Paul is in luck. He is led to a gwala, where, today, a cow is in just such a condition, and Paul bears witness to the unpleasant process; a gwala succeeds in pushing out a precarious beam so rich in yellow that the sun is nearly white in comparison and struggles to shine through. The urine trickles through a burlap sack and collects into a wide-mouthed clay basin below. The palpability of both color and odor cannot be overstated. Other farmhands were tasked with boiling the discharge in a cauldron for several hours, creating a syrup-like reduction that is then displayed in the sun, where it bakes for over 72 hours, congealing. For Paul, this link in the manufacturing chain is by far the worst, but for the workers, it's just another stroll in Pungent Park. The cauldron requires constant supervision. The vapors blasting out are first overwhelming before abruptly turning intoxicating, beguiling, causing the guide to break her confidence to tell the kind of monster story told around weenie roasts. The gwalas are known to sing or whistle to the cows, passing the time and setting the tone for the day. This was true; Paul can vouch for it, having heard it himself—a happy gwala nursed a fat bladder free of its burden, all the while humming *You Are My Sunshine* —The guide continues: a year ago, the gwalas noticed that their cow-side concertos coincided with the appearance of THEM—*On the ridge up there*, the guide said, pointing out a treeline no more than a hundred yards to the east; that's where They saw the *Sootman*, a massive black blob, formless, dark of a thing, dense like a swarm of ten million flies. The Sootman would observe their processes from the lookout, sometimes many times against the day, hiding just out of view beyond the tree line. One morning, the gwalas were alarmed to arrive on the farm to find that their cows had already been drained, a bucket full of piss waiting beside each of them, and from what the gwalas gathered, not a drop was spilled. The tour nears its end, but first—*the bolaroom*! It is just as it sounds: a ballroom where barefoot workers stomp and squish the jelly bile, kneading it under their arches for hours, transmutating it first into sticky cakes, before it's formed into its final shape and color for exportation: a brown sphere. : : : The fire catches and erupts in the iron cauldron's belly. Paul celebrates by sucking down a couple of hard ones. Properly primed, the two painters huddle around their indoor sun to spin a good yarn or two before the self-dosing overwhelms their interests, and the two fade into the French air. The pills & booze-fueled discussion has mutated oblongly into the subject of the Whitechapel Murders and Jack the Ripper; the mutilations happening at that very moment in time, only a short rail ride away. Paul claims intimate knowledge that at least one of the purported Ripper murders has been misidentified. Vincent pops digoxin and returns to an earlier subject: Prado, and tries, again, harder this time, to recall if, yes, maybe they had crossed paths with the condemned killer. Perhaps they have even met or exchanged glances. Paul takes the bait, choosing to focus on Prado's execution and talks at length about the abandoned primitive disposal methods, those much more horrific than what awaits Prado. Paul expresses a particular enthusiasm for lateral bisection. Caligula would dine in his great hall whilst a criminal heathen is, well, divided tableside. Paul questions the idea of cannibalism. Vincent remembers reading an article around 1880 about a Canadian who cannibalized his entire family, even though an outpost was a day's journey away and the area was aplenty in game. The Canadian chose to do this and was hanged. *HANGED for his appetite! ... That's nothing*—India still squishes heads under elephant hooves, and that's only after the beast drags one to their own death stump. *Hanged ... pthhhh, c'est époustouflant, Vincent!* Paul talks of what is in store for Prado, the eternal separation of the bulb from the socket. *The French love a beheading, that is for certain.* Vincent finds it strange to be amused about looking like a known murderer, but he, too, becomes unable to distinguish Paul from Prado, settling on calling his roommate PAULDO from now on—Paul was simply expressing an interest in *mirroring*—the nature of duplicates—that's all, so cool it down, Red. Vincent swallows more digoxin, says that he has lived and died once already, and is a victim of forced reincarnation. He dwells obsessively on his dead baby brother, a cosmic *twin* who shared the exact same name as Vincent and who was born on the exact same calendar day, too, only one year previous. He described a dream in which They, the two Vincent Willem Van Goghs, swapped heads, and now the surviving one believes it was more than a dream. He inspects his neck in a mirror for suture scars, wondering aloud if they would have both been painters.

• •

• • •••

• • •

••• • • •

•

•

•

Paul awakens from his lap-slumber at four in the morning and leaves the brothel, wandering into the mostly quiet courtyard of the Prison de la Roquette. 65-year-old master executioner M. Deibler and his three assistants make a quiet bustle erecting and preparing the guillotine for a decapitation at dawn. They are cautious, moving slowly and methodically, careful not to catch the inmates' attention and trigger hysterics. Deibler's son, Anatole, is likely the next French empire beheader. Only a month ago, Anatole turned twenty-five, having worked steadily as a tailor's assistant, but recently realized that his seated position as a third-generation headsman is coming to fruition. It's futile fighting the fact that he possesses the midas touch. The Diebler name has earned a reputation as a smooth operator. This mantle, at the very least, Anatole, by God, must be maintained. That's how the old man put it before returning to his garden. All three methodically construct and test the guillotine, which is kept, this one at least, on the prison grounds. A bushel of tightly bound hay is loaded into the neck restraint, and down comes the blade, splitting the grain so acutely that a fine mist of fiber hangs in the air. This morning, the mysterious inmate known only to the masses as PRADO (aka Count Linska de Castillon)—*a bandit of the savannah who found his way to the boulevard*—will rest his neck on the lip to stare into the dark corners of a hungry wicker basket. Although Prado will not know his fate for another three hours, a passionate group of the curious has already caught wind and begun filing into the courtyard for a peek. Other onlookers stake out the perfect spot to take in the Big Cut. At daybreak, Prado's severing is set. More than two hundred spectators gather in the prison courtyard. Paul wedged his way to the front of the line and crouched to gaze perfectly between the guards' boots, gaining a clear, proper view of the contraption. Paul contemplates how he arrived at this place, lying belly-down on the dirt, counting the minutes before the separation of a man from his head. Paul stared at the executioner, a young man shy of thirty. He admired the boy's attention to detail. How does this public servant deal with the constant threat of retaliation? Where does he drink in peace or eat free from ridicule? Joan of Arc's executioner, Geoffroy Therage, suffered so from crippling guilt of having possibly killed a messenger of GOD, that on the night of her roasting, Therage claimed that Joan appeared to him in a fever vision as a pure white heifer. Suddenly, Paul's eyes fell upon Prado waiting patiently in the prison yard corridor, smoking a cigarette, chasing puffs with sips of cognac from a tulip-shaped glass. Paul was immediately struck by their physical congruence—nearly identical, just as Gaby had said—except for the perforated line that rang Prado's collar. As Paul compared their uncanny facial similarities, he was trapped in Prado's gaze, and his thoughts raced back to the Chinchorro mummy he once touched as a child in Peru. He remembers how their heads were lobbed off clean and replaced with a bag of straw and seed that would eventually be capped with a clay death mask. Without warning, or a countdown or fanfare of any kind, Papa Deibler drops the plunger, and Prado's rigid body tumbled neatly into a waiting wicker casket out of sight. But the head—the head, when it settles, reveals Prado's face, frozen in a silent, guilty scream; his bulging eyeballs firing at Paul, who falls into the voids and thinks of the two small sunflower paintings by Vincent that he swiped from Yellow House. Paul figures that Vincent only painted them to entice him there, so success, they worked. Vincent should be flattered when he discovers their absence.

SOFT DELETES // A COUNTRY-SHAPED FART

Spring 1969. It will be another unkind year during America's transmutation. T-d dates one of the Fractured Cow waitresses, the 19-year-old daughter of a once-famous television actress-turned-beach bunny who now spends all of her free time (and there's lots of it) at the country club, knocking back tonics and tonguing pimentos from olive belly-buttons. Anyway, she and her looker-of-a-daughter conveniently live across the street. Today, T-d is holed up in his Manhattan Beach bungalow, his traditional black sheets hoisted into position to prevent vitamin D leakage, inside, of course. T-d had barely tightened the last nut on a contraption he had been constructing with broken and discarded junk donated to him by a friend and owner of Triangle Hardware in Hermosa Beach—when a rapture darkened his door.—KNOCK—KNOCK—BANG—BANG—POUND—POUND!—the kind police give at 3 a.m. when they need a cup os sugar. "We know you're in there, T-d!" And, he is, pressing his back against the door to secure it in place because Manhattan Beach isn't exactly what you would call structurally sound. "T-d, T-d, we thought to call first ... but ... well, you know how you are." There is a long pause as the voice processes through T-d's THC-caked membranes, eventually making a match like one of those slot games that aligns torsos and legs and a head of a robot and man and beast; the gears and escapement are rusty on this current model, but they eventually catch ... "T-d, T-d, COME ON, we need your help, sweetheart. WE NEED IT REAL BAD!" Another moment passes inside while T-d stares at the floor for the answer (which he kinda already knows), but tries anyway to read off the raised grain structure and oval knotting of the oak runners—*but what the hell*, T-d thinks. He's always primed for surprises, so he cracks the door open just enough to flash a blue eye and buck-tooth, giving away instantly that it's true; T-d is here. However, T-d isn't so sure these two weirdos are the ones he expected. The little, skiddish moustached ONE ducked and weaved and constantly looked back over his shoulder at the drink of water to his left, who was doing something akin to an in-place watusi, the sun lighting HER perfectly from overhead so that she appeared like a mystical, tall tube of flan. The two of them, side by side, did a perfect impression of the number 10. As evidenced by wrappers sticking outta the little one's breast pocket, these Tweekers are living on sodypop and grape lollies. And then it hit T-d: The little one is LEVIS COAK, looking now much more like T-d remembered, but upon closer inspection, he's older looking—as should be expected—given his line of work. It was COAK's new female partner that threw off the chill front porch vibe.

"Who's your new sidecar, COAK?"

"Sidecar? Fuck you, T-d!" hisher squealed, "It's me ... VALSOU," continuing, cocking its head dramatically, and then repeating in a softer, more disappointed tone, "Hello ... VALENCIA SIOUXX?"

"No shit?"

"Exactly, no shit. Only now it's VALSOU, not VAL SIOUXX." Either way it's diced, *NU-SU* has undergone extensive reappropriations and reassignments to core bodily faculties.

"I guess congratulations are in order, uh, ma'am ... "

COAK let out a heavy sigh, half relieved, half preparing to tell their story. VALSOU, conversely, gulped in air, simultaneously filling up lungs while firing a convincing pointed pair directly at T-d. "As you can see, I'm practically reinvented, from the floormats to the moonroof, but I still have ... IT. We're on our way to JALISCO to have— IT—lanced off like a boyle, and the rest of it filleted like a battered catfish. I suppose I owe it all to you."

"Thank you, that's great—Wait … what?"

We are suddenly transported into the red rented convertible with the three ancillary FREAKS—COAK helms the wheel. VALSOU, fittingly, rides bitch. T-d is laid out across the backseat with his pecker to HEAVEN, the seabreeze lapping over his bow. Thirty-some-odd months ago, T-d was pardoned from his Government service, and the *comfort promises* (as they called their arrangements outlined in both contracts) simply haven't been fulfilled. The thought that COAK and VALSOU might actually be kidnapping him comes and goes once VALSOU turns back to dangle over the seat, addressing T-d directly. Their authoritative confidence drains from both in a wink. "We're in a pickle, my boy," choked VALSOU. "The whistle's been blown!" COAK chimed in, then tilted the rearview down to get a better look, settling the mirror frame on T-d's crotch. "We've been made!" COAK continued, flicking his eyes back and forth between the mirror and the road.

"The wheels have come clean off … "

"Yah, everything's gone sideways … "

"No, gone south, er, pear-shaped … "

"Yes, pear-shaped. And down the drain!"

"OKAY, I GET IT. Christ, I get it," T-d shouted, kicking at the air.

An hour later, they arrived at a beach spotted with tar slicks and buzzing seaweed. THEY located a hidden crag and got mega-stoned on some Government hash under it. T-d wanted to fly a kite. "THERE IS NO KITE!" and then COAK mustered up the courage to tell T-d why there was no kite.

THEY pulled their britches up past cankles and varicose veins, and trudged out to sea, pretending to enjoy wading ankle deep in the frigid Pacific. T-d, on the other hand, was loving it.

"How do you do that?" COAK wondered aloud about T-d, "How do you write like that?"

"It's goddamned poetry," VALSOU whispered.

By studying T-d's novels, by ingesting the endless left-of-center social observations and historical reworkings of the other contributors' works, VALSOU and COAK had been changed on a molecular level. And it wasn't just they, but their entire division that was wholly radicalized after years of exposure to their VIRUS collections. The entire AGENCY has since disbanded, splintering into 23 free-thinking shards before shuffling into the everyday mix, enriched.

Well …

that's …

just …

great …

Simply partners just months ago, THEY are now full-blown lovers on the lam, barreling their way to a new life in the only place where THEY will be left entirely alone: MEXICO. "Nobody wants to go to Mexico. Nobody! Not even Mexicans," VALSOU accentuated, performing a hat dance until T-d interrupted, arguing, "Well, that's where you fellas dug me up. Right?"

"Neigh, it's an altogether different scenario."

When T-d questions THEM about abandoning their families, VALSOU and COAK ignited to put the ol' bruising on T-d, but this time T-d is ready for THEM, and he easily overtook THEM, getting a hard-earned *UNCLE!* outta THEM in seconds.

Later, the TRIO, huddled around a beach fire, wolfed down fat, squishy burritos THEY picked up from a local dive. Through flecks of bean and cheese, the recovering SPOOKS tell T-d that VITO has taken his family and split for Haiti. He's gone; ditched the basement.

T-d gulped a pepperoncini.

"There's more, T-d … "

VALSOU & COAK felt obligated to stop on their way to inform their prodigal son not only of VIRUS's dissolution, but also of DIVISION DIRECTOR PROONE GEISTWHITES' recent fiasco. Their story went that GHEISTWHITES was accused and tried for corruption by the

OFFICE OF GENERAL COUNSEL after a three-year internal investigation. He was found guilty on all thirteen counts, and subsequently removed from office; his two decades with the AGENCY ended in irreparable disgrace. GHEISTWHITES was stripped of all accolades and ordered by the Court to pay $150,000 in reparations. PROONE moved himself and his wife DELLA into a quaint cottage at the edge of the Palatinate Forest in Kaiserslautern, Germany. His problems started up again when it was alleged that GHEISTWHITES lifted several highly-classified documents before his dismissal—among them, you guessed it, T-d's contribution to the PONSONBY COMMISSION REPORT—and GHEISTWHITES had reportedly shopped the dossiers around HOLLYWOOD, UNTIL! two weeks ago, when the GHEISTWHITES were found dead in their wohnungen. The coroner framed their passing as an *accidental death, brought on by carbon monoxide poisoning caused by a faulty furnace.* Their devoutly Roman Catholic landlady auctioned off many of their belongings and donated the proceeds to Lorsch Abbey. Unsold items were distributed amongst the local Die Heilsarmee. The AGENCY is scrambling like mad to locate and secure PACKETS at any cost.

"Please don't act surprised, T-d, you knew there was a chance of something like this happening."

"Yah, he's right. We shouldn't have come … but, then again, here we are."

The pepperoncini T-d gulped several minutes ago came back up.

EDITOR'S NOTE

Congratulations on sticking it out this far. Your reward: more reading. Relax, you're almost to the best part.

By 1975 (now known as the Year of Intelligence), T-d had published three books and gained significant traction in the literary world, becoming the unlikely rockstar/scholar of postmodern writers. By most accounts, he is considered one of the greatest living American novelists and the quintessential anonymous counterculturist.

The following section illustrates the inescapable chrysalis of the period from 1966 to 1980. This compendium of chronological fragments, notations, citations, and personal postulations by T-d was compiled after the CHURCH COMMITTEE of 1975 used Congress to successfully expose clandestine intelligence programs and inhumane experiments, and secure a Supreme Court ruling against them.

BOOK | TWO

To understand a historical event, read it in superstition with other possible events. When something happens, you should always ask yourself: *what other options failed so that this could have happened?*—SLAVOJ ŽIŽEK

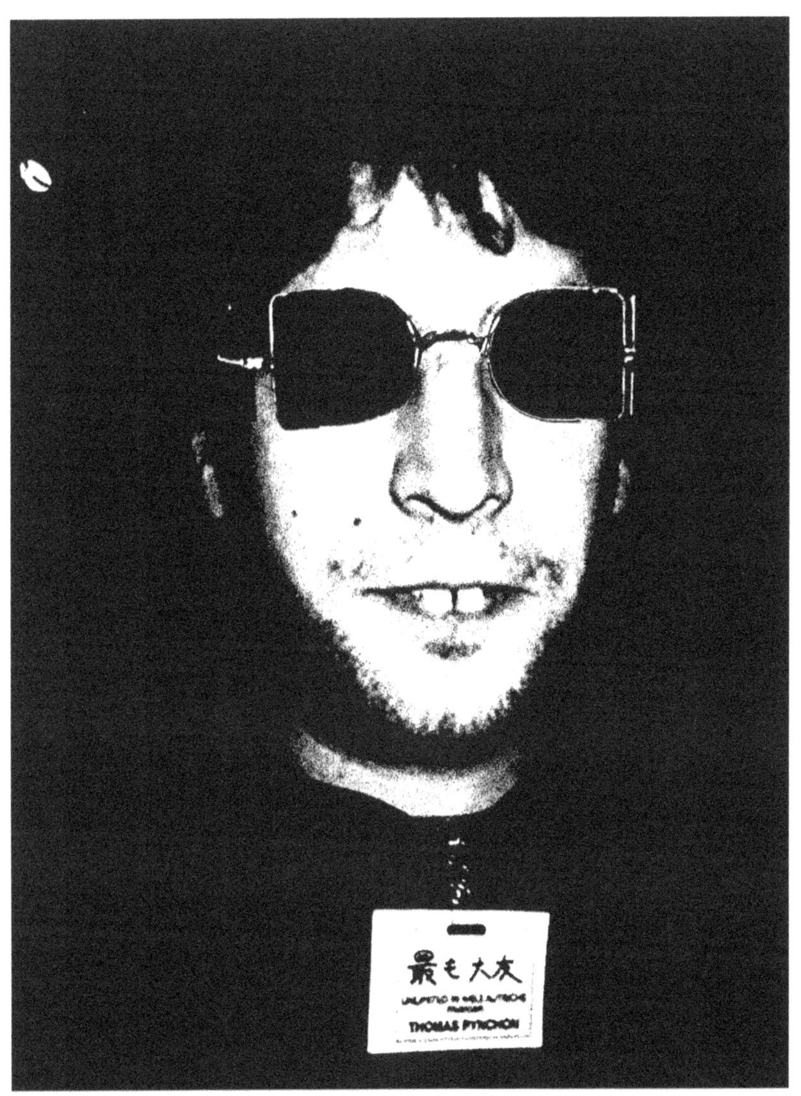

“Portrait of T-d as Claude Raines as Jack Griffin” — circa 1970

1966

On June 20, 1966, LOVE recorded their *7 AND 7 IS* single in HOLLYWOOD at SUNSET SOUND RECORDERS. BEAUSOLEIL, having been replaced by BRYAN MCLEAN, has moved on, putting the need to attain his own rock god status on hold to instead trawl the city for stray pussies. THE MOTHERS OF INVENTION released *FREAK-OUT!*. Frequent FREAK contributor RAY LEONG took the album cover and layout photos. Just as he was in *THE GIRLS ON F STREET,* VITO is listed under ASSISTANTS simply as: VITO. HE, KARL FRANZONI, and KIM FOWLEY are credited as AUXILIARY MOTHERS. The liner notes mention that *HELP, I'M A ROCK* is dedicated to ELVIS PRESLEY, even though FRANZONI cites scribing these words on a stone before giving it to a girl he intended to sack, and ZAPPA thought it was hilarious. FRANZONI insists his version of the story is correct—*I ALWAYS CARRY FELT TIP PENS IN MY POCKET*—Early album pressings included a fold-out map by ZAPPA called *FREAK OUT HOT SPOTS!*—a satirical illustration of all the essential meeting spots given that you are serious about getting in touch with your deep inner FREAK. It crudely details HOLLYWOOD's underground rendezvous, the battle grounds and banal zones—places like CANTER'S DELI and quoting MOI JIMMY CARL BLACK—VITO'S *DUNGEON OF SIN.* Considering ZAPPA's timing in releasing this peculiar propaganda, it's almost as though he put on his flashy subversion coat and started shadow-snitching his balls off. LAUREL CANYON is designated in red ink, so, too, is the *FREAK*

SANCTUARY. To the immediate west of LAUREL CANYON are two sets of red crosshairs, polygraphic registration markers for repress printing—symbols that are almost always cropped from the final publication, but here they—not only included, but highlighted—Maybe ZAPPA thought the crosshairs drove home the authoritative impression that a rifle scope sight might, intstilling that feeling of being monitored; tracked—an existence on par with what the Assholes designated on plot N°·21 had to deal with. This area of the map, N°·21, is swaddled in red, indicating, at least according to ZAPPA's supplied key, that explosions and mega-police activity plague the block. CLAY VITO is smack dab in the center of this war zone. ZAPPA writes:

> VITO'S STUDIO & store & cult HQ & sanctuary & genetic laboratory, which is REALLY THE PLACE TO SEE, is located at 303 N. Laurel (the bomb blast tells us that the status quo agents have made it known that they are checking Vito out)

ZAPPA wears a wig, thou digh? LOVE released the split seven-inch, *7 AND 7 IS* and *N°·14*. JERRY HOPKINS takes to *FREEP*, writing the strange, masturbatory article, *KOOKS, LITTLE GREEN BOOKS AND ZAPPA BLOWS BICYCLE*, about his experiences booking *talent* for *THE STEVE ALLEN SHOW*:

> I am responsible for uncovering and booking some of the show's more interesting people ... From time to time, one of my "kooks" comes back into my life and brightens it. It was through that show that I met Vito and his wife, Sue. Vito, I still see, usually dancing at the Whisky or the Trip, or I go by his house on a Friday night when he is conducting one of his sculpture classes—a kind of terra cotta seminar ... Another "kook" I lost track of was the guy who came into the Steve Allen Theatre and looked me in the eye and said, "I play musical bicycle." I said, "What?" "I blow bicycle, man. I want to teach Steve how to blow a bicycle." I said Okay, go get your bike and show me how it's done. Which is exactly what he did – "tuning" the spokes with a spoke wrench before plucking them. Then he blew a few notes across the open end

> of the handlebars. This went on for some time, with variations. The melody was intriguing, if less than consistent. Two years went by before I saw this fellow again. Now he has a record out and an album. The fellow's name is Frank Zappa, and he is the leader of The Mothers. The album is called "Freak Out" and it is two records (for the price of one) of psychedelic music, for lack of a better phrase. It is a good album. It has original selections titled "The Return of the Son of the Monster Magnet" (being an "unfinished ballet in two tableaux" running 12:17), "Who Are the Brain Police," and "Hungry Freaks, Daddy." Even if you don't like psychedelic music, you should buy the album – just for the liner notes. "Hungry Freaks, Daddy" is written for Carl Orestes Franzoni, and it says about Carl, "He is freaky down to his toenails. Someday he will live next door to you, and your lawn will die." The album also lists 184 people who "have contributed materially in many ways to make our music what it is ... please do not hold it against them." ... There are pictures of charter members of the United Mutations of Los Angeles. Lots of things like this. This is Frank Zappa's gift. Frank Zappa and Vito may be "kooks" in somebody's book. Not in mine, they aren't. The "normal" people are the batty ones.

HOPKINS seems to be the preeminent LA stoner, forgetting that he and VITO were both guests on the same episode of *THE JOE PYNE SHOW* in May 1960, two years before HOPKINS joined *THE STEVE ALLEN SHOW* as talent coordinator. The BYRDS released *FIFTH DIMENSION*, exemplifying the significant influence eastern music phenom RAVI SHANKAR had on them. Their single, *EIGHT MILES HIGH*, becomes the psychedelic rock fire starter. FREEP celebrates its second birthday. Recalcitrant, VITO, and his FREAKS attend the GREAT UNDERGROUND ARTISTS MASKED BALL ORGY (GUAMBO Nº·1) at the AEROSPACE HALL at 7660 Beverly Blvd. ZAPPA has budgeted $1,990 for the event, marking the fee due *H.C.* (HERB COHEN). VITO's name is left off the performance invoice, but he attends the ball in full glory anyhow, sporting a tall conical mask with cut-out oval slits for eyes and fringe dangling over his mouth and jaw, a design nearly identical to the traditional tribal masks that are handmade ONLY by the MANGAI tribe in PAPUA NEW GUINEA.

> LIGHTS SOUNDS DANCING ACTION BOOZE BAR AND COKE BAR and Mother Hopkins Brownie Bar. EVERYBODY: A monster junk sculpture will be assembled in the parking lot. Bring your goodies and add on! FILMMAKERS! Bring your work and show it yourself. TATTOO ARTISTS! Attend with colored markers. POETS ARISE! A side room to read to whoever would gather to listen. MASKS are obligatory—COSTUMES are optional.

Talent booker cum-writer-cum-edibles-baker JERRY HOPKINS tells *FREEP*:

> WHY EVERYBODY DIDN'T GUAMBO ... So the music was shut down, and the main ballroom was cleared by the uniformed police with the aid of many plain clothes vice squad officers who appeared out of the Guambo crowd with long hair and LSD buttons. The party continued for the next hour only on the second floor happening room and the restaurant. It was a great party, and a successful one, for the ones inside, but the Free Press admittedly made a number of mistakes, mainly underestimating the number of people who would attend and not knowing how to handle the crowds when they did appear. A lot of people were undoubtedly disappointed at not getting in, but we hope they understand that we have never held a party like this before, that we faced the enormous handicap of moving it at the last minute, and that we are the kind of people who make mistakes but work hard at not repeating them ... So don't destroy your costumes. You may need them soon.

DON'T DESTROY YOUR COSTUMES. YOU MAY NEED THEM SOON ... As July turned into August 1966, FRANZONI visited LENNY BRUCE at his HOLLYWOOD HILLS apartment. BRUCE was seated on the floor among a sea of scattered court documents. BRUCE was destitute—a pauper who couldn't afford a secretary—so his old pal VITO occasionally made *secretaries* available to help sort through the looming legal battles, although, more often than not, these charity cases developed into charity asses, Ladies are a particular vice for BRUCE (who is affianced with fellow comedian, LOTUS WEINSTOCK). On August 3, 1966, BRUCE was found dead on his bathroom floor by roomie (FREAK dancer and MOI's WHISKY soundman) JOHN *JOHNNY FUCK-FUCK* JUDNICK. The medical examiner ruled BRUCE's cause of death as *acute morphine poisoning caused by an overdose.* JUDNICK called over longtime BRUCE confidant, PHIL SPECTOR, who arrived at the scene and immediately bought the crime scene photographer's first roll of negatives. It proved of little help in dulling the sensationalism, as the death images flooded the entertainment world anyhow. BRUCE's early departure marked a tidal change on the scene. Drugs that were once purely recreational have developed into dependencies, setting well into motion the disintegration of the disenfranchised. It was, as VITO saw it: WORST CASE SCENARIO. The DOORS played a private show at the WHISKY for ELEKTRA RECORDS-head JAC HOLZMAN, but unlike VALENTINE, HOLZMAN was not impressed, and passed on signing them—ZAPPA TRADES ASS FOR LIGHTS—The success of July's GUAMBO encourages ZAPPA to throw a follow-up FREAK-OUT at the SHRINE EXPOSITION HALL (1.4 miles northwest of CLAY VITO): SON OF GUAMBO. A full-page ad in *FREEP* issue 107 boasts a *Light Show* but makes no mention of VITO or his dancers participating. 5,000 over-18 party-goers stuffed the ballroom to max capacity. ZAPPA's expense list clearly indicates a $*5,729* profit on a budget of $*11,239,* of which a measly $*200* is allocated to *dancers (15) Vito + company. $550* has been allotted to the advertised *light show,* and *80 pairs of bedsheets* will set ZAPPA back *$216.* This little piece of parapraxis ephemera exemplifies ZAPPA's total lack of appreciation for the real draw: VITO and his FREAKS. It also beautifully illustrates the beginning of the end. One of the fifteen dancers that VITO escorted to this show is PAMELA MILLER, who is so taken by ZAPPA that she makes it a point to slam into him on the dance floor to get his attention. ZAPPA is on the move to fill the subversive void left by BRUCE after he ditched this dimension. VITO, on the other hand, has turned blue and made a play to separate his FREAKS from the commonplace, all-but-discredited HIPPIES. The DOORS were still opening for LOVE when ARTHUR LEE came to their rescue, convincing HOLZMAN to give the band another shot—this time at BIDO LITO's. HOLZMAN agrees, and the private DOORS show tickles the right part of HOLZMAN this time. He pulls the trigger, signing the band to ELEKTRA RECORDS—HOLZMAN's first order of business: manufacturing MORRISON's look. HOLZMAN immediately hired JAY SEBRING to give MORRISON a hairdo that will bring out his big-dick energy. Three days after signing to ELEKTRA, the DOORS shared the bill with LOVE. MORRISON, already feeling the COMPANY shackles tightening, surprised the tar out of his bandmates and WHISKY staff by adlibbing:

FuckYouMamaAaallllllNightLooonggYyyyyaaaaaahhhh!

Maybe MORRISON was paying a thoughful tribute to the recently sacrificed FIRST AMENDMENT DALI LAMA—BRUCE. Whatever poetic reasoning MORRISON could muster wouldn't have mattered a hoot to VALENTINE, and when the old man gets wind of MORRISON's public OEDIPAL outburst, he's fuming mad, and immediately shows the DOORS the window, relieving them right then and there of any commitments to the house. On August 25, 1966, ROBERT LEE FROST's (credited as DAVID KAYNE) exploitation pseudo-documentary *MONDO BIZARRO* premieres. SAUL RESNICK (also of *THE MAIDENS OF FETISH STREET*) is credited as part of the electrical department; BOB CRESSE co-produces. One of the exploitative segments features VITO in his element:

> NARRATOR: It is here in this great Los Angeles basin that we find the elusive search for love and fulfillment taking forms never dreamed of by Michelangelo, Shakespeare, or Dante ... Art in Los Angeles is by no means restricted to the professional ... This is Vito, a sculptor, painter, poet, dancer, and photographer, truly a Renaissance man. His approach to the arts is joyously creative and spontaneous.

Tiger print bikini bottoms vibrate and erupt on a model's derriere just inches from the camera's eye. We are in CLAY VITO, hanging out in the dim basement studio with VITO, who suddenly manifests with a camera in hand, the MAD SCULPTOR excitedly snapping pics of the topless dancer. She freezes in a pose, he snaps a shot, and then the two return to FREAKING-OUT. The fleshy object bends into another living sculpture, motionless until the next shutter click. We move on to VITO pasting those snapshots onto small, geometric glass shapes before affixing them to a tessellated, sculpted figure-form which HE has named *BENDING DANCER*—the pointy female dancer, bends at the waist, touching her toes, pointing her rigid glass ass skyward toward EASTON GYM's floor. She is raised on a table, allowing VITO to survey her from underneath, and carefully place a triangular picture in an empty spot on her belly. VITO'S booming voice sharpens the air:

> My name is Vito, and I am a sculptor. And the figure that you see here is a glass construction entitled "Bending Dancer." I cut out photographs of girls, and then I tape them onto pieces of glass, and then I glue the pieces together on the figure, which is two-thirds life-size. I also do more conventional kinds of sculpture. This is my protest against prejudice and intolerance in the world. I believe that we should love one another rather than hate. I believe in peace rather than war. I try to put that into my work. Now, I consider myself a deviant from the norm. The word *deviant* is considered an unhealthy word in our culture. But without the so-called *deviated man*, the normal man long would have perished because the deviated is the one who brings an element of beauty, an element of aesthetics into the world. And without beauty, it's pointless for man to exist. I'm interested in adding some element of design to my general attitude in life. Otherwise, it's a bore and mundane, and I'm not particularly interested in it. Many people think that I'm some kind of a nut, but I don't care, just as long as they buy my sculptures.

[END]

LIFE MAGAZINE publishes the feature article, *THE MAD NEW SCENE ON SUNSET STRIP* by ROGER VAUGHAN, highlighting the CALIFORNIAN everyday lifestyle lived by VITO, SUE, and GODO. Ten years back, before VITO was VITO, he appeared in this same popular publication promoting BOCK's WPR release, *THE CHICO HAMILTON QUARTET IN HI-FI*. In this current article, VAUGHAN summarized:

> And what do you know, there are Vito and Sue and Karl and Beatle Bob and Godot, all making the last call at Wil Wright's at 1 in the morning. Godot is 3 1/2, but he can sleep late, what the hell, and he really digs ice cream. These are famous people, the Strip's beautiful people. Vito is a sculptor with very long, scraggly hair and the face of an old seaman, wrinkled and half-shaven and beautiful. He has on a wild furry shawl thing, buttoned and wrapped about him in some mysterious way. Sue is his wife, blond and disarrayed. Sue is 23. She breastfeeds the boy Godot everywhere and any time —at civic meetings where they talk about things like cooperation with the police, or at parties, or in clubs. "Sue," Vito says, as though he were addressing a child, "here is your ice cream. Take the cone, Sue." She smiles a vacant smile and looks through him. "Hi," she says and takes the cone. Karl is their friend in a white leather car coat, high-heeled boots, hair in a mad confusion of long ringlets, and a goatee. Beatle Bob wears a page boy hair-do and has a nice smile. He is six and a half feet tall and 130 pounds. He paints. Godot is the most beautiful child in creation. Pure blond hair to his shoulders, pudgy little cheeks, and blue eyes that are steady and make you want to weep. He is always dressed like his father, in wraps and shawls and boots and things like that, a 3 1/2-year-old bohemian cat. Godot, Godot, how old are you? "Free and a half years old," he says defiantly, and Vito chuckles with pride. Back outside the ice cream place, you suddenly feel yourself coming apart.

In the LETTERS TO THE EDITOR section of *LIFE MAGAZINE*'s next issue:

> Dear sirs: What we need now is an understanding of the environment that produced the Ellies, the Vitos, the Sues, and the Karls. And what will the present environment do to their sons and daughters? How interesting it would be to see an article 20 years from now on Vito and Sue's young baby Godo.

September 1 thru 11—Another hole is poked in the WHISKY fabric when VALENTINE banned the DOORS, but DAVID CROSBY and the remaining BYRDS are more than willing to fill the sudden 10-day vacancy. On September 9, 1966, an advertisement on page 13 of today's *FREEP* features a collage made up of images of FRANZONI, ZAPPA, and LITTLE GARY FERGUSON—captioned under it:

> *Pat Morgan, Dallas Producer, is presenting one of the wildest light shows and dance freak-out performances at the Shrine Exposition Hall Saturday night, Sept. 17,* according to Joe Shugurs, the top West Coast Emcee. The show will feature the Mothers of Invention, Little Gary Ferguson, along with the West Coast Pop Art Experimental Band Count Five, Kenny Dino, and The Factory. Charles Camptin of the L.A. Times says *The West Coast Pop Art Experimental Band is a total experience of incredible crescendos of sound, sustained walls of sound that seem to have a physical presence in the room.* The Mothers of Invention are reviewed elsewhere in this issue.

This summer posed a ZARATHRUSTRIAN moment for PAPA VITO and his ungrateful-but-cunning disciple, *FRANKY-BABY* ZAPPA. Their super-egos tussle over the belle of the ball, MISS SUNSET STRIP, each taking to the media to plead their case for pole position as DISTRICT COUNTERCULTURE AMBASSADOR (since BRUCE cannot orate from the GREAT BEYOND). AND SO IT BEGINS: ZAPPA airs out his dirty, stripped slacks in *FREEP* on September 16. An individual in the MOI camp, *SUZY CREAMCHEESE*, takes out an ad in the form of an article. On page ten, MADAME CREAMCHEESE calls to action a particular revolutionary responsibility when joining in on *FREAKING-OUT*:

> This is about the Mothers of Invention. We have watched them grow, and with their growth, we hopefully have grown. Their honesty has offended some and been provocative to many, but in any case, their performances have had a real effect on their audiences. The Mother's music is very new, and as their music is new, so is the intention of their music. As much as the Mothers put into their music, we must bring to it. The Mothers and what they represent as a group have attracted all of the outcasts, the pariahs, the people who are angry and afraid and contemptuous of the existing social structure. The danger lies in the "Freak Out" becoming an excuse instead of a reason. An excuse inlies an end, a reason a beginning. Being that the easiest way is consistently more attractive than the harder way, the essential thing that makes the "Freak Out" audiences different constitutes their sameness. A freak is not a freak if ALL are freaks. "Freaking Out" should presuppose an active freedom, freedom meaning a liberation from the control of some other person or persons. Unfortunately, reaction seems to have taken place of action. We SHOULD be as satisfied listening to the Mothers perform from a concert site. If we could channel the energy expended in "Freaking Out" physically into "Freaking Out" intellectually, we might possibly be able to create something concrete out of the ideological twilight of bizarre costumes and being seen being bizarre. Do we really listen? And if we really listen, do we really think? Freedom of thought, conversely, brings an awesome responsibility. Looking and acting eccentric is NOT ENOUGH. A mad tea party is valid only as satire, commenting ironically, and ending in its beginning, and that it is only a trick of interpretation. It is not creation, and It IS NOT ENOUGH. What WE must try to do then is not only comment satirically on what's wrong but try to CHANGE what's wrong. The Mothers are trying,
> [SUZY CREAMCHEESE'S SIGNATURE]

There's a protocol, bitches, ya'll can't just freak out, okay? VITO and SUE likely felt a tad jaded since ZAPPA has apparently co-opted their lifestyle, philosophy, and even their nicknames—*SUZY CREAMCHEESE* had been the alter ego for SUE PAULEKAS for some while already. It seems that the FREAKS were in danger of becoming a homogenized, marginalized *movement*, and VITO's always been in it for little more than nipples and pubes; to act as the master coffer for the directionless tickles and slaps rolling outta buses and into his HOLLYWOOD feeding grounds. VITO has embodied the very definition of *FREE LOVE*. To hell with *free thinking*. ZAPPA's bond with FRANZONI has strained, and his need for VITO is seriously waning—at least he thinks that's the case, but it is VITO who is breaking from the culture he spawned—going MONADISTIC—concerned only with self-reinvention, sewing his own new FREAK-flag to protect ALL THINGS VITO. Sep. 16—*LIFE MAGAZINE* is read by tens of thousands of homes in 1966, and VITO proves that he is one of them by following up VAUGHAN's article published three weeks earlier with a pic of GODO, and editorial corrections.

> Sirs: Here is Godot, "The most beautiful child in creation," according to Roger Vaughan. He is two-and-a-half rather than "free-and-a-half" years old.

GODOT PAULEKAS

> Pictures of the "wrinkled and half-shaven and beautiful father," Vito, and of the mother, Sue, "blonde and disarrayed" are available upon request.
>
> VITO PAULEKAS
> Los Angeles, Calif.

EXOTIC LONG HAIR FREAKOS RUNNING AMOK & CRAZY!—take over the SHRINE EXPOSITION HALL on September 17, 1966. The MOTHERS OF INVENTION perform with the seven-year-old dancing sensation from DALLAS, TX, LITTLE GARY FERGUSON. Ten days later, LOVE records at RCA STUDIOS in HOLLYWOOD, taking a well-deserved break from VALENTINE'S daunting WHISKY schedule, allowing for MOI to slip it in and play that venue for the first time. VITO and VALENTINE were cut from the same cloth, but ZAPPA had tremendous difficulty meeting the WHISKY's strict requirements. VALENTINE doesn't want any probable cause for law enforcement to show their ugly blue faces at the WHISKY. Oct. 6—The synthetic hallucinogen lysergic acid diethylamide (LSD) is deemed illegal in any form by the US GOVERNMENT. The next day in the *FREEP*, AUXILLARY MOTHER FRANZONI contributes a letter: *A 'MOTHER' AGAINST LSD*. FRANZONI's piece is given a top-billing slug line on the cover. He takes the opportunity to paint himself as an invisible-but-indispensable member of the MOI. This is FRANZONI'S first big freak-up. There also appears on page nine, an ad depicting the October sales calendar for ZEIDLER & ZEIDLER's clothing store; spotted with pro-narcotics catch phrases such as—*Dope is good for what ails you*—and—*Speed Week*—and perhaps most stingingly—*May the good dope fairly shine her love lite on the Mother of Invention*—Z&Z blatantly bastardized ZAPPA's (borrowed) mantra into things like—*FREAKS UNITE!*—to sling their merch. Another ad repeats the big MOI show featuring *THE SENSATIONAL BOY WONDER FROM DALLAS, TEXAS, LITTLE GARY FERGUSON*. This ad (laid out by VITO) is much easier on the eyes than the previous one for the same event. It is crucial to consider the images depicted here in relation to how VITO may have used *THE GIRLS ON F STREET* as shades of confessions. In this advertisement, a prominent picture of LITTLE GARY FERGUSON screaming into a mic, with a pained expression as he belts one out. FERGUSON's figure is bisected by a banner bearing his name, but the banner does not simply lie over FERGUSON's abdomen; his body (image) is severed into two sections—

pulled apart as if a victim of a medieval torture rack. His right hand hangs beside his hip. A duplicate image of FERGUSON (this one intact) is tilted on its X-axis, making him appear to lie on the ground, with his left foot in the left palm of the upright, bisected FERGUSON. Graphic black swirls leak out from the top of the lying-down boy's cabeza. Featured performers, including the CASS ELLIOT's MUGWUMPS, are listed all over the empty spaces—*THE WORLD-FAMOUS ARTIST AND SCULPTOR VITO with his wife, his child, and his entire entourage of dancers and freakers*—will provide an atmosphere for the *light show nirvana and optical psych-out Dance*. FRANZONI flees his 1000 N. SPAULDING AVE. apartment (less than 1.5 miles from CLAY VITO) to squat in an abandoned mansion at 2401 LAUREL CANYON. Initially serving as the old LAUREL TAVERN, western star TOM MIX bought the vacant watering hole in the 1920s and hired ROBERT BYRD (who would build 10050 CIELO DR. in two decades more) to turn the sprawling structure into what MIX lovingly christened THE TREE HOUSE. In mid-October, tensions between ZAPPA and VITO intensified. Everything about the previous *FREEP* publication appeared to have chapped MR. MOUSTACHE's parachute pants. ZAPPA lost his mind about two Z&Z ads that unified MOI, FREAKS, and DOPE. FRANZONI's article also caused the final rift between himself and ZAPPA. ZAPPA takes out ad space in *FREEP* to clarify a few recent misnomers:

> FREAK OUT OFFICIAL NEWS OF MOI—PUBLISHED WHEN WE CAN AFFORD IT—MOSTLY FOR FUN—MOTHERS FORCED TO CANCEL OUT OCTOBER 15th—from the Earl Warren Showgrounds in Santa Barbara due to a critical acoustic problem and non-existent P.A. facilities. We will, however, perform in Santa Barbara at the San Marcus High School Auditorium. PHONY FREAK INS, ZEIDLER DOPE ADS, & KARL FRANZONI'S LETTER—Kindly read this: A Statement of Policy, from Frank Zappa, for THE MOTHERS OF INVENTION—Last week's issue of the L.A.F.P. contained 3 items in print which, we feel, bear analysis and discussion. FIRST: the FREAK-IN ad for the Shrine Exposition Hall. The MOTHERS OF INVENTION are in no way, shape, or form connected with this ersatz promotion event. We repudiate this

act of mercenary indiscretion on these grounds: 1. We do not wish to be associated in name or spirit with any CORNBALL effort to exploit FREE MUSIC, FREE DANCE, or FREE PEOPLE as we see it being done here: We quote the ad: "The World Famous Artist & Sculptor VITO with his wife, his child, and his entire entourage of dancers and freakers" 2. We find the ad itself, the promoter's attitude toward his audience (of freakers), and the unethical implications of this misguided attempt to CORRUPT something we, as a group, feel is VALID (and worth fighting for), to be totally BULLSHIT... that is to say: FREAK-INs (also FREAK-OFFs & TURN-ONs) DON'T MAKE IT—SECOND: the ZEIDLER & ZEIDLER "dope fiend calendar" ads THESE NIFTY SPECIMENS OF PRE-PUBIC JUVENALIA (hand-lettered and cartooned by a frustrated pseudo-freako from Laguna Beach named Howard James (Baron Von) Lockway, who likes to advertise his radiant Buddha-hood & worldly teen-age knowledge of dope & drugs & stuff, along with ZEIDLER'S threads) HAVE TWICE INCLUDED REFERENCE TO FREAK-OUTS, AND TO US, AS A GROUP. LAST WEEK, ZEIDLER & ZEIDLER, IN A FLUSH OF PSYCHEDELIC BAD JUDGEMENT, DRIVEN BY THEIR INVINCIBLE & UNERVING SENSE OF THE SUPERFICIAL, ARMED ONLY WITH THEIR TOTAL LACK OF TAST & PERCEPTION, SAW FIT (in their infinite lack of WISDOM) TO INCLUDE A DEFTLY SECRETED BLURB WHICH PLEADED: "May The Good Dope Fairy Shine Her Love Lite On The Mothers of Invention" WE ARE NOT (no sir, buddy) FLATTERED OR ENTHUSED BY BARON VON ZEIDLER'S IMBECILE ATTEMPT TO ASSERT (!) HIS teen-age (in the deepest DICK CLARK sense of the word) coolness BY USING OUR GROUP NAME (with all its inherent rural cleanliness & protein value) TO: 1. Hustler Zeidler's MOD monstrosities (with which we find it hard to identify) and/or ... 2. Endorse any psychedelic, narcotic or laxative substance dispensed by FAIRIES or any other superficially aberrated person, by means of LOVE LITE, VASELINE, State Welfare and/or Federal Aid to Education. IT APPEARS THAT BARON VON ZEIDLER WANTS TO GO OUT IN A BLAZE OF PSYCHEDELIC MARTYRDOM (we could be wrong) AS EVIDENCED BY HIS APPARENT FETISH FOR ADVERTISING HIS KNOWLEDGE OF & AFFINITY FOR "DOPE." THIS WILL, NO DOUBT, PRECIPITATE SOME SORT OF MONSTRO BUST AT HIS "PAD" (hep talk) & GIVE

HIM A LOT TO WIMP ABOUT WHEN HE GETS OUT (is the status really worth it? wouldn't it be more fun to go back to surfing & playing with your crayons?) ... THEREFORE: WE HEREBY MAKE THIS KIND AND SUPERFICIALLY GERNEROUS OFFER ... that is to say: We, The Mothers of Invention, agree to play on Mr. Zeidler's front lawn NON STOP during the course of the routine Narco Bust tentatively described above (yes, from the moment they kick down your door till the moment they kick down your nose) ... NON STOP, baby! For only half of what we normally get at the Whisky a Go Go, and all YOU have to do is get a lot of extension cords to the front yard for our amplifiers (providing, of course, that the heat lets us know about it a few days in front). ACCEPTED BY [signature line for ZEIDLER & ZEIDLER to sign] (a swell bunch of guys and a heck of a good sport, GOD LOVE THEM). For further information contact our SuperManager, Herb Cohen, who will also give you a good price on weddings and graduation parties, not that you'll ever need it. THIRD: the article "A MOTHER AGAINST LSD" by Karl Franzoni. Karl's worthwhile and well-intended letter to the editor was, UNFORTUNATELY, incorrectly labeled as a public statement from a member of our group. KARL FRANZONI IS NOT A MEMBER OF THE MOTHERS OF INVENTION Nor does he claim to be ... BUT, FOR THE MOST PART, WE AS A GROUP AGREE WITH HIM IN HIS PLEA FOR A SANE DRUG POLICY (basically: stick it up your ass and fly to the moon). WE, AS A GROUP, DO NOT RECOMMEND ... VERILY, WE REPUDIATE ANY ANIMAL/MINERAL/VEGETABLE/SYNTHETIC SUBSTANCE, VEHICLE and/or PROCEDURE WHICH MIGHT TEND TO REDUCE THE BODY, MIND, OR SPIRIT OF AN INDIVIDUAL (any true individual) TO A STATE OF SUB-AWARENESS OR INSENSITIVITY ... that is to say: WE ARE HERE TO TURN YOU LOOSE NOT TURN YOU ON TURN YOURSELF ON THE SORT OF HIGH YOU REALLY WANT IS A SPIRITUAL HIGH AND YOU ARE BULLSHITTING YOURSELF IF YOU TRUST ANY CHEMICAL and/or AGRICULTURAL SHORT-CUT TO DO IT FOR YOU YOU CAN'T GE BUSTED YET FOR AWARENESS maintain your aristocratic coolness ... Sincerely, FRANK ZAPPA For The MOTHERS Of Invention

What a semi-talented-loser-dickhead—ZAPPA changed significantly when brothers HERBIE and MUTT COHEN took over the band's creative representation. ZAPPA's world and VITO's split into two distinct freaky tribes. In the divorce, ZAPPA got the lion's share of the FREAK girls, which handsome, persuasive CLAY VITO staples like BOBBY BEAUSOLEIL and RICKY APPELBAUM, brought in. MASKS! MASKS! MASKS!—Oct. 15, 1966. Get ready for the next *FREAK-IN* at the SHRINE EXPOSITION HALL, brought to LA by VITO via ZAPPA's current arch-rival, the nomadic promoter, PAT MORGAN. VITO's id explodes across this *FREEP* blip:

> Oct. 21—7 FAR-OUT BANDS IN ORBIT IN A FREAKATHON FRACTURE—JOIN SAINT VITO'S CRUSADE TO FREAK-OFF THE WORLD—Pat Morgan presents the KRLA Monster Halloween Freak-Off Dance at the Great Western Exhibit Center. Vito Paulekas, The Seeds, and others perform. MASKS! $100 CASH EACH TO 2 WIGGIEST MASKED FREAKERS Get your advanced tickets at the Free Press bookstore on Fairfax for $2.50.

There it is, folks. Never has the hide-in-plain-sight tactic been more expertly executed:

> *JOIN-VITO'S-CRUSADE-TO-FREAK—OFF-THE-WORLD*

This slogan, mixed with featured bands, is overlaid atop a hand-drawn spider web that looks more similar to a fanned-out stack of throbbing, plump, MICHELIN MAN-esque dildos. On a different page in this same issue, another full-page ad for the event:

> Vito Sue and Godo present a freak-out freak-in freak-up freak-down Halloween costume mostly painted genitals must be covered dance at the Hullabaloo Sunday, October 30 across from Palladium 18 and over—ID required light show music by the Daily Flash by the Sparrow $3.00 in advance all mutual ticket agencies one dollar if you wear a vito button $3.50 box office.

It is a provocative rectangle of text, surrounded by overlapping, jagged, cut-out images of disembodied arms and legs, creating a frame essentially made up of (or at least the idea of) flesh. Centered on both the top and bottom borders is VITO's NEW SYMBOL of unity; a symbol that he digs so much, that he goes so far as to use it as his letterhead— Imagine if you will four hands interlocking, each one a different hexadecimal tone shaking the wrist of the next, creating four right angles. The thumbs close in on the center of the square, forming a spinning four-cornered star. VITO'S literal trademark is clearly tied to his fascination with the *eternal cycle,* the *WHEEL OF LIFE,* and so on, fundamentally similar to the SICILIAN flag, the demon BUER, and VITO'S cover-worthy piece, *COUNTERPOINTS*. Maybe this hand-wheel-thingee is a symbol not of inclusion, but of conspiratorial complicity—serving as a shorthand identifier for those on the take or willing to be so. To complete the picture of the world at large in October of 1966, at the bottom right corner block of page 14, an ad:

> FREE SPEECH FOR BUTTONS! Get the buttons that say absolutely anything you want. The ultimate button is here! You put the message on yourself—with type-face letters that simply press on. Looks exactly like printing! Four 3" buttons and a Scrabble set full of letters for $2.00. Send name, address, and bread to THE ULTIMATE BUTTON CO. P.O. BOX 62 Kenilworth, Ill. 60043

During the final week of October, *SCULPTOR VITO PAULEKAS* and his *"freak-out" band* appeared on the *JOE PYNE SHOW* on KTTV-11 along with *writer-producer JERRY HOPKINS, PEACE CORPS official RAY HOLLAND, "human physics" exponent DR. CHAMPION K. TEUTSCH, feminist VELMA MENELKOCH*. VITO and the station manager got along very well and communicated in fluent LITHUANIAN. JOE PYNE and VITO, too, are friendly off-air, putting on what was essentially an act intent on helping to define the cultural and political divide—and to bolster ratings. Show me one red-blooded AMERICAN who doesn't like to tune in to a good fight now and again, I dare ya. Besides, PYNE ain't always so puritanical, nor was VITO strictly liberal commie-on-blast. The two gregarious media mavens met in the middle where public figures and celebrities are ALWAYS willing to put their differences aside and unite for a better day: P-A-Y-D-A-Y. At the precise moment when VITO's disappointment with AMERICA has climaxed, he and FRANZONI suffer a major falling-out and the two temporarily split; their JOHN DEE & EDWARD KELLY saga-mirroring will continue, don't you worry. October 28, 1966—On page 8 of today's *FREEP*, the *VITO FUCKS THE WORLD* ad runs once more before the BIG PARTY. Then nine pages later, ZAPPA takes out his own full-page ad (on behalf of THE MOTHERS) railing against what he deems to be adjunct behavior when stood-up next to HIS personal FREAK canon:

> READ THIS FIRST. Many people have been under the impression that THE MOTHERS are engaged in the field of ENTERTAINMENT. This is NOT TRUE. THE MOTHERS ARE STRIVING TO COMMUNICATE WITH (not specifically to entertain) THEIR AUDIENCE ... no matter how small that audience may be. WE HAVE DISCOVERED a small but active AUDIENCE OF DETRACTORS here in L.A. (consisting mainly of IMPOSTERS who would USURP & CORRUPT a number of CONCEPTS & TECHNIQUES which WE DEVELOPED...specifically the "FREAK OUT" & the "LIGHT SHOW NIRVANA"). These CHARLATANS and their STOOGES IN ATTENDANCE have attempted to besmirch OUR STERLING REPUTATION. WE WOULD LIKE TO COMMUNICATE WITH THIS (brak!) AUDIENCE on a higher plane, BUT unfortunately, that is NOT WHERE THEY'RE AT (to use an expression common to this area), THEREFORE: we reluctantly DESCEND (In the interest of higher education), momentarily sacrificing our most treasured principles ... WE DESCEND TO THEIR SUBTERRANEAN MILIEU (such a Machiavellian compromise!) TO RETURN LOGIC & PATIENT EXPLANATIONS FOR THEIR LOATHESOME BEHAVIOR. Next week, they will say we play dirty. Zappa goes on to complain and whine more and eventually circles back around to Pat Morgan and his TOP MINISTER OF

> PROPAGANDA (stooge) writing, For what seemed an eternity, SEAN MACGREGOR stooged his way through the TINSEL CITY column ... finally finishing in a pool of rank perspiration (from which he derived his opening lines about "VICTORIOUSLY STREAMING ARM PITS" quote) he rushed to the side of his master for approval (as he had done so many times before with TV producers) only to find the sinister Texas FREAK MERCHANT on the telephone....craftily SUCKING VITO (" ... we'll call you KING KARL—maybe getcha a little crown or something or a robe ... ") INTO HIS GRANDIOSE SCHEME TO FAKE OFF THE WORLD. SEAN MACGREGOR stood by, his soiled little paper in one hand, listening intently as THE BIG MAN contributed his telephonic hype ... "We'll put a bunch of ads in the Free Press where your whole entire entourage of dancers & freakers can see it and get turned on by it, and then we'll go to a BIG radio station that all the kids really dig—like KRLA—and we'll get them in on it, AND WE'LL ALL MAKE SOME BREAD ... I know you could use a little extra with Halloween coming up and all, and later Xmas has a lot of expenses, and you'll be wantin' to get a littlesomething for the Mrs' & your baby ... HOWSABOUT IT?" Somehow it worked ...

We should understand that it was far too simple for VITO to be exactly what everyone thinks him to be. ZAPPA says that VITO was *duped*, but the joke's on HIM. VITO, 53, is now after the big bucks and little fucks, having returned to his youth-roots to again fully embrace free capitalism —knowing all too well that the COMMUNIST model works out just fine on paper, but the equation collapses under the weight of REALITY and BIG GOVERNMENT. Taking a page from the PATSY-MAKING PLAYBOOK, ZAPPA chases an altogether different dragon, believing himself to be in the spearhead of a youth revolution, convinced that he and his merry musicians are fundamentally changing the ESTABLISHMENT, the very same ESTABLISHMENT, that, if without, would leave ZAPPA devoid of social commentary. If the illusory thing that ZAPPA *fought against* disappeared tomorrow, from what creative wellspring would he drink? All of the clownish dots and stripes would dry up (and they do; eventually). LOVE plays their final show at the WHISKY on October 30, headlining for BUFFALO SPRINGFIELD and SONS OF ADAM. At the GREAT WESTERN EXHIBIT CENTER, VITO oversees the *KRLA MONSTER HALLOWEEN FREAK-OFF DANCE*; the HALLOWEEN costume ball HE promised in *FREEP,* which sparked the FREAK FIGHT. At the end of October 1966, AL MITCHELL, owner of the FIFTH ESTATE COFFEE SHOP, printed and disseminated thousands of leaflets into every LOS ANGELES district high school:

PROTEST

PROTEST

POLICE MISTREATMENT OF YOUTH
ON SUNSET BLVD.

SAT. 9 P.M.

NOV. 12th

IN FRONT OF

PANDORA'S

BOX

8118 SUNSET STRIP

NO MORE

— Shackling of 14&15 yr olds
— Arbitrary arrests of youths
— Disrespect and abuse of youths by police

In November of 1966, LOVE released their second album, *DA CAPO,* which showcased the band's musicianship improvements in only months —da capo: ITALIAN; *from the head or the beginning, to go back and start again*—Just as VITO's 1956 sculpture, *COUNTERPOINTS*, da capo is a variation of the musical symbol *coda*, which is often indicated on sheet music by the initials DC. This tells the musician to return to the start of a section, or sometimes to the beginning of the entire piece. The coda is another reference to the ETERNAL WHEEL—the life cycle—the ZODIAC. D.C. also happened to be the initials of LOVE's drummer, DAN CONGA. On November 12, nearly 1,000 enraged teenagers flooded the corner of SUNSET and CRESCENT HEIGHTS boulevards, near PANDORA'S BOX, rallying against its upcoming scheduled demolition and the increasing police violence seemingly directed at the LA youth. A mandatory municipal curfew was enacted, pressing the teens up against the proverbial and physical white picket fence. When a heavy police presence turned up after the *TEEN RIOT* started, VITO made that 1.5-mile straight shot south on CRESCENT HEIGHTS BOULEVARD to the subterranean comforts and security of CLAY VITO. Less than a week later, the fuzz sank their blue hooks into one of the FREAKS; the stinky, greasy, broken gasket is none other than KARL O. FRANZONI. YOINKS! This is bad news for FREAKS and MOTHERS:

> Nov. 18—*Long Beach Independent,* Singer Gets Indicted for Mail Fraud—LOS ANGELS—A part-time North Hollywood singer was indicted by a federal grand jury Thursday for allegedly selling two ineffective "sex machines" through the mail. Indicted on 30 counts of mail fraud was Carl Franzoni, 33, purportedly a part-time singer with a local group known as "The Mothers." According to Assistant U.S. Attorney Arthur I. Berman, Franzoni lived in North Hollywood, but his whereabouts are now unknown, and he is sought on a $1,000 fugitive warrant. The indictment charges Franzoni with selling the machines through the mail from March of 1963 through February of 1965. Franzoni allegedly used the business names "Hydromedic Institute" and "Cecelia de Stefano."

The *LA EVENING CITIZEN NEWS* ran an identical indicting report on page three. One week later, FRANZONI went on the lam—to CANADA—and, by doing so, cleared a path for LAW ENFORCEMENT to put pressure on FRANZONI's contacts and acquaintances. Not groovy, man, not groovy at all. Late November 1966—Between the closing of the teen sanctuary PANDORA'S BOX, the general civil unrest, PLUS! FRANZONI's bust for mail-order busts; it's all too heavy for ZAPPA, and he books it with wifey GAIL for NYC. IT'S THE ONES YOU HATE LIVE FOREVER—December 23, 1966—THE WINTER SOLSTICE. Today marks the final day of SATURNALIA, if you follow that kind of thing. While *unattended* on the roof of the SMITH BUILDING, VITO and SUE's three-and-a-half-year-old son, GODO, walked over a painted skylight/trapdoor and crashed through it to the landing 12 feet below. The CHILD survived the initial fall, but suffered severe cuts to HIS head. HE was rushed to nearby PRESBYTERIAN HOSPITAL for emergency care, but shortly after admittance, GODO PAULEKAS died.

> Dec. 26—*The Los Angeles Evening Citizen News,* 3-Year-Old Boy Killed By Home Fall—HOLLYWOOD—A 3-year-old boy was fatally injured Friday when he fell through a skylight on the roof of his apartment home and fell more than 20 feet to a stairway landing. Godo Paulekas, 303 N. Laurel Ave., was rushed to Hollywood Receiving Hospital and then transferred to General Hospital, where he died of head injuries. Police said the tot was playing on the roof of the building while his mother, Susan, 25, was helping a photographer take some pictures of a group of young teenagers. While the mother was occupied on one portion of the roof, the youngster was playing with an unidentified 8-year-old child near the skylight. The mother reportedly told police she heard the crash of shattering glass and found her son's body amid the broken glass of the skylight on the landing.

Authorities use the tragic *incident* to malign VITO's reputation even furtherand to stir up intense speculation on the goings-on inside the

BASEMENT. High-profile LA COUNTY CORONER, THOMAS NOGUCHI, conducted an extensive autopsy at the demand of LA DISTRICT ATTORNEY, EVELLE J. YOUNGER, only to find, as most expected, the three-and-a-half-year-old's system clean of drugs. *MONDO HOLLYWOOD* director, ROBERT CARL COHEN, claims that GODO choked on his own vomit after having been restrained in a supine position—HOSPITAL ADMINISTRATORS claim the CHILD was uncontrollable, and repeatedly shouted—*FUCK YOU*—at the hospital staff. On December 30, only four days after the FREAK tragedy, PAULEKAS family friend, JERRY HOPKINS, wrote an article for *FREEP* that appeared in the euphemistically titled section, MAKING IT. It is also worth noting that, for being such a dear friend, HOPKINS misspells GODO's name five times, adding a *t* at the end of it every chance he gets. He also managed to describe GODO while avoiding the obvious noun—*child.* HOPKINS, in essence, reduced GODO to an incommunicative object beholden by all who encountered him—an idol; a twentieth-century, falcon-headed HORUS THE YOUNGER:

> GODOT CAN'T COME TONIGHT—'My Flower ... My Butterfly', Godot achieved some fame in his young, full life this past summer when he and his parents, Vito and his wife Sue, were featured in a LIFE magazine spread about the Sunset Strip. Before that, and since, Godot truly earned his little place in life by being what he was, a small man exposed to what was happening, clapping his hands at everything. And then, before Christmas was over, there he was, dead—dead at just over three years of age from a fall through a skylight. He was, to me, a small blonde figure in hip-swaddling clothes (made by Sue) popping around Vito's studio on a Friday night when Vito conducted sculpture classes, a happy child eating clay. Vito called Godot "my flower ... my butterfly." He was a small figure at State Beach in the summer heat, nibbling at his mother's breast. He was the reason for celebration every night of the year, but especially in early December when there were birthday parties at his home at 303 North Laurel in Hollywood. He was the small person at the Great Underground Arts Masked Ball & Orgy who played the drums with the Mothers of Invention. He was a little man

> in his father's arms, hearing but not truly reacting yet to talk about the wrong in mankind being hatred and avarice and prejudice, the splendor of dancing, the immorality of the Vietnamese war, the joy of love. He was three. He was playing on the roof with his parents nearby. There were other children and grown-ups there, waiting for a photographer to come to take pictures for this newspaper. Little Godot climbed onto a skylight, and it collapsed. The people at the hospital said he was going to be all right. But he died. Clapping his hands and laughing, playing drums and eating clay, "My flower ... my butterfly" died.

In the same issue, the interview, *ZAPPA ZAPS THE BIG LIE*:

> WILLIAMS: Do you think the whole thing will die out—
> light shows and Freakouts?
>
> ZAPPA: Yeah, I hope it does. Dies tomorrow.

KENNETH ANGER claims that the preschooler was his first choice to play LUCIFER in his (maybe) upcoming film, *LUCIFER RISING*, which ANGER based on ALEISTER CROWLEY's book of the same name, depicting the writing of *THE BOOK OF THE LAW*:

> The first one was six years old, and he died in an accident, thinking he was an angel and could fly. His name was Godo. He had a hippy mother and a hippy father, who were both artists, and he was an absolutely stunning child. He had platinum blonde hair. It's never been cut since he was born, so it was down to his shoulders, and he looked like a Blake cherub. He was so awesomely beautiful. People would see him and just go, 'ahgh!' This kid had that charisma, that magick, but he died before I could use him. I told him I wanted him to be in the movie, and he agreed; he said yes. And I didn't suggest that he would try rehearsing flying on the roof, but that's where he died, in an accident, he fell off the roof. And you know, it's just heartbreaking. Everyone was in mourning; in fact, we never got over it.

1 9 6 7

VITO continues on a media blitz, appearing with SUE and FRANZONI in a US GOVERNMENT-produced 16mm scare-educational film, *LSD-25*. Filming took place around the BAY AREA, primarily in SAN MATEO COUNTY. The January 6 and 13 issues of *FREEP* advertise VITO's debut rock album (produced by long-time FREAK dancer KIM FOWLEY):

You've seen him, heard about him
Now! — Live on Record

Now! While they last

The album is available exclusively at *FREEP*'s new bookstore, THE KAZOO, which sits directly across the street from the favorite FREAK hangout, CANTER'S DELI. THE KAZOO operates daily from 10:00a to 2:00a, at which time the employees head to CANTER'S DELI and then VITO's studio (less than half a mile southwest). The January 22 *SACRAMENTO BEE* reviews the newly released 12" LP, *WHY DID LENNY BRUCE DIE?* Although VITO provides only a single point of insight, he is listed on the album gatefold as being a close compadre, stating: *To sculptor Vito Paulekas, Bruce was "a great rabbi."* At the 3:57 mark of the LP:

> RICHARD WARREN LEWIS: Other intellectuals, like sculptor Vito Paulekas, unflinchingly endow Bruce with the qualities of a messiah.

> VITO PAULEKAS: As recently as just a matter of two or three weeks before his death, Lenny Bruce influenced my thinking tremendously. I learned about myself. I learned about my own hypocrisy. I listen to him as a student. I listen to him as a great teacher, and I have remarked over and over to my students throughout these years that there was really one great rabbi, one great teacher. And, look to him. He'll be placed amongst the great thinkers of mankind. But, you know, pay homage to him now. Lenny Bruce is really a rabbi.

In mid-February, *THE NEW YORKER* published *FLY TRANS-LOVE AIRWAYS* by 28-year-old journalist RENATA ADLER. ADLER laid out the SUNSET STRIP and described the HOLLYWOOD FREAK scene with her usual elitist-cum-trippy journalistic flair—An excerpt describing the freakiest moments of her visit:

> By 5 a.m., six groups had played, and the Monkees, the Miracles, and the Mama's and the Papa's had joined the audience. Vito's group had been taken offstage earlier when it was announced that all further dancing would be done by two union dancers, in red spangles, on the balconies of the dance hall. Within moments, however, the two union dancers had been supplemented by a dancer in a silver costume and silver boots, who materialized onstage, and since no one seemed to know whether she was union or not, Vito took this as a cue to send his group back onstage, where they remained. The size of the audience had not diminished in the slightest, nor had the volume of the radio concert in the parking lot. At five, there was a pause, and both the audience and Vito's group seemed tense; everyone was quite sure that it was the Love's turn to play. By five-twenty, when there was still no sign of the Love, the management was trying to divert the crowd with jukebox music. The audience, however, appeared quite accustomed to delays of this sort; the pause seemed to bear out their expectation that the Love would be the next group

> to go on. It was. A record was cut off abruptly, the front curtain rose, a group of four whites and three Negroes was revealed, and the lead singer, dressed in a black stocking cap and brown pants and vest, leaned slightly sidewise, yawned briefly, and began to sing. The group, with what seemed a kind of driving, electronic desperation, played a song called "I Flash on You." When the song was over, the audience cheered a kind of desperation cheer, as one might cheer an acquittal verdict for a defendant against whom the case looked bad. The group played two more numbers, and then, in the middle of a song called "She Comes in Colors," the lead singer walked off. He did not return for several minutes, but the group played on. Then, when he did return, he ignored the microphone and sat down abruptly on a crate amid the electronic equipment. Several times, as the group still played, he seemed on the point of rising but sat down again. Finally, he rose, walked carefully forward, and, grasping the microphone, leaned forward a few moments, with teeth bared, and began to sing. He sang a long time, then stopped and let the group play several minutes more. Suddenly, in a calm speaking voice, he wished the audience a Merry Christmas and reminded them that Halloween might soon return. The front curtain dropped. The audience cheered again.

ADLER reported that at one point, VITO produced one of his personalized buttons for her friend MEG to use as a trouser mend:

> "Fix your pants, baby," Vito said quite calmly, producing what he called a "fraternity button," designed by him. "Just relax." Meg took the button, pinned her pants, and returned onstage.

It's safe to assume that MEG'S modesty kept her from making the FREAK cut. To pull things into focus—VITO's first daughter, ANN, is now 16 years old and a student at GUNN HIGH SCHOOL in PALO ALTO, CA. At the close of February 1967, BEAUSOLEIL's rock band ORKUSTRA plays *THE INVISIBLE CIRCUS/RITE OF SPRING* event at GLIDE MEMORIAL UNITED METHODIST CHURCH in SAN FRANCISCO. ANGER, *by chance,* was in attendance, and so impressed with BEAUSOLEIL's performance that ANGER accosted *CUPID* in the parking lot, and right there on the spot, offered the young guitarist the role of LUCIFER in his next film. ANGER recalls:

> Bobby was a very beautiful boy with beautiful blue eyes. He was nineteen years old, and he had long hair to his shoulders. He was very cocky and very self-confident, but he was a Scorpio, and he had a lot of Scorpio traits, which are charismatic, but they're not always easy to work with (and I have a half Scorpio in my horoscope). But on the other side was a toad, a beautiful golden toad ... I knew there were these two natures, and he could be either this poisonous toad or an angel.

ROGER MCGUINN of the BYRDS said LA *was an amazing music town, almost more than it was a movie town.* The FREAK moment had plateaued and dissolved into our current understanding of a HIPPIE, just as the BEATNIKS usurped the BEATS. VITO has permanently blipped on local law enforcement's radar—His family, neighbors, students, and acquaintances are routinely surveilled and pressured to give up dirt on him. After 20 years of building his monster underground, DR. PAULEKENSTEIN has steered rock gods and disenfranchised youth, but the creation, a formless mass, is coming for its creator. VITO questioned the next, proper FREAK move. He is interviewed in *TORRID FILM REVIEWS*, a magazine devoted to subversive, d-market movies, illustrating how VITO was pivoting from music into the world of nudies, softies, and roughies. Actor and CLAY VITO regular, SAL MINEO, has become something of a counterculture enthusiast, and according to PAMELA DES BARRES (née MILLER), MINEO shot freakloads of 16mm footage at CLAY VITO for an abandoned (then eventually *lost*) documentary film about the FREAK scene.

VITO & SUE

Wish to announce an

EXHIBITION

of

Drawings & Paintings

BY THEIR SON

THE LATE GODO

SUNDAY - February 26, 1967

1 to 5 P.M. and 8 to 12 P.M.

AT THE ORACLE

840 N. Fairfax Av.

VITO & SUE take out a full-page ad in the late February edition of *FREEP*. THE ORACLE is a quarter of a mile due north of JAY SEBRING's now world-famous salon at 725 N. FAIRFAX AVE.

March—At the edge of SAN FRANCISCO's prestigious ALAMO SQUARE, at 1198 FULTON STREET & SCOTT, sits a fine example of ITALIANATE VILLA architecture, with its great wooden palazzo, tall vertical lines, and squared bay windows. The 28-room mansion was built by GERMAN candy baron WILLIAM WESTERFELD for $10,000 in 1889. At one point, a handful of CZARIST RUSSIANS squatting in the mansion began running a roukus nightclub out of it. It quickly acquired the nickname: THE RUSSIAN EMBASSY. WESTERFELD'S original build included a tower and a carriage house (which was eventually converted into the first automobile garage in SAN FRANCISCO). Horny, hetero, 20-year-old BOBBY BEAUSOLEIL boards there at the RUSSIAN EMBASSY, free of charge, with ANGER, 40, who foots BEAUSOLEIL'S rent after he agreed to replace GODO as the ANGEL OF LIGHT. In addition, BEAUSOLEIL has conceded to serving as ANGER's personal chauffeur. On EASTER SUNDAY 1967, LOS ANGELES COUNTY stages its first *LOVE-IN*, and VITO and his DANCERS show up, front and center, dolled up and down in full FREAK regalia. Filmmaker LES BLANK captured it all, and much of VITO'S dancing is featured in BLANK'S documentary, *GOD RESPECTS US WHEN WE WORK, BUT LOVES US WHEN WE DANCE.* VITO throws a proper FREAK-fit, thrusting his pelvis at the camera, which struggles to take in all of VITO's freakiness. A pink pentagram painted across the whole of his chest has faded, but the ꜥ-n-ḫ—known otherwise as an ANKH symbol—is highly visible, embroidered on a codpiece flap dangled over VITO'S unit. The EGYPTIAN icon itself mimics the appearance of a cock & gonads. ZAPPA and MOI are, of course, absent from the festivities; ZAPPA having flown the coup earlier today, his flapping chicken wings darkening the sky on his way outta LA and into the BIG APPLE (where worms are more at home)—Elsewhere in AMERICA—If you're going to SAN FRANCISCO ... be sure to take notice that drugs, paranoia, and guns have rapidly replaced the body paint and flowers in your hair. Artist BURT SHONBERG got a lorious write-up in the April 18, 1967 edition of the *LOS ANGELES CITIZEN NEWS*.

HE does an impression of a pretentious rubber dong:

> One by one, the basic ingredient is an unknown painter who likes to call himself a "magic realist" or a "living surrealist," his brush dipped in mixed mysticism ... "The artist is supposed to struggle and suffer and all that crap—the stuff of pulp magazines," beams Shonberg behind a few five-o'clock shadows. "An organization that supports him is a beautiful set-up." As guidance for critics and audiences alike, the incorporated creator offers a line from the Tibetan Book of the Dead: "Be not attracted to, nor repelled by anything." Then, nodding and smiling, the artist advises, "Let it all be news."

In May of 1967, ELMER VALENTINE closed the TRIP. VITO and SUE attend the art opening for one of the many young devoted FREAKS at his WHITTIER HIGH SCHOOL. The out-of-place FREAKS make a splash and get more looks than the artworks. WHS student and part-time FREAK, DAVID DOTY, is thrilled to see that his strange basement brethren have shown. VITO, as always, was turned on like a hunter scanning their arena for the best angle, eyes peeled for the choicest take-downs. RUMPLEDFORESKINE and his band of FREAKS have become omnipresent, gobbling up acres of NOTORIETYBURG. VITO'S unexpected presence no doubt caused unease amongst WHS administrators, as well as attending parents who saw through (or at least questioned) what was likely really going on behind VITO's lupine lookers. For one week in May, the DOORS headlined the WHISKY for a final time, taking a backseat opening for the BYRDS (who agreed to share the bill this time—ONLY). JIM MORRISON was scheduled to meet JACK KEROUAC at CLAY VITO right after the DOORS' finish at the WHISKY. KEROUAC showed up, early and drunk, only to be lured into the NEW AGE TARTAROS by topless SIFREAKS posted up in the basement's steel doorway, their softening, tempera-painted nipples air-drying, pointed artistically at the lingering sun—creating six glorious googly eyes staring back at KEROUAC. THEY draw him downstairs inside CLAY VITO, where a HIGH

PRIESTESS SIFREAK was painting shapes around an assembly line of innies and outties. The artist got her brush tangled in a patch of healthy, tight pubes that stretched over the panty waistband of one of the models. KEROUAC could barely blink. The alcohol had evaporated the moisture from under his lids, leaving his buttered ass to take in the VOLTAIResque performance with unobscured clarity. He seized the opportunity to illuminate their *art* with tales of a teenage VITO as he is carried to a dark corner—telling stories of the BEANTOWN lad who KEROUAC (or LITTLE JOHN as he was known in adolescence) would watch apostatizing from an applebox that had been dragged to a street corner in LOWELL, MA—It was *VITO: THE MAGIC PAGAN*!, KEROUAC expelled, cupping his mouth with his hand so the bourbon reeking from his bowels didn't kill the angels as THEY stuffed his empty trouser pockets with fistfuls of wet clay. The SIFREAKS made their move to devour KEROUAC bite by bite, but SUE suddenly interrupted the coven, reminding them of almighty MORRISON'S expected appearance at any moment. KEROUAC passed out, his flaccid unit sucked back into his body, disappearing (lending, perhaps, reason for his juvie nick: *LITTLE JOHN*). They then tried giving him a basement shower, but it was of no use; he had OD'd on epididymal hypertension, MASSACHUSETTS memories, and stiff drink. Despite their violent rigor, the SIFREAKS couldn't revive the shrivelled-up, plastered poet, and soon their futility mutated, once again, into creativity. THEY returned wth LITTLE JOHN to their tempera palette, making HIM up to look like a proper SOLOMON ISLAND CHIEFTAIN—painting a wild, blocky smile and crescent moon across KEROUAC'S face before floating upstairs to ready THEMSELVES for MORRISON. KEROUAC awakened later, alone, and stumbled his way out through the steel door onto the alley, where he found a bike resting against the SMITH BUILDING. He mounted it and stole it without haste, pedalling west down the long LAUREL AVENUE alley into the darkness, making for the coast he's heard so much about.

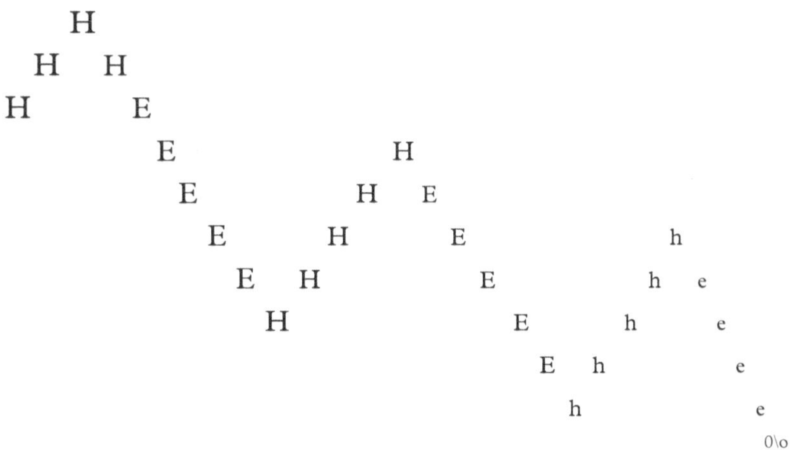

A light rain fell as MORRISON arrived at CLAY VITO with a collection of poems under arm for KEROUAC'S review—the lot of loose leaves bundled with a strap; on it, embossed in gold: JAMES DOUGLAS MORRISON. He knocked on the storeroom window with a coin (just as VITO instructed everyone to do) for a long, long time, but an answer never came. On the SUNSET STRIP, bands that were once summertime roster club staples were instead playing big, popular venues and music festivals (like THE MONTEREY POP FESTIVAL, which WHISKY enthusiasts, and music mogul, LOU ADLER, orchestrated). The record deals were maximized, allowing once destitute musicians to move into established affluent neighborhoods. RENATA ADLER claimed her personal stake in responsibility for manufacturing the *important movement*:

> ... In 1966, I proposed to the then-managed editor of Esquire, Byron Dobell, that I do a piece on a colorful group of Angelenos, led by Vito Paulekas, who dressed in strange clothes and spent their time dancing to folk-rock music. Dobell liked the idea but was forced to report back to me that Esquire's editor, Harold Hayes, nixed the idea with one phrase: "Just another bunch of California weirdos." When 70,000 people who dressed, danced, and acted like Vito

> showed up in San Francisco the next summer and had a colorful name attached to them—hippies—every magazine editor got the idea.

Independent journalist, RICHARD GOLDSTEIN, sat in on VITO's basement class, taking notes for what became *THE HEAD FREAK WAITS FOR A NEW SON*, published in *SOUNDS ON CAMPUS*. GODO died only twelve weeks before its publication. GOLDSTEIN, a stranger to the PAULEKAS tribe by all accounts, somehow mustered enough respect to leave the BECKETTIAN *t* off the memorialization, and managed to refer to GODO as a *child* and not simply as an object (like *family friend* JERRY HOPKINS):

> LOS ANGELES—The three-year-old kid, as the story goes, answered the door, took a cool look at the policeman standing there, raised his full blue eyes, and declared: "Fuck off," he repeated, without blinking. So, naturally, the policeman left. The legend is one of many traveling the Los Angeles underground these days concerning a sapling who struck like a wet branch and went by the name of Godo.
>
> For the time being, Godo is dead.
>
> His father, one Viautus Alphonsus Paulekas, is the chief of a vague tribe known as the Freaks. In the legend, Vito is part teacher, part artist, part dancer. His hands and feet are instruments of magic; his eyes are sorcerer's eyes. Vito is not the most articulate of insurrectionaries, but he comes on booming like a big-city rebel. His theories make meager sense, but they are expounded with a galactic joy that threatens to burst into thunder any time he opens his mouth. His eyes jolt from briar patches of wrinkles, and there is a phosphorous giggle tacked onto every statement to let you know that behind the dogma is the fizz of experience. His apartment, crammed below a busy men's gymnasium, has the look of a shrine. The living room is slung with webs of beads and drapery. The bedroom is small and dark, like the passage of a good-sized sewer; its only window is shrouded in leaded glass. The whole place resounds with canned patter from a

radio turned up Up UP to compete with the bouncing of medicine balls and barbells above. All over the house, on every wall, hand-painted pictures of Godo's immaculate face. In the basement, where Vito teaches sculpture, work by father and son stands in a row along walls caked with clay. Godo's watercolors run to bold, resolute patterns. No merging shapes or colors - just simple, certain forms. Vito's busts look like Ed Roth's busy work. They are leering, lipless people with gaping teeth and breasts. They are super-detailed, bug-eyed monsters crying out in Los Angeles terror. The art of Los Angeles, inherent in every brazen boulevard, celebrates the grotesque. Those sun-baked Pacific people will have none of that Brancusi perfection in their sculpture. There will be no breeze-like Calder mystery, no Giacometti bone-marrow angst. Vito's scene could double as a set for one of those 1950 Hollywood exposés that took you behind the scenes into a "real" beatnik pad, where chicks danced bra-less to bongos while some collegiate-looking cat read poetry and smoked a jade pipe.

Vito comes on like a living cliche. He is everybody's favorite professional beatnik. This adherence to form explains the attention Vito gets from filmmakers, TV producers, and editors of girlie magazines. He looks too much the rebel to be one. His familiar blend of Love-Work-Marxism actually renders him benign because that is what we expect from artists. Vito is cast as a nut and tolerated as one. He has made frequent appearances on the Joe Pyne Show ("to establish communication with the people of Los Angeles"), where he makes an ideal sparring partner. The rumored friendship between "Iconoclast-Vito" and "Joe-the-Brute" is no coincidence; both are roles that seem too simple to be real. So it comes as no surprise to learn of Vito's forays into exploitation. A skin magazine features a photo spread about "a name that represents nonconformity, artistic freedom, originality...one of the most diversified sculptors the world has ever known." Vito is featured in films like Girl on F Street or Mondo Bizarro, neither of which will make them drool at the editorial office of Cahiers du Cinema. "Any publicity is good publicity," he reflects. "You go through all this routine with naked girls, and they pan over and show your sculpture. I believe in the object itself; once they show that, they can say anything."

If there were no Vito, the L.A. cops would have to invent him. His peculiar fraud is what the scene has made of him. He takes his wife, Sue, and his people (a group of 35 kids, costumed, energized, and ready to dance) and hops from club to club, grooving with the city's best rock bands. To watch the tribe dance is a revelation. There are leaps and bounds, swaying strands of hair, and bouncing, stomping feet. Sue moves like Fay Wray caught in some frenzied Kong embrace: neck taut, shoulders erect, hair streaming free. In the center, Vito flays the smoky air and roars. It is pure, awkward energy, but under all that rampant spasticity is a certain go-go grace. This is because when Vito dances, he lets his eyes take over his body, and all that glittering blue shows. To the kids, Vito's people are the most brazen exponents of a lifestyle that is somewhere between reprehensible and forbidden. Teen culture demands of its heroes that they be a menace to adults, but though Chief Vito defines his tribal code as an "exorbitant, unpredictable, whimsical way of behaving," he neglects to mention defiance. Still, just by being themselves, the Freaks haunt Los Angeles. They are likely to turn up anywhere, and they are sure to panic the straight people. They have no skill at physical destruction, but whenever the Freaks appear, they cause such loathing and terror in the general populace that they might as well be shouting, "burn, baby, burn!"

Vito claims he is "the most checked-out man in this city," elaborating: "There are plainclothesmen in all my classes, and whenever we dance somewhere, the management is threatened with all kinds of injunctions." His distaste for Heat goes back a long way. At 18, he spent a year and a half in a reformatory, and after that, he admits, he was busted a few more times before he went straight. Vito's childhood is a hazy fairytale. He is the son of a Lithuanian sausage maker who settled in Massachusetts. He recalls: "My father's fingers became shaped for stringing frankfurters. He used to walk home with sausages wrapped around his legs." Vito's formal education encompassed four blurred years of his life. All he chooses to remember is an early penchant for sculpture. "I used to fool around with clay. While the other kids were busy learning to be useful citizens, I was sculpting naked women."

His are successes whether or not it is inspired because it is uniquely his. His dance technique needs no esthetic: it was perfected during Vito's career as a marathon dancer. "I had to place myself entirely in the possession of my partner for three hours. I carried her through the milkman's matinee, and then she carried me. After six months of that kind of trust, I learned to let go completely."

Dancer, sculptor, danger, scofflaw. He will never come of age, says the legend. His eyes will never wrinkle. It is beautiful to watch Sue and Vito play. His son Godo was a child's child. Life magazine described him as "the most beautiful child in creation, with pure blond hair to his shoulders ... pudgy little cheeks and blue eyes that are steady and make you want to weep." Godo is still central to the Freak mythology. He is Apollo-Jesus, the golden boy, the realization. At two-and-a-half, Godo was reputed to be an expert drummer. Amid Vito's ugliest statuary stands an angelic bust of his son. It is a stylistic reversal: no torment, no suspicion, none of the envy-condemnation Vito feels and shows the straight world. Just a father looking at his son. "Every place he went, Godo had an intensity with every human being," says Vito, "He sized up people long before I did, and he would tell me about them. He made love to everybody." Once, Godo kissed an old lady in Kanter's delicatessen in medias bagel.

"Godo is dead," Vito mutters. The wrinkled lids blink shut. A silent cough. A rasp in Vito's throat. It happened last December on Vito's roof. Godo encountered a rusted trap door and started to play with it. It opened, and Godo fell in. At the hospital, the doctors called it nothing serious and let Vito see his son. Godo lay strapped and spread-eagled on a metal table. A sterile towel covered the hole in his head. His fists were pale and clenched. Vito opened his blue eyes wider than ever as his son cried over and over: "Help me." An hour later, Godo had hemorrhaged and died. No earthquake, no fire-and-brimstone accompaniment, no final revelation. Just a real baby dying and two infant eyes asking a father to help. Absurdity kills myths.

"Godo is dead." Vito hardens, straightens, narrows. "The D.A.'s office is trying to get something on me for this," he explains in spurts. "I heard from people in their office that they tried to find evidence of drugs on Godo's body. It wasn't a rotten trap door they were after; that's legal. But drugs ... " No one has to accuse Vito; the subject of responsibility comes up by itself. Why wasn't a tracheotomy performed at the hospital? Why did they tie Godo down to the table? Why was the door left to rot? "An old friend of mine came to see us afterward," Vito recalls. "She said, 'Vito, your baby is dead. God punished you for doing the things you did with him.'" Vito's laugh becomes a nervous giggle. "My son was killed by a bum trap door, not by any God," he demands. No one says anything. No one accuses. But Vito feels the weight on his shoulders anyway. Somewhere behind those brash blue eyes lies Vito's wound. The superstition: God is punishing him for immeasurable evil. Godo is dead, and God, in the form of a cop, isn't through with Vito yet. But myths never die; they only transmigrate. Godo was a necessary solder. He held the legend together. He was living proof: the second Freaky generation. So, the underground awaits his resurrection, and the occasion may not be far away. Sue is six months pregnant and sewing clothes. A box of lacy nightshirts waits in anticipation. "My baby is dancing already in Sue's belly," Vito exalts. "Sue was dancing right in this kitchen while she was in labor. When Godo was born, he came out with his mouth already open, making noise."

The living legend has a new inspiration. A child messiah will be born among the Freaks. Lightning will strike Beverly Hills. Thunderbolts will shatter over Sacramento. Sunset Strip will hiss, crack, and split. Chief Vito's sorcerer's eyes will twinkle as - amid the stucco ruins - God is risen.

HELEN SWEET, VITO's live-in girlfriend from a decade earlier, designs fashionable women's shower caps for a PASADENA retailer, or so says an ad in the *LOS ANGELES TIMES*. At SUNSET SOUND RECORDERS in EAST HOLLYWOOD, LOVE tracked the first two songs for what was to become

FOREVER CHANGES. At the start of the sessions, the band members (except ARTHUR LEE) were high as kites, struggling to lay down anything LEE deemed usable, pissing him off to holy hell, forcing LEE to hire session musicians to motivate by humiliation; the ploy works. On June 23, as VITO observed his new baby girl resting on SUE's bosom, born just minutes ago in the corner of 303's kitchenette, he christened her—GRUVI NIPPLES PAULEKAS. Two weeks later, on the 7th of July, VITO appeared on *The JOE PYNE Show* with *students* FRANZONI and KEN ATTERSON. VITO and the GENERAL MANAGER of KTLA had maintained a close relationship, speaking fluent LITHUANIAN with each other and so on. But, when VITO made harsh remarks on tonight's show that are in direct opposition with the US GOVERNMENT'S policies on the VIETNAM WAR and *parent-forced* abortions, agents from MAYOR SAM YORTY's office assured VITO that he will never again appear on KTLA-TV (This television station was founded in 1947 by GERMAN JEW, KLAUS LANDSBERG, after PARAMOUNT PICTURES hired LANDSBERG and stuck him in a backlot garage to develop an experimental TV format. He does, and KTLA becomes the first broadcaster in LOS ANGELES to televise live coverage.) VITO crossed a fundamental FCC line and fixed his FALL GUY appeal squarely on the map. In 1967, media colloquialism deems a bad LSD experience as a *FREAK-TRIP*, or a *FREAK-OUT*, or a *BUMMER*, and talk of what they call—*flashback phenomena*—which may suddenly rear its ugly multi-colored head up to eighteen months after the initial dosing. JIM LOUDIA's multi-page spread, *PSYCHEDELIC FREAK-OUTS!* in the August 1967 edition of *MODERN MAN: THE ADULT PICTURE MAGAZINE,* depicts the swelling HOLLYWOOD underground anti-war scene. It only took PYNE one month to find his controllable, KTLA VITO replacement; one more inspired by self-destruction and his own massive id than anti-warisms—none other than VITO's longtime pal-turned-trippy-dippy-painter, BURT SHONBERG:

> Aug. 9—*The Decatur Daily Review*, THURSDAY RADIO HIGHLIGHTS—JOE PYNE SHOW—Foreign Correspondent Elaine Shepard, who wrote the popular "Doom Pussy" tells Joe of her experiences with a Marine unit in Vietnam. Artist Burt Shonberg gets inspiration for his paintings from psychedelic drugs. 7:30 a.m. WDZ.

Even with all of the sensitive topics SHONBERG and PYNE discussed (such as FREE LSD, MAN!, and repeating the tactile word: *pussy*), these subjects are still regarded as less offensive than VITO's speaking out against nationally mandated murder. LOVE, the band, not the emotion, has labored through three grueling months at SUNSET SOUND RECORDERS, adding twelve tracks in addition to their previous two singles. Despite (or maybe because of) the *teen riot,* PANDORA'S BOX is demolished in August, leaving behind a concrete island that looks like a kicked-over headstone, forking CRESCENT HEIGHTS BOULEVARD into a Y-shape. At the end of August, the BYRDS are billed as a solo act for three straight WHISKY shows. Come September, spiritualism once again pours over greater LOS ANGELES, coming from the EAST outta a bowl—the HOLLYWOOD BOWL to be precise—RAVI SHANKAR and ALI AKBAR present *FESTIVAL FROM INDIA*. An ad in the *FREEP* touts SHANKAR as the festival's art director, lending the event major cultural clout. On September 21, 1967, the AUTUMNAL EQUINOX, ANGER performs *THE EQUINOX OF THE GODS* at the STRAIGHT THEATRE in SAN FRANCISCO. ANGER intends to raise funds for the remaining production costs for completing *LUCIFER RISING*. RICK GRIFFIN designed a flyer promoting the performance, which was circulated in the *SF CHRONICLE*. GRIFFIN's finished illustration shows sunflowers climbing masonic pylons capped with stone finials engraved with *666*, each flanked by the EYE OF HORUS. A log line describes the film as: *A Love Vision.* ANGER's brooding roomie, BEAUSOLEIL, assembled and fronted the night's headlining band, THE MAGICK POWERHOUSE OF OZ. ANGER once said of BEAUSOLEIL: *BOBBY was the second choice (to play Lucifer) ... He was more on the demonic side. And I thought I could handle that, and I couldn't. It sort of blew up in my face!* BEAUSOLEIL was *CUPID* to some, JASPER DANIELS to others (according to STRAIGHT SANTANS biker ALAN SPRINGER, who knew BEAUSOLEIL by that name via DANNY DECARLO). So, the pretty-boy, whom VITO insisted that ARTHUR LEE oust from LOVE, has recently replaced VITO's now dead son GODO in the part of LUCIFER in ANGER's (future) opus. *Far-out, man—like, far-fucking-out—* To supplement that public fundraiser, ANGER hosts a private *basement* screening of fragments at the RUSSIAN EMBASSY for occult artists and experimental filmmakers ALEJANDRO JODOROWSKY, DONALD CAMMELL (who was raised in the CROWLEY world), and the black-clad bunco artist and founder of the CHURCH OF SATAN, ANTON LAVEY. Fueled by amphetamines, ANGER ran about the stage like a madman during the performance, shouting—*I LOVE YOU!*—at the esoteric peanut gallery that ANGER was ultimately unable to rally together for big-dollar action. 383 miles to the south in LOS ANGELES, FRANK ZAPPA married 21-year-old WHISKY receptionist, GAIL SLOATMAN. Autumn 1967, the first issue of *FREAKOUT MAGAZINE*—published by science-fiction author ROBERT *DOC* AUGUSTINE WARD LOWNDE's NYC-based HEALTH KNOWLEDGE INC.—features multiple layouts about GUAMBO, as well as articles and snapshots of the general WEST COAST FREAK-OUT experience. VITO and FRANZONI are featured prominently. Actor-cum-filmmaker TITUS MOEDE is also interviewed in this same issue. (This may be when VITO and MOEDE'S lives first intersected, or it could've happened years earlier during their RAY DENNIS STECKLER days, when both men—plus ZAPPA—were in the employ of TIMOTHY CAREY, contributing to the making of *THE WORLD'S GREATEST SINNER*. Also, MOEDE is known to run with the bikers who deal with BEAUSOLEIL. Oct. 6, 1967—Season two, episode four of *STAR TREK—MIRROR MAN*—stars JAY SEBRING's ex-girlfriend (and former first employee of SEBRING INTERNATIONAL), BARBARA LUNA as LT. MARLENA MOREAU. Oct. 9 thru 12—A new incarnation of the BYRDS is billed for three consecutive nights as the solo band at the WHISKY. Original BYRDS members DAVID CROSBY and MICHAEL CLARKE were dismissed from the band after constant friction became unbearable. GRAM PARSONS was brought in. Fan demand dropped off as the venues were saturated with newer, and in many cases, better live acts. By now, the draw that the FREAK DANCE TROUPE brought to both the BYRDS and MOI should have been painfully obvious. On October 1, 1967, ROBERT CARL COHEN's *MONDO HOLLYWOOD* was released to less-than-favorable reviews. The *LA TIMES* said of VITO's participation: *VITATUS ALPHONSUS PAULEKAS enjoys a limited sort of fame. Writer RICHARD GOLDSTEIN, the secretary-general of pop culture, once described him as everybody's favorite professional beatnik: "VITO comes on like a living cliche."*—OUCH!—The zeitgeist is shifting away from VITO: KING OF FREAKS! ... to VITO: KING OF NUTS. Since wrapping production on *MONDO HOLLYWOOD*, AMERICA'S news cycle has metastasized. The world's needs are choking out entertainment. *MONDO HOLLYWOOD* developed into a kind of LIBERAL recruitment film; a plastic arts pied-piper to call future FREAKS to LOS ANGELES from all corners of the country, operating on the BERNAYSIAN plane. The film exploits the general *live-your-greatest-you* commie idealisms, while avoiding the real underbelly of TINSELTOWN and community's endless local social conflicts and inability to grow out of its adolescent phase—Or maybe COHEN couldn't gain access to the real COUNTERCULTURE, and had to, instead, settle on manufacturing a synthetic one, or at least one aesthetically pleasing to those on the fringes and familiar with radicalization, but not yet. Perhaps it's something else entirely, something even more nefarious than sleight-of-hand social engineering.

EXAMPLES:

ENTER THEODORE CHARACH—*this melodramatic cat sits in a small room with 8x10 glossies taped up all around him. He plugs away steadily on his typewriter as his voice-over recounts his plethora of accolades as an impresario actor.*

Then things get wacky, turn dark as CHARACH *flips through the pictures he hopes will validate his wilder claims*:

> One of my broadcasts triggered a full-scale riot inside a Saskatchewan penitentiary. Like Orson Welles, I was called the Boy Genius. But the Royal Canadian Mounted Police always get their man, and they eventually got me. I became a special undercover agent in the Communist Party for the Mounties. I've conceived and played almost every dramatic role. The leading man. The character part. The Hollywood heavy. A few years ago, I met my lifelong idol, America's number-one newsman, Walter Winchell. Governor Nelson Rockefeller, one of the world's richest men, took me on the flight over Hollywood in his special jet plane. But I'm still searching. Searching for an image that will set the world on fire.

CHARACH *pauses—gazing at the picture—an illustration of a skull with its left eye socket hollow. From the right cavity peeks a female eyeball; we know its gender because above it is a patch of glamour make-up, complete with long, full mod lashes.* CHARACH *smuggly gasps in recognition of something*:

> Horror! That's it … Horror!

CUT TO: *Latex Halloween masks displayed in a shop window.*

> There are monster books, monster magazines, monster movies, monster television shows. I'll need help, of course; help from those who have confidence in me. From people who promote culture and talent.

CUT TO: *A child's backyard birthday party.* MASKED CHILDREN *loom and lurch into the lens. A group of translucent masked kids cheer on the aggressors.*

> In Hollywood, where children have monster birthday parties, there is obviously a need for a dynamic young villain. I am the director of the Devil!

The MASKED CHILDREN *push and yell at a dummy suspended from a noose; a FRANKENSTEIN'S MONSTER mask is affixed to its face.*

> I am the eye of evil. I am the face of gloom. I am the voice of doom.

One KID *uses a pencil to encircle the pelvic region of an articulated skeleton cut-out, which is taped to a slatted fence. He is highlighting the area where a penis or vagina would or should be, where he/she is not a chain of bones. The* ONLOOKING KIDS *get a big kick outta this interaction.*

> I WILL BECOME THE NIGHT STALKER!

As if that wasn't enough, MONDO HOLLYWOOD's absurdity climaxes when we are confronted with VITO *and* FAMILY, *er, playing THE STAR-SPANGLED BANNER on a bed stuffed into a corner of 303, beads and orange are everywhere.* VITO *is on his knees playing violin,* SUE, *droll as ever, coming across less animated than a* HANNA-BARBARA *cartoon; she twitches every few hundred frames as she strums a dulcimer resting in her sedated lap. Baby* GODO *bounces wildly on the bed at* VITO's *knees, plucking a mandolin.* VITO'S VOICE OVER:

> I've known Carl for about five years, and we see eye to eye on most things. He's bitter about injustices. Bitter about people who are dishonest and hypocritical. My name is Vito. This is my wife, Sue, and my son Godo. I think that Hollywood, perhaps more than any other city in the United States, lends itself toward the so-called variant, the deviate. I mean, deviate in the healthy sense. I mean it as deviant as departing from the norm and exploring other possibilities. And I think I can function more comfortably here than I could function in practically any other city in the United States. I am convinced of that.

CUT TO: *In the outdoor* LACMA *commissary,* SUE *takes a moment to breastfeed* GODO *through her macrame shawl that doubles as a blouse:*

> People are curious about Sue nursing Godo. He's two-and-a-half years of age, and in most instances, the child has been weaned long before they're two years of age. But, they both have such an enjoyment from one another that she's decided that she's gonna nurse him til he's ready to get married. [nervous laugh like a sheep bleat] Isn't that something?

ON SCREEN, VITO *laughs it up big, and glad-hands a balding old* LACMA *patron who has seized the opportunity to indulge in a little public smut photo session—snapping a few pics of* GODO'S *lunch break.*

> There is considerable drug addiction and alcohol addiction in our society. The only thing is that since I want to be as close to reality as possible and since I have some knowledge about what drugs have done to Man in the past, how they have innovated Man, I'm really very much concerned about this fashion for taking benzadrine, amphetamines, and various other kinds of drugs. It's perfectly obvious that the major drug corporations are involved, and they are the major pushers of most of the drug traffic that doth ennovate [sic] the American people.

VITO'S VOICE OVER *is cut off by* CHARACH, ON SCREEN—*dressed as* DRACULA, *stalking a LA prop house in a choreographed segment meant to make Hollywood appear as his 24-hour stage. An hour and thirteen minutes into the movie,* VITO, SUE, FRANZONI, *and* GODO *creep back into the film. At first, we only get glimpses of them under* RAM DASS' VOICE OVER. *The* ROYAL FREAKS *are posed in several strange portraits, like MADONNA WITH CHILD or ISIS NURSING HER SON HORUS.* VITO'S BOSTONIAN *drawl returns as a disembodied voice*:

> LSD is being treated as if it's something new, as though it was an intellectual experiment; as though the taking of drugs somehow or another broadens and expands man's consciousness, which is a lot of nonsense. The Chinese of a hundred years ago, who didn't get loaded on opium, had the most fantastic kinds of fantasies that LSD never will touch

> upon. I'm particularly disturbed by the rationalizations that are taking place because, in some of the so-called best intellectual circles, there are discussions about taking LSD in order to make a special kind of person out of you. This is the great LIE BEING TOLD TO YOU.

Thirteen minutes of footage of ANTI-WAR PROTESTERS *picketing in* HOLLYWOOD *near* FRANKLIN *and* CAHUENGA *avenues pass before we join a mock dance class in session down in* CLAY VITO—VITO *is clad in a black neoprene catsuit, his arms stretched out as if crucified on air, instructing a small faction of* FREAKS *behind him who hang on the* BOSTONIAN'S *command, follow his every direction. For the first time, we get a good look at the* BASEMENT *interior. Then, just like that,* VITO & CO. *disappear until the closing* DANCE, *a scene cut from the aforementioned wrap party at* COHEN'S LOS FELIZ *pad. At the two-hour mark, the psy-op, er, documentary ties a bow on* FREAKINESS *with a succession of shots of a shirtless* CHARACH, *making the pilgrimage walk along the ridge above* CAHUENGA AVENUE, *strolling directly under the leftover relic of the ontological* HOLLYWOOD THEOSOPHIST'S—the STEVENSON CROSS. *Just seconds before the credits roll, over this stark image of the* STEVENSON CROSS *lurching over the half-naked* NOMAD—VITO'S VOICE comes in sharp, and *in a moment of Nostradamic clarity,* HE MAKES THIS PROMISE:

> There's no question in my mind that the revolution is going to take place here in the United States, and it is going to surpass the Russian Revolution, the Chinese Revolution, and it's going to happen very soon.

VITO *lets out a nervous, staccatoed bleat-laugh. The camera pulls back to reveal the hilltop STEVENSON CROSS overlooking the busy 101*—CHARACH'S *obnoxious goon voice vibrates back in to put a period on* VITO'S *threat*:

> I'm going to catch a dream ... and make the whole world, THE WORLD OF HOLLYWOOD!

Amidst all of the interviews painting vivid descriptions of tripping experiences, surrounded by LSD proponents, VITO stood alone as the detractor, saying virtually the same things as AMERICA'S PARENTS and the POLICE, but with a different tact. VITO didn't plead with the youth culture; he schooled THEM. HE showed THEM that THEY are ill-informed, dis-educated—BUT, good news!—It's not THEIR fault. THEY have been and are currently being manipulated, weaponized by industries such as BIG PHARMA and the MEGA-MEDIA.—Why did COHEN lean so heavily into featuring VITO and his FREAKS in the film's advertising—explicitly on the poster and vinyl LP cover—but offer so little personal insight into the FREAKS world? Despite COHEN and VITO's relatively close friendship, VITO'S STUDIO and SCULPTURES, as well as SUE'S hugely popular HIPPIE/FREAK/BOHEMIAN stylings, are altogether dismissed—THE BASEMENT IS TO LIVE-ON INFINITELY A PLACE THAT SIMULTANEOUSLY EXISTS AND DOES NOT EXIST TO OUTSIDERS—On the first of November, JAY SEBRING co-founded and presided over THE INTERNATIONAL HAIR DESIGNER'S GUILD at 400 SOUTH BEVERLY DR. in BEVERLY HILLS. In December, The (NEW) BYRDS played a series of solo act shows at the WHISKY, without VITO & THE FREAKS. *SOMETHING'S HAPPENING* is released while the iron is hot, another documentary featuring in small part VITO and the FREAKS bouncing around SAN FRANCISCO. VITO is featured doing things like performing as an ordained freaky minister and marrying off ANY PERSONS who so desired in a public *wedding*. On December 29, episode 15 of *STAR TREK*, season 2, *THE TROUBLE WITH TRIBBLES*—written by science-fiction novelist DAVID GERROLD—aired. It is safe to assume that GERROLD and fellow *STAR TREK* writer, GEORGE CLAYTON JOHNSON (BURT SHONBERG'S LONG BEACH roommate), and cast member/SEBRING's ex-girlfriend, BARBARA LUNA, all likely know each other, or at least *of* each other. On NEW YEAR'S EVE 1967, the YOUTH INTERNATIONAL PARTY was founded by NEW LEFT LIBERTARIANS PAUL KRASSNER and ABBIE & ANITA HOFFMAN. YIPPIES soon follow.

1 9 6 8

Enter the hardships after a year of spoils—The YOUTH have taken up public spaces, blocked sidewalks, superimposing a weak projection of their philosophy (*peace & love*—whatever the fuck that means) onto the existing fearful and violent climate. In March of 1968, FRANZONI is broke as a joke, squatting in an abandoned LAUREL CANYON house (designed and built by ROBERT BYRD) that had been nicknamed the *LOG CABIN*. In its glory days, its original owner, Western star TOM MIX, wined the likes of WYATT EARP in its dining hall, but now decades later, FREAKS and ANCILLARY FREAKS began collecting there, soon turning it into a proper crash pad, temporarily relieving CLAY VITO from the swarm of HEAT, who are coming around CLAY VITO more often these days to check on the whereabouts of students reported as *tardy* by their parents. Sometimes THEY are found staying over for a weekend-long art class, sometimes not. In early spring, the ZAPPAS returned to LA from NYC, desperate for stylish digs. ZAPPA had visited FRANZONI at the LOG CABIN not long ago, and if memory served him right, the place was perfect for the growing tribe—they moved into the detached guest pad near the main cabin, but soon found the quarters much too cramped for their freaky needs, and bullied their way into the main house, forging the final major rift between the mad main MOTHER and the stinky OG AUXILLARY. PAMELA MILLER turned her back on VITO, the FREAKS, and THE LAUREL CANYON BALLET COMPANY, clutching at new, greasier coat tails. MILLER is only one of a handful of FREAK converts who will attempt to eclipse (and in some ways succeed) the real movers and shakers. Other LAUREL CANYON BALLET COMPANY girls stayed behind at the LOG CABIN, finding employment by the ZAPPAS in one capacity or another. FRANZONI's squat-mate insists that they cannot continue living at the LOG CABIN under these conditions, so the two bail, allowing FREAK COMMUNE II to be colonized by pseudo-radical, fame-starved bullies. MILLER moved into the guest house in the back, earning her board by acting as a *governess* for the growing ZAPPA clan. Just to turn the screw on VITO a tad more, the ex-FREAK GIRLS do their hair up in pigtails and dress like babies and are brought up onstage to dance with MOI. ZAPPA gobbled them up, fusing them into the rinky-dink all-girl band—GIRLS TOGETHER OUTRAGEOUSLY (aka GTOs)—and arranged studio time for them to record their (only) full-length album, *PERMANENT DAMAGE*. MILLER remembers—*He* (ZAPPA) *wanted everyone to experience their creativity as far out as they could get it. I considered him and Gail my main mentors during that period.* June 7, 1968—THE ROLLING STONES complete recording *BEGGARS BANQUET* for DECCA RECORDS one day after ROBERT KENNEDY's murder in the kitchen of the AMBASSADOR HOTEL (which sits directly across the street from DICK BOCK'S THE HAIG). The STONES have relocated to LA to mix *BEGGARS BANQUET* at SUNSET SOUND RECORDERS in HOLLYWOOD. JAGGER and girlfriend, MARIANNE FAITHFULL, needed a *chauffeur* and (like the ZAPPAS) an *executive nanny*. They offered ex-con PHILLIP CLARK KAUFMAN the job, which he accepted. As summer geared up, BEAUSOLEIL fled the RUSSIAN EMBASSY, stealing ANGER's van along with his UNEDITED MASTER FOOTAGE that was to be *LUCIFER RISING*. BEAUSOLEIL'S gone for LA, man—gone, like, in the head and feet. Legend (according to ANGER) has BEAUSOLEIL stopping at the MOJAVE DESERT to bury the film somewhere sure never to be found by ANGER—the human artifact left for future ancients to unearth when the MOJAVE is tilled up to build the new MIDWEST NEFARIUM. ANGER:

> Because his dark side of his nature took over, he stole my van, he stole the film, and he betrayed me. I gave him money to buy some musical things for his band, instead, he went and bought a huge amount of marijuana in Mexico, and drove up in my van with my license plates on the van, full of bales of marijuana (at that time, as big as this couch, you could buy these huge things, wrapped in black plastic). He stored them in my studio. He sneaked them in and stored them. Our dog began sniffing these wrapped-up plastic packages, and then I cut one open, and there was all this grass. It was my apartment, and if anyone was gonna get busted, I was gonna get it- he would get off as a minor, and I was 'seducing' him or 'corrupting' him in some way. So I picked up the bales, threw them down the front step, and I'm not particularly a physically hefty hunk of a guy or anything like that, but when I'm mad ... I picked him up by the scruff of his neck when he came home after a late date and tossed him down the front stairs. And that was the end of our relationship. But you know Scorpios are sneaky, and so he waited. He had a really old car that kept breaking down and everything, but I had the van that I bought for the first "Lucifer Rising" film production. He knew I never cooked, and he waited until I went out to dinner with a friend. Then he broke into the place, stole all the film, and then stole the van. So I came back, and there was no van, no film, and he was gone. I knew he did it; nobody else could have done it, or wanted these cans of film with "L.R." on them for "Lucifer Rising."

Two days later, on the 14th and 15th of June 1968, LOVE headlines at the KALEIDOSCOPE near VINE STREET at 6230 SUNSET BLVD. NEIL YOUNG sat in on guitar, playing the solo to *REVELATIONS* alongside LOVE'S JOHNNY ECHOLS. BEAUSOLEIL, freshly back in LA, has picked up some new friends along his journey, and is, by self-admission, *on a serious drug hunt.* June 24—THE FRATERNITY OF MEN released their self-titled debut album, produced by the well-seasoned TOM WILSON (reuniting him with MOI guitarist ELLIOT INGBAR since recording *FREAK-OUT!* two years previous). This is yet another *band* on which VITO has made an indelible impression—According to FOM guitarist and former MOTHER, LAWRENCE *STASH* WAGNER:

> A local L.A. artist, Vito was the leader of a group of freaks who had danced with Frank Zappa's Mothers and then became a fixture for Fraternity of Man. He had a sculpture of 4 hands (white, black, yellow, and red), all united by holding the wrist of the next. The sculpture was a great political statement, and since we were a politically active band, the name seemed to fit... I was in San Francisco, playing on the streets of the Haight/Ashbury district, when I saw a group of freaks walking on the street towards me. In the midst of the freaks was Mark Rugio. He was the drummer in a band we had in high school. After our embrace, he introduced me to Vito, Carl, and some of the other freaks. He then told me that the guitarist in his new band had just left Mothers of Invention and was the greatest guitarist in the world. He then invited me to see them play. At the gig, I was blown away and stuck around helping them pack up their equipment. When they asked me if I would be interested in being their roadie, I quickly accepted the offer to be able to sit at the feet of a real guitar god. Elliot and I hit it off immediately because we shared the same sick sense of humor. A very talented photographer by the name of Ray Leong took us out to 21 Palms, deep in the California desert. There, we were fed LSD and watched the rocks melt into various forms. The album cover was simply the rocks in the desert melting into a giant phallic symbol.

FREEP reports: *Free Press Bastille Day Bash—1 p.m. to Midnight.* It's all free, and MOI headlines. *Plus Groups Prohibited (by Contracts!) from advertising.* VITO and the FREAKS are nowhere to be seen, having moved on in July to partying with THE FRATERNITY OF MAN, CANNED HEAT, RHINOCEROS, and, of course, LOVE (whose guitarist, song co-writer, and BEUSOLEIL's replacement—BRYAN MACLEAN—lives in a small rental unit at the Smith Building). VALENTINE had a change of heart (desperation will do that), inviting newlywed ZAPPA and THE MOTHERS back to the WHISKY to headline for groups such as the ALICE COOPER-fronted folk band, THE SPIDERS. When the CALIFORNIA DEMOCRATIC PRIMARY

ELECTION results came in at the end of August, showing that comedian PATRICK LAYTON PAULSEN won, VITO and his FREAKS celebrated by losing their shit on the boards of the KALEIDOSCOPE. In early September, LOVE played several solo shows at WHISKY with the FREAKS in tow. BARRY FEINSTEIN's docudrama, *YOU ARE WHAT YOU EAT* (produced by PETER YARROW and TINY TIM), premiered on September 24, 1968, and received considerably better than its MONDO-FREAK FILM predecessors. FRANZONI has taken the FREAK FRONTMAN reins in the film, leading a group of BAY AREA FREAKNIKS around SAN FRAN rooftops, to climb down fire escapes, and gallivant through hepatitis drenched alleys. Aside from a body-painting segment leading up to the insane dance climax, VITO appears sparingly, his participation and representation limited almost entirely to the final fifteen minutes. Was VITO distancing himself from the MONSTER HE CREATED? Could he sense an uneasy change in the tide? Is LAW ENFORCEMENT watching him 24/7? Autumn—After the BEAUSOLEIL debaucle, ANGER was down but not out. HE scoured LONDON, seeking solid financing for his revamped *LUCIFER RISING*. Two of his temporary LUCIFERS (both, remember, were directly linked to VITO) have failed to turn up. ANGER managed to pull together some fragments of the film (that BEAUSOLEIL missed taking in haste) to show art dealer and swinging '60s king, ROBERT FRASER. FRASER introduces ANGER to his future benefactor—billionaire oil magnate J. PAUL GETTY. While on a stay-over in LONDON, ANGER discovered his newest maybe-LUCIFER, a young steelworker named LESLIE HUGGINS. But, HUGGINS, too, will abandon the project (*pulling out* is probably an applicable term here), shipping ANGER back to the STATES scorned and minus another leading man. Oct. 26—ANGER takes out a full-page in *THE VILLAGE VOICE*:

In Memoriam

Kenneth Anger | Filmmaker

(1947-1967)

At that time, his half-completed "Lucifer Rising" had been stolen, and it seemed as though we had seen the last of his dazzlingly beautiful, highly symbolic images. But now we have this new film, apparently salvaged from "Lucifer Rising."

Nov. 5—REPUBLICAN presidential candidate RICHARD MILHOUS NIXON is elected 37th PRESIDENT of the FREE WORLD. FRANZONI suffers *a major bust* at an unidentified house (likely RICKY APPELBAUM's), sending FRANZONI on the lam, north to TORONTO.

> Style is when they're running you out of town, and you make it look like you're leading the parade—WILLIAM BATHE

November 28, 1968—VITO informs his BASEMENT TROLLS that after 20 years of community service, CLAY VITO (or as JIMMY CARL BLACK put it, his *den of sin*), will be shutting down at the end of the month. VITO blames HIS rash decision on our nation's election of anti-Lib NIXON as HEAD OF STATE. The leftover FREAKS—KEN PATTERSON, DAVID DOTY, RICKY APPELBAUM, and RANDY BLACK FOX (aka RANDY PEREZ)—sign a lease with building owner, JD KUBERNICK, taking over responsibility for the footprint of the former CLAY VITO. FRANZONI has migrated affiliations, this time from KOURT ZAPPA to KAMP BURRITO (those of the flying brothers breed). PATTERSON arranged for the FREAKS to perform two final shows at GRATEFUL DEAD concerts at THE BANK nightclub in TORRENCE, CA, on December 13 & 14. On the following day (Sunday), VITO threw one last blow-out party at CLAY VITO before HE, SUE, and GRUVI *escaped* to HAITI by way of LOUISIANA, then from FLORIDA by boat, BUT, JUST BEFORE VITO AND FAMILY GO OFF-GRID: Dec. 20—Two TEENS are murdered just within BENICIA (Latin; *blessed one*) city limits, SOLANO COUNTY in NORTHERN CALIFORNIA. At 10:15p, HOGAN HIGH SCHOOL students BETTY LOU JENSEN (Scandinavian; *sons of John (God is gracious)*) and DAVID FARADAY (a unit of electrical measurement named after its 19th-century discoverer, ENGLISH chemist, MICHAEL FARADAY) are on their first date at the gravel turn-out on LAKE HERMAN ROAD, when THEY are both gunned down in FARADAY's mother's AMBASSADOR RAMBLER. At 11:00p, STELLA BORGES discovered the DEAD TEENS near her home. Nine days later, in LOS ANGELES, at 10:00p, 17-year-old MARINA ELIZABETH HABE and her date, 22-year-old

JOHN HORNBURG, watched comedian LARRY HANKIN perform at THE TROUBADOUR (a FREAK favorite club—AND! it is DIRECTLY NEXT DOOR to THE CORONET THEATRE, where VITO taught his CAN YOU DIG IT? dance class up until two weeks ago). At 11:30p, HABE and HORNBURG left THE TROUBADOUR. At midnight, a murder mystery takes shape. HABE's autopsy reports:

> The decedent went out for the evening, Sunday, Dec. 29th, 1968, in her car ... Sometime after midnight (into the 30th), the descendant's mother heard descendant's car come into the driveway. Seconds later another car was heard in the front. Possibly an old car with loud pipes. The car was heard driving off. Descendant's mother checked and found keys in daughter's car but daughter was gone ... (at 3 AM) ... The mother of descendant filed a missing persons report with the sheriff.

HOLYWÖD

The only place where being at the top feels like the pits.

THANKS FER EVERYTHING, FREAK!

1 9 6 9

The 366-day year was over, and the year of paranoia got off to a rough start. On NEW YEAR'S DAY morning, MARINA ELIZABETH HABE's corpse was discovered by MRS. KLUTE while *sightseeing*:

> Mrs. Klute of 7534 Trask Avenue, Playa Del Rey went to Venice Division Station LAPD with descendant's purse that she found in the area where the body was found. Mrs. Klute was in area looking at view of city—when purse was found. Body was in the brush area down the side of a hill approx. 20' from aux. road. Descendant was lying in supine position. Clothed except for one shoe being off but near her. Descendant's throat had been cut and she had been stabbed numerous times in the chest. An old motorcycle frame was found at descendant's feet and will be impounded by Sheriff's Dpt. Evidence Lab.

TERRY MELCHER and CANDICE BERGEN have split up and moved out of the ROBERT BYRD-designed 10050 CIELO DR.—MELCHER lands in MALIBU. VITO and his family successfully fled AMERICA mercurial. Jan. 23—*THE RAMRODDER* premieres in SAN FRANCISCO. The WESTERN roughie climaxes with a man being tied to a tree and castrated by a knife-wielding killer injun—PLAYED BY BOBBY (*BOB*, as he is credited) BEAUSOLEIL. The film co-stars red-headed nudie-cutie, CATHERINE SHARE, in her blue film debut. SHARE and BEAUSOLEIL were friendly before shooting this film; both are squatting on a commune out on

BARKER RANCH in the PANAMINT RANGE of DEATH VALLEY, CA. ROMAN POLANSKI and HARRY FALK, current owner of 1600 SUMMITRIDGE DR. (and husband of SHARON TATE's *Valley of the Dolls* co-star, PATTY DUKE), could not agree on a sale price, so POLANSKI instead signed an extended one-year/$1500-a-month lease for 10050 CIELO DR. with owner and INDUSTRY talent manager, RUDOLPH *RUDI* ALTOBELLI. POLANSKI and TATE moved into the main house, but the smaller guest house at the northernmost end of the property is not included in the lease. It is where ALTOBELLI stays when in town, but tended to & lived in by 18-year-old caretaker WILLIAM GARRETSON, whom ALTOBELLI hired. In March of 1969, SUE PAULEKAS became plus one, carrying HER and VITO's third child. At the end of March, a postcard is delivered to *SF CHRONICLE* reporter PAUL AVERY, stapled to a packet advertising the new FOREST PINES condominium development at INCLINE VILLAGE, NV, on LAKE TAHOE. Summer—MELCHER was escorted to SPAHN RANCH by biker and bit-part actor, MARK ROSS, so that MELCHER could dig on some of these wild songs dreamed up by the compound's guru, CHARLIE MANSON—the same compound to which both BEAUSOLEIL and SHARE belong—BEAUSOLEIL and MELCHER are surely not strangers, being connected by both having frequented CLAY VITO in the early hay days. In HOLLYWOOD, the forsaken FREAKS had established a commune in the ruins of CLAY VITO, just as the ROMANS built ROME atop yesterday's rubbled theatres and corner markets. VITO's absence had created a counterculture vacuum, too extreme for some. The one-time SPEAKEASY had returned to its former shade, its original conception: to provide damp walls around folks getting chemically tanked off their asses. According to FRANZONI, under its new management, the BASEMENT quickly devolved into a popular *shooting gallery* for junkies. It was around this time, with VITO long gone, that BEAUSOLEIL started circling back around to the old dugout—but, this go-round, HE's on a mission to collect ragged, stray young things to lasso and drag all the way back to SPAHN RANCH. Now, without VITO's pesky regulations, endless entrepreneurial opportunities suddenly lie at BEAUSOLEIL's funky feet. THE US GOVERNMENT threw out FRANZONI's MAIL-ORDER FRAUD case at the end of 1969, or so FRANZONI claimed—*but I stayed underground in Canada until January 1, 1970.* HAITI, as it turned out, is the last place anybody peddling *free love* and community laundry wants to lay down roots:

> *Intercontinental Press,* DICTATORSHIP IN HAITI DECREES DEATH FOR COMMUNISTS!. "The rubber-stamp legislature of Haitian dictator François Duvalier voted unanimously on April 28 to make 'communist activities' a 'crime against the security of the state' punishable by the death penalty. This "crime" is to include the "promotion of Marxist or anarchist doctrines." Anyone accused of spreading Marxist ideas or of aiding or harboring anyone so accused is liable to be tried by a military tribunal and executed. Only a few days after this head-hunting warrant had been issued, the Duvalier regime gave a demonstration of the enforcement of its new policy. Dispensing with the part about a military trial, it proceeded directly to the executions. The May 3 issue of Le Nouveau Monde, a semiofficial government organ published in Port-au-Prince, reported that police had surrounded a house in the Haitian capital and killed thirty-five "communists." Police opened fire on the house and then demolished it when the occupants would not surrender. The people inside were buried in the rubble. Four survivors were taken prisoner.

VITO knew he had to bail ... again. SUE was two months pregnant with their next chess piece when it suddenly dawned on VITO that it was precisely GAUGUIN'S lack of familial ties which allowed the artist to survive—thrive even—in a remote, destitute island setting, one such as here. Arriving in HAITI and hearing that all of the wealthy ANGLOS lived high up on the hills naturally caused VITO to shuffle his family in with the commoners at sea level—but after months wallowing amongst deplorable living conditions, VITO had nightmares on the regular of his toddler, GRUVI NIPPLES, falling into a gutter. In half a year, SUE will bring another into the game—The time fer gettin' IS NOW! The

PAULEKASES first gave JAMAICA a whirl, but soon found conditions comparable to those in HAITI and jumped ship to COSTA RICA. It wasn't until SUE entered her second trimester, in June, that the ROYAL FREAK FAMILY finally returned stateside, making landfall in LOUISIANA, tunneling their way to FLORIDA so VITO could retrieve his VW van from a friend who was storing it during THEIR voyages. Six months later, nearly to the day, the PAULEKASES looped back to CALIFORNIA, turning the motor off up north in SAUSALITO. While dancing at the FILMORE, former LA FREAK, ROBERT AMINZADE, was shocked to find VITO and SUE there dancing with him, given their international status. VITO informs AMINZADE that they are looking for a community to set up shop. On a matchbook, AMINZADE scribbles the name of the poultry-centric town with a hexagonally designed downtown—COTATI—A PLAQUE in COTATI's DOWNTOWN PLAZA leans against a boulder, greeting tourists with:

> COTATI'S HEXAGONAL TOWN PLAN, ONE OF ONLY TWO IN THE UNITED STATES, WAS DESIGNED DURING THE 1890S BY NEWTON SMYTH AS AN ALTERNATIVE TO TRADITIONAL GRID LAND PLANNING. THE SIX-SIDED TOWN PLAZA WAS DESIGNED FOR FOUNDERS THOMAS PAGE, AND EACH OF THE SURROUNDING STREETS WAS NAMED AFTER ONE OF PAGE'S SONS. "COTATI" DERIVES FROM "KOTATI", A LOCAL POMO INDIAN CHIEFTAIN.
>
> CALIFORNIA REGISTERED HISTORICAL LANDMARK NO. 879
>
> PLAQUE PLACED BY THE STATE DEPARTMENT OF PARKS AND RECREATION IN COOPERATION WITH THE CITY OF COTATI AND ALL ORGANIZATIONS.

Flying over the PLAZA, the chemical composition of meth or LSD might come to mind:

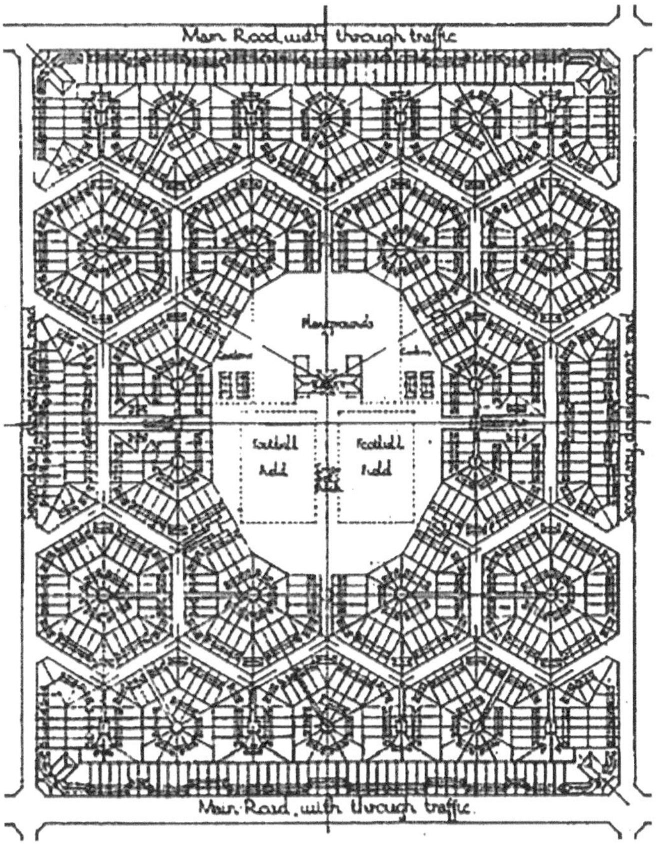

34-year-old SANTA ROSA resident, FREDERIC MANALLI's short story, *STRATEGIC WITHDRAWALS,* was published in the June edition of the international journal of contemporary writings: *THE LITERARY REVIEW.* MANALLI's story ends on the top quarter section of page 504. On the nude three-quarter page left below appear two prominent symbols:

The top ONE is the zodiacal symbol for *LEO*; the bottom SYMBOL is NORSE for *SUN*. Was it the publisher or the author who placed these here? Per ROBERT AMINZADE's suggestion, VITO and SUE bought a house in COTATI in SONOMA COUNTY, and moved in. On INDEPENDENCE DAY, teenagers DARLENE FERRIN (Albanian; *hell*) and MIKE MAGEAU (French; *mage*—or *wizard, magician*) are shot at close range while parked off a road in BLUE ROCKS SPRINGS PARK, VALLEJO, CA. MAGEAU survives, but FERRIN dies from sustained injuries. Two weeks later, on July 18, 1969, 20-year-old BOB BEAUSOLEIL is living at 964 OLD TOPANGA RD. in TOPANGA CANYON, with the owner of the house, GARY HINMAN—a 34-year-old reformed drug addict-cum-music teacher, and born-again NICHIREN SHŌSHŪ BUDDHIST. July 23 thru 27—Since the disbandment of the FREAKS, the club experience has taken on an entirely different tone—The SIR DOUGLAS QUINTET headlines for FLOCK at the WHISKY—Are the poles shifting?—THE WHISKY'S BIG BREAK—Since the inception of this hugely popular dance/rock club, there has not been a six-week dry period between shows likes the one about to place the moment after DOUGLAS walks his ass quietly off the raised stage. July 28—BEAUSOLEIL got burned in a drug deal by HINMAN, scoring a shit load of bad dope from the evangelical Buddhist music teacher—and then selling that sour batch to a hardened biker gang, which is demanding a refund. Perhaps this is why BEAUSOLEIL is confronting HINMAN today.

THEN, THREE DAYS LATER, ON JULY 31, 1969: TWO EVENTS ...

HINMAN's mutilated corpse is discovered at his home by concerned FRIENDS who entered HIS TOPANGA CANYON home by climbing through a window which THEY broke. HINMAN, from THEIR inspection, has been stabbed through the chest; a laceration runs the length of his face from above the ear down past his chin. Cellophane tape was used to keep HINMAN's divided ear as intact as possible. *POLITICAL PIGGY* has been scribed in HINMAN's own blood on a wall near HIS corpse, which, by all indications, had been rotting in that room for at least THREE DAYS. Then, three similar handwritten letters are delivered to THE *SF CHRONICLE, VALLEJO TIMES-HERALD,* AND *EXAMINER*, each with a slightly different cipher. In the letters, the writer demanded that THEIR ciphers are to be published on PAGE ONE of their following editions—or THE WRITER will go on a killing spree. These ZODIAC LETTERS (as they will come to be known) had crept from obscurity into publicity, mocking HIPPIES, LAW ENFORCEMENT, and both CULTURES—POP & COUNTER. On the first of August, HINMAN's employer, GLENN KRELL, told investigators that HINMAN owned several vehicles, of which two were inventoried as *missing.* Three days after the first set of taunting letters, the *SAN FRANCISCO EXAMINER* received another, this one from an author calling themself *the ZODIAC*, and claiming responsibility for the recent killings and correspondences. On August 6, 22-year-old ROBERT KENNETH BEAUSOLEIL (aka *BOBBY*, *BUMMER BOB*, *JASON LEE DANIELS*) was arrested in SAN LUIS OBISPO COUNTY after being pulled over while driving one of HINMAN's missing vehicles—another van gets BEAUSOLEIL in trouble. The LA SHERIFF'S DPT. takes SUSPECT N°·1 in the HINMAN HOMICIDE INVESTIGATION into custody—THEN!—we are sold the narrative that school teacher DONALD G. HARDEN, and his wife, BETTYE, of SALINAS, CA, successfully decoded ZODIAC's first cipher using a simple substitution key—The solution is published in the next *SF CHRONICLE*:

> I LIKE KILLING PEOPLE BECAUSE IT IS SO MUCH FUN IT IS MORE FUN THAN KILLING WILD GAME IN THE FORREST BECAUSE MAN IS THE MOST DANGEROUE ANAMAL OF ALL TO KILL SOMETHING GIVES ME THE MOST THRILLING EXPERIENCE IT IS EVEN BETTER THAN GETTING YOUR ROCKS OFF WITH A GIRL THE BEST PART OF IT IS THAE WHEN I DIE I WILL BE REBORN IN PARADICE AND ALL THEI HAVE KILLED WILL BECOME MY SLAVES I WILL NOT GIVE YOU MY NAME BECAUSE YOU WILL TRY TO SLOI DOWN OR ATOP MY COLLECTION OF SLAVES FOR MY AFTERLIFE. EBEORIETEMETHHPITI.

On the morning of August 8, 1969, in EL MONTE, CA, 18-year-old STEVEN EARL PARENT prepared for his first job of the day at VALLEY CITY PLUMBING SUPPLY COMPANY, four miles to the west in ROSEMEAD. Last June, PARENT graduated from ARROYO HIGH SCHOOL on CEDAR AVENUE in EL MONTE. HE lived with his folks at 11214 EAST BRYANT RD., and planned to attend CITRUS JUNIOR COLLEGE in AZUSA in the fall. Before leaving home, PARENT asked his mother, JUANITA, to *get him a change of clothes*. At 9:00p, PARENT had put in a full day between both jobs. HE left his second place of work, JONAS MILLER STEREO at 8719 WILSHIRE BLVD., and headed almost an hour home to EL MONTE—HE had a delivery to make. This celebrity mule scenario was set into motion several weeks prior (around mid-July) after PARENT picked up 19-year-old hitchhiker WILLIAM *WILLY* GARRETSON in BEVERLY HILLS, and gave him a ride to home/work at 10050 CIELO DR. Peek between the thickening pines and blooming cherry trees draping the hills of BENEDICT CANYON. At the end of a cul-de-sac, you'll see the fruits of architect ROBERT BYRD's two-and-a-half years of labor. 10050 perches on a cliff, facing the sun as it rises daily over the flats of BEVERLY HILLS and BEL AIR. (Sat directly below on a parcel of plateau owned by BEDROCK PROPERTIES, is 10048 CIELO DR., a *twin house* simultaneously built by separate crews dedicated to each site.) MICHÈLE MORGAN purchased the original 3,200-square-foot house on a three-acre lot in November of 1941, and then invested an additional $32,000 to have BYRD design and install a swimming pool, plus a 2,000-square-foot *recreation cottage* at the rear of the main house, which it replicates aesthetically. BYRD's additions transformed the one-time *AMERICAN farm-type dwelling* into a *FRENCH country-style structure,* a *EUROPEAN farmhouse*—GARRETSON explained to PARENT that he stays there temporarily in the guesthouse in exchange for working as property caretaker for the owner while he is away frolicking on business; the folks staying in the main house are famous, by the bye. PARENT met SEBRING, TATE, and other guests, and saw dollar signs dripping from the walls. PARENT's not-so-dormant delinquency switch is flipped; he's engaged, activated. PARENT gets this information about the wealthy druggies dojo, and was subsequently charged with laying a trap, opening the door on the treasure trove—9:45p—Tonsorial artist JAY SEBRING, actress SHARON TATE, coffee heiress ABIGAIL FOLGER, and writer/artist WOJCIECH FRYKOWSKI finished their meal at the EL COYOTE CAFE at 7312 BEVERLY BLVD., and make for 10050 CIELO DR.—10:00p PARENT drove to DALE'S MARKET, where HE spoke shortly with friend JOHN LE FEBURE, before meeting up with SOURCE, obtaining a butt-load of MDA, and running through the movements one last time before the BIG SCORE—PARENT is to *gain access beyond the gate, make the MDA drop, and then dick around with the caretaker kid for a half hour while the drugs are ingested and fully kick-in. KILL TEN MORE MINUTES—then leave, alone, casually driving out and leaving the gate ajar and unattended.* It's all elementary. THEY will be there, waiting in the bushes, at midnight, to handle the rest. PARENT will get his significant cut, his *finder's fee* for HIS undetectable involvement—At 10:15p PARENT began the haul from EL MONTE back to to 10050 CIELO DR.; FRYKOWSKI eagerly awaited the delivery, and when PARENT arrived at 11:15p, HE was immediately granted access through the main gate, and parked HIS father's white RAMBLER just inside, much closer to the MAIN HOUSE than GARRETSON's GUESTHOUSE at the opposite end of the driveway. FRYKOWSKI ushered PARENT into the main house, where business was conducted in the living room; a transaction which secured a couple of big'ol doses of the hug-drug for FRYKOWSKI and FOLGER. TATE and SEBRING were straight for the night, politely passing through the haze, saying *hi* and *bye* in the same breath, before continuing to go on to do their own thing quietly in another dark corner of the HOUSE. When FRYKOWSKI rolled a tiny yellow pill between his thumb and middle finger, HE considered PART ONE: COMPLETE—FOLGER and FRYKOWSKI GET WASTED—All parties are satisfied—*THEN KILL THIRTY MINUTES*—PARENT excused HIMSELF and made HIS way, alone, out to visit GARRETSON in the GUESTHOUSE—THE PLAN: PART TWO—According to the *TATE HOMICIDE INVESTIGATION PROGRESS REPORT*:

> Garretson told the investigators that Parent had come to the guest house at approximately 23:45, 8-8-69, and that he displayed a clock radio to Garretson ... Parent has an arrest record as a juvenile for burglary. The chief object of attack during the five burglaries he was caught at was electronic equipment. He served two years in the California Youth Authority program. He was described as having both sadistic and homosexual tendencies by a probation officer.

Ten minutes into August 9, 1969, after spending half an hour in the GUESTHOUSE with GARRETSON—uh, doing things, PARENT placed a call to 25-year-old JERROLD *JERRY* DAVID FRIEDMAN (better known by his writing credit—DAVID GERROLD—for penning the wildly popular *STAR TREK* episode, *THE TROUBLE WITH TRIBBLES*. This call is later traced to a building near the intersection of DOHENY DRIVE and SANTA

MONICA BOULEVARD, which happens to be the exact location of two FREAK hot spots—THE TROUBADOUR and THE CORONET THEATRE—the very theatre where MARINA HABE was last publicly seen alive.) According to the *FIRST TATE HOMICIDE INVESTIGATION REPORT*: at 12:15a, PARENT saw HIMSELF to the door; GARRETSON claims not to have watched PARENT as HE headed down the side path back to his NASH AMBASSADOR—IN THE WEE HOURS—GARRETSON is asleep in the *garage-like structure* at the rear of the property.—At roughly 5:30a, GARRETSON awakened and dialed information for the time, but found the landline dead—At 8:00a on August 9, POLANSKI's housekeeper, WINIFRED CHAPMAN, is late for work. By a stroke of luck or brutal fate, CHAPMAN runs into *someone* at the mouth of BENEDICT CANYON, whom she has known only as—*JERRY*—and this *JERRY* has been a guest at 10050 CIELO DR. several times, so she feels comfortable hitching a ride with *JERRY* to work:

> The housekeeper, Winifred Chapman, arrived from her home at the intersection of Santa Monica Boulevard and Canon Drive (1.3 miles from the Doheny/Santa Monica location Parent called 8hrs earlier) at approximately 0800 on 8-9-69. She saw a male acquaintance, "Jerry," last name unknown, and asked him to drive her to the Polanski residence as she was a little late for work. She arrived at the front gate of the Cielo address at approximately 0830. Upon her arrival, she noticed an electrical wire hanging loosely on the ground going from the telephone pole near the push button for the gate onto the Cielo property and hanging across the gate. She pressed the electric button, which operates the gate, and entered the driveway. She picked up the morning newspaper, walked to the garage (Addendum 1A), and turned off the overhead lights.

So far, only two *JERRYS* have entered our storyline: JERRY HOPKINS, a friend of VITO's and former showrunner for *THE STEVE ALLEN SHOW*—a show on which SEBRING often appeared. And secondly, this new one, the *STAR TREK* writer and science fiction novelist, JERROLD *JERRY* DAVID

FRIEDMAN (aka DAVID GERROLD). Both *JERRYS* would have a vested reason for hanging around the mouth of BENEDICT CANYON. So, we know it's somebody named *JERRY*—and only *JERRY*; like CHER—and someone whom WINIFRED CHAPMAN felt comfortable getting a ride from and granting access to the property. JERROLD *JERRY* DAVID FRIEDMAN wrote for *Star Trek* (as DAVID GERROLD), which SEBRING was linked repeatedly to, not least by a former lover/co-worker—8:30a—WINIFRED CHAPMAN discovered STEVEN EARL PARENT dead in HIS father's RAMBLER MPK 308; six slugs, seven empty casings, and two live rounds were found at the scene. PARENT was shot four times and stabbed once in the center of HIS hand. The car has been turned off but left in second gear. HIS wristwatch was cut free and flung onto the backseat. It appeared that PARENT opened the gate, then got back into the vehicle just before HE was attacked by at a minimum of two assailants—multiple weapons were used. PARENT's blood level record showed that HE had consumed at least one alcoholic beverage shortly before his killing. Had PARENT become a liability? Did SOMEBODY silence HIM before being given a chance to hush up on HIS own? If gunfire happened BEFORE the ASSAILANTS entered the MAIN HOUSE and murdered the other FOUR, how could THOSE inside NOT hear the shots fired upon PARENT? If PARENT's car had made it out through the gate and HE was killed there, then the RAMBLER would have been pushed back onto the property. That course of action could account for THE OTHERS not hearing the gunshots ... Written in blood across the exterior face of the front door, the single word: *PIG*—a word that in 1969 was a common derogatory slang for *rich white folk*.) POLANSKI's *business agent*, 28-year-old BILL TENNANT, was called on by investigators to identify the FIVE CORPSES—At some point on Sunday, August 10, LENO and ROSEMARY LABIANCA were murdered in their LOS FELIZ home at 3301 WAVERLY DR.; attacked in the living room. ROSEMARY had been stabbed multiple times in her back—one cut so deep that it severed her spine (something that just twenty years before, in the case of

ELIZABETH SHORT, was deduced as possible only by a medically trained mastermind). A LAMP CORD shared by a PAIR OF HEAVY LAMPS was tied loosely around ROSEMARY'S neck, just as a rope had been around SEBRING's corpse. Unlike the TATE murders on the night before, the killers washed their hands at the LABIANCA house; ROSEMARY's blood was found in the bathroom sink, LENO's in the kitchen. Only one weapon was used, and it wasn't one that the KILLER(S) brought. It was a steak knife from the LABIANCA's kitchen drawer, but now it was jammed into LENO's carotid artery. LENO lay on his back with his hands tied behind him, a pillow case had been pulled down over his head as had been done to both TATE and SEBRING. A couch cushion may have been used to prop up his head, as the knife could be inserted into his neck more easily—this method is commonly used in the field by hunters to bleed out fresh kills. ROSEMARY's purse was rummaged through, but her wallet was the only item stolen. Again, just as at the TATE crime scene, a message was written in the VICTIMS' blood: *DEATH TO PIGS* across a wall, *HEALTER SKELTER* on the refrigerator door. The extra *A* in the spelling is often overlooked (maybe even ignored). A fork protruded from LENO's belly, the single word—*WAR*—carved into his flesh and fat. NEWSPAPERS have already picked up on several questionable details comparing the two slaughterhouse scenes, going so far as to call both scenes *ritualistic*.

> A second suspect in that case is still believed at large. The second suspect is a man whose name was mentioned by William E. Garretson.

Who was this second suspect named by GARRETSON? Did the police seek out and talk to the aforementioned *JERRY*? Aug. 11, at 2:00p, the prime suspect in the CIELO DRIVE MURDERS, 19-year-old caretaker, WILLIAM GARRETSON, is released from LAPD custody. After GARRETSON had been free for two weeks, he filed a $1,250,000 *false arrest* claim against the city of LOS ANGELES for his initial implication as the murderer of five adults and one fetus. Three weeks after the slaughter, 10050 CIELO DR. owner RUDI ALTOBELLI moved back into his now-infamous house while the killer(s) remained at large. At 4:00p on September 27, the fourth *associated* ZODIAC killing occurred on an artificial oak island: LAKE BERRYESSA in NAPA COUNTY. College student, BRYAN CALVIN HARTNELL, and his sweetheart, CECILIA ANN SHEPARD, were brutally attacked—tied up with PRE-CUT LENGTHS OF CLOTHESLINE before being stabbed multiple times by an ASSAILANT, reported by HARTNELL as dressed from head to toe in a strange black costume complete with gloves and a rope belt. It is the PERP's unusual headress that makes the most memorable impact on HARTNELL—It was a squared-off, tall HOOD with a fabric flap that draped over the WEARER's neck and upper breast plate—on the front of this neck-flap, embroidered: the ZODIAC SYMBOL, which BAY AREA RESIDENTS were now all too familiar with seeing in all the local papers. The two eye holes were cut out and then affixed with a pair of clip-on sunglasses. HARTNELL stressed in interviews that the SYMBOL on the EXECUTIONER'S-STYLE HOOD was made with crafting care, neatly sewn on, not crudely painted—Is this MASK/HEADCOVERING a reference to the CAPIROTE PENITENCE HOOD worn in the MIDDLE AGES by SPAINARDS who were condemned to death and led through towns? Another such CAPIROTE is the kind worn by SICILIAN STREET PERFORMERS during THE HOLY WEEK as THEY publicly act out the humiliation of CHRIST during his supposed ascent of GOLGOTHA. THEIR tall HOODS are flapped back over their neck, creating a squaring of the top. THEY, too, brandish ESOTERIC and HOLY SYMBOLS on a neck/breast cover—Before leaving the scene, the MASKED ASSAILANT used a permanent FELT-TIPPED PERMANENT MARKER (the kind FRANZONI bragged recently of carrying on his person—AT ALL TIMES) to scribble a message on the door of HARTNELL's white VW KARMANN GHIA:

Vallejo
12-20-68
7-4-69
Sept 27-69-6:30
by knife

BRYAN HARTNELL survives the attack, but CECILIA SHEPARD succumbed to her wounds two days later. DIANE LINKLETTER, daughter of ART LINKLETTER (on whose variety television show VITO occasionally appeared), was reportedly depressed, despondent, and not herself, and swan dived from the sixth story of her WEST HOLLYWOOD apartment on October 4, 1969. The next day, her FATHER told media trolls that LSD was to blame for DIANE's death, pointing his finger squarely at the drug's manufacturers and dealers. In early October, JARVIS THURSTON published volume 16, issue two of *PERSPECTIVES,* a quarterly of modern literature, which included the short story: *PARADISE: IT'S A NICE PLACE* by FREDRIC MANALLI. In DENMARK on October 10, ANGER premieres his 11-minute experimental cinematic curse, *INVOCATION OF MY DEMON BROTHER,* intending to beam an evil invocation directly at BEAUSOLEIL, who sat locked in a prison on MURDER ONE charges, 5,500 miles away. This visualized curse was a pastiche of fragments and outtakes that ANGER had salvaged from the stolen cut of *LUCIFER RISING.* MICK JAGGER (whose nanny/chauffeur, PHILLIP KAUFMAN, happened to be a one-time cellmate of CHARLIE MANSON's) provided the accompanying minimalist and endlessly pulsating electronic score. Maybe the curse was deflected somewhere in the stovepiping ether, because on the following night, Sunday October 11, 1969 at 9:58p, 29-year-old taxi driver PAUL LEE STINE is shot in the back of the head with a 9mm by an unknown *passenger* at the intersection of MAPLE STREET (although entered on STINE'S log book as CHERRY STREET) and WASHINGTON

STREET in SAN FRANCISCO'S PRESIDIO HEIGHTS district. STINE moonlighted as a cabbie while working on HIS ENGLISH LITERATURE thesis for SAN FRANCISCO STATE COLLEGE. According to STINE's rider log, HIS KILLER was picked up near the corner of GEARY STREET and MASON STREET, where the newly opened all-night PINECREST DINER sits. Four days later, the *SF CHRONICLE* received another handwritten message (postmarked 10.13.69) taking credit for STINE's murder. Included with the letter was a bloody swatch torn from STINE's striped shirt. The inscription is signed with the same SYMBOL that HARTNELL reported to have been sewn onto the KILLER'S HOOD, as well as matching, exactly, the signature left on HARTNELL's car door. (This SYMBOL will henceforth be known in this text as: CODA) Nov. 8—What is soon referred to as the *DRIPPING PEN CARD* is delivered to the *SF CHRONICLE* from ZODIAC. Included with it: a 340-character key block cipher centered above a large CODA. On November 9, the *SF CHRONICLE* received its fourth handwritten letter from ZODIAC; this one is seven pages in length, and one of those pages included a DIAGRAM depicting a *DEATH MACHINE* EXPLOSIVE DEVICE that ZODIAC intends to DETONATE for maximum carnage. A week later, a 14-year-old boy discovered a fully clothed FEMALE CORPSE while birdwatching along on a remote stretch of MULHOLLAND DRIVE. The VICTIM had been stabbed over 150 times, clustered heavily around the neck and collar. HER identity is unknown. SHE is registered with the L.A. COUNTY CORONER'S OFFICE as JANE DOE #59. On November 20, ALTOBELLI sued POLANSKI to the tune of $848,000 over the unauthorized printing of photographs in *LIFE MAGAZINE.* ALTOBELLI claimed that three months of back rent are owed to him, and that damages have decreased his property's value significantly. LA LAW OFFICIALS have had nearly four months to secure their official narrative, so THEY had better get it right. On December 1, an announcement came connecting a disenchanted hippie guru named CHARLES MANSON as the brainwashing mastermind behind this summer's slaughters. On December 6, with MANSON and members of his media-deemed *FAMILY* locked up and declared the deviants responsible for the high-profile HOLLYWOOD murders, VITO materialized back into the public sphere at the ALTAMONT SPEEDWAY free concert in TRACY, CA; HIS re-appearance immortalized in 1970s documentary film, *GIMME SHELTER*—Brother MAYSLES panned and zoomed his picture pistol past JEFFERSON AIRPLANE on stage, only to land on VITO in all his freaky glory; dancing atop a make-shift platform, hovering over tens of thousands of MUD HONEYS and GRANOLA GOONS, HIS flacid fabric-dick codpiece of sorts waving at them from HIS waist. ANGER, too, is in attendance as evidenced by a photograph taken from the foot of the stage as ANGER filmed THE ROLLING STONES' performance that infamously devolved into a PUBLIC SACRAFICE at the behest of the HELL'S ANGELS, whom THE STONES have employed for band security. After the pot was stirred, 18-year-old MEREDITH HUNTER was stabbed and beaten to death after reportedly drawing a pistol and charging the stage. Like OSWALD'S execution-as-theatre, 300,000 festival attendees breathed in HUNTER'S last breath that day—just another blip of AMERICAN discourse piled on the heightening heap. LOS ANGELES venues on SUNSET BOULEVARD and SANTA MONICA AVENUE, once plagued with lines circling city blocks, have taken it on the chin in the wake of the *MANSON FAMILY MURDERS*. However, VALENTINE is steadfast, believing that business at the WHISKY never faultered—the street-level kids who just wanted to hear music *didn't care about that shit*, VALENTINE claims, but the paranoia of RADICALIZED/KILLER/DEADHEAD HIPPIES was the final nail in COUNTERCULTURE's coffin. In mid-December, ROSEMARY LA BIANCA's change purse was found by a gas station attendant while cleaning the women's restroom; it had been shoved into the tank, obstructing the ball and causing the toilet to run endlessly. MANSON appears on the cover of *LIFE MAGAZINE*'s December 19 issue, depicted as a guilty, wide-eyed madman even before DAY ONE of his trial. Mid-December 1969—VITO was unable to secure a teaching position at either SANTA ROSA JUNIOR COLLEGE or SONOMA STATE

UNIVERSITY, probably due in no small part to his checkered past. While *lying low* in TORONTO, FRANZONI put on an opera with MOI bassist ROY ESTRADA. ZAPPA visited FRANZONI there in an attempt to collect monies ZAPPA felt owed to him. *CAPTAIN FUCK* feels otherwise, believing that ZAPPA been fully compensated since FRANZONI contributed to published MOI recordings without monetary gains, and HIS dancing at MOI shows drew in innumerable more people to watch the band that wouldn't have otherwise. Five days before CHRISTMAS DAY, AMERICAN television personality and celebrity lawyer MELVIN M. BELLI received a handwritten letter from a WRITER claiming to be ZODIAC (Note: Recall that LENNY BRUCE cited BELLI as a prime example of the elite's social disconnect in his public address to UCLA students three years before this letter. Also, *belli* is derived from—causus belli—*is an event or action that justifies or allegedly justifies a war or conflict* … Maybe ZODIAC knew this little ontological nugget, too.) COTATI, CA's population at the close of 1969 is a minuscule 1,368, but on December 29, the township needed to tick one more on the census counter—BENJAMIN *BUB/BB* PAULEKAS was born to VITO and SUE at SANTA ROSA MEMORIAL HOSPITAL. B.B. arrived nine days after the BELLI letter. Could this correspondence, like those of recent, perhaps be brought forth by this uncanny correlation with a common stressor in VITO's life: PREGNANCIES AND CHILDBIRTH? FREDRIC and SOU MANALLI of 428 EIGHTH ST. in SANTA ROSA, CA, filed for divorce but quickly reconciled, retracting the decree and remaining together … for the moment.

1970

> VITANTAS—A variation of the Lithuanian name, *Vytautas*, composed of the elements *vyti, to pursue* or *to cross or twine*, and *tauta*; *people*, hence creating the compound meaning: *a pursuer of the people*. It is interesting to note that the Lithuanian word, *Vytis*, translates in English to *knight*. Similar or related names: *Vito*

58-year-old VITO PAULEKAS taught his dance class, *CAN YOU DIG IT? deep in THE BASEMENT* of IVES HALL at SONOMA STATE UNIVERSITY. This was as close as VITO could get to joining the faculty. Some PRIVATE PARTY COLLECTORS are already offloading their BURT SHONBERG pieces:

> Mar. 11—*Los Angeles Evening Citizen*, 311-Antiques—PAINTINGS, ETC.—Bert Shonberg Original Oil painting (1961) $350. 874 6178—BERT Shonberg original oil painting (1961). $350. Pvt. pty. 874 6178

THE SONOMA COUNTY/SANTA ROSA HITCHHIKER MURDERS BEGIN—On March 12, when 17-year-old SONOMA STATE UNIVERSITY co-ed EVA LUCIENNE BLAU left JACK LONDON HALL at 780 E. COTATI AVE., SHE told her study partners that SHE was heading less than half a mile west to HER apartment at 395 E. COTATI AVE. If you continued west another half mile down the exact same road as BLAU's apartment—COTATI AVENUE—ONE will arrive at KARL FRANZONI'S doorsteps at 238 W.

COTATI AVE. (So, BLAU disappears from SONOMA STATE UNIVERSITY property—where VITO teaches an EXTRACURRICULAR dance class in an on-campus basement—as SHE is headed to HER apartment, which sits a half a mile from VITO'S long-time, dedicated, and fucking freaky-to-the-core friend—FRANZONI? Okay ... I'm sure there's nothing more to that ... Coincidentally (or perhaps not), BLAU disappeared on the same day that MANALLI mailed off his manuscript of *THE PRISONER AND THE KEEPER* from the SONOMA COUNTY jurisdiction.) On the day following BLAU's vanishing, AL GROVE, owner of GROVE'S DRYING YARD in SONOMA COUNTY, discovered a PARTIALLY NUDE CORPSE *posed* on his property at 3395 PETALUMA HILL RD., just west of the shale pit, and less than six miles from where VITO had recently moved his family. BLAU's case gets much attention in the press, but SHE will ultimately be written off as another overdose victim. April 20—Another hand-written letter is received by the *SF CHRONICLE*, taunting inspectors and readers both to decode THEIR NAME from the included 13-character cipher:

> This is the Zodiac speaking
> By the way way have you cracked the last cipher I sent you ?
> My name is ———
>
> A E N ⊕ ⊗ K ⊗ M ⊗ ⊥ N A M
>
> I am mildly cerous as to how much money you have on my head now . I hope you do not think that I was the one who wiped out that blue meannie with a bomb at the cop station . Even though I talked about killing school children with one . It just wouldnt doo to move in on some one elses teritory. But there is more glory in killing a cop than a cid because a cop can shoot back . I have killed ten people to date . It would have been a lot more except that my bus bomb was a dud.
>
> I was swamped out by the rain we had a while back.

Some points here are deserving of singling out: The WRITER's NAME CIPHER features what could be interpreted as three TAURUS (bull) ZODIAC SIGNS; the very star sign to which VITO belongs, being born on May 20. The writer also includes their own SYMBOL—or CODA or CHOP—as a character within the cipher itself. If we believe ZODIAC to be arrogant, bragadocious, a real FIRST-RATE TYPOMANIAC who must see their name published in print, then what better way to add THEIR name REPEATEDLY to a document that will be seen by thousands—millions eventually—subliminally. This reduction of a complex idea to an artistic, qualified symbol coincides perfectly with VITANYAS ALPHONSE PAULEKAS' pushing to be recognized by the monodistic—VITO. ZODIAC, a TYPOMANIACAL writer, would most certainly include THEIR identity (or a SYMBOL of it) IN EVERY SINGLE CORRESPONDENCE, so that the MESSAGE is transmitted each & every time, even if everything around it turns out to be meaningless—THE SYMBOL IS THE NAME—To demonstrate this clearly: first scribe a V on a sheet of paper; just a regular V. Next, turn the paper clockwise 135 degrees, and drag that right leg of the V up as you would write the letter I. Rotate the paper clockwise another 90 degrees and complete the letter T using the combination V & I. Finally, circle the entire T with a strong O to complete the CHOP. Here, have a look-see at these scribbles in action:

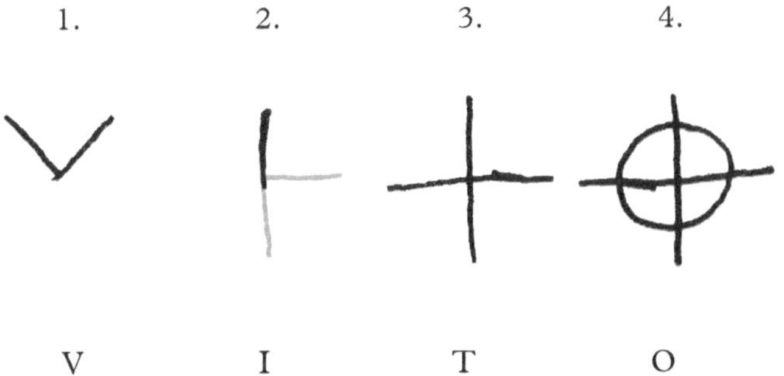

Like circular time, each preceding letter layer becomes part of the one harmonious SYMBOL. Good luck ever seeing the ZODIAC SYMBOL without PAULEKAS'S name shuffling to the surface. To illustrate even further that the name theory also works out on the X-axis—enter the name VITO A. PAULEKAS into the 13-character WRITER'S NAME CIPHER, and that, too, just so happens to fit:

V —	I —	T —	O —	A. —	P —	A —	U —	L —	E —	K —	A —	S
1	2	3	4	5	6	7	8	9	10	11	12	13

Eight days later, on April 28, 1970, ZODIAC'S *SORRY MY ASS IS 'A DRAGON* card arrived at the *SF CHRONICLE*, and then two months passed without any correspondence from ZODIAC, before sending another handwritten message to the *SF CHRONICLE* on June 26:

> This is the Zodiac speaking.
> I have become very upset with the people of San Fran Bay Area• They have not complied with my wishes for them to wear some nice [small coda] buttons.
> I promiced to punish them if they did not comply, by anilating a full School Bus. But now school is out for the summer, so I punished them in another way .
> I shot a man sitting in a parked car with a • 38 •
>
> — 12 SFPD — 0
>
> The Map coupled with this code will tell you where the bomb is set • You have untill next Fall to dig it up.

Note: This year opened with VITO PAULEKAS teaching his dance class, *CAN YOU DIG IT? deep in THE BASEMENT* of IVES HALL at SONOMA STATE UNIVERSITY. Is it just me, or has HIS class title mutated in its meaning over the years?—*CAN YOU DIG IT?*—Perhaps once relative to VITO's WWII HAZARDOUS MATERIALS RETRIEVAL LEND-LEASE MISSIONS, now maybe points instead to ZODIAC'S BURIED BOMB challenge to find and DIG THEM UP by FALL—*CAN YOU DI...* oops, almost said too much—It's also worth noting that VITO PUSHED HIS OWN NOVELTY BUTTONS throughout the articles and ads that we have read already—RENATA ADLER mentioned her friend MEG was given one by VITO himself in 1966 to keep her britches up. And, VITO's HALLOWEEN FREAK-OUT ad promised a discount to ANYONE WEARING A *VITO BUTTON*—Not a *FREAK* BUTTON, or a *FREAK-OUT* BUTTON ... but a *V—I—T—O* BUTTON. July 24, 1970, ZODIAC is pissed that nobody is wearing HIS BUTTONS and sends in another letter voicing his disdain. July 26, the *SF CHRONICLE* received yet another letter, this one containing several blatant references to the comic opera, *THE MIKADO* (of which VITO'S old acquaintance, GROUCHO MARX, recently released a wildly popular recording). On October 29, RICKY J. APPELBAUM, one of CLAY VITO's FORSAKEN FREAKS, gets busted while journeying up to KING VITO in COTATI:

> Oct. 27—*The Fresno Bee*, ALERT CUSTOMERS SPEED ARREST OF BANDIT—Several customers are credited for the prompt arrest of four robbery suspects early this morning in Fresno, less than half an hour after J's Coffee Shop at Floral Avenue and Freeway 99 north of Selma was robbed of $85. Michelle Valenzuela, a waitress at the 24-hour restaurant, told sheriff's deputies a young woman entered shortly before 3 a.m. and purchased three cups of coffee. She said as the woman walked out, two men entered. She said one of the men displayed a small pistol and ordered her to open the cash register. She said the gunman scooped out the money, and both bandits fled. VEHICLE SEEN—A customer, Lowell Nelson of Selma, saw the suspects' panel truck speed away. Two other customers, Dwight Brown of Hanford and James

Wallace of Selma, then followed the panel truck, noting the license number as it headed toward Fresno. Arrested at 3:15 a.m. at Freeway 99 and Ashlan Avenue by the Highway Patrol were Ricky J. Appelbaum, 23, Los Angeles, Adam H. Lee, 26, of Berkeley, and his wife, Marion, 27, and a 16-year-old youth, a runaway from Frontana. All are held on suspicion of robbery and possession of marijuana and dangerous drugs, which deputies say were found inside the panel truck. Investigators said Mrs. Lee is believed to have been the woman who purchased the coffee before the robbery.

1971

On March 13, the *LA TIMES* received the first handwritten letter from ZODIAC in eight months. ZODIAC hints that the previous ciphers are bunk loaded with MCGUFFINS. With that notice, ZODIAC's LETTERS TO EDITORS abruptly ended. 17-year-old LISA MICHELE SMITH goes missing from PETALUMA on March 16. SHE was last seen hitchhiking on HEARN AVENUE just a short distance from HER FOSTER HOME in SOUTH SANTA ROSA, near MANALLI'S residence.

> March 28—*Press Democrat*, MISSING GIRL TREATED IN NOVATO HOSPITAL?—Sonoma County authorities are investigating whether an assault victim treated at Novato General Hospital Saturday was Lisa Smith, a 17-year-old Petaluma girl missing since March 16. The girl, taken to Marin County hospital, allegedly was beaten after she was picked up by a man while hitchhiking. She identified herself to hospital authorities as Lisa Smith, but she was released after treatment. Hospital authorities believed she was 21. Photos of the missing girl were being sent to the hospital for possible identification. Miss Smith was last seen hitchhiking on Hearn ave, the night of March 16.

APRIL FOOLS!

> April 1—*Press Democrat*, MISSING GIRL, 17, SAFE AT HOME —The 17-year-old girl reported missing by her Petaluma foster parents on March 16 has turned up and was returned to her own home in Livermore, according to sheriff's officers. Lisa Michele Smith was reported missing and last seen hitchhiking on Hearn ave. Her picture ran in Sunday's Press Democrat. Sheriff's juvenile officers said she apparently left her boyfriend and his disabled car and hitchhiked to San Francisco, where she stayed with friends on Third ave. On March 26, Sheriff's Juvenile Officer Shirley Andreatta said the girl set out hitchhiking from San Francisco to Sausalito and was picked up on 19th ave in San Francisco. The man drove past Sausalito, according to sheriff's officers, and later threatened to rape the girl while brandishing a gun. The girl became frightened and jumped out of the truck as it was going some 55 mph. near the Highway 101 intersection with Highway 37 south of Novato, Mrs. Andreata said. The girl was taken to Novato General Hospital for treatment of a minor brain concussion, but apparently, before hospital officials could identify her, she left the facility. Mrs. Andreatta said the girl hitchhiked back to San Francisco and took up residence with her friends on Third ave., again. San Francisco police were sent there several times trying to locate the girl without success. Her parents finally found her and returned her to their home in Livermore. She was checked by doctors at Kaiser Hospital and released to her parents, Mrs. Andreatta said.

April 7—The feature film, *THE ZODIAC KILLER,* directed by TOM HANSON, premieres in CALIFORNIA. HANSON, founder of the PIZZA MAN restaurant franchise, released the picture with the hopes of luring the real ZODIAC out from the shadows—surely ZODIAC can't help but go to see a movie about ITSELF. The STAKE-OUT garnered no identification or apprehension, but does it hold the distinct honor of coining the now-ubiquitous moniker: ZODIAC KILLER. Interestingly, the film takes place, of course, in the BAY AREA, despite featuring a scene of the *ZODIAC KILLER* worshipping under the THEOSOPHIST'S STEVENSON CROSS on CAHUENGA in HOLLYWOOD, an interesting choice considering that

HANSON was well aware that this landmark is a five-hour drive south from the killing fields. On the first day of December, SUE PAULEKAS gave birth to her and VITO's 8-pound and one-half ounce son, SKY, at HILLCREST HOSPITAL in COTATI—SKY'S conception occurred last March, corresponding with SMITH's disappearance from PETALUMA. The name—*SKY*—could be a reference to the ZODIACAL STAR SYSTEM, which breaks the—SKY—into the twelve equal segments NECESSARY TO READ ZODIACAL TRANSITIONS.

1 9 7 2

On NEW YEAR'S DAY, *THE WHITE HORSE GANG* premiered in SAN FRANCISCO. The film is produced and directed by actor-turned-softcore pornographer, TITUS MOEDE. BRITISH novelist NINA BAWDEN penned the screenplay based on her 1966 children's novel of the same name. SHE augmented the original coming-of-age premise—three KIDS kidnap THEIR annoying, younger SCHOOLMATE as a prank—into adults abducting someone to hold for ransom monies that they desperately need to satiate this jonesing—a relevant social commentary, maybe even too relevant; the new overarching theme seems to mirror the BEAUSOLEIL/HINMAN ordeal on some basic level. VITO is featured in a primary role, with HIS wife, SUE, supporting as an uncredited *DRUG MULE*. VITO's one-time *STEVE ALLEN SHOW* assistant, KEN PATTERSON, appears as an uncredited *STREET CORNER HIPPIE*. *THE WHITE HORSE GANG* is considered a *LOST FILM*—but ONE has to wonder—is it really LOST, or just sequestered away because it paints a picture too revealing? Throughout the 1960s, VITO allowed CLAY VITO to be used as a set for low-budget film productions, as long as HIS sculptures were featured in the final film in some capacity. Was CLAY VITO a production mecca to *PRIVATE COLLECTORS*? To wit, VITO and MOEDE had been connected for years before the making of *THE WHITE HORSE GANG*. Both were featured interviews in the first issue of *FREAKOUT MAGAZINE*, 1967. They are linked even earlier—circa 1961—by way of TIMOTHY CAREY's *THE*

WORLD'S GREATEST SINNER, in which MOEDE had a small role, while it also served as FRANK ZAPPA's first real gig. Not to forget, *TWGS* was shot in STEVEN PARENT's hometown of EL MONTE, CA, by MOEDE'S old friend and frequent collaborator, RAY DENNIS STECKLER, who used VITO's sculptures in his second feature, *THE INCREDIBLY STRANGE CREATURES WHO STOPPED LIVING AND BECAME MIXED-UP ZOMBIES* (1964)—VITO, SUE, and FRANZONI appear on a *DICK CLARK SPECIAL* and then JOHNNY CARSON's first LA taping of *THE TONIGHT SHOW*. JERRY HOPKINS begins researching and writing *NO ONE HERE GETS OUT ALIVE*, an autobiographical account of his experiences with JIM MORRISON and THE DOORS. On January 25, 1972, CHARLES MANSON, SUSAN ATKINS, PATRICIA KRENWINKEL, LESLIE VAN HOUTEN, and CHARLES WATSON were each found guilty of *first-degree murder* and *conspiracy to commit murder*. A story develops that the 10050 CIELO DR. hit was a warning shot meant for TERRY MELCHER, since he lived at the infamous address shortly before TATE, and since MELCHER had just previously rejected a bid for him to produce MANSON's album after MARK ROSS's eye-opening tour of SPAHN RANCH. MELCHER squashed this claim, stating:

> I should probably put the record straight ... The Manson family knew I did not live in my house. They knew I'd been living in Malibu for a year. If I had to, I'd blame it all [the end of the Hippies] on David Crosby—He broke up the Byrds and joined Buffalo Springfield and broke them up ... I'd have to say that, personally speaking, Crosby was worse for the good feelings of [L.A.] rock 'n' roll than Manson was.

// THE SANTA ROSA HITCHHIKER MURDERS BEGIN //

February 4, 1972—At around 9:00p, 12-year-old HERBERT SLATER MIDDLE SCHOOL students MAUREEN LOUISE STERLING and YVONNE LISA WEBER disappeared after skating at the REDWOOD EMPIRE ICE

ARENA. Both GIRLS were last seen hitchhiking on GUERNEVILL ROAD in SANTA ROSA, CA. March 4, at approximately 5:20p, SANTA ROSA JUNIOR COLLEGE art student KIM WENDY ALLEN, 19, disappeared after being seen accepting a ride home from HER job at LARKSPUR NATURAL FOODS, with two men. The next day, near an embankment off ENTERPRISE ROAD in SANTA ROSA, ALLEN's brutalized CORPSE is discovered. SHE has been raped and strangled to death. RICKY J. APPELBAUM makes an after-hours pharmacy pick up in HANFORD, CA, 120 miles to the southeast of his destination of VITO's in SANTA ROSA:

> March 6—*The Hanford Sentinel*, Police—Alerted by a burglar alarm, Hanford Police Officer Douglas Hamblin made a timely arrival at Hanford Pharmacy, 1028 N. Douty St., at 4:30 a.m. today and came face to face with Rick Appelbaum, 24, of Los Angeles inside the building. Appelbaum, a musician who said he had been in Kings County for two days, was booked at the county jail on charges of burglary and possession of restricted dangerous drugs after a bottle of codeine tablets identified as belonging to the pharmacy was found in his pocket. In another drug case, sheriff's officers are investigating a forced entry at Hanford Veterinary Hospital, 9086 Lacey Blvd., where the office had been ransacked and 20 morphine tablets and 20 disposable syringes were taken.

After three weeks of local lock-up, APPELBAUM appeared before a judge:

> March 28—*The Hanford Sentinel*, Court Reports—Kings County Superior Court Criminal Calendar—Criminal proceedings were suspended, and two doctors were named to examine Ricky Appelbaum, 24, of Los Angeles, after he pleaded guilty in Kings County Superior Court to second-degree burglary. A hearing to determine whether he is a narcotics addict or in imminent danger of becoming one was set. Appelbaum was caught inside the Hanford Pharmacy on March 6 after a burglar alarm was triggered. Police found in his possession a bottle of codeine tablets identified as having come from the pharmacy.

APPELBAUM is released from the local pokey. The SANTA ROSA HITCHHIKER MURDERS were on hold during APPELBAUM's incarceration. But on April 20, another SANTA ROSA JUNIOR COLLEGE student, JEANETTE KAMAHELE, 20, disappeared just off Highway 101 in COTATI—APPELBAUM's DESTINATION. KAMAHELE (Hawaiian; *the traveler*) was witnessed by a friend getting into an older-model CHEVROLET pickup that had a makeshift wooden camper affixed over the bed (perhaps akin to a PANEL TRUCK?). The WITNESS described the driver: a WHITE MALE with an Afro, aged 20 to 30. At the time of this writing, KAMAHELE's body is still unaccounted for. On July 12, VITO struck a deal with the ROHNERT PARK COMMISSION, clearing HIM for building the BANDSTAND, but local bureaucracy, of course, stalled the progress:

> Aug. 18—*The Press Democrat*, COTATI—Whether or not Cotati citizens are going to build a bandstand for the Plaza and, if so, how soon became the topic of discussion in a town meeting atmosphere at last night's City Council meeting. After Mrs. Lorraine Leivas, chairwoman of the Parks and Recreation Commission, had presented plans showing a bandstand to be built of donated materials by volunteer labor, a debate began with both council and audience participating, "I've got a pick and a shovel, and I'm ready to go down and start digging a foundation," declared Vito Paulekas, who stated that he was "between jobs" and could begin work immediately.

> Sep. 8—*The Press Democrat,* ... Mr. Salfren spoke in favor of the bandstand, and a general discussion ensued, in which various estimates of the cost were put forth, ranging from Vito Paulekas' "four dollars for a saw blade and five for nails" to "$2000 for beams and other things." The council voted to approve the concept of the bandstand over the negative vote of Mr. Dolinsek and directed the planning commission to submit a more concrete plan and estimate of costs.

In October 1972, BALLANTINE BOOKS published DAVID GERROLD's (aka JERROLD *JERRY* DAVID FRIEDMAN) debut novel, *WHEN HARLIE WAS ONE*. The novel suffered grand acclaim and garnered a NEBULA AWARD for BEST NOVEL. The cover for the first edition trade paperback featured artwork by JAQUES WYRS depicting a thinly veiled image of BAPHOMET. *WHEN HARLIE WAS ONE* is only the second work of fiction—preceded by GREGORY BENFORD's 1969 novel, *THE SACRED MAN*—in which a computer program specifically designed and implemented for digital destruction is referred to as a *VIRUS*. The novel's dedication page is a posthumous message from GERROLD to his DEAD BUDDY; someone who knew the author when he was *JERRY* FRIEDMAN, the same FRIEND who phoned the author from 10050 CIELO DR's GUESTHOUSE on August 9, 1969:

> IN MEMORY OF STEPHEN EARL PARENT
> *—one of those very special friends.*

Maybe since GERROLD changed his name after the MANSON murders, why not change PARENT's name, too, choosing to spell STEVEN's name as *STEPHEN*.

> Oct. 20—*The Press Democrat*, The matter of dogs running loose seems to be a sore point for Vito Paulekas, who gave an eloquent oration against dogs being brought to the plaza to deposit "excreta."

VITO managed to build the BANDSTAND with the help of FRANZONI, ALPPELBAUM, and OTHERS, using reclaimed wood and wire from the abandoned, unused chicken coops that littered the HIPPIE hideaway village. On page 5C of SANTA ROSA's *PRESS DEMOCRAT*, we get a mouthful from and about VITO:

November 5, 1972—THE INEXHAUSTABLE BANDSTAND BUILDER—By DONNA KARASEK Staff Correspondent 545-7420, COTATI—Who is building the bandstand? Vito is. Well, Vito and Robert and Ward and ... But mostly Vito. It was his idea, and his was the original drawing shown to the City Council. Vito is building the bandstand of used lumber in the plaza, hoping that concerts, plays, dancing, and all sorts of acts will be available there for the enjoyment of the citizens of Cotati. Yet, such is Vito's personal philosophy that he says it wouldn't matter to him if the bandstand were torn down the week after it was finished. The fact of creating is the art, he says; after that, it is finished, and the city can do with it as it wishes. That's getting ahead of the story. Who is Vito? He is Vitautus Alphonsus Paulekas—a wiry, fit 59 with long, stringy, brownish-gray hair, a gray beard and mustache, a Boston accent, and an endless supply of energy. Let's start at the beginning of this interview. In a room deep in the basement of Ives Hall on the Cal State, Sonoma, campus, Vito leads a dozen young people in a dance class—a no-fee, no-credit, extracurricular project for all of them. NON-STOP Vito wears purple slacks and a purple web shirt. He is barefoot, as are most of the students who wear a busy variety of jeans, shorts, and leotards. Loud rock music sets the beat. Vito jerks, sways, and whirls in a modern dance mode that is half ballet, half rock and roll. The students, with obvious delight, try to imitate his every move—but no one can imitate his muscular, angular grace and perfect rhythm. Bouncing, jumping, posing, the action goes on. Students drop out in exhaustion, but Vito never stops. Then the class is over. Collecting up his family—wife Sue, 29, and the children, Gruvi, 5 1/2, B.B., almost 3, and S.K.Y., ten months—Vito drives them all home in his 1950 Chrysler. Home is a small, dark-grey cottage at 8165 El Rancho dr. Vito, Sue, and the children lead us into a small living room, walls covered with pictures, rugs, and webbed hangings. Vito unslings a hammock from a wall, hooks it up across the room, and lounges.

A CELEBRITY—Then we learn what a celebrity Vito really is. Out come the albums, and there are the clippings—stories from Los Angeles newspapers and from the "New Yorker" magazine. Vito tells of interviews by BBC and by Swedish and

French TV interviewers in Los Angeles. He tells of bringing a group of dancers onto the Johnny Carson show and of appearances on the Steve Allen show. Once, he sculpted the head of Steve Allen while on the show. He claims a number of appearances on the Joe Pyne TV talk show while in Los Angeles. Dancer, sculptor, TV personality—has he always supported himself in these ways? Oh, no. He is a violinist, too. And he has worked as a busboy, housepainter, carpenter, a merchant seaman during the war—you know he means World War II. Vito mentions working in the Civilian Conservation Corps during the Depression. And the marathon dancing—he tells of staying on the floor for 4800 hours, or five months and three weeks, in 1932. The arithmetic doesn't quite check out, and the vision this presents is almost unbelievable. Without a sign of shame, he admits to having been a welfare recipient for over two years now. He has described himself as "between jobs." He explains that that means he has built two rooms and a porch onto his house, attends many City Council meetings—and, of course, is now building the bandstand. "That's what I mean by 'between jobs'." The Vito energy again.

THE ACCENT—Let's go back to beginnings. Vito's is back in Lawrence, Mass., and then in Cambridge—hence the accent. He refers vaguely to schooling between the fourth and eighth grades. "I escaped school before that ... and after ..." Then to Los Angeles in the thirties. But he mentions living in the Caribbean, including Haiti, and a year or two here and there in Europe. He and Sue have been married 13 years. Briefly, he refers to another child, Godo, who lost his life at the age of three. Vito has two other children, a son, 28, and a daughter, 24, from a previous marriage. From Los Angeles, Vito and family came to investigate San Francisco. In a dance hall there, he met Bob Aminzade, now of Santa Rosa, who suggested Cotati. And so the Paulekas family has lived in Cotati for nearly four years now. The interview turns to other topics. On drugs, Vito says, I am very dogmatic about drugs. Even the wonder drugs, like penicillin, have some side effects. I am against drugs. But I am not opposed to marijuana. Even taking a couple of aspirin that you buy at the drug store is worse for you than marijuana." On his own vigor: "I believe we were endowed with our physiques to do something with them. If you let them just sit around, your heart will think everything has died and will stop beating." On dogs, a subject about which Vito spoke eloquently at a recent City Council meeting: "Students have been brainwashed into thinking they have a right to their own trip. They don't have the right to commit a nuisance. It's a gesture of hostility to bring a dog where he isn't wanted." And finally, back to the bandstand: "It's going very well. People stop by, and I get them to clean wood and pull nails. Someone else hammers for a while. Someone brings Cokes. It's becoming a social center. "The bandstand represents to me a kind of nostalgia, a trip to the past when the environment and man's relationships were not as corrupt." This is the bandstand that Vito is building.

HE'S VITAUTUS ALPHONSUS PAULEKAS
But Just Call Him 'Vito'

November 11—13-year-old student LORI LEE KURSA is reported missing by HER MOTHER when SHE does not return home from LAWRENCE COOK MIDDLE SCHOOL. It was not uncommon for KURSA to hitchhike. Multiple witnesses report having seen KURSA on or around the second week of December being pushed around and possibly abducted into a van from PARKHURST DRIVE by TWO MEN—the DRIVER fitting the description of JEANETTE KAMAHELE's abductor. The vehicle headed north on CALISTOGA ROAD. On December 14, KURSA's body is found at the foot of an embankment below CALISTOGA ROAD, near SANTA ROSA's RINCON VALLEY. KURSA's corpse is frozen. HER neck had been broken, HER spinal cord compressed to the point of hemorrhaging. SHE had most likely been killed at the time of HER abduction a week previous. An ad placed in the December 21 *SONOMA WEST TIMES* edition (published in SEBASTOPOL, CA):

> TRUCK, haul, move, chop, build, clean, paint, wreck, rig or fix, complete odd job service. Free estimate. Call Freestore Village Idiots. 874-3046. 10-14

December 28, the SKELETAL REMAINS of MAUREEN LOUISE STERLING and YVONNE LISA WEBER—the two 12-year-old STUDENTS missing since February—were found at the bottom of a steep embankment below FRANZ VALLEY ROAD. The CAUSES OF DEATH could not be determined due to the condition of the BODIES.

1 9 7 3

Jan. 5—*The Press Democrat*, ... Strong anti-Vietnam-war statements were made by Thomas Dunphy and Vito Paulekas, and requests were made for the city to donate aid to the North Vietnamese people. "Don't send a dollar; send a letter," Paulekas then said dramatically, but he was reminded that the council had already gone on record as being opposed to the Vietnam War and that a letter to that effect had already been sent to the president.

Don't Send a Dollar; Send a Letter—Sounds like advice somebody fixated on correspondence might give.

Jan. 31—*The Press Democrat*, COTATI BANDSTAND HELP APPRECIATED—EDITOR: We would like to thank all who participated in and supported the building of the bandstand in Cotati. Many types of donations were received: some in the form of money, many in building materials, and many people participated by donating a few hours of labor or an encouraging word of enthusiasm. The original idea and impetus for construction came from Cotati resident Vito Paulekas, who worked tirelessly for months before the construction of the bandstand, having plans drawn up, cutting through red tape, and eventually approved by the City of Cotati. Vito feels the process of creation to be more rewarding than the completion of the finished product. Regretfully, there were some hard feelings from some factions; hopefully, these can be resolved with the completion of the bandstand. In any case, the City of Cotati desires that the soon-to-be dedicated bandstand in Cotati be enjoyed and used by all—to bring the town together instead of dividing it.

March 1—*The Press Democrat*, COTATI PARKS COMMISSION MUTINIES, COTATI—Vito Paulekas showed sample works of two stained-glass workers, Wayne Schoech and Jake Holtzman, and suggested a stained-glass inlay in one of the bandstands as a starter at a cost of $40. The commission voted to recommend this to the council. He also suggested a bocce ball court in the plaza and was asked to bring details of this idea back to the commission.

March 2—*The Press Democrat*, ... A proposal to put a window fashioned of stained glass by Wayne Schoech and Jake Holtzman into one of the triangles near the top of the bandstand was discussed. The possibility of vandalism was brought up, to which Vito Paulekas, builder of the bandstand and backer of this proposal, replied in horrified tones, " I can't conceive of anyone throwing a rock through a stained glass window. I'm shocked that the question could be asked." The proposal, at a cost of $40, passed on two yes votes, a no from Councilman Frank Dolinsek, and an abstention by Dunham.

April 6—*The Press Democrat*, ... Several others spoke in favor of all commercial zoning, one referring to the council treating investors in a "cavalier fashion." A few were speaking against the commercial zoning there, such as Vito Paulekas' comments that he didn't want to see Cotati become another Rohnert Park. Commented Councilman Herb Winter, "As a councilman, I don't see how we can go against the taxpayers on East Cotati." He said the city needed more commercial property to keep the tax rate from going up. Dolinsek agreed, adding, "If you give it (commercial zoning) to one, you have to give it to the other."

At the beginning of April, SUE was impregnated with her and VITO's fourth child. By mid-month, VITO had developed a severe hernia while teaching *CAN YOU DIG IT?,* and the hernia quickly worsened to the point that surgical intervention was inevitable. VITO backed off the scene momentarily allowing APPELBAUM to fill in as RESIDENT ACTIVIST:

> April 20—*The Press Democrat*, IN LIEU PARKING—An ordinance to provide an in-lieu parking fund, whereby owners of commercial property could pay into the fund for parking lots rather than provide on-site parking, passed over Winter's negative vote. An ordinance regulating conduct in parks and plazas, including a prohibition against camping in local parks, passed, but not until Ricky Appelbaum had angrily pointed out that these rules cut people sleeping in the parks "because they don't want to pay a landlord." A cry of "riffraff" was heard from the back of the crowd. "I think it's unfair of you to tell people where they can sleep and where they can't," added Appelbaum. A woman objected to "kids who want to drift" and pointed out sanitation problems, and the ordinance passed.

Mid-May—VITO was bedridden, recovering from a botched hernia fix after SURGEONS missed feeding a tube through HIS bronchial sphincter and instead plunged the length into HIS stomach. VITO died on the operating table, affording him HIS SECOND DEATH—It was only for a moment, then HE returned to life already in progress, but hardened now and with an irritability off the charts. During the last week of May, 20-year-old LETTERMAN GENERAL HOSPITAL keypunch operator, ROSA VASQUEZ, goes missing. Three days later, HER strangled CORPSE was discovered discarded in shrubbery several feet from the ARGUELLO BOULEVARD at the entrance of GOLDEN GATE PARK in SAN FRANCISCO'S PRESIDIO. On July 15, 14-year-old CAROLYN NADINE DAVIS was dropped off at a GARBERVILLE USPS office in SHASTA COUNTY by HER GRANDMOTHER so that DAVIS could hitchhike a ride southbound on HIGHWAY 101 toward MODESTO, CA, where SHE was to board with friends—hiding out—because DAVIS believed SHE was targeted and chased after witnessing a double murder. On or around July 20, DAVIS died from straight STYCHNINE POISONING administered either by injection or ingested. Eleven days later, CAROLYN NADINE DAVIS's decomposing CORPSE was discovered in the exact same locations where the SKELETONS OF MAUREEN LOUISE STERLING and YVONNE LISA WEBER were found over the new year. DAVIS, like many of the other recent SANTA ROSA victims, was tossed like a sack of garbage down the embankment, coming to rest in a patch of lowland brush. Like clockwork, guess who makes a media blitz on the heels of the murders? —On the first of August, 1973, a LETTER was mailed to *THE TIMES UNION* in ALBANY, NY. The upper left corner of the envelope bears the small CODA SYMBOL instantly associated with ZODIAC:

> YOU Were WRONG I AM NOT DEAD OR IN THE HOSPITAL I AM ALIVE AND WELL AND IM GOING TO START KILLING AGAIN.
> Below is the NAME AND LOCATION OF MY NEXT VICTIM
> But you had Better hurry be
> cause Im going to kill Her August 10th at 5:00 P.M. when the shift change ALBANY is Anise Taun
>
> 
>
> [A block of 51 cipher characters]

ALBANY might be a reference to where VITO was stationed for CCC service in 1931, as well as the SAME CITY where GEORGE ESTABROOKS began his well-documented hypno-abuse. VITO's botched surgery and recovery, when set against ZODIAC's hospital remark, align very neatly.

> Aug. 3—*The Press Democrat,* ... Lee Gray announced that Vito Paulekas has cleaned the Marie Tadlock fountain and filter, which is now operating properly, and has expressed intentions to keep it up. Paulekas himself then asked what report had been received from the Sonoma County Sheriff's Office in the matter of Jake Speaks, a black whose apartment was invaded by Sheriff's officers searching for a wanted black man last May 18. Gray indicated that he had received a confidential reply from the Sheriff's Office and that he himself could not reply to Speaks' complaint against the Sheriff's Office. The council will attempt further to obtain satisfactory answers to the questions presented to the Sheriff's Office.

Aug. 10—*The Press Democrat,* SANDBOX—It was unanimously decided to install a sandbox in the plaza after Commissioner Robert Davis had volunteered that he and Vito Paulekas, builder of the bandstand, might be able to build it.

AND, THEN MAYBE ... JUST MAYBE:

Aug. 17—*The Press Democrat,* ... HEARD Vito Paulekas refers to "crackpot mail" being received, allegedly with no return address or signatories, making "scurrilous attacks" on the mayor. It appeared possible that he was referring to a circular recently published by the Citizens for Sound Government, the recall committee, which announced a change of position on Dunham to "no opinion," still calling for the recall of the other two young members of the council. Dunham explained that the tactic was probably to set up the council to appoint its replacements for recalled members, if any, and recommended that voters, however, they vote on recall, vote to fill the vacated positions by new election, not appointment. He endorsed Miss Lombardi and Laughlin.

Aug. 31—*Petaluma Argus-Courier,* ... DISPUTES COSTS—Dunham also disputed the charge that $700 was spent on the bandstand. He and the others have consistently claimed that no more than $47 was spent on the facility, with most of the materials and all of the labor donated. Recall Committee Chairman Herb Winter said, however, that he believed the city had purchased at least $200 worth of lumber, which the bandstand's builder, Vito Paulekas, said was to be donated, and that another $400 to $500 had been spent in sending out city crews to work on the project. He also said that a $23 saw was purchased and never returned to the city. Miss Lombardi denied saying that all materials and labor were donated except for $47 worth, part of which bought only a saw blade to replace one Paulekas had broken while working on the bandstand. She is the most pessimistic of the three and believes that the recall, at least for her and Laughlin, may be successful because of the tactics used by her opponents. "We might lose," she said, "because of the fact that we've done the right things, but we haven't made those things public."

> Sep. 2—*The Press Democrat*, ... Vito Paulekas, builder of the bandstand, present at the press conference, loudly backed up the statement that the sum was $47 and angrily claimed that Winter, as a member of the council himself, was aware of this.

On the front page of SAN RAFAEL'S *DAILY INDEPENDENT JOURNAL*, BONNIE BARD described the COTATI TOWN HALL between nine applicants (one of whom is VITO) duking it out for only two open seats on the CITY COUNCIL PARKS AND RECREATION COMMITTEE. KARL FRANZONI has quietly served as COTATI'S PARKS AND RECREATION COMMISSIONER under the just-left-of-center aliases: *ROBERT FRANZONI DAVIS*, *KARL FRANZONI DAVIS*, and *ROBERT DAVIS*.

> Sep. 17—CALL FOR HARMONY IS HEARD IN COTATI—Nine Seek Council Seat Appointments—Three young councilmen—in hopes of mending hard feelings—called the unique town meeting to get opinions from residents on which candidates should be appointed ... Paulekas, 68, an unemployed artist and carpenter, said he could work in complete harmony with younger members of the council. He led the effort to build the bandstand in Plaza Park. Paulekas said he would work to further arts and crafts in the city on both a mercantile and cultural basis. He said he would also work to keep Cotati's population as low as possible...

THE PRESS DEMOCRAT reports that this TOWN HALL question was put to each candidate: *What have you done for your city before the recall election?* After eight fairly bureaucratic replies, VITO gets his turn, and makes an interesting selection of words, the paper reporting that: *Paulekas said he contributed rope to people downtown as leashes for their dogs.* Sep. 30—Another COTATI TOWN HALL is gathering, this time to vote in favor of or against charging ARTISTS a vendor's fee for selling wares at the PUBLIC PLAZA. VITO will have none of it:

The Press Democrat, Cotati Group State Need For Resale Permits—P.D. Bureau—COTATI—Artisans, tradespeople, and vendors who normally need a resale license to sell their wares may find the City of Cotati endorsing a resale permit under which all may operate. The idea was unanimously approved at Wednesday night's meeting of the Cotati Park and Recreation Commission. The body recommended the Council approve a $25 expenditure for the purchase of a temporary resale license ... Audience member Vito Paulekas suggested the need for artisans to secure resale permits was red tape and added, "This is ludicrous. It can be very disheartening to these people to have to go through all these just to sell a few wares." He said it "wipes out the initiative of the tradesmen." ... One of the biggest headaches to come from the Commission to the City Council in the form of a recommendation is a recommendation to reroute traffic around the Plaza on Sundays. Paulekas proposed to circumvent the plaza between 9 a.m. until almost dark on Sundays ... Paulekas said Sundays would be a good day for closing the plaza since no heavy industrial trucks would travel other arterial streets that can't handle the tonnage. He added traffic on Sundays is also lighter. The Commission endorsed the idea unanimously, and Paulekas said he would take it to the Council. Councilwoman Lombardi said she thought the idea was great and said she would introduce the motion to the Council.

Nov. 21—*The Press Democrat,* APPOINTED—Vito Paulekas and Carol Stansbury were named to the Parks and Recreation Commission to put the seven-member body back at full strength.

Dec. 19—*The Press Democrat,* ... In other action, an anticipated long delay by Golden Gate Transit in installing bus shelters in Cotati was taken up. The Council authorized the expenditure of $125 for payment to Vito Paulekas to build the shelters. However, Paulekas had just been reappointed to the Park and Recreation Commission. Mayor Geoffrey Dunham expressed concern this might be a "conflict of interest." But just before the vote, Paulekas said, "I have some questions about the Mayor reappointing me without consulting me first." Paulekas then submitted his resignation,

> and it was accepted. The Council then authorized him to build the shelter. Paulekas' move to build the shelter by resigning his Commission seat was obvious. Asked if he planned to reapply once the shelter is completed, he said, "I don't think I dare."

On December 22, 1973, three days after VITO went on a local media rant decrying the local COTATI GOVERNMENT and resigned in fury, 23-year-old MIRANDA, CA resident, THERESA DIANE SMITH WALSH, is seen for the last time in MALIBU on ZUMA BEACH. WALSH is reportedly desperate to hitch a ride to GARBERVILLE to visit HER family for the CHRISTMAS BREAK, and tragically does so. Six days later, WALSH's CORPSE is found by kayakers in MIRANDA's MARK WEST CREEK. WALSH's body was partially submerged in water; SHE had been hogtied with a clothesline, strangled, and, by all signs, sexually assaulted. WALSH was also likely killed the day she disappeared. After dumping her body, it drifted several miles after the high water mark rose significantly from heavy rains. After WALSH's discovery, the SANTA ROSA HITCHHIKER MURDERS suddenly cease. Remember that beanpole, first-generation FREAK, ROBERT *BEATLE BOB* ROBERTS? Well, he's been studying traditional tattooing under legend, DON ED HARDY, and is officially ordained a *jagger*. ROBERTS begins tattooing professionally at THE PIKE in LONG BEACH at 95 SOUTH PINE AVE. He works alongside living legends in the inking industry, BOB SHAW and COLONEL BILL TODD. (ROBERTS soon moves back to HOLLYWOOD and opens his popular SPOTLIGHT TATTOO at 5859 MELROSE AVE.)

1 9 7 4

FRANZONI takes two of the *highest members of HIS theatre troupe* to ask big-time concert promoter, BILL GRAHAM, to make good on old favors and get HIS FREAKS *a fucking gig*, but GRAHAM refuses to see THEM. THE SALAD DAYS ARE OVER. Jan. 28—PHREEKUS *MARK* MAGEEKUS PAULEKAS is born in SONOMA COUNTY to VITO, 61, and SUE, 30. The growing family lives in PETALUMA at 8165 EL RANCHO DR. (If you are curious about the formula for mixing a PHREEKUS MAGEEKUS (aka SEX MAGICK) cocktail: Take one PHREE MESSEN (or *Child of light*; or *Lucifer* if you can find 'em), and add a pinch of a special *K* to the *magic* (just as CROWLEY did, differentiating HIS WORKS). Be sure to have plenty of spare PHREEKUS/ PHREEKING/PHUHKING on hand AND! USE ONLY WITH THE CROWLIAN *K*) THEN ON JANUARY 29, 1974: the day after a new PAULEKAS took HIS first breath, ZODIAC mails THEIR first correspondence in two years. In this letter to the *SF CHRONICLE*, the WRITER hints at retiring ZODIAC in favor of another PERSONA; ONE which has yet to materialize in the media. The WRITER ditched THEIR unfortunate famous pick-up line—*THIS IS THE ZODIAC SPEAKING*—and THEY DID NOT sign the MESSAGE with THEIR usual CODA.

> June 12—*Petaluma Argus-Courier*, COTATI ADOPTS PLAN TO CONTROL AMPLIFIED MUSIC by MARTIN BRODY Staff Writer—COTATI—The Cotati City Council unanimously adopted a plan to control the amplified music at the

bandstand in the city's center Tuesday night after a lively discussion on the controversial matter. Loud music coming from the bandstand on weekends has drawn considerable protest from citizens in both Cotati and Rohnert Park. A petition, signed by some 100 people from Rohnert Park, was read. It called the bandstand music a public nuisance and stated that Cotati should enforce some kind of regulation controlling it ... Vito Paulekas was designated as "keeper of the bandstand" and given responsibility of the key to the bandstand fuse box to provide electricity when directed by permit. Mayor Steve Laughlin, who expressed doubts about the effectiveness of the policy, and Vice Mayor Harry Fassio both pointed out that the adopted plan does not concern the type of music (in this case, rock), and there was no intent in barring rock music. Loudness was the issue.

July 8—*THE SF CHRONICLE* receives a handwritten LETTER:

Editor—
Put Marco back in the hell-hole
from whence it came—he has
a serious psychological disorder—
always needs to feel superior. I
suggest you refer him to a shrink.
Meanwhile, cancel the Count Marco
column. Since the Count can
write anonymously, so can I—

the Red Phantom
(red with rage)

Sep. 22—*The Press Democrat*, Police Advisory Committee to Meet—P.D. Bureau—COTATI—The revitalized Police Advisory Committee, a standing city committee formed more than two years ago to improve police-community relations, will meet at 7:30 p.m. Tuesday at City Hall to consider police brutality charges. The charges were made at two recent City Council meetings by citizen Vito Paulekas about three separate events, none of which he personally witnessed.

VITO really hates the *Blue Meanies*, like, dig man?

Sep. 24—*Daily Independent Journal*, POLICE BRUTALITY HEARING SLATED—The Cotati police advisory committee will meet at 7:30 p.m. today in City Hall to consider a brutality accusation against a member of the city police department. The charge was laid before the city council recently by resident Vito A. Paulekas of 8165 El Rancho Drive. Paulekas, a sculptor, said he knew of two residents who had been harassed and beaten by a city officer. Paulekas told the council he had not witnessed the harassment himself. The committee, which reviews cases and advises the city council, has been inactive during the past year ... Mayor Dunham said that mentioning specific cases would be permissible in a public meeting so long as the cases were not currently under litigation. Resident Vitatus A. (Vito) Paulekas, 61, objected the loudest to Corrigan's attempt to prevent public accusations. As the chairman attempted to persuade Miss Gree to be circumspect, Paulekas screamed, "I want to hear these people with no interruptions from you or anyone else on this committee. If you want to (investigate complaints) in a closet, then call this meeting off and go meet in a closet." Miss Green and Paulekas repeatedly told the committee they believed Officer Standish was the source of the brutality ... Corrigan decreed that the committee, strictly an advisory group under the city council, could not act on hearsay evidence but needed complaints from victims themselves. His position especially outraged Paulekas, who accused Corrigan and other committee members of not making sufficient effort to seek out and question alleged brutality victims. Paulekas rose from his chair at one point and shouted, "We've got a nut on the police force named Rich Standish—we're not safe on the streets from him, and we're not safe in our homes from him. How do you expect these people to come to you when they are terrorized by the police? If you don't clean this thing up, then the city government is done for." ... The police advisory committee, after two hours of arguments, decided to meet again.

IMPROVISED EXPLOSIVE DEVICES // CLOWNS IN PRIVATE LIFE

1975

On the seventh of February 1975, VITO'S newest incarnation of FREAKS THE FREE STORE THEATRE COMPANY (henceforth FREESTORE)—a street theatre troupe made up of *avant-garde* ACTIVISTS born out of *CAN YOU DIG IT?* VITO PAULEKAS, KARL FRANZONI, GLENN SACCO, PEGGY *BIG RED* FARRAR, RICKY J. APPELBAUM, KATHLEEN HOLLAND, CLAY GEERDES, LORETTA MERY, and LOREEN ALLEN began performing throughout SONOMA and MARIN counties in a fashion not all that different from the COMMEDIA DELL'ARTE—the eleven-person group of masked clowns that trolled the medieval Italian countryside. On February 20, VITO filed an insurance claim against the surgeon who botched his herniorrhaphy. March—*SUANNE C. SHAFFER* files for divorce from VITO using her maiden name, explicitly expressing HER intent to drop the PAULEKAS surname.

THE FREESTORE HIT PARADE:

A Compendium of Appearances, Performances & Public Threats

> May 14—*The Press Democrat,* Entertainment—THE NEW SKY RIVER BAND will headline a free concert beginning at noon Saturday at the plaza in downtown Cotati. Also appearing will be the hard rock trio Starfire Express; Freestore, a group of players from Cotati who specialize in avant-garde, revue-type theater; and two acoustical acts, Sandy Nelson and Tom &

Rod. The emcees will be David and Lindsey. The concert is sponsored by various Cotati business people ...

May 16—*Daily Independent Journal,* FREE STORE, a group of Cotati actors, will perform a revue featuring avant-garde and political skits. The affair is being sponsored by several Cotati businesses.

May 19—*The San Francisco Examiner,* FOLK, ETD: Morning Glory, Gangband, Freestore at Inn of the Beginning, Cotati, Tuesday, 9 p.m.

July 6—*The San Francisco Examiner,* Vito, and Getz—THE FREE Store Theatre Company, specializing in the street theatre style, is headed by Vito Paulekas (right) and will perform Wednesday at noon in Sproul Plaza of UC Berkeley. Others in the group include Karl Franzoni, formerly of the Mothers, and lyricist Rick Appelbaum.

July 7—*The Berkeley Gazette,* THEATER IN THE STREET—The Free Store Theater Company will perform on Wednesday at noon in Sproul Plaza on the UC campus in Berkeley. "Free Store" was written and choreographed by Vito Paulekas, the Los Angeles sculptor who originated the "freak-out" style exhibited by such 1960's ensembles as Frank Zappa and The Mothers of Invention. Karl Franzoni, who danced with the Mothers for several years, is with the Free Store Company. Others in the company include Rick Appelbaum, who wrote the lyrics for numbers like "Palace of Love" and "For a Nickel I Will." The show is done in the street theater style popularized by the San Francisco Mime Troupe in the 1960s. The company has been performing for five months in Sonoma and Marin counties.

Sep. 19—*Daily Independent Journal,* Town Meeting, Dinner Bring Cotati Factions Together ... A little over a year ago, the two other young councilmen resigned—on the same day as Richard Nixon—after being arrested for stealing marijuana plants from a police evidence locker. "All concerns people had back then are still there," Dunham said, "but there's not the schism between the divergent lifestyles—if you don't believe me, just look over there, man." He pointed to a nearby table. Around it, eating and conversing animatedly but pleasantly, were several policemen, a couple of long-tressed young women, oldtimer Ramie Ahlstron, and the inimitable

Vitatus A. Paulekas. Vito, as most know him, is an embroidery-bedecked hippie who is Cotati's chief protector of unwanted dogs, resident one-man guerrilla theater company, and unofficial dance master laureate and general purpose crazy person.

Sep. 25—*The Press Democrat*, FREE STORE, street vaudeville troupe which evolved from a free modern dance class taught at Sonoma State College by sculptor Vito Paulekas, will perform at noon Friday in Santa Rosa's Old Courthouse Square. Free Store, named for a community swap shop, has performed at the Last Great Hiding Place, in Cotati Plaza and at Union Square, San Francisco.

Oct. 2—*Daily Independent Journal*, SONOMA STATE PROTEST—Arming Campus Police Hit—By ERNEST MURPHY—Sonoma State College students yesterday staged what may have been the largest student protest rally in the school's history ... As it was, estimates range from a turnout of 500 to about 1,000 students, 10 to 20 percent of the total population attended the noon rally outside the campus cafeteria. Big as the rally was, it almost got upstaged by the Cotati Guerrilla Theatre Company. For an hour before the rally, the company, led by Cotati's Pied Piper, Vitatus (Vito) A. Paulekas, cavorted and pranced in a bawdy performance satirizing everything from guns to venereal diseases. "The CIA," bawled Vito as the troupe did its routines clad in leather jackets, garter belts, and other exotica, "is xxxxxxx in your drinking water." It was a coincidence that Vito and company had got permission to use the cafeteria terrace before the rally organizers did, and so Vito decided to help them out with a little pointed satire. The rally people, though, seemed unappreciative. "Man, we gotta stop this. We're gonna lose our audience," one said to another as the weirdness continued. Once Vito's mummers finished and the rally actually started, the students found the object of their anger, college President Marjorie Wagner, wasn't there to see the show. "She's out of town this week, " Daitz told the crowd. "I think maybe she's a relative of Mayor Yorty of Los Angeles."

Oct. 5—*The San Francisco Examiner,* 'Lollipop' From the Free Store—FREE STORE, a song and dance troupe created by Vito Paulekas in the tradition of early American vaudeville, will perform Wednesday at noon in front of the new Student Union Building San Francisco State University, with Kathleen Holland doing her "Co-co Lollipop" rendition. The group will be performing in Union Square in December.

Nov. 2—*The San Francisco Examiner,* FREE STORE THEATER COMPANY—A vaudeville-type satirical revue by this street-theater troupe. Noon Tuesday. San Francisco State University. Holloway near 19th avenue.

December—SUE PAULEKAS (who is in NO WAY part of FREESTORE, but still crazy-as-ever) files for divorce ... again: SUANNE C. SCHAFFER from VITO A. PAULEKAS. Dec. 13—VITO is reimbursed $125 for materials purchased for the BANDSTAND build, and then, without VITO's consent, the CITY renews HIS COUNCIL SEAT.

Dec. 20—*Petaluma Argus-Courier,* Clubs—INN OF THE BEGINNING—Sat. Dec. 20: The Moonlighters, Tommy Thompson and the Sonoma County Line; Sun. Dec. 21: Christmas Party with Freestore, Street Music Rainbow Trancee Dancers ... 8201 Old Redwood Highway, Cotati. 795-9955.

1976

Jan. 26—*The San Francisco Examiner,* "Walkers have arrived at Sonoma Grove, a funky trailer encampment near Sonoma State College. Led by Vito and his Free Store, an outrageous repertory group, which has played in Union Square and Sproul Plaza and does regular turns in Cotati, walkers are paraded into Cotati, escorted by a hundred or so residents, to The Last Great Hiding Place, local coffee house. Here, a benefit is held to raise money for walkers with food, music, poetry readings, etc. Monks rise, and older one makes little speeches, with younger monks translating, as in foreign movies with subtitles: "We are beating the drum of peace ... Pray for the peace, pray for the happiness of all mankind." That night, some walkers stayed at our house. Most seem to be "going all the way" or at least a considerable distance.

Feb. 19—*Sonoma West Times and News,* A benefit dance for salmon—A benefit dance and entertainment to finance the raising of silver salmon at a new site north of Jenner will be held Saturday night, 8 p.m. to 1 a.m., at the Occidental Community Center. Dance music will be furnished by the Starfire Express. A theatrical group, Freestore, will provide entertainment, and Tom and Rod, a singing group, will perform. Money is being raised to buy a pool in which to raise the salmon. Marine Resources & Engineering Development, sponsors of the event, was incorporated last August as a non-profit organization to raise salmon to be released off the Sonoma coast. The operation so far has been financed by memberships.

Feb. 21—*Petaluma Argus-Courier,* ON THE COVER—No, it's not Halloween. It's street theater. And Free Store Theater Company, a Cotati-based troupe, has become one of the leading practitioners of the style in the Bay Area. At the top of the page is a scene from "The Assassination of Santa Claus."

VAUDEVILLE LIVES IN COTATI by CHRIS SAMSON Staff Writer—They call themselves "the new vaudeville." And that may well be the best way to describe the Cotati-based Free Store Theater Company, a unique group of entertainers who defy standard categorization. Indeed, the spirit of old-time vaudeville still lives with this 11-member ensemble, which was formed a little over a year ago. They have revived that dying art that thrived in earlier days by offering theatrical productions that combine musical comedy, contemporary satire, song and dance, nostalgia, and "outrageous fun." Social and political commentary is also thrown in for good measure. The form of entertainment provided by Free Store is uncommon these days and may be the reason for their growing popularity. In the last several months, they have been answering invitations to perform throughout the Bay Area. They are regulars on Saturday nights at the Shot in the Dark, a Cotati nightclub. Tonight is an exception, however, as they will be doing a benefit in Occidental. They will be back in Cotati at the Last Great Hiding Place Monday night and next Saturday at the Shot in the Dark. But their increasing reputation is such that they have also fulfilled requests to perform at the San Francisco Art Institute, U.C. Berkeley, San Francisco State, Mills College, Laney College, and this past week at Indian Valley Colleges in Novato. Their next "big-time" engagement will be at the Intersection Coffeehouse in San Francisco on March 7. Using the street theater style popularized by the San Francisco Mime Troupe in the 1960s, Free Store is flexible enough to perform just about anywhere. "We're acoustic and provide everything," explained one member of the group. "All we need is space like a gym floor." Free Store is also non-commercial. Their shows are usually performed in exchange for modest donations received by "passing the hat." Members of the ensemble also display an enthusiasm for their craft to a degree not often found even in professional theater. "It's a celebration every time we do a show," said Peggy, one of the performers. "The whole show is an affirmation of beliefs." This street theater genre usually gains the attention of the audience quickly. The Free Store numbers are short and compact and lend themselves to this style. Each member is dressed and made up to their own imagination with painted faces. Free Store usually begins their show with a warm-up number where characters weave through the audience, stretching and leaning to the rhythmic beat of percussion. This sets the stage for both the performers and the audience for what is to follow. A rapid-fire succession of about 20 or so numbers ensues, most on contemporary subjects. Topics range from rock stars, disarmament, and politicians to bare skin, dogs, and womanhood. The shows are never the same either, Peggy said. We're continuously evolving, and our repertoire and people change." Free Store is the brainchild of 62-year-old Vito Paulekas, one of Cotati's most colorful citizens. Paulekas is a former Los Angeles sculptor who originated the "freak out" style exhibited by Frank Zappa and the Mothers of Invention and other 1960s groups. Karl Franzone, who used to perform with Mothers, is another key member of Free Store. The Cotati vaudeville ensemble is an outgrowth of a dance class, "Can You Dig It," that Paulekas began instructing at nearby Cal State Sonoma four years ago. "It just evolved from that," one member explained. In December, the Free Store staged several performances of "The Assassination of Santa Claus." Their regular shows combine old numbers like "Goodnight, Irene" and "Five Foot Two" with new songs such as "For A Nickel I Will" and "Palace of Love," written by Rick Applebaum. Peggy summed it up by saying, "It's the kind of show you'd want to bring your children to see, but probably not your mother."

March 30—*Daily Independent Journal*, Bawdy theater from Cotati By Ernest Murphy—One of these days, enthusiastic local fans may dub it the Cotati Metropolitan Opera Company. But for now, it's simply Free Store, and until recently, it was one of Cotati's best-kept secrets. The word got out the day tourists at San Francisco's Cannery were alarmed to see a bunch of seeming lunatics prancing through the brick promenades. The dozen or so paint-faced mummers, dressed in top hats, G-strings, tassels, and garter belts, made strange noises like a howling horde of hopped-up hyenas. That's how a typical Free Store performance—if there is such a thing—begins. It quickly progresses into a song and dance revue interspersed with short skits, which are usually bawdy and always satirical. Some who have seen it compare Free Store to vaudeville. The creator of the dozen-member troupe thinks otherwise, and rightly so. Free Store is to vaudeville what Country Porn is to Roy Rogers. "I'm not into nos-tal-gia, man. I'm into con-temp-o-rary the-at-re." That's the explanation of Vito A. Paulekas, an elfin 62-year-old man who neither looks nor acts like anyone else that age. Vito talks that way when he's making a point, emphasizing key syllables in a rather declamatory style. Vito came to Cotati about seven years ago after more than two decades as a Los Angeles sculptor. He'd left the southland to move to Haiti—as an artist, he is interested in the symbolism used by primitive peoples—but the island nation was too costly. Vito came back and tried to settle in Sausalito, but he couldn't find a place to live. Someone told him about Cotati, and he moved. He's been there ever since. Vito also is a carpenter and a dancer. He began dancing during the ballroom marathon craze of the early 1930s. A year and a half ago, Vito got together with several of his dance students and others involved in drama at nearby Sonoma State College. They formed Free Store, named after the no-money second-hand shop Vito built behind A Shot in the Dark, a Cotati night spot. Free Store performs every Saturday night at the tavern, and other performances happen during weekdays around the Bay Area. At noon on Thursday, the troupe will give an April Fool's Day performance at the College of Marin. What is a Free Store performance all about? Gun control, incest, electroshock therapy, welfare bureaucrats, rock and roll, all kinds of things. "The show is about the kind of everyday problems people in the community can relate to," Vito explains. "Problems with landlords, with mommies and daddies; with the clap—it's a satire on everything, but with an undercurrent of serious concern." There are no sacred cows among the Free Store folk. The troupe's regular parody on gun control usually involves the simulated machine gun assassination of some easily identified figure in keeping with the season—Santa Claus, for instance. Or the Easter Bunny. Or Jesus. The way Vito looks at it, Free Store is nothing less than government-subsidized art. Most troupe members live off of some form of public assistance, and Vito is especially proud that several are recipients of what used to be called Aid to the Totally Dependent, persons who, for one reason or another, can never be expected to support themselves. "There should be something like this in every town," Vito postulates. "Theater created by welfare people who have a lot of time on their hands and who need some way to contribute to the community. "The United States government is our Medicis—

we are artists, and it is our patron."

April 3—*Petaluma Argus-Courier,* FREE STORE THEATRE COMPANY, comedy-satire-vaudeville. Saturdays at 9 p.m., Shot in the Dark, Cotati. 795-8346.

April 11—*The San Francisco Examiner,* The Free Store Theatre Company begins a new season of song, dance, and contemporary satire when the troupe appears in Union Square at noon on Wednesday. The script is by Vito Paulekas and Rick Applebaum, with choreography by Vito.

April 12—*The Press Berkeley Gazette,* THE FREE STORE—Choreographer Vito Paulekas, pictured with a young audience member, is among members of the Berkeley-based Free Store Theater Company to perform at noon Wednesday in San Francisco's Union Square. The musical comedy group is noted for outrageous costuming and painted faces. The free program leads up to a noon April 21 performance at the San Francisco Art Institute, 800 Chestnut St.

April 13—*The San Francisco Examiner,* FREE STORE: A performance of "Free Store," a satirical musical, by Free Store Theater Company, Wednesday, noon, Union Square. Free.

April 18—*The San Francisco Examiner,* FREE STORE THEATRE—Satirical vaudeville revue. Noon Wednesday. S.F. Art Institute, 800 Chestnut street.

April 25—*The San Francisco Examiner,* FREE STORE THEATRE COMPANY—Satirical revue. Today at 2 p.m. Aquatic Park.

May 9—*The San Francisco Examiner,* FREE STORE THEATRE COMPANY—Satirical vaudeville revue by this Cotati troupe. Today at 1 p.m. Hippy Hill, Golden Gate Park.

May 16—*The San Francisco Examiner,* FREE STORE THEATRE CO.—Revue. Shot in the Dark. Saturday at 9 p.m.

> June 3—*The Press Democrat*, Entertainment—Free Concert is Saturday—COTATI—A Free "Fun in the Sun" concert at the outdoor bandstand in Cotati Plaza is planned at noon Saturday. Many performers are donating their time for the six-hour performance. They include Cotati Freestore, the community street theater group of 11 actors, singers, and dancers.

> June 26—*Petaluma Argus-Courier*, Concerts—BENEFIT CONCERT for Cotati Tenants Union, featuring Free Store Theater Company and Funktion. Cinnabar Theater, 3333 Petaluma Blvd. North, Petaluma. Sat. June 26, 8:30 p.m. $2. 795-7717.

> July 3—*The Press Democrat*, Free Concert is Saturday—COTATI—A free "Fun in the Sun" concert at the outdoor bandstand in Cotati Plaza is planned at noon Saturday. Many performers are donating their time for the six-hour performance. They include:... Cotati Freestore, the community street theater group of 11 actors, singers, and dancers.

> July 17—*Petaluma Argus-Courier*, FREE STORE THEATRE COMPANY, comedy-satire-vaudeville "street theatre" group performs Saturdays at 2 p.m. in Cotati Plaza. 795-8346.

After using the words *SATIRE* and *SATIRICAL* extensively throughout previous NEWSPAPER articles and ads to describe the FREESTORE style, they are all but dropped completely from the PRESS' vocabulary going forward:

> July 26—*Berkeley Gazette*, The Free Store Has Some Outdoor Problems, By RICHARD RAMELLA I-G Feature Editor—The Free Store Theatre Company will not be performing in Berkeley's parks from now on. Members are afraid they might get into trouble because of a so-called "obscenity clause" in the agreement they were asked to sign. A parks and recreation spokesman noted that the Free Store folk were overreacting to the situation. Perhaps so. But the Free Store knows what

it's like to get in trouble because of a performance on public grounds. There was a time when the group's performance coincided with the presence of about 300 children around the Band Shell in San Francisco's Golden Gate Park. The group is made up of colorfully garbed members who perform a kind of "contemporary vaudeville" show. Vito Paulekas, the 62-year-old ringleader of the classically motley group, recalls with pleasure that the show was a hit with the children. "They danced. They ascended the stage. They performed with us. We passed the hat, and the kids gave us nickels and dimes. We collected about $5." That was the good part. The bad part was "a disturbed woman who ran around, screaming obscenities about what children should look at." What could have offended the woman? The brief costumes of some of the performers? The outrageous face paint? The anti-venereal disease song? The ditty that rhymed "plucking" with "college?" Vito isn't sure. "I tried to give her the money we'd collected," he recalls with a laugh. "'Here,' I said, 'let me bribe you at least. Take the money and leave us alone.'" The woman complained to the Parks and Recreation Department in San Francisco. On the strength of that complaint, says Vito, the Free Store's permit to perform in San Francisco has been halted until park board members can review it in September. Vito asked an official if this was "restraint?" No, she said. It was "interruption." Then, the Berkeley misunderstanding occurred. Seeking a permit to perform in public here, says Vito, the Free Store group was put off by the agreement it had to sign. Said papers contained what was taken to be an obscenity clause. In addition, says Vito, a city official, wanted to see the script beforehand. He claims this "touches" on a prior censorship of the material. An official here called it an overreaction and noted a 1967 incident alleging "profane language" by the San Francisco Mime Troupe was resolved in its favor by the city's recreation commission. No free speech prohibitions exist in city parks, says the official. Though hat-passing is not technically legal, the city apparently would not go to the bother of interfering with any group that informally passed the hat after performances. Meanwhile, the Free Store is looking for indoor outlets for its brand of contemporary vaudeville. The group performed recently in Sproul Plaza at the University of California. It is an area in which free speech is no longer an issue. The future, says Vito and associate Clay Geerdes of

Berkeley, will hopefully include more club dates. The company has been performing for about a year now. It was all Vito's idea and grew out of a free modern dance class he taught at Sonoma State College. It was something else interesting for Vito to do after he left his Los Angeles sculpting studio in 1967 [sic], took a trip to Haiti, and eventually settled in Cotati. He began the class in 1971 for anyone who wanted to attend. It continues. The class engendered the show. Vito wrote some material, Ricky Applebaum wrote some new lyrics to singable standards, and everyone worked on the choreography. The show changes as numbers are dropped and added, but a certain Free Store identity remains.

Aug. 12—*The Press Democrat,* Cotati councilmen 'launder' donation to theater group By MIKE McCOY—COTATI—A desire to donate $75 to Freestore Theater, prohibited by law, forced the city council to "launder" the money by deciding to sponsor a bicentennial performance of the group at 2 p.m. Sunday in the plaza. The issue arose when Vito Paulekas, representing Freestore, a community theater group, appeared before the council Tuesday to request funds. Paulekas said he was unable to solicit funds from the city's Bicentennial Commission, which has continually failed to have a quorum to hold a meeting. And City Mgr. William Cavalli informed the council that money earmarked for the commission's distribution to promote bicentennial events for fiscal 1975-76 has been re-budgeted for other uses in the 1976-77 budget. But Mayor William Payne, citing Freestore's community contributions and association with the city of Cotati, moved to donate $75. City Atty. Jay Cantor then interjected that "private organizations are not proper recipients for public monies." Payne, however, jokingly responded that he's seen where "Rohnert Park got the money laundered through the chamber of commerce to finance a lawsuit." Payne's reference was to Rhonert Park's lawsuit against the Santa Rosa Urban Renewal Agency's regional shopping center project. A large portion of that suit's cost has been paid by the owners of Rohnert Park's proposed regional shopping center property. The money has been collected by the Rohnert Park Chamber of Commerce and turned over to the city to finance the suit. Payne asked if it was possible to "launder" the donation to Freestore, possibly by giving the

> money to the non-profit Kairos Community Center but earmarked for disbursal to Freestore. Cantor responded that the city "can make gifts of public money to non-profit organizations" and indicate general uses such as promotion of the arts." But before Payne could make a motion, Councilman James Barrett moved to pay Freestore $75 to perform Sunday. The motion was defeated 2-3, with Barrett and Payne the only supporters. Minutes later, after a verbal harangue by Paulekas, Barrett reintroduced the motion but specified the city would sponsor a "bicentennial" performance by Freestore. Councilman Frank Gleason changed his vote, and the measure passed. Gleason later said he changed his vote because the "performance would be a special performance related to some historical event" in keeping with the efforts of the Bicentennial Commission. Freestore reportedly gives weekly performances in the plaza anyway.

Aug. 24—At 8:30p, 41-year-old SANTA ROSA JUNIOR COLLEGE creative writing professor, FREDRIC STEVEN MANALLI, was driving eastbound along the two-lane HIGHWAY 12 when his van careened into the westbound lane, colliding head-on with another vehicle. Five hours later, MANALLI died *from SHOCK due to MULTIPLE TRAUMATIC LESIONS* at SANTA ROSA MEMORIAL HOSPITAL. The FEMALE DRIVER of the other car sustained serious injuries but survived. In three more days, on Aug. 27, an uncanny ad for its timing in relation to MANALLI's death, is placed in the classified section of today's *SF CHRONICLE*:

> ZODIAC, your partner is in DEEP REAL ESTATE. You're next. The Imperial Wizard can save you. Surrender to him or I'll terminate your case. R.A.

This is perhaps too simple an observation to mean anything, BUT: but we know of exactly two *R.A.*s in this community, who BOTH have direct ties to VITO—an aging and altered magnet whose behavior over the last few years appears to be consistent with that of the BAY AREA ZODIAC NARRATIVE & ACTIVITY TIMELINE: a) Original HOLLYWOOD FREAK and current FREESTORIAN—RICKY APPELBAUM (German, from *apfelbaum; an apple tree*)—or—b) ROBERT AMINZADE (Persian; *offspring of the faithful*)—the person who suggested in the first place that VITO should move his family to SANTA ROSA COUNTY; COTATI in particular. In October 1976, MANALLI's home address at the time of his death was 6665 SEBASTOPOL RD., a modest plot in the SHADY REST TRAILER PARK. MANALLI'S ex-wife, SUZANNE CARLSON, and MANALLI's former boss, DON EMBLEN, cleaned out MANALLI'S former home, allegedly turning up a backpack that belonged to murdered SANTA ROSA JUNIOR COLLEGE student, KIM ALLEN. Along with it, they reportedly found several sketches depicting a female figure trussed and bound in S&M fashion. On October 13, buried on page seventeen of the *THE PRESS DEMOCRAT*: KARL FRANZONI DAVIS failed to gain the support of COTATI CITY COUNCIL and was passed up for appointment to serve with VITO on the COTATI PARKS AND RECREATION COMMISSION.

> Nov. 29—*The San Francisco Examiner*, SAN FRANCISCO FREE SPIRIT: "SF Good Times," a film about rock music, Peoples' Park, Black Panthers, Tim Leary, Bill Graham, and other local heavies, plus a TV short on "Emperor Norton's Bridge." Tuesday, 8:30 p.m., at Shady Grove, 1538 Haight. Also, a live performance by the Free Store theatre collective.

1977

KARL and SHILA FRANZONI are listed in the US CITY DIRECTORY for SONOMA COUNTY as living in PETALUMA, CA at 228 WEST COTATI AVE. —*Occupations: retired*—I guess *freeloader* wasn't an option yet. Upon learning that ANGER released ROBERT PAGE from composer obligations for the *LUCIFER RISING* soundtrack, BEAUSOLEIL eagerly offered his services to his OLD ROOMIE, citing that he had the lenient and fame-hungry WARDEN's blessing to record at the DEUEL VOCATIONAL INSTITUTE in TRACY, CA, where BEAUSOLEIL was incarcerated. ANGER employs BEAUSOLEIL, who pulls other INMATES together to form the FREEDOM ORKUSTRA—(One of the IN/BANDMATES was a one-time fellow MANSON gang alumn, now convicted murderer, STEVEN *CLEM/ SCRAMBLEHEAD* GROGAN. GROGAN joined on the condition that BEAUSOLEIL build him a custom geetar, and dispensed with some free lessons.) The motley group of the damed recorded 45 minutes of music, the results of which tickled ANGER.

> Feb. 2—*The San Francisco Examiner*, Stage—FREE FREESTORE: A free performance of street theater by the Freestore company, Thursday, noon, Civic Center Plaza.

VITO celebrates FREESTORE's second anniversary at THE LAST GREAT HIDING PLACE:

> Feb. 5—*Petaluma Argus-Courier*, Street Theatre—Freestore, the Cotati-based "street theatre" troupe, will mark its second anniversary Monday with a gala celebration at the Last Great Hiding Place in downtown Cotati. The entertainment, which begins at 8:30 p.m., will include music and refreshments. Freestore has successfully kept alive the spirit of old-time vaudeville with their outrageous and original theatrics, which combine musical comedy, contemporary satire, song and dance, nostalgia, and just plain fun.

> March 3—*The Press Democrat*, Free dance concert—COTATI —A free dance concert Saturday at the Cotati Plaza will feature the Wild 'n Wolly Band and the Free Store theatre troupe. Noon to 5 p.m.

—and then on page 18:

> Artists' Union to Hold First Show—COTATI—The Cooperative Artists Union holds its first group show this month at the Inn of the Beginning. The show opens Sunday with a no-host reception from 1 to 6 p.m., with music by Avatah Jazz and Tom Doris Rock. Other entertainment includes a show for children by Vito Paulekas of Free Store from 3 to 4 p.m.

March 19—VITO and SUE PAULEKAS are granted the divorce, and the finalization allowed VITO to put all of his creative and destructive needs into FREE STORE and the local government.

> March 22—*Daily Independent Journal*, Clown Files For Council—Karl Franzini Davis, an unemployed clown, filed yesterday for the May 31 Cotati City Council election. Davis, a Cotati resident for three years, is affiliated with the Freestore Theatre Group. The special election will fill the seat of Councilman Frank Gleason, who has resigned effective March 31.

> April 21—*The San Francisco Examiner*, STREET THEATRE: The Freestore Theatre Company performs Friday, noon, in Union Square.

> April 26—*The San Francisco Examiner*, STREET THEATRE: The Freestore Theatre Company performs Wednesday, noon, in Portsmouth Square, Kearny and Washington Street.

> May 11—*The San Mateo Times*, Ms. Klein lives at Lake Tahoe and teaches art. A former psychiatric nurse, she began studying art while earning her R.N. degree. Later, she studied sculpture with Vito Paulekas in Los Angeles and painting with Minerva Herzog in Venice, Calif., developing her present expressionistic style.

> May 17—*The San Francisco Examiner*, STREET THEATRE: The Freestore Theatre Company, Wednesday, noon, in Union.

In the May 27 *PETALUMA ARGUS-COURIER*, a crazy-ass close-up portrait of FRANZONI appears. HE is done up in HIS FREESTORE clown getup; face caked with make-up, mouth agape—the article above the wild pic reads:

> 'Freestore is the Ideal I Go By' (EDITOR'S NOTE: Karl Franzoni Davis is a candidate for the Cotati City Council and

> has submitted the following statement for publication. Davis resides at 228 West Cotati Ave.) + + + "Freestore" is the ideal I go by. Whatever you want, you know you're going to find at the "Freestore." Whatever you need, you know you're going to get, and it's free. It's my motivation.

Elsewhere on the page:

> Cotati Election Set Tuesday—Four persons are seeking election to one seat on the Cotati City Council in a special election to be held Tuesday, May 31. The candidates are Robert Davis, Karl Franzoni Davis, Martin Tusler, and Sandra Walton. The special election is being held to fill the council position, which was vacated by the resignation of Frank Gleason in March. All of the candidates were invited to submit statements to the Argus-Courier, which appear on this page.

So FRANZONI, who has used the alias ROBERT DAVIS in the past to run for local public office, is suddenly running against another ROBERT DAVIS for the same local public office.

> June 10—*The Press Democrat,* Groups to play in Cotati—A free afternoon of entertainment will be presented Saturday from noon to 5 p.m. at the Cotati Plaza bandstand. Bands are Brother Music, Bad Boogie, and Wild 'n Wooly. The Asfura troupe will be present, belly dancers and mid-Eastern musicians, and the street theater group Freestore will perform.

> July 27—*The Press Democrat,* Final election results credited Davis with 253, Sandra Walton with 244, Martin Tusler, 64, and Karl Franzoni Davis, 8.

1978

Except for VITO, 65, and LORETTA, FREESTORE is all but defunct.

> Feb. 2—*The Press Democrat*, VITO AND LORETTA of the absolutely insane street-theater group known as Freestore will be on the Gong Show Friday (11:30 a.m. Channel 4), and somehow, it seems inevitable that this would happen. The crazies appear regularly on Saturdays at the Inn of the Beginning. Their last brush with the big-time was when they shot Santa Claus in Union Square. They could win.

> May. 23—*The Press Democrat*, LORETTA AND VITO, also known locally as Freestore, are getting to be regulars on the Gong Show. They'll be on the Channel 4 madness Friday night—billed as The Two Aristocrats.

Oct. 26—VITO was appointed to COTATI's DOWNTOWN REVITALIZATION COMMITTEE.

1979

Tattoo artist and former FREAK DANCER ROBERT *BEATLE BOB* ROBERTS joins SAN FRANCISCO *punk* band THE OFFS as saxophonist. Feb. 15—SOPHIA (*sofia*: ABRAXAS's SHIELD OF WISDOM) CREME (CREME, BENJAMIN: a key figure in the MAITREYA-CENTRIC, NEO-THEOSOPHY) PAULEKAS was born at COMMUNITY HOSPITAL in SANTA ROSA, SONOMA COUNTY, to VITO and LORETTA. July 2—SKELETAL REMAINS are found in a ravine off CALISTOGA ROAD in SANTA ROSA. The BODY has deteriorated beyond identification, but shows traces of having been bound and tortured. Oct. 3—Grievances are aired with COTATI CITY COUNCIL on page ten of the November 14 *PRESS DEMOCRAT*. The closing comment made by VITO is an unusual one, as expected—directed at the recently overthrown PERSIAN leader, MOHAMMAD REZA PAHLAVI (AMINZADE is of PERSIAN descent):

> SHAH OF IRAN—Took no action on the request by resident Vito Paulekas that the city request President Carter "to immediately return the monster, the Shah of Iran, to justice."

1980

Jan. 31—*The Press Democrat*, Welcome to Cotati—Chief Kotate welcomes visitors to the city that bears his name. The 350-pound chief was donated to the city by local artisan Vito Paulekas, who worked daily for two months to ready the nine-foot-high sculpture for placement in Cotati's plaza. The sculpture honors Cotati's forebearers, the Kotate Indians, members of the coastal Miwok tribe who settled in the area 2,000 years ago. Paulekas said the sculpture symbolizes "Chief Kotate dancing on the nipple of the breast of Mother Earth, which gives life to all of us."

YOUR KUNDALINI IS SHOWING // DIVISION BY ZERO

T-d has had the rare privilege of living on two Manhattans; this one—the place of the whirlpools—provides fewer opportunities for him to bury his work, as it is entirely crusted over with a single massive mesh of concrete and steel, not covered with a natillion grains of sand as the other. T-d and his family have lived in this modest Upper West Side corner penthouse for the last 18 months, moving here shortly after the birth of their son. T-d is still on the fence as to whether that decision was a stroke of genius on his wife's part, or a self-loathing attempt to hide among an island of 1.5 million Metropolitans, like a Mexican in a teepee. Their spot is bookended by a rising pop star, whose double entendre songs give pubescents a bright place to hide from the current Grunge expunge—and a real estate agent who occasionally, over a casserole, shares his time machine schematics that are, based on T-d's understanding, practical and possible needing only a few tweeks and good hardware store visits—Wholesome, everyday, pepper of the planet types—But, beyond these double-insulated walls, T-d is endlessly terrified of being recognized, or worse yet, hounded, now that his reputation as an enigmatic writer-in-hiding has transcended his existence to one of mythical proportions. With four successful novels and a collection of short works linked to his Roman Catholic name, the goal is, was, and forever shall be, to remain physically forgettable, undetectable, and unapproachable—or, at the very least, to convince those concerned that he's doing fine, and there's nothing to see here.

Worse than being made is the threat of being photographed. T-d isn't at all comfortable with the idea of his earlobes being broadcast and scrutinized the world over by the LOBAL ELITES. Besides, national news has more pressing issues to report: Americans have been subjected to a real red-letter year, learning how to surf on a web, or the proper attire for listening to music from Pacific Northwest timber mills, or how to debate the fate of a Milwaukeean cannibal who kept his fridge stocked with dark meat—All that's left of Ouroboros' lunch, is for Georgy "Twice Fooled" Porgy to hand the cabinet keys over to Big "Willy" Bill in January.

On this damp Thursday evening, out here on his pad's back fire escape, T-d speed-tokes a pin joint, singing the wiry white hairs from his kuckle.

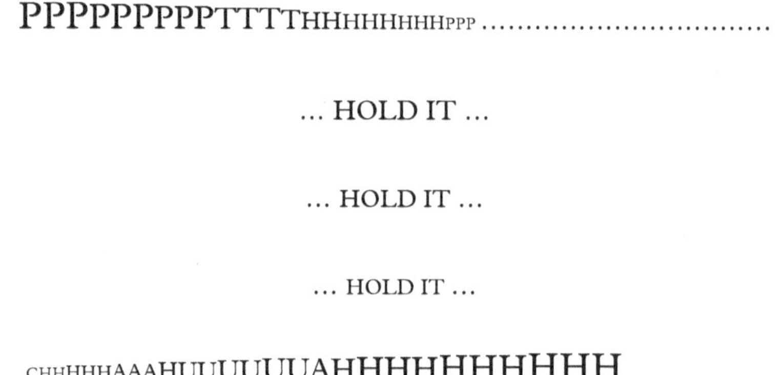

A bomb goes off, his neurons fire—he wanders from thought to thought, stopping for only a moment to consider what fatherly advice he will first admonish on the one-year-old baby boy; one made in his own lanky, buck-toothed shadow—something important, like: "If you burp and sneeze at the same time (to *breeze*), you will die."

2 He and Him

Another heavy toke makes his thoughts take a hard 90 toward the memory of the murder that occurred this morning right outside his building. Short of personal crises, Thanksgiving Day is the only morning of the year that you'll find this vampire up before the sun, leaning out his windows to watch the rubber giants of the parade being pumped plump with hundreds of cubic feet of helium, and then being moved to the holding area near 79th Avenue, before their huge asses are literally paraede through prime East Coast real estate. Last year, Garfield's head drifted so close to T-d in the window that he could have burned a hole with his roach in the fat feline's hooded eye. In 1924, elephants from Central Park volunteered their time to make the six-mile trek through N.Y.C., with advertisements slung over their hides, cutting a swath between pockets of communal hallucinations, such as the tap dancers and the steam train that had been freed from its tracks, barreling down Broadway. By 1928, vehicle-sized helium-filled balloons had replaced the livestock attractions (which were deemed *too frightening for children*). Until 1931, Macy's released those balloons into the city air after the parade, offering a $50 shopping reward for their retrieval. That gimmick, though popular, came to a tragic end when an idiotic bi-wing pilot attempted to lasso a freed grinning pig, but he instead tangled his prop in the tethers, crashed, and died—never redeeming his gift cert. Very sad, I'm told. In 1942, '43, and '44, the surviving decade-old balloons that remained in custody were dispatched, and the department store donated its entire helium and rubber catalogue to the U.S. war efforts; after all, a country's global standing is measured, rightly so, by its natural resources surplus. Suicide-by-helium only happens in provinces where the gas is plentiful, which is why Poles primarily hang themselves, and Asians take to bridges. During WWII, America made a run for inhaler's gold, baby.

—6:13 a.m. A commotion was heard coming from the steps of the First Baptist Church In the City of New York at the corner of 79th and Broadway, directly across the street from T-d's vantage point. He spied the Lever Bros' balloon, Snuggle Bear, peeking out of a stocking, waiting next in line in the holding tank. 13 nervous handlers secured their bones, when a sudden collision of gusts caught Snuggle Bear under his curls, turning him into a tethered bowling ball—rolling over filling staff noggins, smashing handlers to the pavement. The bad bear managed to dismantle a street lamp post before settling back into place, hovering in the early morning mist like he ain't done nuthin'. Two handlers were injured badly enough that they really should have sought medical attention, but instead walked it off. One of them returned to rope management, the other suffered through a panic attack brought on by a sudden case of CASADASTRAPHOBIA—the fear of being sucked up into the great wide yonder, or falling into the sky, or looking up at tall objects. A recent incident reported in the tabloids concerned a pair of hangliders who were carried up 30,000 feet by a rageful gust, sucked into the clouds where the fliers passed out from a lack of oxygen, and then froze to death before sailing violently back to land to die a second death somewhere in the Outback—Additional safety factors were quickly established and demonstrated by the captain handler, wrapping the balloon's tether tightly around his bone, as they call the stick thingee, shortening the line significantly to drag the inflated stocking much closer to them than in rehearsal. With a loud: "Y'INS WATCH OUT FOR KIDS AND BUS STOPS, OKAY?" Snuggle Bear begins his miles-long journey to NBC's Media Center.

Parades create a safe space for shared hysterias; a place to exploit the universal relationship between the observed and the observer through a dizzying crisscross of eyelines and individual perspectives that spaghetti-bowl into a singular, unified illusion.

Near the parade's mid-mark at Columbus Circle, the crowd turns bloodthirsty, *oohing* and *ahhing* when the balloons temporarily misbehave.

—6:39 a.m. The next balloon to get the old gas-blast is the unofficial grand-daddy of the parade, the one They call—THE HAPPY DRAGON (from here on out: THD). Legend has it that THD hated Thanksgiving for decades, and when the ruckus of the Macy's parade woke HIM from HIS deep cave slumber, HE vowed to avenge his lost beauty rest. HE had prepared to swoop down and crisp those merrymakers to bacon strips, but when THD arrived at the parade, so overjoyed was HE by the festivities and HIS welcoming, that THD called a truce and, for the next 33 holiday shopping seasons, joined in the fun. The stupidly optimistic DRAGON had no clue that on that chilly Thursday morning, HE had signed HIS own death warrant.

As the helium flattened HIS folds and raised THD's head, T-d got a good look at ITS bulging, bloodshot eyes; old boy's looking tired. After a few minutes, the beast is filled, lifting off the pavement just enough for the crouching safety crew to walk under. A rainbow-colored ellipse—designed to mimic a gaping wound—runs the length of THD's belly, threatening to ingest any passersunder when raised to street-flight height, so beware.

At sunrise, the attack came suddenly, as they often do, lasting no more than a minute. A mass of masked ECO protestors descended from dumpsters and phone booths, flooding the church steps like a swarm of flies, brandishing sling-shots and sickels and machetes. THD takes a direct hit to the head and multiple deep incisions about ITS body; the numerous gashes instantly release hundreds of cubic feet of helium into the atmosphere. T-d watched helplessly as the concentration mixed with the charged air and ignited for a microsecond, burning a 20-story pylon into the very fabric of space, flashing through millions of colors in a blip. The murderers missed the strangest fruit of their labor while too busy fleeing, shouting eco slogans and bio propaganda—*depletion this … save that*—disappearing back into their dumpster and phone booth holes to wait out the next gas party. THD free-fell like a detonated building, his heavy, flaccid rubber carcass collapsed to the street, settling at the foot of T-d's windows, giving the 55-year-old writer an even clearer vantage of the next and final step in THD's public desecration. Locals seeped out from the neighborhood buildings armed with shears and butter knives, trampling the DRAGON to carve the commercial heirloom to ribbons. Some dissectors voiced plans to make flags; others, T-shirts, drapes, tablecloths, and so on, until all their crafting needs are met. When the scavenger sea parted, and They filed quietly satisfied back into their dwellings. A faint outline like that of a Hiroshima blast shadow was all that remained of THE HAPPY DRAGON.

At 10:00 a.m., nine floors closer to G-d, T-d's bedroom boob-tube projected the glowing illusion of a parade passing by outside in real-time, but processed through the prism of lenses and videotape, adding more distortion to an already partitioned reality; one on the brink of snapping. What if this same public behavior were underway, but unprompted and unexpected? What if clowns spontaneously burst into song and dance, and giant balloon beasts were aided by helpful *pot-bellied freaks of common clay*, trotting down a rat-maze of avenues taken over by a department store, to amaze and astonish that coin outta your purse and all the way to the bank? No matter how it's sliced, T-d has loved the chaos for years, and this morning is no exception.

For reasons known only to T-d, he has kept a running, consecutive tally of the commercials littering the broadcast so far, beginning with the main sponsor, Cotton Incorporated, and then:

NORELCO RAZORS—HALLMARK—LUDEN'S—WENDY'S MELT—OLDSMOBILE AURORA—*SUPER MARIO LAND 2* for GAME BOY—BLOCKBUSTER VIDEO—GOTTA GETTA GUND—DISCOVER CARD—CHEVY LUMINA—MACY'S AFTER THANKSGIVING SALE—FRUIT OF THE LOOM—PEPPERIDGE FARMS GRAVY—*BOB HOPE PRESENTS THE LADIES OF LAUGHTER* promo—*SAVED BY THE BELL: THE MOVIE* promo—PONTIAC BONNEVILLE—NY TELEPHONE —HESS TRUCKS—*DONAHUE* promo—COTTON INCORPORATED—WENDY'S MELT—HONEY BUNCHES OF OATS—NORELCO RAZORS—DISCOVER CARD—DISNEY'S BEAUTY AND THE BEAST trailer—MACY'S AFTER THANKSGIVING SALE—GEO PRIZM—CAMPBELL'S HOME COOKIN' CHICKEN VEGETABLE SOUP—POLAROID PARTY FILM—*SAVED BY THE BELL: THE MOVIE* promo—HESS TRUCKS—NYNEX—*THE MIGHTY DUCKS* trailer—MACY'S AFTER THANKSGIVING SALE—WNBC-TV HAPPY THANSKGIVING bumper—*DONAHUE*—BUICK REGAL—LUDEN'S—FRUIT OF THE LOOM—WENDY'S MELT—COTTON INCORPORATED—MAYTAG—HALLMARK—*A RIVER RUNS THROUGH IT* trailer—GOTTA GETTA GUND—PONTIAC BONNEVILLE—*I'LL FLY AWAY* promo—CADILLAC SEVILLE STS—AT&T VIDEOPHONE—METLIFE —WNBC-TV HAPPY THANKSGIVING bumper—SNUGGLES SINGLES—TRIAMINIC—NORELCO RAZORS—PEPPERIDGE FARMS GRAVY—MACY'S AFTER THANKSGIVING SALE—OLDSMOBILE EIGHTY-EIGHT LSS —WENDY'S MELT—COTTON INCORPORATED—*CATS* on BROADWAY—CAMPBELL'S CHUNKY BEEF NOODLE SOUP —GOTTA GETTA GUND—*HOME ALONE 2* trailer—THERAFLU—*THE TONIGHT SHOW STARRING JAY LENO* promo—MACY'S THANKSGIVING DAY PARADE sponsor COTTON INC.—GEO PRIZM—WENDY'S MELT—NORELCO RAZORS—HANES—HERSHEY'S CHOCOLATE SYRUP—*HOME ALONE 2* trailer—GOTTA GETTA GUND—BUICK PARK AVENUE ULTRA—NBC THURSDAY PRIMETIME promo—OLDSMOBILE 95th bday—NYNEX—CITIBANK CARD—WNBC-TV HAPPY THANKSGIVING bumper—CAMPBELL'S DOUBLE NOODLE SOUP—HALLMARK—BUDDY L. VOICE COMMAND—SNUGGLES SINGLES—WENDY'S MELT—COTTON INCORPORATED...

At 11:07 a.m., aware of it or not, millions of NBC viewers witnessed a ghost at the telecast's second hour mark—T-d knew it. He watched with mouth agape, because in all HIS green and yellow splendor, THD was centered in the t.v. frame, bounding down a bone-dry Broadway Avenue toward the 6th Avenue Media Center at the head of Herald Square. Onlookers held their breath as the winged latex LIZARD easily made the turn onto Columbus Circle. NBC was ill-prepared to report the slaughter, so They had opted for cutting in a segment of last year's THD appearance footage. Couric and Scott's obnoxious voice-overs do their damndest to blur the distinction between the fake realities. Couric, of course, took the deceptive lead:

> 'The grand old man of the Macy's balloon family brought out in honor of this anniversary year. The 72-foot fire-eater made his first appearance in 1960. There was a dragon among the very first balloons designed in the 1920s, but in 1942, with rubber and helium in short supply, he was sacrificed along with the others and donated to the war efforts.'

—and then Scott put a period on it:

> 'That's a nice thing. I like a patriotic fella. And that's why he was just a dragon. This guy is the HAPPY DRAGON. He lived to wag his little tail. Wiggle that tail for us, Dragon.'

T-d remembers muttering out loud to an empty apartment—*What the goddamn fuck is going on here?*—before completing his useless list:

> *HOOK* on home video—NORELCO RAZORS—MACY'S THANKSGIVING DAY PARADE closing credits (which contains its own set of clandestine adverts, making this layer three)—NFL LIVE promo—*I'LL FLY AWAY* promo—MACY'S THANKSGIVING DAY SALE—CADILLAC SEVILLE STS—MACY'S THANKSGIVING DAY SALE—*DONAHUE* promo—and to close it all, an NBC bumper.

The broadcast ended at noon sharp. T-d turned the set off and ate half a pumpkin pie all by himself. He spent the rest of the afternoon waiting by the telephone for a call from his wife, which finally came much later.

... HOLD IT ...

... HOLD IT ...

... HOLD IT ...

Now, at 5:47 p.m., T-d sits crouched on the fire escape with his back against the door. He was told to expect both WIFE and BABY back home any minute, so he peeled the bitter brown nub from his lips, dragged his sleeve across his mouth, and wedged his Birkenstock between the slick slats of the fire escape to try to stand. Erect, eventually, T-d's vision zeroed in on the neighbor's back door: Hunched over, tinkering with the bedroom door knob, was what T-d could only describe as a tall PATCH OF INK—a BLOT—in the shape of a human. T-d stumbled at ITS sighting, the noise drawing the BLOT's attention to him. IT stood straight, but did so in a movement difficult to put into words. IT was slow and exacting, as if animated with extra frames to create a motion smoother than any human T-d knew was capable of. From what little T-d could make out, BLOT measured in height similar to his own, but IT did not appear equal in mass; for BLOT seemed not to have any. As the rain began beating down around IT, T-d watched as the raindrops vanished when they passed in front of the motionless void. T-d struggled to make out a single detail—Something. Anything—a nose, or a chin, but there was nothing discernible indicating that even a face was there to be looked upon. BLOT was a total and complete lack of third-dimensional substance, a featureless photon vacuum of characteristics, a THING beyond our current comprehension. The immeasurable absence of light was astonishing, and it troubled T-d. And, then, without using words, at least as we understand them, BLOT spoke to T-d: IT was only one of infinite bottomless holes that connect all things here and all things not here—all things before, and all things to come, but T-d and his kind know the present, the fleeting now—intimately; something BLOT craves to the point of need. T-d wept quietly with acceptance, but still, BLOT did not move, reacting instead by producing a tiny red spark—like the glow from a cigarette's cherry tip when it's dragged on—a dull dot at the center of where T-d estimated a face should have been. Staying absolutely still, totally frozen in time as both beings watched each other with matched intensity until the sound of the front door's deadbolt unlocking nudged the Universal escapement forward, suddenly reminding T-d that he was to leave his sandals on the welcome mat before going back inside.

The End

IMAGES | FIGURES | TABLES

VIKON VILLAGE BOOKS | California, U.S.A.

www.ingramcontent.com/pod-product-compliance
Lightning Source LLC
LaVergne TN
LVHW100503110826
845146LV00002B/503

9798218946029